NO REMORSE

Decker's War — Book 6

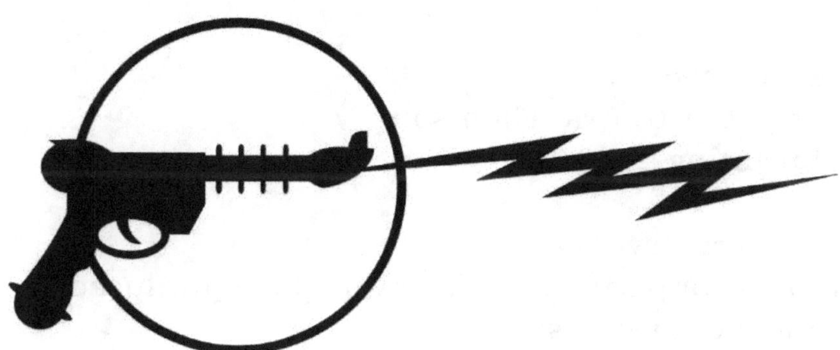

ERIC THOMSON

No Remorse
Copyright 2018 Eric Thomson
First printing 2018

Published in Canada
By Sanddiver Books
ISBN: 978-1-7751355-2-4

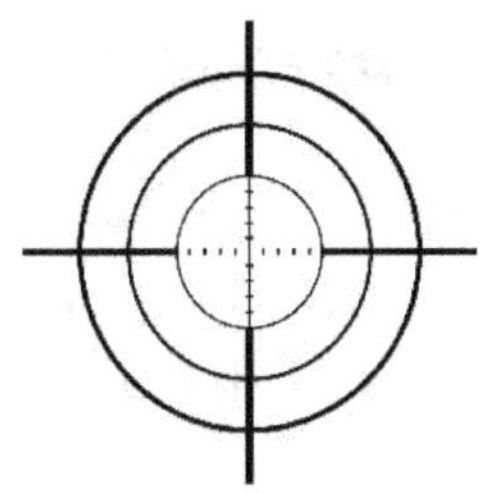

—ONE—

The faint, almost imperceptible sound of muffled footsteps reached Major Zack Decker's ears. Alone in a rundown part of the city teeming with danger, the Naval Intelligence operative stopped and listened, trying to find the source of the furtive noise.

Small, rat-like creatures scurried around in the shadows, occasionally emitting high-pitched squeals that triggered an instinctive revulsion. Or at least a queasy feeling all too common when faced with species native to ecosystems far different from Earth's.

A thick, almost nauseating aroma of overripe sewers, rotting food and perhaps even rotting corpses assailed his nostrils. No matter where humanity settled, it seemed to keep its knack for taking the worst problems along and repeating the same mistakes on new worlds.

This slum might be anywhere on one of the twenty or so habitable planets colonized during the first wave of migration after the discovery of faster-than-light travel. But after almost four centuries of uncontrolled growth, those star systems were even now facing inevitable decay, especially in the social and political realms, since the two were always closely intertwined.

He heard the sound again, closer and distinct enough to tell him two humans were on his trail. Were they footpads, muggers, or something worse? Had he been spotted by an opposition ready to unleash assassins? They had tried often enough in recent times, especially since he and Talyn broke the Black Sword conspiracy wide open.

That she wasn't here to watch his back made Decker more vulnerable. His enemies only needed to be lucky once. He needed to be lucky every time. Lucky and ready to terminate any threat with extreme prejudice, a fate about to befall the duo tracking him, even if they were merely after the contents of his pockets. The local police rarely ventured into dimly lit alleys and didn't much care about lowlifes killing each other or visitors doing the same. It saved them the effort. A self-correcting problem, as some would call it.

The corrosion eating away at the Commonwealth's core hadn't quite reached the outer systems yet, those colonized in the second great migration wave. They had earned their right to self-rule two centuries earlier by winning a bloody war responsible for more deaths than every other human conflict since the dawn of time put together.

But the older worlds weren't shy about exporting their undesirables to the more pristine frontier, whether or not settlers there were in agreement. And so the sickness spread, helped along by forces wanting to restore centralized authority and dispense with the niceties of an often chaotic confederation. Forces who'd prefer to see Decker and Talyn dead as punishment for thwarting them at every turn.

He slipped into a darkened doorway, careful not to touch the leprous concrete, so he didn't leave traces for enemy hunters eager to spill his blood, and loosened the dagger strapped to his left forearm. In an era of ubiquitous power weapons, even here where the dispossessed eked out quiet lives of desperation, the

Marine preferred a silent blade. Used by a master of the art, it could kill instantly and leave little, if any traces.

A hint of soft, human breathing came from around the corner, just beyond his reach, and he tensed. Then, he heard the rustle of clothes. Sloppy. How did they expect to creep up on him? Decker sensed, rather than saw the first of his two stalkers step into the filth-strewn alley where he'd taken shelter.

He freed his blade, reached out from the doorway with his left hand to grab hold of a tunic collar, and yanked the shadowy figure off its feet. The Marine's dagger flashed in the dim light and the pursuer, a man, went limp. He dropped him and stepped out to confront the other stalker who briefly froze at the unexpected turn of events, torn between fight and flight. Decker struck again, relieving the second one, a woman, of the need to choose. Two for two.

"End scenario," he shouted into the darkness.

Lights came on and his surroundings dissolved, leaving only tubular skeletons on which holographic projectors could build realistic scenes, such as an inner system slum.

The trainees at his feet looked up with sheepish expressions while they waited for their sim suits to reactivate so they might stand. Decker shoved his fake dagger, another simulation tool, back in its sheath, and headed for the control platform, where Command Sergeant Rolf Painter, his chief instructor, waited.

"No improvement," the latter said when Decker came within earshot.

"None. Our friends Nikarov and Suli simply don't have the right instincts, and I doubt they'll ever develop them. You'll do the debriefing?"

"In detail, Major. I took the most beautiful three-D rendering of their latest failed pursuit. They'll wish you'd sliced them up for real once I'm done."

"Try not to enjoy yourself too much."

"No promises. Remember what you told the staff — if we can convince marginal cases to quit on their own, so much the better. And those two are the least capable candidates in the current draft. Best they figure it out themselves. The real world isn't known for giving second chances."

"Especially not these days."

"Roger that, Major. I figure when they pull a guy like you from the field and make him teach the fine art of killing, it means the universe is giving birth to a whole new level of pain." Painter tossed off a salute. "I'll have an update for you later."

— TWO —

A familiar voice cut through Decker's empty-eyed stare at the training installation's main quadrangle. "Wool-gathering on duty, Major? That'll cost you."

He turned away from the office window and gave his partner, Commander Hera Talyn, a mocking smile. "What are you now? The boss' inspector general on top of being his temporary chief of staff? Or are you slumming with us field pigs?"

"I needed a breather, a little getaway from the fog of treason permeating HQ. So I figured why not visit my favorite Marine at Camp X where he's having the time of his life while I'm trying to balance operations with rebuilding the division?"

"You could have taken a stroll through downtown Sanctum to clear your head instead of a long trip into the boonies."

Talyn took the chair facing Decker's desk and exhaled. "Sanctum is just as foggy as HQ's corridors these days, Big Boy. You may recall we're still hunting for Black Sword members on Caledonia. There's no telling how many of them are wandering around the capital, pretending to be loyal members or employees of the Commonwealth Armed Services. At least here, I'm reasonably sure the air is clean and the people true to their oath."

"We hope. Considering Manfred Yang turned traitor on us, I'd say our vetting process has been compromised and is still full of glaring holes. The only folks around here who clearly aren't Black Sword come from the 1st Special Forces Regiment or the Pathfinder School."

She gave him an ironic smile. "The great Pathfinder family."

"To which you belong, honey." His reply was devoid of its usual bantering tone.

Talyn examined him with concern in her eyes. "For a man who's been teaching our next generation of special intelligence ops people to kill and keep from getting killed, your mood seems strangely subdued. This has to be a reasonably decent tour of duty, considering you could be riding a desk with me back at HQ. What gives?"

Decker grunted wordlessly, his eyes drawn back to the window overlooking Naval Intelligence's remote and highly secret training facility. "Did I ever tell you that in my younger days, I nurtured delusions of familial adequacy?"

"No." Talyn turned a curious stare on her partner, wondering where this was leading.

"A quarter-century ago, I married a lovely lady by the name Ingrid Lagman. Together we produced an even lovelier child, Saga, my daughter."

"I'm aware of that. It's in your file. By the way, your girl has a pretty name."

"It's what they called the Norse goddess of poetry and history. Ingrid always nurtured a deep attachment to her family's ancestral culture. Her attachment to me proved a lot shallower. One year after I transferred to the 902nd Pathfinders, while the squadron was away on a six-month deployment, she packed everything up and took a starship home to Scandia with Saga in tow. I found out via subspace message she petitioned the Scandian courts for sole custody, based on my inability to parent my child while I was chasing rebel scum light years away. The courts, quite naturally, granted the motion, and Ingrid told me in crystal-clear terms I was to refrain from contacting my daughter — at least while she was still legally a minor."

"Which she would no longer be today."

Decker nodded. "Saga is twenty-five now, and since she took after her mother rather than me, she'll be a true Scandian beauty."

"And you didn't reach out to her when she turned eighteen?"

"If you'll recall, I was otherwise occupied playing janissary for alien slavers back then. After that," he shrugged, "I was too busy keeping you out of trouble."

"This is old news, Zack, yet you look as if it happened last night?"

Decker slumped in his chair, turned his gaze back on Talyn and let out an uncharacteristic sigh. "I received a subspace message from Ingrid this morning, the first since she told me to fuck off and die twenty years ago. Saga's gone missing. She was preparing for her orals — believe it or not, my girl is doing a doctorate in pre-diaspora political history..."

Talyn gave him a crooked grin. "I can guess where she picked up that fixation."

"But a week before defending her thesis, she simply vanished. That was almost two weeks ago. Neither Ingrid, nor Saga's research supervisor, or her university colleagues for that matter, have seen her since then. There's no trace of Saga on the entire damn planet."

"Surely it's a matter for the Scandian Police Authority."

The Marine's hand rose in a dismissive wave. "The cops are investigating. But so far, zip. They checked her apartment, and nothing was out of place. Their forensics people did a scan and found no evidence anyone had been there since she was last seen at the university. Her financial accounts remain untouched, and she's not shown up on any surveillance sensors. It's like she evaporated somewhere between the university gates and her home."

A surprised frown creased Talyn's forehead. "That doesn't sound good, Zack."

"Tell me about it. I'm worried this isn't just an ordinary missing person case. Ingrid claims Saga is one of the most grounded people she knows and wouldn't go walkabout on a whim, not with the culmination of her hard work in sight. She has no dodgy friends, bad habits, or anything else that might attract unwanted attention. Hard to believe she's my daughter, but her studies are everything."

"Why did your ex- contact you after such a long silence?"

"The inspector in charge of the investigation suggested advising me after he found out Saga's biological father was a Marine. I suppose that's in case her disappearance is related to my work for the Fleet, or she's done a runner and wants to look me up. Never mind there's been no contact in two decades, and Saga took on her mother's last name. And before you ask, Ingrid has no idea what I'm doing these days. She addressed her message to the HQ communications center in the hope of them forwarding it as required. But she sounded scared."

"And you'd like to ask permission for a trip to Scandia?" Talyn grimaced. "Until the next few trainee classes are ready to graduate, I can't spare you."

"What if it's the Coalition, either through Black Sword or the *Sécurité Spéciale*, trying to draw me out? Draw us out? By now they're aware we're the ones who uncovered

Black Sword's existence and triggered the great cleanup. They'll be looking for revenge. Yang would have known about Ingrid and Saga since he could access my personal file at will. Why not pass that sort of information to his asshole buddies?

"That's the other reason I can't spare you, let alone ask the boss to assign another victim as his temporary chief of staff. We are unquestionably the biggest targets for termination with extreme prejudice. The Coalition needs us dead yesterday, and to quote a certain Marine fond of historical trivia, eventually, even the most inept shooter will hit something. Until we've rebuilt the Special Operations Division's strength and barring emergencies, you and I are benched, whether it's business or personal."

Decker gave his partner the mulish stare she expected, but he nodded once. "Got it."

"Promise you won't sneak off or go absent without authority?"

"Promised."

Talyn examined her partner with sympathetic eyes.

"I understand you're worried about Saga, even though you've not seen her for so long, but Scandia isn't exactly next door. Then there's the possibility she might simply be hiding because she couldn't handle the pressure of defending her thesis. It happens to even the most grounded individuals. She'll re-emerge once she's dealt with her issues." When he gave her a skeptical grunt, Talyn added, "Sure, sometimes paranoids have enemies, but most often, they only have fears. Let the Scandian cops deal with it. But if it makes you feel better, I can reach out to one of my contacts in the Constabulary and ask her to take a gander at the case."

"How will your Professional Compliance Bureau friend on Cimmeria help?"

Talyn gave him a reassuring smile. "Scandia is part of Chief Superintendent Morrow's jurisdiction. She'll know who to ask and what to ask. Besides, she's a sharp lady. You'd like her."

"Fair enough. I suppose I should send Ingrid an acknowledgment. And then write the latest batch of evaluations. Sadly, the only ones in the current class ready for the next stage are Markku and Fresal. Unsurprising, I suppose, considering both came to us straight from the Special Forces and are already trained to fight dirty, unlike the desk analysts you recruited. At least two of them won't pass, no matter what I do. They're neither the right species of psychopath, or can't shut out their emotions, which means they'll always hesitate when it comes time to kill. And I'd rather not put them up against the opposition's best cutthroats — they wouldn't live long enough to justify the investment. The others will likely make it."

"That's precisely why I can't cut you loose. You're best placed to tell me who won't survive under real conditions. Which two won't pass your phase of the course?"

"Nikarov and Suli. They're bright, eager, fit, but they lack the right temperament to develop a killer instinct. That's not something I can teach. It's either in you, or it isn't. If it isn't, I can't help. My evaluation will recommend they cease training and return to their previous duties unless they withdraw on their own first."

"You're sure?"

Decker nodded. "I am. But if you're about to say we should keep them at it for a while longer in case they suddenly discover their inner sociopath, don't. We'll only be wasting time and money."

"Shame. Suli, in particular, struck me as the sort with enough wiles to infiltrate the *Sécurité Spéciale*."

"And die the moment things go sideways. She'll never get off the first shot or slit a throat before the other guy knows what's up. I've seen her sort before. Their brains can't override the social conditioning that says thou shalt not kill. They're usually the ones who freeze in a firefight or can't seem to hit the side of a starship even though they're dead accurate during training."

"What does Pavlik say?" Talyn asked.

"Commander Hineman and I don't necessarily see eye to eye on certain matters, Hera. He's not seen real action for years. The game has changed since he last ran a mission."

Decker's tone told Talyn everything she needed to know about her partner's relationship with the man in charge of the division's training wing.

"Maybe I should chat with Pavlik, old-timer to old-timer. What does *he* think about Nikarov and Suli not having the killer instinct, as you put it?"

"He hasn't shared his opinion with me. But I've told him if he passes anyone I consider unfit, and they die in action, their blood will be on his hands."

Talyn winced. "I see you've lost none of your forthrightness, Zack. How did Pavlik take it?"

"Like someone shoved a super-heated tungsten rod up his ass because he knows I'm right. If I tell him Nikarov and Suli won't pass the close quarters combat phase, then he'll wash them out. He can't afford to watch me and the guys I borrowed from Fort Arnhem walk out on him."

She snorted. "And I know you well enough to believe you'd bundle your Pathfinder buddies into a skimmer, take the controls, and head for home. After asking Josh

Bayliss to hide you from anyone not of the tribe, like Pavlik. By the way, how is our distinguished Pathfinder School sergeant major?”

“Looking for any excuse to come down and help me train our fledgling operatives in the fine art of assassination. And he’s not the only one wanting in on the action. When I spoke with Josh the other day, he mentioned Ari Redmon might volunteer to join our merry bunch. She’s finding life as a senior instructor on the command Pathfinder course too tame for her liking.”

“I hope you told him Ari getting entangled with Black Sword, no matter how unwittingly, makes her a lousy candidate for intelligence work.”

Decker raised a placating hand. “Let’s not stumble over the past. You realize she’ll never fall for that trick again, right? I’d say it makes her twice as safe as anyone we recruit from elsewhere.”

“But her involvement with the late Colonel Wynt’s schemes means she doesn’t qualify for a high enough security clearance to work with us. It’s why she’ll never go back to the Special Forces Regiment either.”

“Commodore Ulrich can waive the restriction on her eligibility for a clearance, Hera. And if we ask, he will. After all, Ari helped us blow the Black Sword mess wide open. It’s what got him his first star, and his command expanded into a division. Which resulted in yours truly teaching at Camp X instead of doing dastardly deeds out there in the big, bad galaxy.”

“That and our losses to Black Sword treachery. And the fact you and I have targets painted on our backs. So I need not speak with Pavlik?”

Decker shook his head. “Unnecessary. We don’t agree on several issues, but Hineman is no idiot. He won’t overrule me if I stand my ground, especially with the guys backing me.”

Talyn laughed. "As if your Pathfinder buddies would disagree with you in front of a Navy officer foolish enough to challenge the tribe's unity."

"*Our* Pathfinder buddies, honey." He blew her a kiss. "Even though you keep forgetting or you pretend to do so, you'll always be one of us, whether or not you want it. And that reminds me — we're both due for a refresher in the next couple of weeks. I should book us a room and find space on a few of the School's training jumps."

She groaned theatrically. "You're just looking for an excuse to hold court at the Pegasus Club. The grand old man of the Pathfinder branch surrounded by an admiring multitude. A multitude that can't quite fathom how an old, evil-tempered noncom ended up as a major working some of the most hush-hush missions ever."

"Sure." He grinned at her. "And maybe recruit a few likely candidates while we're there. I've noticed smart Pathfinders with combat experience need less time than career intelligence officers to learn the fine art of doing what we do, me being a case in point. If the boss wants to make up for our casualties and grow the Special Operations Division, we can't put people through the long course you took."

Talyn shrugged. "Perhaps. But your sample size is still small while your pool of candidates in the Special Forces community is deep. We're skimming off the top percentile."

"That still doesn't change the fact every single Pathfinder coming through Camp X finishes the course faster than career spooks. And that's because our job is direct, covert action rather than intelligence gathering and analysis. It means anyone with a few years in the Special Forces has an advantage. Again, if the boss wants fast growth that won't leave us with dangerously under-trained operatives, we should focus our recruiting efforts on Fort Arnhem. Looking for likely candidates inside Naval Intelligence doesn't give us the same rate of return, let alone searching the Fleet at large for recruits with the right psychological makeup. People like you are surprisingly rare."

"I'll run it by the commodore when I'm back in Sanctum. If he agrees and you can afford to leave for a few days, we'll take a drive up the valley and join the other lunatics who enjoy jumping out of a perfectly good shuttle from low orbit."

"And Ari? In case she approaches us to volunteer while we're at the fort?"

"I'll ask the boss about that as well." She climbed to her feet. "You need to work on your evaluations. I should make my manners with Pavlik and observe a few classes. Do you think I can stay overnight?"

Decker grinned at her. "Sure, we have guest rooms if you're after a few hours of sleep."

"I wasn't exactly thinking of sleep, buddy."

"That's what I was hoping you'd say. How about I show you to my room instead?"

"When both of our working days are over, and I've sampled the Camp X cuisine."

"Good thinking. We'll both need our strength."

— THREE —

Talyn's hand traced the old scars on Zack's bare chest as she lay in the crook of his arm, one leg draped over his. "I didn't sense you were fully there just now. At least not with your usual intensity. Would that be related to your daughter's situation, perchance?"

Decker grunted. "What do you think? Twenty years without a word and Ingrid's first message after all that time is to tell me my daughter's missing. Considering who I am and what I've done in the last few years, it's hard not to wonder whether there's a link. Kidnapping an opponent's child to coerce him is a story as old as humanity."

"In that case, rushing to Scandia headlong would be inadvisable. I sent a message to Chief Superintendent Morrow before the evening meal. Maybe in a week or so, we'll hear more."

"In a week it could be too late," Decker snapped back.

"My, my." Talyn raised her head to stare at his stony face. "That message from your ex- really got to you."

"Those of us who aren't dead inside can still fret about our children, even if we haven't seen them since they were five years old."

"If I weren't dead inside, my feelings might be hurt right now." She gave him a light kiss on the cheek. "A wise man once said it's futile to tie yourself in knots over things you can't change. You're here, on Caledonia. Saga is on Scandia.   How many light years between those systems? And how long would the trip take, considering there's probably no direct connection via civilian passenger shipping?"

"Did I ever mention how much I hate it when you go all logical with me?"

"When one doesn't experience normal human feelings, logic is pretty much it." She gave him a sad smile.

"You sure were feeling things a short time ago."

"I was." Talyn let her fingers dance across Zack's muscular abdomen again. "But that's not the same thing. Mind you, I'm ready for a rematch when you are." When he didn't immediately answer, she added, "It might take your mind off things and tire you out enough to sleep."

Later, well after Caledonia's moons had set, and nocturnal silence blanketed Camp X, Talyn said, "I didn't think to ask earlier, but was the message from Ingrid text, audio only, or audio and video?"

"Audio and video. Why?"

"And it was the Ingrid you remembered?"

"Sure. Twenty years older, of course, but still the same woman I used to love. Her voice and mannerisms were unchanged. If you're wondering whether the whole thing is a fabrication to lure me out into the open for an assassin's knife, I'd say it's possible but unlikely. The person in the message felt real, with none of the telltales that betray even the best artificial intelligence avatars."

"If you don't mind, I'll send a copy of the message to the lab for analysis. If it's a simulation, they'll figure it out. And if it's a real person coerced into feeding you a load of horse manure, they'll catch that as well."

"How about we ask the damned Scandian Police Authority if they're investigating Saga Lagman's disappearance? None of this beating around the bush bullshit — just an open and honest question. That'll confirm whether it's real and lay to rest the late-night musings of an oversexed spy."

"This oversexed spy wonders if they'll tell you anything about an ongoing investigation, especially via a subspace packet."

"Can't hurt to try. I'm Saga's father, even if she grew up without me."

"Fair enough, but let's take our precautions, okay? Stick to a text message transmitted via the central HQ communications node. If we're faced with unholy doings, the less information on your whereabouts we let slip, the better."

Decker turned his head toward her and smirked. "Please. I wasn't about to record a video message with Camp X as a scenic backdrop."

"Just making sure, darling. In fact, come morning, why don't you write it and I'll bring it to the communications center myself. That way we'll be sure no inadvertent routing tags make the trip to Scandia."

"That'll work. When are you headed back to Sanctum?"

"After breakfast. The boss was nice enough to let me slip the leash for a day, understanding enough to let me turn it into an overnighter, but he's not generous enough to make it two. Besides, whether or not I'm there, the administrative work keeps coming."

Decker chuckled. "Everyone has a cross to bear. Make sure you thank the commodore on my behalf for the loan of his chief of staff and suggest he should send you on an inspection tour of Camp X more often. It would improve my morale immensely, and a happy Zack means well-trained, happy little spooks."

"How about I don't and let him keep the illusion we're nothing more than co-workers?"

The Marine's uproarious laughter shook their bed. "Commodore Ulrich hasn't nurtured illusions about anything since before you and I signed up for a life of fun and adventure in our fine, interstellar Fleet. And now that Mannie Yang's no longer around to spread a puritanical damper on everything, the boss might loosen up."

**

A few days after Hera Talyn's visit, as Decker watched his close quarters combat instructors put the last of the slow learners through their paces, his communicator vibrated in a particular pattern. It signaled the arrival of a message via the secure channel between HQ and Camp X.

With a nod at the command sergeant leading the exercise, Decker excused himself and left the training range. Once in his office, he called up the message only to see a miniature holographic Talyn materialize over his desk.

"I figured you'd be busy with trainees, so I made this a recording rather than a direct call. If you want to talk after I'm done, feel free. But I'll be leaving the office in thirty minutes and I'd rather we didn't discuss this over anything other than the secure channel. We've heard from the Scandian Police Authority. They confirm investigating a missing person case about a Saga Lagman, daughter of Ingrid Lagman. However, the individual who wrote the reply expressed curiosity at your query, considering Ingrid Lagman stated for the record you've been out of the picture for twenty years."

Decker paused the recording and sat back in his chair with a thoughtful frown. Perhaps the reply didn't come from the officer in charge of Saga's case — the one who supposedly suggested Ingrid tell him — but from someone unaware of the investigator's advice. Knowing how bureaucratic organizations worked, Decker was willing to bet on it. He brought Talyn's image back to life.

"The lab has done its thing with Ingrid's message, and your instincts hit the mark again. It wasn't an AI avatar but a real human, although without a baseline image for comparison, they can't confirm it was indeed your ex-wife. They also ran a stress analysis on her choice of words, voice, gestures, and eye movements. The technician said she exhibits the signs of someone under considerable emotional strain, which is to be expected, I suppose."

She paused.

"So that's it. Saga's disappearance is real, at least as far as the Scandian Police Authority is concerned. If you're sure it was Ingrid in the message rather than a professional grade doppelgänger, then I'd go with what your gut says. As to the technician's impression, your guess is as good as mine. He's been doing this for a long time but has experienced the occasional false positive, because even under identical circumstances, behavioral clues will almost always differ between individuals.

"And before you ask, no, I can't clear my calendar for another visit to Camp X. But the commodore, who is aware of your affection for his chief of staff, by the way, authorizes you to visit Sanctum the next time you find two days to spare between classes. Just make sure you practice the tradecraft you're teaching our trainees, so you don't pick up any vengeful parties along the way. Talyn, out."

The hologram faded, leaving Zack to stare at the desktop, lost in thought. Even the fastest aviso, capable of outrunning anything with hyperspace engines in the known galaxy, couldn't transport him to Scandia in much under a week, assuming he could commandeer one in the first place.

The Navy used the tiny FTL starships with the oversized drives to move high priority people or cargo. Sometimes, they even carried information too sensitive for the most secure subspace encryption algorithms, but their assignment was controlled at the highest levels, well beyond the Chief of Naval Intelligence.

Once he reached Scandia, then what? The local cops wouldn't want him anywhere near the investigation; Ingrid likely wouldn't want him to hang around her; and since routine missing person cases were rarely referred to the Commonwealth Constabulary, even Hera's contacts were of limited use. A knock on the door jamb snapped him back to reality, and he looked around.

"Hey, Rolf. How are they hanging?" Like everyone at Camp X, Command Sergeant Painter wore an unmarked and unadorned battledress uniform.

"I thought you'd like to know Tatya earned herself a pass at last. She made it through the urban simulation without a scratch. Something in her brain switched on at one point. Surprised the heck out of us. Unfortunately, her partner Bree failed just short of the safe line."

"So it wasn't a complete pass. Tatya gets points for surviving, but I want to see both make it together before I sign off. Put them through the simulation again."

Painter glanced at his timepiece. "Today? It's getting close to the evening meal, and they're worn out."

"There's no time like now, Rolf. If Tatya's pass isn't a fluke, she'll be able to run the course once more this afternoon."

"And Bree?"

"Too many failures. Easing the pressure won't do her any favors. If she can't switch into kill mode even when she's tired, then there's no point continuing. Let her know she's on the bubble."

An approving smile tugged at Painter's lips. "You're a hard man, Major."

"Train hard, fight easy, live longer." Decker let a grim chuckle escape his throat. "I like that. Perhaps we should write it on the camp's main gate, to remind the professional spooks that life isn't an endless round of cocktail parties, with the occasional search through underwear drawers. One more run through for Tatya and Bree before supper. Let's see if they want it bad enough."

"Will do. What doesn't kill you makes you stronger, right, Major?"

"Except Pathfinders. We *will* kill you."

Painter grinned and pumped his fist in the air. "Ooh-rah, sir."

Moments after the noncom left Zack's office to put their two laggard trainees through the urban survival simulation one more time, the communications system chimed softly, announcing an incoming call. He touched the controls. A holographic Talyn materialized again, this time as part of a live connection and not a recording.

"You received my message?" She asked without preamble.

"Yep."

"A second subspace transmission just arrived from the Scandian Police Authority, this time signed by the inspector investigating Saga's disappearance. I guess the first one came from their public affairs division, which probably funneled your query to the case officer, a man by the name Jakob Harms. Inspector Harms would like us to transmit Ingrid's missive. He hasn't been able to contact her for several days, and neither friends, nor family knows where she is."

Decker sat back, eyes on his partner's hologram and rubbed his chin while a grimace split his square face. "Did this guy say how many days?"

"No, but he obviously assumed you sent your message right after receiving Ingrid's and calculated the time required for a round-trip subspace transmission."

"Meaning the Scandians lost track of Ingrid before she contacted me."

Talyn nodded. "That's what I figure."

"Crap."

"For what it's worth, Ingrid's message had the expected tags for a transmission from Scandia, including the city, Kollsvik."

"Right on the edge of the Great Northern Ice Sheet. That's where Ingrid was born. It means Saga was probably studying at Kollsvik's Jökul University." Decker exhaled with an air of frustration. "Give Inspector Harms what Ingrid sent me and ask him to keep us abreast of his investigation. If both vanished, we're no longer talking burnt-out doctoral candidate hiding from her orals. We're looking at enemy action."

"Don't jump to conclusions with both feet, Zack. There likely still is a rational and benign explanation."

"Bull! You and I set off Black Sword's implosion, damaging if not outright destroying schemes long in the making. As a result, we're removed from operations for our own safety, because Commodore Ulrich thinks the Coalition's foot soldiers are keen on terminating us before we cause even more dhamage. Then, a few months later, both my ex-wife and my daughter vanish. Tell me that's not an attempt by the opposition to flush us out for a kill. And don't give me your once is happenstance and twice is coincidence crap. That only works in spy stories, not real life."

"It's actually your quip, not mine, honey, and your life is a spy story. Or did that fact escape your notice?"

Decker gave Talyn the rigid digit salute and received a blown kiss in return.

"I love you too, Zack. But we're still not traveling to Scandia. Let the Police Authority do its work. They know how to find people."

"And we don't?" He snorted with derision. "What's their success rate compared to ours? If this is the opposition's handiwork, Inspector Harms and company don't stand a chance."

Talyn didn't immediately reply, but when she spoke it was in a gentle tone. "If it is the opposition's handiwork, Zack, you should face the possibility Ingrid and Saga are already dead. Or that they will be the moment you set foot on Scandia and the bad guys take a bead on your thick skull."

"Don't you think I know that," he snarled back with uncharacteristic vehemence. "Too many of the people I love are dead already because these Coalition assholes want a piece of me. They won't take my only daughter as well, and should they make the mistake of killing her, I will go to Pacifica with a tactical nuke in my rucksack. The ComCorp tower in downtown Hadley desperately needs to be turned into a parking lot, along with every other Amali holding around it."

"I won't argue with the sentiment, but working yourself into a rage based on the evidence we've seen so far won't help your blood pressure. Go for a run around the camp, spar with one of your Pathfinders, get shit-faced on cheap whiskey, whatever will help bleed off the stress and worry. You won't do your trainees or the rest of the staff any good stomping around like a maddened carnosaur." She absorbed his ferocious glare with her usual equanimity, then said, "Besides, we don't hold the tactical nukes, and those who do are smart enough to keep them from the grasping hands of half-crazed spooks."

"Then forget cleaning up Hadley. How about I take a bunch of my Pathfinder friends from the 1st Special Forces Regiment on a paid vacation to see Scandia's ice age wonders? Or perhaps hook up with the Scandia Regiment for a little cold weather training? I'm sure I could convince Colonel Martinson to loan me a few troops, perhaps even an entire squadron. From what I remember, the Scandia Regiment is a solid outfit, always ready for a new challenge."

Talyn's hologram emitted a low chuckle. "That's the Zack I prefer. Thinking like a trooper rather than a nuker. Tell you what, I need to brief the commodore on this anyway, just in case there's a Coalition angle. I'll suggest we might want to think about a contingency plan or two. If the opposition has decided families are fair game, we can't just let it pass without brutal retaliation. They've obviously forgotten the lessons we taught them when we eliminated both Harmon and Walker Amali, meaning we need to stomp on their ugly faces again."

An unexpected grin lit up Decker's face. "Stop it, darling, you're turning me on. I might feel the urge to chat up one of the lovely trainers from the cryptography wing."

"Or I could be at Camp X in two hours."

The Marine's face brightened even more. "Really?"

"No. I'm chief of staff to the flag officer commanding the Special Intelligence Operations Division, not your designated bed warmer. Run four laps around the camp and take a cold shower. I'll call you when I have news.

Until then, nothing has changed — you keep on turning normal people into soulless assassins. And stay away from the crypto trainers. They're a little too strange for my liking, especially the women."

"Be nice, Hera, there's a difference between someone who's strange and someone who's a cipher."

Talyn's parting grimace at his pun left Decker with a smile, but it vanished soon after his partner's hologram. With nothing else on hand to relieve a growing sense of frustration, he pulled on his scout armor, complete with helmet, and swung a heavy pack over his shoulders. Then, he headed for the camp's perimeter road and a long, hard run.

— FOUR —

"Traveling to the fleshpots of the big city, Major?" Command Sergeant Painter poked his head through the open door to Zack's room two days later.

"Business, mostly. The commodore wants to speak with me in person. Besides, I figure I earned a break." Decker tossed his packed overnight bag aside before hauling his favorite Shrehari blaster from the issue battledress holster lying on the table. "That last class was just one shaky student after the other once Fresal and Markku made it through to the next phase."

"At least Bree passed."

"By a micron-thick margin. I'm not entirely convinced she'll survive her first contact with the opposition, not with the nastiness going around these days. She can do it, but I don't think she'll ever fully embrace her dark side."

"Bree still managed better than Nikarov and Suli."

"Which isn't saying much. Those two should thank us for saving their lives instead of giving Commander Hineman grief because we washed them out of close quarters combat and recommended a return to their regular duties."

Painter nodded. "True. And maybe one day, they'll understand this business isn't the sexy fun and games they make it seem in bad fiction."

"Let's hope we're given the green light to increase recruitment of our guys. At least they're already trained not to hold back when it's killing time."

"Is that why you're going to Sanctum, Major? So you can convince the commodore this outfit needs more Special Forces operators?"

"That, and other matters." Decker's fingers, moving of their own volition, checked the blaster's ammunition supply and power pack before tucking the large-bore weapon into a shoulder holster under his left arm.

He shrugged on the waist-length black leather jacket he preferred when out of uniform, one in a long succession of similar garments either lost, stolen, or destroyed over the years. It hid his blaster while allowing easy access.

"I'm signing out one of the unmarked combat cars pretending to be staff skimmers. If you, Lara, and Ejaz want to spend forty-eight hours on parole, I can give you a lift."

"Thanks for the offer, sir, but we plan on taking it easy and stick around the area. Lara wants to visit Thurso tomorrow, and Ejaz is trying to convince us we should hike up Mount Caravel so we can clear our minds."

Thurso, the nearest town to Camp X, boasted a famous mineral spa, while Mount Caravel was one of the highest peaks in the area. Decker could understand the allure for people with no one to visit in the big city, unlike himself.

"Enjoy." The Marine slung his bag over one shoulder and, once Painter backed into the corridor, he pulled the door to his room shut. "I'll be back by oh-eight-hundred on Monday at the latest."

"Give Commander Talyn my best."

Decker smirked at him. "Why should I give her *your* best, Rolf? It's not even in the same dimension as mine."

The command sergeant chuckled with delight. "You want to compare dimensions, Major, sir?"

"Enjoy your day at the spa with Lara, my friend. Try not to feel inadequate beside Ejaz."

Decker left a grinning Painter in the hallway of the staff quarters and stepped out into the late afternoon sunshine. The lengthening shadows of the mountains surrounding Camp X told him it would be full dark by the time he reached Sanctum and the staff officers' quarters where he kept an apartment next to Talyn's.

The skimmer waiting for him in Camp X's motor pool looked like something with decades of hard use. The boxy ground effect vehicle would blend with the sort common in the backwoods, hollows, and small-hold farms that dominated this part of Caledonia's main continent, well away from Sanctum.

Once in the city, however, it might attract the attention of bored police officers looking for entertainment in the form of a traffic inspection on a dreary Friday night. But there was little Zack could do about that.

At least the thing was hardened against small arms fire beneath the dull, dinged outer hull, and boasted most of the same sensor gear and ordnance as a combat car, albeit hidden. The driver's door opened at his touch, proof the motor pool had already keyed the skimmer to his biometric information.

He tossed his pack on the passenger seat and switched on the power plant. After watching the telltales come to life on the primary display, he walked around the vehicle and inspected every square centimeter visible to the naked eye. Decker was looking for anything that might come loose or otherwise cause him mischief while he sped down the main strip to Sanctum.

Satisfied the worn appearance was nothing more than cosmetic, he slipped in behind the controls and donned the safety harness. Then, he made his way to the main gate at a sedate pace, mindful of the posted speed limit.

There was no point in giving Camp X's commandant any more reason to look askance at him whenever he entered the staff mess. The commandant, a Navy captain, wasn't known to be fond of Marines in the first place, and the influx of Pathfinders destined for intelligence's Special Operations Division filled him with dismay.

Once past the automated sentry post and through the chicane preventing anyone from ramming the gate at high speed, Decker accelerated. He quickly vanished down a winding road almost entirely hidden from view by native foliage growing on either side of the mountain pass that connected Camp X's secluded nest with the rest of the planet.

The peaks around the camp were part of a restricted-access military reservation surrounded by a fence and sensor perimeter. He therefore passed another automated sentry post upon emerging into the Thurso Valley.

To his left, the lights of Thurso already sparkled in the premature twilight brought on by the sun setting behind Mount Caravel and its equally massive neighbors. But the road leading to the Nestor Valley and thence to Sanctum skirted it. So after a quick, almost wistful glance at the town's welcoming glow, he focused his attention on escaping the highlands altogether and reaching the plains where he could push the skimmer's drives.

Once past Thurso, he merged with regular traffic and switched on his transponder so he could join the controlled network and travel at the fastest allowable speed without attracting attention.

No one knew the Coalition's most wanted man was aboard and by acting like any other anonymous, law-abiding traveler, he aimed to keep it that way. Hera Talyn wasn't a prissy pain in the ass like the late and unlamented Manfred Yang. But she wouldn't hesitate to reprimand him for taking unnecessary risks just so he could shave half an hour off the trip home. The Black Sword traitors turned double agents in the counterintelligence branch were clear about the threat still hanging over his and Hera's heads.

Once out of the Thurso Valley and in the lowlands surrounding Sanctum, Decker left the secondary road in favor of the main north-south highway and let his AI take control. He settled back in the driver's seat, hands folded in his lap and wondered how he could persuade Commodore Ulrich to authorize a training mission on Scandia along with a troop or two from the 1st Special Forces Regiment.

Joshua Bayliss, the Pathfinder School's sergeant major, could easily take Zack's place as head of the combat and explosives training section at Camp X for a few months. He'd relish the chance to escape Fort Arnhem and dabble in black ops again, even if it was at a remove.

With the last rays of the setting sun vanishing in the west, leaving nothing but a purplish band above the mountains, Decker thoughts strayed deep into the past. He dredged up memories of the few happy years he'd enjoyed with Ingrid and their precocious daughter.

Saga had been so pretty, so gentle, and so damn smart he couldn't believe he was her father. But her intense blue eyes matched his, and whenever he stared into them, he knew there was no mistaking her for anything but a Decker, even if she'd grown up with her mother's name. And she'd developed the same love for pre-diaspora history, to the point of choosing it for her doctoral dissertation.

The AI's soft chime pulled him from the depths of his mind palace, signaling the skimmer's imminent arrival in Sanctum. Decker hadn't even noticed the glowing lights of the capital as they neared it in the early evening darkness.

He took over the controls again and directed the skimmer onto the ring road rather than cutting through downtown even though it added several kilometers to his journey. The fewer eyes, both human and electronic who saw him, the better.

Finally, he left the highway and soon found himself at the main gate to the sprawling Armed Services HQ installation. Here, armored military police troopers backed up the automated sentry stations. They subjected his credentials to careful scrutiny, ensuring the biometric data on file matched the man in the old car before letting him into the most secure facility on the planet.

He found an empty spot for his vehicle near the door to the senior officers' apartment complex, a utilitarian building that appeared, at least outwardly, to be no different from any other on the base. Polarized windows prevented any light from escaping and kept curious eyes from prying, but Decker nonetheless glanced up at where he knew Talyn's unit to be.

Was she still sitting at her desk in the Naval Intelligence wing of the main HQ complex, or was she home and ready to make Zack's forty-eight-hour pass memorable?

The Marine let himself into his suite next to Talyn's and opened his side of the doorway connecting both. He tossed his jacket on a sitting room chair before hanging his shoulder holster and blaster on his bed's headboard. Then Decker called up his music collection and selected a piece by a late twentieth century performer he'd recently come across during his idle evenings at Camp X. The beat and lyrics suited his mood, now that he was in the only remaining place he could call home, and about to spend quality time with his partner.

When the music started, loud enough to make whiskey glasses on the sideboard vibrate, Decker belted out the song, eyes on the connecting door. With one side open, the soundproofing no longer protected Talyn's unit from stray decibels. If his partner was home, she'd appear momentarily, no doubt shaking her head at Zack's antics.

So it proved. Talyn's door opened, and she leaned against the frame, arms crossed, one eyebrow cocked in mock disapproval. However, a fond smile appeared when Zack pointed a thick finger at her while singing the song's main refrain. Then, he motioned her to enter and join him in an impromptu dance session. Though still in uniform, she sashayed toward her partner, snapping her fingers to the beat of the song and a broad grin split his face.

When the music finally died away, Decker gave Talyn a bear hug and kissed her with enthusiasm. After releasing her he said, "Honey, I'm home."

"I heard. A new discovery?"

"Late twentieth century. The guy's stage name caught my attention while I was trawling through the historical music database at Camp X one lonely night when I was probably a bit hungry."

"And his name was?"

"Would you believe Meat Loaf?"

Talyn snorted. "That's my partner all right, attracted to musical acts named after food, and not just any kind, but comfort food."

"That was a rip-snorting song, admit it. There's more where it came from. Marvin Lee Aday, also known as Meat Loaf, is now on my favorite classical musician list."

"Only you would go looking for five hundred-year-old tunes."

"What can I say? Artists were talented back then."

"You need to find yourself a rogue wormhole and travel back to the pre-diaspora days, honey. You're obviously too cool for the twenty-sixth century."

Decker winked at her. "I'm too cool for any century. Besides, time-traveling wormholes are a myth."

"They're not, as I found out since taking over the chief of staff role and reading my way through files everyone thought memory-holed. Would you believe Admiral Dunmoore found verifiable evidence of their existence during the Shrehari War?"

"Bullshit."

"Hardly. That incident is just as real as your ability to communicate mentally with Sisters of the Void."

"I should read those files when I'm alone and bored back in the wilds of Camp X."

"Volunteer to do a stint as the commodore's chief of staff, and you can read whatever you like. Otherwise, find something else to keep you from chatting up cryptanalysts." She studied him for a moment. "You seem incredibly cheerful for a man whose only daughter went walkabout."

"Just trying to keep my spirits up in one of only two ways I know. And now you're here, I can indulge in the second one."

"Let me hang up my uniform before you get frisky."

"No need to slip on your civilian clothes just yet."

His stomach rumbled without warning, and she laughed.

"I'm about to put on something nice instead, as are you. Then we'll join the commodore for supper at the HQ officer's mess."

Decker glowered at her. "That sounds less than thrilling. After months in the boonies, I was dreaming of *L'Habitation*'s five-course table d'hôte."

"And how did you expect to reserve seats at such short notice? Not to mention we shouldn't spend more time than necessary where an assassin can find us."

"I was counting on your ability to beguile the maître d' as usual."

"Sorry. The boss is expecting us. Besides, it'll be a working supper, something else we can't do out in the open." She glanced at Zack's clock. "Time to make ourselves respectable. And before you even think of it, no you can't ask the chef to prepare meatloaf."

— FIVE —

The Fleet HQ officer's mess occupied a building resembling nothing so much as a substantial Victorian mansion transplanted from Earth to Caledonia. Even its interior seemed seven hundred years out of date although the quaint decor hid the latest of twenty-sixth-century technology.

When Decker and Talyn checked in with the AI in the vaulted lobby, it directed them to a private alcove off the main dining room, which was large enough for an entire wing of assault shuttles.

Raucous noise from the bar taking up almost half of the ground floor created a background buzz that pursued them up the winding stone staircase. On a Friday evening, officers with no families waiting for them at home celebrated the end of the week in traditional happy hour style. By imbibing generous amounts of ethanol while noshing on mounds of free finger food. Mercifully, sound dampeners kept the upper levels safe from the perils of second-hand revelry, which suited Decker just fine.

They found Commodore Konstantin Ulrich, head of the Special Intelligence Operations Division, already seated at a table set for three with a glass of red wine in hand. As soon as he spied Talyn from the corner of his eyes, his head snapped up and the tablet he was reading vanished into a pocket of his sober civilian business suit.

"Good evening, sir."

"Commander, Major." He nodded in greeting. "Thank you for joining me. Please sit. And welcome home from the back of beyond, Zack, even if it's only on a forty-eight-hour pass."

"Camp X has its charms, sir." He took the chair to Ulrich's left. "But the entertainment leaves much to be desired."

At an unseen signal, a serving droid appeared, bearing a glass of gin and tonic for Talyn and a bottle of vintage Shrehari ale for Decker.

"Is this your doing, Commodore?" Decker asked, taking the proffered drink with something approaching reverence. "Or has the mess somehow programmed its AIs to anticipate our requests?"

"Look at the vintage, Major."

Decker examined the label with a connoisseur's eye. "A five-year-old *T'klach* bottled on Shrehari Prime. The mess doesn't normally carry it; I've never asked for it here, and the only one who knows I consider this to be the best vintage ever is Hera." He turned to his partner and blew her a kiss. "Thank you, sweetie. This almost makes up for not greeting me in the accustomed manner."

Talyn cocked an eyebrow. "Almost? Careful there, *Major*. Lack of proper gratitude could make your weekend feel rather chilly."

"In that case," Decker bowed his head in thanks, "may a thousand blessings rain on your head." He uncapped the bottle and inhaled the pungent, alcoholic aroma. Then he sighed with contentment.

Ulrich raised his glass. "I propose a toast. To my deadliest team of operatives. May they be back in the field as soon as possible."

"I'll drink to that." Decker, a wolfish smile on his face, brandished the green, twisted alien bottle.

After a solemn sip, they sat back in their chairs and Ulrich said, "Pavlik Hineman speaks well of your efforts in training our prospective agents to fight dirty and win."

"I didn't know Hineman spoke well of anyone, least of all me."

"And yet he does. Pavlik's not been in the field for years, but you'd be wrong to think he can't appreciate that the game has become deadlier. He knows it now requires a more ruthless, less refined approach to survive and win. Pavlik therefore understands that's where the training you and your Pathfinders dispense takes on added importance. In fact, Pavlik would like to see you permanently assigned to Camp X, but I can't afford to waste one of my best officers training others while he can still strike fear in the hearts of the opposition."

"Glad to hear you say it, sir. I'll go stir crazy up there in due course. Any experienced Pathfinder can teach my stuff."

"Minus what you learned through experience by running covert ops," Talyn said.

Decker glared at her. "I thought you were on my side, *Commander*. While I won't deny the experience I amassed working with you nice psychopaths is useful, I wouldn't overstate its importance. The instructors I poached from the Pathfinder School are doing most of the work now. Under my supervision, of course. And they're better at it than Pavlik Hineman's staff. Someone like Sergeant Major Bayliss, for example, could do pretty much everything I can. And he's not the only old-timer kicking around Fort Arnhem with a bagful of dirty tricks in his pocket."

Ulrich nodded. "I'll take the suggestion under advisement. Hera tells me you think we should also look to the 1st Special Forces Regiment for new operatives rather than recruiting likely candidates from within Naval Intelligence."

"It's easier to teach trained killers the weirding ways of spookdom than to take analysts and turn them into killers, sir. And it's faster than combing the Fleet at large for people like my kind, compassionate, and saintly partner. The pass-fail statistics prove it." When Talyn made to speak, Decker raised his hand. "Admittedly, our sample size is small, but it points at a trend."

"Did you discuss the matter with Commander Hineman?" Ulrich asked.

"No, sir." Decker shook his head. "I didn't think he'd be interested, considering I'm only an adopted member of the intelligence tribe."

"You're as much an intelligence officer as anyone under my command," Ulrich replied in a dry tone, "and you've earned the right to speak up, perhaps more so than many in this organization. Without you risking your life to find Major Redmon, Black Sword might be well on the way to destroying us. You think we should recruit more Special Forces operators? Done. Work something out with Hera and make the next training serial a Special Forces only group. Then we'll see if your theory is valid."

"Thank you, sir."

"Don't thank me. Prove that we can shorten the production pipeline and put enough agents out there to regain the upper hand. Who knows what the Coalition and its imps are doing while we're rebuilding our strength."

"They're probably busy kidnapping a Naval Intelligence officer's daughter and ex-partner," Decker said, deadpan.

"Ah, yes. Hera briefed me on that matter. And we will discuss it after we order our meal. The mess is offering a fixed menu five-course table d'hôte tonight that might not rival your favorite restaurant's, but it'll beat whatever they've been feeding you at Camp X, Major."

Decker shrugged. "Since I've been forbidden to order comfort food, I guess I'm in."

Ulrich gave the Marine a curious look, then glanced at Talyn who responded with a mysterious smile. The head of the Special Operations Division shrugged. "I suppose that comes under the heading of don't ask, lest you hear things you'd rather not. Three tables d'hôte it is."

"Now that we've committed ourselves, what are the courses?" Decker asked.

"You'll find out as each is brought in, Major. Enjoy the mystery." The serving droid reappeared at that moment, bearing three plates. "And here is our first taste."

"Fast little bugger, isn't he?" The Marine remarked as the droid carefully placed an artistically arranged serving of smoked fish in front of him. "You were that sure we'd go with the fixed menu, sir?"

"Let's just say I took a chance based on my chief of staff's knowledge of her long-time partner. *Bon appetit*, my friends."

Decker took a bite and said, after swallowing, "Very nice. I could almost fancy myself at *L'Habitation*. Did the kitchen staff take cooking lessons while I was in the boonies? This is fancier than anything I've ever eaten here."

"It's a matter of incentive. Grand Admiral Larsson is hosting a private dinner in the VIP room, and we're the unintended beneficiaries of a highly motivated executive chef who likes his job."

"You mean everyone eating in the mess tonight gets the five-star treatment?"

Ulrich chuckled as he shook his head. "No. Only the Grand Admiral's party and us. As I said, the executive chef likes his job."

Zack took another bite, then glanced at Talyn. "Remind me to keep the boss happy. Not only does it help prolong life, but it also gets us fancy food at a fraction of what they charge in town."

"Or it could be a condemned man's last meal."

"And what fresh hell are you condemning me to now? I've done the slave soldier thing; spent quality time in exile with the Commonwealth's worst criminals; fought giant insects; overthrew a government or two; redid basic training as a convict recruit, and tangled with psychotic mind-meddlers. Not to mention that these days, I put my life at risk every time I try to teach a wide-eyed intelligence analyst how to slit throats without making a big, noisy mess." Decker swallowed the last of his fish and sighed with contentment. "I don't think there's anything left for me to experience. Other than good food. That was incredible. Hopefully, the remaining courses will be just as fantastic. Now, can we discuss my daughter?"

Talyn said, "I heard from Chief Superintendent Morrow this afternoon. She confirms through her sources that the Scandian Police Authority is treating Saga Lagman's disappearance as a missing person case."

"And Ingrid?" Decker asked.

"We didn't know about the police losing touch with her when I queried Morrow. And I've seen nothing from the inspector charged with the case since sending him a copy of Ingrid's message."

"Hera tells me you suspect foul play." Ulrich took a sip of his wine.

"Gut feel, sir. Who knows what personal information Yang passed to his Black Sword buddies, and through them to the *Sécurité Spéciale* or whatever henchmen the Coalition uses for the really slimy stuff."

"You haven't seen your daughter in twenty years, Major. She'll not be the person you see in your mind's eye. She'll definitely not be a young, female version of a fearless Marine who finds his entertainment by jumping out of perfectly good shuttles from low orbit. Perhaps she *has* dropped out of sight to deal with personal issues. She wouldn't be the first doctoral candidate to feel overwhelmed by the pressure. Saga may be your daughter, and half of her DNA comes from you, but she'll not be Zack Decker, someone capable of dealing with just about any situation that comes his way."

"Maybe, Commodore, but my gut tells me this is something else, and I'll remind you I've not been proved wrong often in my years working for you. Then there's the Scandian inspector saying he hasn't been able to contact Ingrid since before she recorded her message."

"You think the opposition is trying to flush you out?" Ulrich asked. "Plausible, I suppose. You and Hera have caused the Coalition more grief than the rest of the Special Intelligence Operations Division combined."

"I'm the one with a weak spot. A child, however much estranged. Hera has nothing that can be used to pressure her."

Talyn laid her hand on his. "Except for you, Zack. I've become rather accustomed to your presence."

"Is that what they call it nowadays?" He asked with an ironic smile.

The next course appeared at that moment, once more delivered by the silent droid who removed the empty appetizer plates. Decker examined his bowl with an appreciative smile. "I could become accustomed to this level of catering."

"Don't. But back to your daughter's disappearance. If there's foul play involved, what is it you'd like to do that the Scandian authorities can't?"

"Find her, sir. If she's been kidnapped, terminate the kidnappers with the most extreme prejudice I can muster, something that's beyond a cop's ability."

"But if you're right and she was abducted to force you into the open, then embarking on a quest to free her will play into the opposition's hands, no?"

Decker snorted with derision. "They've tried to eliminate me how many times now? And how many of theirs died instead?"

"Assuming I let you go to Scandia, what then?" Ulrich asked in a reasonable tone. "The police won't want you interfering or freelancing. Besides, how long has it been since your last visit?"

"It's been a while, sir," Decker grudgingly admitted. "A few years before my involuntary transfer to intelligence."

"So you may not find many contacts you can rely on."

"I'm sure the Scandia Regiment will adopt me with pleasure. There's bound to be noncoms who'll remember me from the 902nd. Of course, I could bring friends of my own. A troop or two from the 1st Special Forces Regiment for example. I'm sure Colonel Martinson would grease our way with his bosses at the Joint Special Operations Command. Scandia has some of the best cold weather training facilities anywhere."

"Yes, Hera mentioned your notion of taking a trip to the Rim Sector under innocent military pretenses." Ulrich nodded at their bowls. "But right now, eat before it gets colder than Scandia's Great Northern Ice Sheet."

With the second course behind them, Ulrich sat back, wine glass in hand, and studied Decker.

"What if the police find your daughter while you and your troop or two are in transit to Scandia? The Special Forces Regiment need not send its operators to the Rim Sector for cold weather training. Caledonia has perfectly good polar regions apt to give any foolish Marine enough frostbite for several weeks in a regen tank. It would be a wasted trip during a time you're needed here, teaching the next generation of agents to survive and prosper. Besides your friends in Fort Arnhem, like the rest of JSOC, are already dealing with a high operational tempo."

Decker, eyes locked on Ulrich, took a swig of his ale and exhaled loudly. "I guess this five-star meal is my consolation prize for being told going to Scandia is not only a no but a hell no."

"The needs of the many..." Talyn said in a soft tone. "You're usually the first to remind everyone it has to be mission before self."

"Yeah." Decker's tone was tinged with bitterness. "And if the Corps wanted us to have families, it would issue them along with the rest of our gear."

"Then you understand my situation," Ulrich replied. "If your daughter vanished through her own volition, she'll reappear. If ordinary foul play is involved, the matter belongs to the Scandian Police Authority, and if the Coalition is involved, it can only be to hasten your death along with Saga's. Any reasonable person in my position would conclude there's no point in allowing you to get involved. And I won't insult you by saying I'm sorry it has to be this way."

The Marine drained his ale and glanced at Talyn. "Since this is my party, I suppose there's more of that five-year-old *T'klach* stashed away somewhere?"

She nodded and touched a hidden screen embedded in the table's edge. "But try not to exceed three bottles. More than that and your snores are loud enough to wake the dead. You may be as large as a Shrehari, but their metabolism can handle it better."

He glowered at her. "Bugger the Shrehari and their damned metabolisms."

**

As they walked back to their quarters under a starlit sky after a meal more notable for its offerings than the conversation once Commodore Ulrich gently but firmly rejected any notion of traveling to Scandia, Talyn wrapped her arm around Decker's.

"Did you consider that your reaction and urge to do something might stem from subconscious guilt at having missed your daughter's formative years?"

Decker snort of derision sounded false to Talyn's ears. "A psychopath giving me psychology lessons? Will wonders never cease?"

"Wonders, no. But ask yourself this, smart ass. Do you want to spend the weekend staring at your living room walls, or make an early return to Camp X? Or do you want to engage in a reasonably grown up discussion? We can't spend the entire time in bed, nor can we gad about town. I raise the possibility of subconscious guilt as a driver to suggest your gut instinct could be influenced by other factors, things unrelated to Coalition minions lurking in the bushes. This is new territory for you."

They walked on in silence, crossing a quiet, darkened headquarters complex seemingly placed into suspended animation for the weekend. However, beneath their feet, in an operations center hardened against the strongest of kinetic strikes from orbit, the duty watch, several hundred strong, stood guard while the rest of the staff enjoyed two days off.

Talyn and Decker should have been in one of the underground passages that crisscrossed the base, connecting all buildings, in keeping with their orders to avoid giving a long-range sniper a chance at a kill. But the Marine had decided otherwise, calling the risk of being shot infinitesimal and his need for fresh air overwhelming.

"Okay, Hera. I'll play along," he finally said in a resigned tone. "Am I experiencing a sudden feeling of parental responsibility after twenty years? Probably. I didn't want to dissolve the marriage — that was Ingrid. If only she'd talked to me first, given me a chance to end my tour with the 902nd and take a shore billet so we could find some normalcy, but by then it was too late.

"At first I blamed her. Oh, boy did I ever blame her. Until Josh Bayliss pointed out the truth — that my priorities were out of sync with Ingrid's. I placed the Corps ahead of my family and ignored growing problems. Did I feel guilty after Josh made me face reality? In spades. Being asked to stay away from my daughter during her minority merely compounded it."

He sighed.

"But remember, this was the old Zack, the one with a temper and the urge to burn his bridges. If my family wanted nothing to do with me, then I'd take my lumps and carry on alone. With no choice other than wallow in self-pity, something I don't do well, I consigned Saga and Ingrid to my private memory hole, where they stayed until I read Ingrid's message. It revived a lot of old feelings, unresolved stuff. Regrets, self-recrimination, and yeah, guilt."

"So now you want to make amends by rushing headlong to your daughter's aid, even though she's light years away. You don't know what's happening. But your mind has concocted the absolute worst-case scenario. One which, if it's true, could mean she might even be dead by now, or will be once the opposition has taken you down."

Decker stopped to look at her. "Maybe."

"I can't tell you how to deal with your feelings, honey. That's not my area of expertise, as you've pointed out more than once. But you're sufficiently self-aware to figure things out." She reached up and touched his cheek with her fingertips. "And I'll help in any way I can — except by letting you abscond on the next starship, that is."

He gave her a half-hearted leer. "I know how you can help me right now."

She chuckled. "Out here in the open? Do you want another stint in the brig?" Talyn took him by the hand and nodded toward the brooding apartment block down the street. "Try to restrain yourself until we're in our quarters."

— SIX —

Sunday evening came around with surprising speed, and Decker, who'd kept his disgruntlement under tight control in Talyn's presence, climbed aboard his skimmer, lost in thought, after a quick supper at the officer's mess.

He was almost convinced, thanks to Talyn, that guilt was clouding his Pathfinder's instincts, and that Saga's disappearance was due to more prosaic reasons than the Coalition.

But his skeptical half wasn't buying it. Besides, his partner was eminently capable of feeding him lies to make sure he didn't go absent without leave. She was an expert manipulator and used her talent without a shred of compunction, even on the man who cared for her more than anyone else.

He gunned the drives and pulled out of the parking lot without a backward glance at the dark apartment block. As he passed through the security checkpoint, rain began to fall in thick, greasy drops that tried to wash out the fading twilight.

Decker turned control over to the vehicle's AI, preferring to let it navigate through Sanctum in the low visibility while he parsed thoughts that matched the chill of an early autumn's weather. He was barely cognizant of the car merging into traffic on the ring road and becoming just one more anonymous dark vehicle speeding along with mechanical precision.

After a short drive, the AI switched him from the ring road to the main north-south highway and soon, Sanctum's lights faded into the damp darkness, swallowed by distance and rolling foothills.

Traffic became sparse. For a while, Decker felt as if he was the last surviving human on Caledonia, hurtling through the night alone in his skimmer, with nary a light to be seen. What vehicles he met were as dark as his and visible only to the AI's sensors.

Eventually, Decker's skimmer caught up with a massive road train also heading north. As with most of these heavy duty, multi-trailer transports, he assumed it was pulled by an automated traction unit under the control of an AI dedicated to driving. One unlike the AI in his vehicle, which devoted part of its artificial brain to the sophisticated sensor gear and defensive weaponry hidden under the innocuous shell.

Decker checked with his AI to confirm it was in contact with both traffic control and the road train before they passed it. He didn't trust automated vehicles and wanted to be sure the road train's programming wouldn't experience an electronic brain fart and suddenly swerve into his lane, sending him caroming into the wood line bordering the highway.

Seconds before his AI was due to move left, the back end of the rearmost trailer dropped, forming a ramp whose edge rode a mere centimeter or two above the ground. Then, Decker felt his skimmer lurch, as if gripped by an invisible hand, and the sensor suite's threat detector began to howl.

Tractor beam, the Marine decided. *The damned road train is big enough to carry a beam generator and its power plant. Someone wants to haul me aboard, and not because they're offering a ride back to Camp X.*

His skimmer and the road train were traveling at speeds close to two hundred kilometers an hour along a narrow clear strip through a dense forest, making evasion, let alone ejection impossible. He tried reversing thrust to reduce his forward momentum, but merely triggered vibrations that shook the entire vehicle to the point of rattling his teeth.

The tractor beam held him firmly in its grip, and was hauling him toward the lowered ramp. Decker had only seconds to find an escape plan. Once inside the trailer, he would be at the mercy of his abductors. He made sure his safety harness was snug and took a last, quick glance around the passenger compartment, looking for loose objects that might take his head off.

A heartbeat later, the front end of his skimmer touched the ramp and angled upward, aimed at the black maw of the waiting trap. Decker opened a hidden compartment by his right arm and touched a recessed button, activating the well-camouflaged weapons system.

He would have one chance only.

A pair of twenty-millimeter plasma cannon emerged from either side of the front compartment while a fire-control hologram materialized before his eyes, its red aiming pip centered on the middle of the trailer's opening. He took hold of the joystick that popped out of the console between his knees with his left hand, half expecting it to be sabotaged and refuse his touch, but the red aiming pip turned green.

The skimmer was almost entirely on the ramp when he took a deep breath, braced himself, and fired a stream of plasma into the trailer, lighting up a massive tractor beam generator occupying its front half. The first dozen rounds splashed off the generator's armored sides, gouging divots and sending up a rain of gleaming metal droplets.

But Decker kept his finger on the firing stud until the plasma stream penetrated the protective shell and destroyed its innards. An unexpected and sudden beam reversal, the result of cascading failures brought on by critical damage, violently shoved his skimmer backward, off the ramp, and sent it spinning out of control.

Then, the night lit up with the brightness of a thousand suns as the tractor beam generator failed, transforming it and the rear trailer into a mess of disintegrating shrapnel. Much of that hit the next one in line, which carried the power source.

The explosion sent the road train careening out of control, its AI unable to process the situation. It plowed into the woods, driven by secondary explosions as the portable reactor, lightly protected to make it mobile, lost the damage control fight.

But the Marine saw none of it. His vehicle's artificial brain, the same as any combat car's, could deal with emergencies better than any human, yet at two hundred kilometers an hour, even almost instantaneous reflexes weren't enough.

He struck the tree line a few dozen meters from where the road train was cutting a fiery path into the forest with incredible violence. Thankfully, the security harness prevented Decker from suffering critical injuries.

The reactor's shielding finally gave up the ghost and a pillar of flame tall enough to be seen in Sanctum erupted. The shock wave sent Decker's skimmer spinning head over teakettle away from the inferno. He bounced off the road, then the trees on the opposite side before the car righted itself and skidded for a good hundred meters, leaving its sole occupant stunned and confused, his body a mass of bruises.

Decker's right hand throbbed with the familiar pain of broken fingers after striking the center console repeatedly while his left hand maintained a death grip on the joystick strong enough to make his muscles scream. His neck and head felt like those of a piñata abused by a particularly vicious Shrehari corsair, leaving him with blurred vision further smudged by the white flames turning night into day.

When his eyes could focus once more, he glanced at the status screen and saw his skimmer wasn't moving from the spot without help in the form of a recovery sled. His only way out was on foot. If the folks behind the kidnap attempt were in the vicinity...

At least the car still offered protection. He activated the emergency military communications channel and asked for a link to Talyn's quarters.

Within moments, her face replaced the status display. When she saw Decker, her eyes widened.

"What happened?"

"Look out any north-facing window. I'm within spitting distance of that spectacular blaze." He quickly told her about the incident. "My ride needs a ride. Can you ask someone to fly a recovery flat and fetch me on an emergency basis? If the bad guys are watching this, I can't afford to try hoofing it. Staying in the skimmer is my best protection. Besides, I don't want to answer questions from the police which will swarm this place like flies on a manure pile."

"Why try an abduction instead of simply taking your car out with a heavy anti-armor gun?" Talyn asked absently, eyes to one side, proof she was calling the HQ quick reaction force. "Tractor beams and portable reactors aren't exactly easy to mount on a ground vehicle."

"To flush you out. They hoped that by making me vanish, you'd expose yourself trying for a rescue mission. If they just kill me, your incentive is a lot different." He winced as he shifted his position and a muttered curse escaped his lips.

"Makes sense. And you obviously need medical attention. The quick reaction force's recovery sled will take you straight to the base hospital before delivering the skimmer to the repair section. There, they've been alerted. Make sure your beacon is working and stay on this channel until they arrive. If anything else happens, I want to see it."

"I doubt this was specifically targeted at me. They were waiting for either one of us to show up on their sensor screen. They didn't go after you when you visited Camp X the other day, meaning no one had eyes on your movements, or at least no one could make a clean ID of your car. Plus you stayed overnight, and a daytime snatch is a lot riskier."

"Since they knew which car to capture, do you think there's a traitor at Camp X?"

"Maybe. It's obvious someone fingered my ride, but that could have happened in Sanctum, while you and I were having deep philosophical discussions about human procreation." He paused for a moment to pull a stray thought from his bruised cerebral cortex. "Change my last. They definitely saw me over the weekend. Otherwise, they wouldn't know to set the trap until they saw me leave HQ. But that doesn't cancel the possibility of a snitch back at Camp X. I suggest our forensics specialists go over this skimmer the moment it reaches the repair section, just in case there's an electronic stowaway that allowed the opposition to track me."

"Will do." Her eyes slipped to one side again. "The QRF has lifted and confirm they see the conflagration.

They also say a number of civilian vehicles are inbound to your location with a lot of chatter on the first responders' channel. They'll arrive before our guys."

"I can either play dead and hope the rescue folks don't decide to cut my skimmer open before the QRF takes me away. Or someone could slap a national security designation on me and tell the authorities to stay away on pain of prosecution. At this point, we can't even begin to hide Fleet involvement in the accident — hell, I probably expended at least a hundred rounds of twenty millimeter — so we might as well be brazen about it."

She nodded. "True. Wait one." Her face turned to the right, and he saw her lips move, but without hearing a sound. She looked at him again. "The boss knows what's up. He'll warn the CNI," she said, referring to the Chief of Naval Intelligence, Vice Admiral Kruczek, Commodore Ulrich's immediate superior. "And he'll alert the Civilian Affairs duty officer, but I'd say your best bet is to play dead. By the time word gets to the first responders, the QRF will be there."

"What a fucking mess." Decker winced again. "And the adrenaline's fading away, which means..."

"You're starting to feel the pain, honey. I know. But at least you're alive."

"With one of the worst cases of whiplash I've ever experienced. Know a good ambulance-chasing lawyer?"

Before Talyn could answer, a new voice broke through on the emergency military channel. "Major Decker, this is Command Sergeant Seppala, B Company, HQ QRF. We've locked on to your vehicle beacon. Confirm code alpha three theta seven five one."

Decker touched a side screen with his left hand and called up the unique identifier his AI was transmitting. "I confirm code alpha three theta seven five one."

"Your skimmer looks like it's been through the wars," Seppala replied.

"That's what happens when you shoot up a tractor beam generator at point-blank range with twenty mike-mike."

"Heck of a barbecue too, sir."

"That'll be mostly from the reactor powering the damned thing. It took damage and went critical." A trio of bright red rescue vehicles festooned with flashing lights landed around Zack's downed car. "The civilians are here."

"We're about two minutes out, Major. Stand by."

Three lightly armored Caledonian police troopers climbed out of the grounded vehicles, one from each, and cautiously approached Decker's skimmer to the howl of approaching aerial trucks, dispatched by the Sanctum Fire Department. Though they couldn't see in through the polarized windows, Zack could make out their every feature thanks to the fiery blaze creeping toward his position.

One of them held what looked like a small battlefield sensor. He stopped, carefully scanned the skimmer, then, he reached out and pounded on the driver side door, his lips moving behind a lowered helmet visor. When Decker didn't respond, he made a waving motion with his left hand. Two more troopers appeared, one carrying a laser drill, the other a portable power pack.

"Shit," the Marine swore when he identified the implement. "Bastards look to cut my ride open. So much for playing dead."

"Still a minute to go," Seppala said. "I suggest you at least talk to the cops, Major."

"Yeah." Decker switched on the car's external speaker. "Hello, Caledonian police. This vehicle is a classified military unit and must under no circumstances be cut open. A Fleet quick reaction force is inbound to retrieve me. Address any questions to the proper Civilian Affairs office in Sanctum."

The cops backed off at his words, surprised and uncertain. It gave Sergeant Seppala and his platoon enough time to swoop down and land. In the space of a few minutes, the skimmer, with Zack still strapped to his seat, was secured on an aerial flatbed transport.

Soon after that, they were airborne, flying away from an inferno still raging out of control, headed for the safety of the Fleet HQ installation. A safety that had been compromised, if Zack was correct. Somebody had watched him leave the HQ compound, another one of the Black Sword traitors still infesting the command staff.

With the last dregs of adrenaline evaporating, he slumped into his harness, closed his eyes, and made a mental inventory of every ache and pain intruding on his consciousness.

The gentle pleasures of a forty-eight-hour liberty, after months confined to a backwoods training base, now seemed illusory. His next bed would be of the diagnostic kind, under the gentle ministrations of a Navy doctor assigned to the Fleet's premier hospital. Ooh-rah!

— SEVEN —

"Perhaps letting you escape Camp X even for a weekend was a mistake." Commodore Ulrich swept through the door and into Decker's hospital room, Talyn hard on his heels. Both wore naval uniform even at this late hour. "The Civil Affairs people are having the most exciting Sunday night of their lives, trying to keep the police and rescue services from turning your little accident into a rehearsal for the apocalypse. You never do things by half, do you, Major?"

Decker, lying on a diagnostic bed, his bare body covered by a white sheet and one arm in a regen sleeve, made a face at his visitors.

"You can't escape a tractor beam unless you put it out of action. It's hardly my fault if they removed most of its shielding and that of the reactor so they could fit the whole mess inside a road train. Twenty-millimeter rounds will eat through thin armor before you can release the firing stud."

"The doctor says you're a mess of internal bruising, but otherwise everything is in working order," Talyn interjected, before her partner and her boss embarked on a discussion about the relative merits of various escape methods. "Whiplash and a mild concussion notwithstanding. They want to keep you under observation until the morning, after which it'll be light duties for a week or two. You're lucky to be alive. The repair tech took one look at your skimmer and declared it beyond salvaging. I'd hate to think of the outcome if your car's passenger compartment wasn't reinforced to military specifications. And in case you're wondering, I retrieved your overnight bag. It's in considerably better shape than you are."

"Any stowaways?"

"The tech is still examining the wreckage. But if someone planted an external tracker, forget about finding it after your car bounced around the highway."

Ulrich pulled up a chair and sat. "In any case, you're in no condition to continue training new operatives at Camp X for a while, especially if there's another traitor in the ranks."

"Call Bayliss down from Fort Arnhem. He can do anything I can, some of it even better, and he's tired of the Pathfinder School routine. Other than jumping with the odd trainee serial, there's not much action for a school sergeant major. In the meantime, Rolf Painter should be able to handle matters, as long as Pavlik Hineman doesn't ride his ass. Rolf's not one of old Pavlik's biggest fans."

"And Sergeant Major Bayliss?"

Decker chuckled, then winced at the sudden surge of discomfort. "Josh has a lifetime of experience dealing with senior officers. Pavlik will be asking him for advice within a day or two."

"If the commodore has no objections, I'll call Colonel Capurso in the morning and arrange for Bayliss to join us on a short assignment. And I'll chat with both Commander Hineman and Command Sergeant Painter."

"The commodore has no objections. Zack is stuck here for now, and we must continue producing field agents.

Now, Major, Hera tells me you think they tried to abduct you without leaving a trace to draw her out as well."

Decker nodded, triggering a coughing fit. When he recovered, he said, "Stands to reason. There's no other way to justify the trouble they took with their rolling trap. If they merely wanted me dead, an anti-armor gun would have done the job with little fuss."

"But they didn't expect you to be armed."

"If there's a traitor at Camp X, he or she will know my skimmer was a combat car under the skin. They probably didn't expect me to open fire at such close range and risk blowing myself up with the rest of it."

Talyn's thin lips twisted into a smirk. "Funny how they still haven't figured out you're a rabid fan of explosive solutions to every one of life's little problems."

"And this time, I solved two problems in one go."

"Oh?" She cocked a questioning eyebrow. "And what would the second one be?"

"I've escaped Camp X duty."

"For now." When she saw the glint in his bloodshot eyes, she added, "But you're still not traveling to Scandia."

"I'd say this latest incident pretty much supports the notion my daughter's disappearance isn't just a random event. They counted on my reacting as I did, hoping I'd leave Camp X, with or without authorization. Maybe they even thought I'd be recalled to Sanctum for a personal talk with the commodore. Whatever. It worked up until I decided opening fire was my sole alternative."

"Or our enemies had an abduction plan lined up just waiting for one of us to be vulnerable. And when you showed up here on Friday night, one of theirs, someone still at large, spotted you, called it in, and they pulled the trigger. Nothing to do with Saga."

"Either alternative is plausible," Ulrich conceded with a nod. "But if the Black Sword mole is at Camp X, why wait until Sunday? Why not try on Friday evening?"

"Time for one thing. I requested the skimmer only an hour before my departure. That was the first anyone at Camp X knew I was heading to Sanctum. Between the time it would take to warn the opposition and then set the trap, I'd be here already. Then, they probably also figured I wouldn't be as alert on Sunday night, after a weekend of carousing."

"I doubt they'll try a similar trick again," Ulrich said. "Not after it failed with such spectacular results. And speaking of results," he climbed to his feet, "Hera and I are meeting the Chief in ten minutes. It's all hands on deck for Naval Intelligence tonight — now that there's proof of further Black Sword rot in our midst. Try to rest, Major, and don't leave the hospital until Hera fetches you in the morning. You're officially on lockdown, complete with guards in the hallway. I'm sure you don't need an explanation why."

"No, sir."

"We can't afford another towering inferno. I'm sure the Governor General of Caledonia is already giving Grand Admiral Larsson an earful about the Fleet turning Highway One into a flaming mess."

"Understood, sir. But I can't control the enemy's actions."

"Just make sure you control yours. Good night."

Talyn blew Decker a kiss, then followed her commanding officer out the door, leaving the Marine to his thoughts. And to his inflamed nerve endings.

******

Monday morning turned into Monday afternoon before Talyn stuck her head through the doorway to Decker's hospital room. "You're not AWOL. Good. Does that mean you're turning into a responsible, mature senior officer?"

"No. It means I'm still feeling my aches and pains, and can't take on the two meatheads standing guard in the hallway. One, maybe, but not both. Did you come to spring me?"

She stepped into the room with a bundle tucked under her arm and nodded. "Yes, and escort you back to your apartment, where you'll find everything you need to convalesce. You're confined to quarters until further notice, by order of the Chief of Naval Intelligence."

Decker put on a wounded air. "Hey, I'm the victim here, remember? Why is the Chief punishing me?"

"Something about avoiding a flare-up of violence at the heart of Fleet HQ, no doubt. Josh Bayliss will take over from you at Camp X for the next six weeks. He's wrapping up things today and handing responsibility for the Pathfinder School to the Standards Squadron sergeant major tomorrow. I spoke with Rolf Painter, and he'll run things until Josh shows up. Pavlik Hineman has no issues with the changes. They send their regards and wish you a speedy recovery."

The Marine snorted. "What? No snide remarks about my propensity for causing big bangs?"

She gave him a mischievous smile. "Josh did touch on your unfortunate habit of overdoing things."

"That's more like it." Decker threw back the covers and sat up, then swung his legs over the edge of the bed with a soft groan. "I will need gentleness from you, my dear."

"That goes without saying. Exerting yourself is forbidden."

"If you do all the work, I won't need to." He smirked at her as he climbed to his feet.

She tossed the bundle she'd been carrying on the bed and nodded at it. "Clean clothes. Get dressed so I can take you home and return to work."

"My sidearm?"

"In your quarters, along with what you were wearing yesterday."

While Decker swapped the hospital pajamas for a set of loose workout clothes, he asked, "Anything new on my misadventure?"

Talyn shook her head. "Not much. The repair section found no indications of a tracking device. But like I said, it might not have survived your bouncing around."

"If they knew what my car looked like and saw me leave the base, the buggers wouldn't need a tracking device. What about the road train?"

"There's not much left. The police and fire service will do the usual forensic analysis, of course, but from what I've seen, I doubt we'll find any clues about the generator and reactor's origin."

"You went up there?"

"At first light. Don't worry, I took a platoon from the quick reaction force along as bodyguards."

"Which is why you're late springing me from this place." He stepped into a pair of light shoes. "Done. Let's go."

His first few steps came with a barely suppressed grimace as bruised muscles made their displeasure known.

"Tender?" Talyn asked.

"A little stiff, nothing more." When she didn't reply, contenting herself with a sympathetic smile, he asked,

"You're not turning my comment into a acerbic joke? Are you actually feeling empathy for others?"

"No. I can't feel empathy for anyone, not even you. But I can feign it well enough to fool most, and that means no crude remarks when an injured man misspeaks."

Decker gave her a broad grin. "Bullshit. I know there's a soft spot for me somewhere inside that soulless void."

"Whatever helps you sleep at night."

They crossed the base via its underground transportation network, this time availing themselves of the silent, smooth, automated passenger carriers instead of walking.

Once in the senior officers' apartment block lobby, Talyn asked, "Can I trust you to go straight up and settle in? Or do you need an escort to make sure you obey orders? I really must return to work."

The Marine raised a solemn hand. "I'll go to my quarters without making any detours, promised. But if I'm missing a few things in the food and drink department, can I ask the commissary to make a delivery or should I call on you to shop for me?"

"Everything you need is already there." She gently touched his cheek with her fingertips. "Try to relax, Big Boy. Catch up on your historical readings. Or if you insist on feeling useful, put a briefing package together for Josh, so he can at least pretend to follow your lead at Camp X. I'll see you when I'm done with the latest crop of brush fires, not least those resulting from last night."

"Sucks to be the commodore's chief of staff, doesn't it?"

"Would I rather be in the field? Yes. But he needs me at his side right now." When Decker opened his mouth to reply, she pointed at the lift. "Off to your quarters."

"Aye, aye, Commander, sir." As Talyn turned to leave, he added, "And if you want to feel even more useful tonight, I might enjoy a massage…"

"I'm sure you would," she tossed over her shoulder before vanishing down the stairs again.

As promised, his apartment was fully stocked with a week's worth of meals and his favorite tipples. He also found a hand-written note from Commodore Ulrich pinned to the wall, a not-so-subtle reminder he was confined to quarters by order of the CNI.

Decker found a dozen Shrehari ales in his refrigerator bearing the alien label identifying them as five-year-old *T'klach* vintage. Talyn's doing again. He took one of them, uncapped it, and raised the greenish, twisted bottle in a sardonic toast to his would-be abductors.

"May you dumb assholes continue to fail in the most spectacular way possible."

Before Decker could swallow a single sip of the potent brew, his apartment's comlink chimed for attention. The Fleet's starburst, anchor, and crossed swords insignia swam into existence before his eyes, followed by words announcing an incoming personal message routed through the HQ communications center. He presented his credentials and accepted the missive, then took that delayed sip of ale while staring at his console with suspicious eyes, wondering whether it augured more bad news.

"Play the message."

"It is text only, accompanied by a static image," an AI's voice replied.

Words suspended in midair shimmered before his eyes.

Congratulations on surviving the highway holocaust you created yesterday, Major Decker. We should have expected you to take the risk of firing on the tractor beam generator at point-blank range, trusting in your car's hardened passenger compartment for survival. But the game is merely beginning.

The holographic image of a young, long-haired, blond woman with deep blue eyes replaced the words. Though Zack Decker hadn't seen his daughter since she was a child, the Marine recognized her immediately. Saga's features faintly echoed his own. But the hard lines she'd inherited from him were mercifully tempered by her mother's softness, although without entirely disguising an innate air of stubbornness Decker recognized whenever he looked at himself in the mirror. And she seemed scared.

"Open a link with Commander Talyn," he ordered the AI in a tight tone, "and then ask the communications center do a full trace-back on this message."

— EIGHT —

"The preliminary analysis of the hologram shows it's a human and not an avatar," Hera Talyn said, not bothering with a greeting when Decker accepted her call later that afternoon. "However, the image has been sanitized of any traces that might show where it was taken. The message itself was cleansed of tags, but the communication center's trace-back points at it originating on Caledonia. Although from where remains a mystery. It bounced several times around the planet via the satellite constellation, obscuring the point of transmission. The signals intelligence folks will keep at it, but don't hold your breath. Are you sure it was Saga?"

"As sure as I can be after twenty years. She looks like such a convincing blend of Ingrid and me that I can't see her being anyone else."

"You of all people should remember how easily a good disguise can fool even the best biometric scanners."

"I'm not a biometric scanner, honey. Parents are a lot harder to fool. We can recognize our offspring even years later because we see ourselves. If that wasn't Saga, then whoever made her up to look like my daughter needs to come work for us." Decker shrugged with irritation. "Besides, it's clear the opposition know who my daughter is, whether or not that was Saga, and are using her to reach me. It's no longer speculation but hard fact. Stuff that up your plasma conduit, Chief of Staff."

"No need to invoke unnatural acts, Zack. I'm well aware of the situation, and I think the message is merely part of whatever they've hatched to draw us out after their abduction attempt failed."

"Aye," he nodded. "And I expect them to reach out again at any moment with part two, designed to trigger a rash move on my part."

"Which you will not act on," she warned in a tone that brooked no reply. "Further communiqués come straight to me. You will not leave your apartment, or call anyone other than the boss or me, in case Yang wasn't the only turncoat in Special Operations. The opposition still has people close to us as last night's events prove." When he didn't speak, she added, "The expected response, Major, is *yes, sir.*"

"Yes, sir," he parroted without the slightest trace of irony in his tone. "Of course, keeping me confined to quarters works better with incentives."

"Drink another ale, watch a bit of entertainment. I'll be home when I've put out today's fires." Her image faded away, leaving the Marine alone once more with his worries.

Inaction never suited Decker, even if his entire body ached from bouncing around the highway, but he knew better than to drown his worries in alcohol. Becoming a booze hound ultimately saw him shanghaied into Naval Intelligence years earlier, albeit via an incredibly twisted route. If he hadn't staggered into an old buddy's bar on Aramis looking for a drink or ten...

Decker made himself another cup of coffee and dove into the latest literary find he'd dug up from the HQ archives, hoping it would help settle his troubled thoughts.

It didn't, but reading about the follies and foibles of a long-gone military intelligence organization serving a totalitarian state kept him mildly entertained. Especially since he saw the Fleet's future reflected in that historical account, should the Coalition attain its goal.

A stab of hunger pulled him back to the present. He glanced at the time display, then noticed darkness settling over Sanctum. Yet so far, no sign of Talyn.

Decker threw together a solitary meal and ate while watching the local newscast. Last night's incident still topped the list of current events, but thanks to the HQ Civil Affairs officers, it was petering out into nothing more than an unfortunate accident. One that caught a member of the Armed Services returning to his duty station.

At around eight in the evening, Decker's AI finally piped up. "Commander Talyn has entered her quarters."

"Open our side of the connecting door." He pulled a bottle of Glen Arcturus, his favorite whiskey, and two tumblers from the drinks cupboard, then set them on his sitting room table.

Talyn's side of the connecting door hissed open. She stepped through, face etched by fatigue, and unfastened her tunic with a sigh of contentment. Decker pointed at the bottle, eyebrows raised in question, and she nodded.

"Tough day in the bureaucratic trenches?" The Marine asked while he poured a healthy measure into each glass.

"There might be an as yet undiscovered black hole in the Scandia system." She dropped into a chair across from him.

Decker handed her a glass, then raised his in salute. "*Smert Chyohrniy Mech.*"

"Right now, I'll drink to anything, but that needs translating."

"Death to Black Sword. It's Russian." He pointed at his reader. "I spend the afternoon getting an education on the ruthlessness of military intelligence agencies in dictatorships, specifically the Soviet *Glavnoye razvedyvatel'noye upravleniye,* circa second half of the twentieth century.”

“You've been studying the past to predict the future?” She asked after swallowing a healthy mouthful of the potent, amber liquid. “Perhaps not a bad idea, considering.”

“What's this black hole in the Scandia system?” He settled back in his favorite chair, the whiskey tumbler cradled in one hand.

“First your daughter vanishes, then the Scandian cops ask us if we've heard from your ex-wife and now one of ours disappears.”

“Maybe Shrehari corsairs are trolling for slaves on our side of the border. Which one of ours?”

“Remember Garrett Montero?” Talyn took another sip.

“Yeah.   Lieutenant commander, likes to work solo under deep cover, almost as big as I am, but only half as mean.”

“Though with a lot more roguish charm. He's back aboard our favorite undercover Q-ship and has been building a new identity to go with his new face, but still working his old job ferreting out intelligence under a smuggler's guise. And he's still operating alone. Or at least he was operating alone.” She sighed again.

Decker studied her through narrowed eyes. “Are you saying Garrett and *Phoenix,* or whatever Amali's old yacht is called these days, went walkabout without leaving a forwarding address?”

Talyn nodded once. “Garrett has. He established his new home base in the Scandia system. I asked him to keep an ear to the ground for anything about your daughter and possible activity by the opposition. It was more as a matter of course than anything else since he's our only operative out there. Call it 'a be on the lookout bulletin' if you like. Garrett acknowledged my transmission, then went silent. I pinged his ship, now named *Haukka*, a few days ago, posing as a potential customer, but received a reply from the Breidablik port master's office instead. *Haukka* is still sitting in her berth, but there's been no sign of Garrett anywhere since shortly after my first message. The port master is wondering who will take over the ship and pay the docking fees."

"Breidablik? Isn't that a free port on Scandia's moon?"

"It is. And before you ask, the harbormaster's office found no evidence of Garrett leaving the habitat or anything to show he was still there either. Like I said, there's something sucking up people in that part of the Rim Sector." She drained her glass, then allowed herself a heartfelt, half-whispered curse. "If anyone could dodge those Sécurité *Spéciale* bastards and their hirelings, it should be Garrett Montero. He's settled into his new identity by now and can pass for a true scoundrel. I'd hate to think what his falling into the enemy's hands means for the thin smattering of less experienced officers out there."

"It means you and I need to get off our asses and back in the field." He grabbed the bottle and held it up. "Another slug?"

"Sure." She slid her glass across the smooth tabletop.

"Consider this." Decker poured her a generous measure. "I'm being replaced by a guy who can teach my stuff as well if not better than me. The boss can surely find another minion to fight his bureaucratic battles — perhaps Pavlik Hineman. We recruit an officer from the 1st Special Forces Regiment to replace him at Camp X, and everything's sorted. There's no one with enough experience available we can send to Scandia other than us. Not if the enemy is operating against Naval Intelligence in full force out there. And with Garrett gone, someone needs to recover *Haukka*."

Talyn sipped her drink, suspicious eyes gazing at Decker over the tumbler's edge. "And not coincidentally, our traveling there would allow you to pester the Scandian Police Authority. What if Garrett's disappearance is part of the opposition's plan for us?"

"Then we'll be extra careful to avoid setting off their trap. But unless we ask JSOC's naval arm to pick up *Haukka* within the week, or God forbid, let her be impounded by the Scandian Transportation Agency, a qualified starship pilot from our division still needs to go. And you're the only one on Caledonia right now. What we need is a fast, anonymous ride out to the Rim - maybe one of the unmarked avisos assigned to HQ for classified messenger duty."

"Or Garrett will show up full of smiles and apologies for having worried us. After an impromptu holiday with someone he picked up at a Breidablik bar." Her dubious tone proved she didn't put much faith in the possibility.

"You don't actually believe that, right? This is a huge galaxy, too big for coincidences involving a small, circumscribed number of interrelated people. Not to mention Garrett isn't a flaky character prone to wander off without warning. We're looking at enemy action."

Talyn let out a long, sorrowful exhalation. "I know. And I'll speak to the boss first thing tomorrow morning."

Decker gave her a subdued grin. "That's what I'm talking about. Let's rejoin the galaxy and kick ass again. Now about that massage you promised..."

She climbed to her feet and drained her glass. "Make me supper while I wash, entertain me while I eat and then we'll talk."

**

"I still think having the aviso pick us up here merely serves to warn the enemy, if you're right about them having a mole inside Camp X, Zack."

Talyn and Decker watched the tiny speck that was *Arke* stream toward them in the cloudless blue sky several days after the Marine's attempted abduction. They stood on the edge of the training installation's rammed earth landing strip, travel bags at their feet, the damp scent of the surrounding forest heavy in their nostrils.

Decker shrugged. "So? No matter how we leave Caledonia, the buggers will quickly figure out we're in play again. At least this way, they see us leave with our normal faces, and aboard one of the Fleet's precious avisos. That's bound to make them wonder what we're planning. When was the last time intelligence operatives snagged a ride on one of the fastest starships in the known universe?"

"Since before my time as the commodore's chief of staff, that's for sure. And if the Fleet has authorized aviso joyrides for our folks in the past, no one's bothered to note the fact in our mission files. I checked."

"Speaking of the commodore — do I dare ask how you changed his mind on keeping us under wraps?"

"I threatened to implement every single recommendation contained in the *Staff Procedures Handbook* on the proper structure of a flag officer's daily routine."

Decker winced theatrically. "Ouch. That's harsh. They've shot chiefs of staff for lesser offenses. I hope you passed that idea to Pavlik Hineman, in case he regrets volunteering to take over from you."

"I'm sure Pavlik can come up with his own methods of channeling the boss' decision-making process in the right direction." Movement on the far side of the landing strip, at the start line of the camp's thoroughly nasty confidence course, attracted her eye. "Isn't that Josh Bayliss and our latest crop of wannabes? How's he settling in?"

"Josh, being a top-caliber sonofabitch, is approaching the job with the appetite of a man eager to inflict pain and suffering on anyone holding delusions of adequacy. He'll probably end up doing better than I was." Decker jerked his chin at the tall, dark complexioned man with a lean, angular face haranguing a small cluster of battledress-clad trainees. "Case in point, I wasn't cruel enough to make the wannabes run through the confidence course before each meal. Once a day was plenty."

Talyn's chuckle sounded both grim and amused at the same time. "You mean he makes them do it even before breakfast?"

"Yep." The Marine nodded. "After he's warmed them up with a five-kilometer run. Mind you, I used to take them on a ten click morning jog myself, so I suppose this might be an improvement of sorts. Unless, of course, Josh makes them take the obstacles backward. Things like that amuse him and with another inmate from the Fort Arnhem Pathfinder asylum now in charge of the training wing, he's free to improvise."

A low rumble reached their ears, and they looked up again. The speck had grown considerably, to the point where the elongated shapes of *Arke*'s massive hyperdrive nacelles stood out clearly. The ship's primary hull, wedged between them, seemed unbelievably tiny in contrast.

"Seriously, though.   What convinced Commodore Ulrich to let us go?"

"An urgent message from *Haukka*'s AI informing us someone was trying to board without authorization. Apparently, Garrett programmed her to self-destruct rather than fall into unfriendly hands. The commodore didn't want his unit to be responsible for taking out a chunk of the Breidablik docks and since we're the only available agents capable of sailing her..."

"You intended to tell me about this when, exactly?"

"Once we were underway and I could open our mission orders."

Decker let loose a soft whistle. "Sealed mission orders? What next? A matching set of licenses to kill?"

"Matching? Hardly. You forget that I'm a designated assassin, while you're merely a guy who's handy with his gun."

"I'm handy with plenty more than just my gun, sweetheart." He winked at her.

"So you keep saying, but where's the proof?"

The roar of the aviso's landing thrusters washed out Decker's reply, but his hand gestures conveyed an unmistakable message and Talyn's lips twisted in a sardonic smile.

Unable to speak over the noise, they watched the small starship's descent slow to a crawl before it settled on the ground in a cloud of dust, its hyperdrive nacelles doubling as landing gear.

Then, the din from *Arke*'s overpowered engines faded away, leaving humans and animals stunned by the sudden silence. A portion of the ship's keel dropped to form a ramp, and a figure in civilian spacer clothes emerged from the unmarked vessel. Upon spotting the two agents waiting by the edge of the strip, he waved at them to join him.

When they were within earshot, the man, who appeared well into middle-age, with a face weathered by space radiation, asked, "Commander Hera Talyn and Major Zack Decker, I presume?"

"You presume correctly," Talyn replied.

"Welcome.   I'm Lieutenant Gallus Perr, *Arke*'s commanding officer. They didn't tell me where I was to take you, only that it was a top secret, undercover mission, and you were on a short timetable. I've never transported intelligence officers before, so please forgive me if I'm not up on the relevant protocols."

"I'll tell you our destination before we lift," Talyn said. "And you're right, we need speed over anything else."

Perr nodded. "Speed I can give you. *Arke* and the rest of the Hermes class avisos are the fastest ships around but have little by way of comfort. She's essentially a life pod connected to a battlecruiser's engines. If you'll follow me..." He turned to walk up the belly ramp.

Calling *Arke* a life pod was an exaggeration. But not by much. Her crew of six lived in cramped quarters, and the cabin set aside for passengers made a standard closet seem spacious.

"It's a good thing you and I are already tight with each other, Hera, darling." Decker dumped his bag on the lower of two stacked bunks. "Otherwise we might find this a tad too close for comfort."

Perr, standing in the open door, seemed puzzled by the Marine's comment and glanced from one to the other before deciding it was none of his business.

Instead, he said, "The mess is two doors down. You're welcome to use it at any time. Please don't enter the engineering space — it's clearly marked. You can visit the bridge, but please ask the watchkeeper before entering.

It's not much bigger than a shuttle's cockpit, so if we're maneuvering, every station will be taken. That means no room to spare. Besides the mess, you can access an extensive entertainment library, and we've converted one of the spare cabins into an exercise room, although it can only be used by one person at a time. Each crew member has a daily two-hour block reserved, but you're free to enjoy our makeshift gym when it's vacant."

"Excellent." Decker rubbed his hands together. "Can't let entropy turn our finely honed bodies into so much useless flab."

"For liftoff and landing, I'll ask you to strap yourselves into your bunks," Perr continued. "Avisos can be pretty bouncy. Now about our destination..."

"The Scandia system," Talyn replied. "Specifically, the free port of Breidablik."

"No problems. You'll be there in half the time it takes the fastest frigate. But understand that *Arke* will stick out in Breidablik like a Sister of the Void at a nudist convention, even if we pretend to be a civilian courier ship."

She nodded. "I know, but that's a necessary risk."

"In the interests of time, no doubt."

Talyn inclined her head. "Just so."

"Then let's not waste any more in idle chatter." He nodded at the bunks. "If you'll secure yourselves for takeoff, we'll be on our way."

A few minutes after Perr left them, Decker and Talyn felt *Arke*'s thrusters spool up, though mercifully the noise that assaulted their ears outside was mostly dampened.

Then, giant hands pushed on their prone bodies with unexpected violence as the aviso tore itself from the landing strip and rose on columns of pure energy, reaching for the heavens.

— NINE —

"Only two jumps?" Talyn studied the navigation plot alongside Lieutenant Perr in *Arke*'s little command center. The aviso was moving away from Caledonia toward her hyperlimit at a velocity few FTL ships could boast after a liftoff as mercifully short as it was uncomfortable. "Impressive."

"I could easily do it in one." Perr's tone spoke of a quiet pride and confidence stemming from experience. "But we'll be passing near a subspace communications array, and as per standing orders, I'm required to go sublight and ping it for fresh orders."

Talyn nodded. "Of course. That makes eminent sense."

"It'll lengthen our total run by only six to eight hours, Commander. That's not much compared to the overall trip." He gave her a fleeting grin. "Especially when you think how long it would take a regular FTL starship to reach Scandia."

"A mere trifle, I agree."

"What's a trifle?" Decker asked from the corridor, his bulk almost completely filling the doorway to the bridge.

"The quick dip back into normal space so *Arke* can pick up the mail from a subspace array we'll pass between here and Scandia. It means the trip will be in two jumps instead of one," Talyn replied.

"You can do the whole trip in one jump?" Decker asked Perr, an air of surprise on his square face. "That's remarkable."

"Routine work for the dashing messenger ships of our mighty human Fleet, Major," the chief petty officer third class occupying the command chair said over her shoulder. "By the way, welcome aboard, Rookie Trooper. We rarely carry delinquents who graduated from the Fort Arnhem School for Wayward Marines."

A frown creased Decker's forehead as the woman's voice evoked the memory of a time long ago, before his forced hiatus from active duty. Then the rumble of an amused chuckle escaped his barrel chest. "Nita Kallani. Is that you? When did they make you respectable?"

The stocky, gray-haired chief turned in her chair and smiled at the surprised Marine. "I put up my chief's starbursts eighteen months after you walked off *Musashi* between two military police bruisers. You seem to have done even better than I did — from disgraced command sergeant to wearing a major's finery. I guess miracles happen and to the strangest people. You still owe me twenty creds from the last game we played before you slugged that idiot Sarratt."

"I see you know my executive officer, who also doubles as *Anke*'s chief engineer and coxswain."

"We spent quality time in *Musashi*'s senior enlisted mess taking money off each other back in the day."

"Dare I ask why she called you Rookie Trooper and who the idiot Sarratt is?"

"The first is my nickname. There's a long, boring story behind it, one better told around a cold ale in the mess. Or Nita can fill you in during a dull, uneventful night watch when we idlers are in our bunks, snoring. The other is a Marine captain who made questionable choices that caused casualties during a mission. As a result, he's a captain for life."

Kallani snorted. "Sarratt didn't make the only questionable choice that day. But God watches over fools and drunks, with a distinct bias in favor of the latter." She glanced at Perr. "And while we're on the subject of drunks, skipper, keep Major Danger away from our booze reserves. Otherwise, he'll clean us out before we skip past the Eratosthenes subspace array."

Decker winked at the chief then nodded toward Talyn. "I'm a reformed man, Nita. You can ask my commanding officer here."

"I'll believe *de*formed before I buy the outlandish idea you're a new man, *sir*." The Marine gave her a rigid digit salute accompanied by a broad smile. Kallani burst into laughter. "Some things never change. We can catch up over a coffee once we're FTL, which will happen within the hour. I must find out how you pulled off the best career recovery in living memory."

"And mightily bored you'll be." Talyn smirked. "Most of it is covered by such a high-security classification that Zack isn't even allowed to reminisce in private. And now that I've satisfied my curiosity about our navigation plan, the miraculous major and I will leave you to sail your ship." She nudged her partner. "C'mon, you paragon of virtue. I spotted a working coffee urn in the mess. Let's leave these hardworking spacers to do their thing without annoying hecklers from Spook Central watching their every move."

Once ensconced in their cabin with matching coffee mugs, Talyn retrieved a data chip from her tunic pocket.

"Our orders."

She mated the small plastic wafer to a paper thin reader and unlocked its contents.

"No big surprises," Decker said, reading over Talyn's shoulder. "Secure *Haukka* and establish contact with home base; find Garrett Montero and figure out what happened to him; find what, if anything, the Coalition is doing in the Scandia system and take appropriate action to counter immediate threats; be prepared for further direction. Pretty broad. It's basically a permit to go hunting, with no mention of Saga or Ingrid."

"I believe that comes under the heading 'determine what if anything the Coalition is doing,' don't you think?"

He grinned and gave her a roguish leer. "I love it when you turn barracks lawyer on me, darling. It somehow makes you more irresistible."

**

"Strap me to a missile and shoot me at a black hole." Chief Petty Officer Kallani shook her head in disbelief after draining her coffee mug once Decker finished recounting a suitably redacted version of his life after leaving the patrol frigate *Musashi*.

"That's a heck of a story, Zack. Although ending up as a Naval Intelligence field operative isn't nearly as much of a surprise as a lot of folks might think. Your talents were wasted in a Pathfinder Squadron, which may partly explain your temper issues back then. Sarratt merely brought things to a head. Whatever happened to him anyway?"

Decker shrugged. "No idea."

"You weren't tempted to look him up after putting on those major's oak leaves? Give him an object lesson on the wisdom of letting things slide in the interests of everyone concerned?"

"I was, but my partner convinced me running across Sarratt by accident would be much more satisfying."

Kallani picked up her and Decker's mugs and stepped to the urn for refills. "Shame what happened to Hal. He was one of the truly good guys."

"He was." Decker felt that twinge of anguish mixed with guilt worm its way through his guts again at the mention of his former troop sergeant and best friend. "But he went out the way he wanted — making sure the bad guys couldn't interfere with our rescue mission."

"Hal was another lost soul, Zack, just like you, except he coped in different ways. It explains why the two of you were close. Perhaps working for the spooks is your way of finding redemption for the missions that didn't have a happy ending when you were with the 902nd."

The Marine chuckled. "When did you turn into a philosopher?"

"Working on avisos gives you plenty of time to contemplate life, the universe, and everything else. We spend most of our time in hyperspace, where there's often sweet fuck-all to do except monitor the systems, what with us getting priority for repairs between courier runs every time something hiccups. I figure we humans are aboard only because AIs can be suborned by hackers."

Decker accepted the proffered coffee cup with a nod of thanks. "How did you end up in avisos anyhow?"

"My chief's starbursts came with a shore billet at a Fleet repair facility. Plenty to do, but boring as hell. So on a whim, I studied for my enlisted watch keeping ticket after talking to the crew of an aviso in for a refit. Once I passed the examinations, I put in for a transfer to the Navy's Courier Group so I could haul my ass back into space doing something more useful than pushing administrative garbage.

"They liked my psych profile and took me almost straight away. Executive officer and chief engineer of an FTL starship, even if it's a non-combatant, is a good billet for a chief third class. I'm accumulating enough bridge time to qualify for a direct commission and my own aviso within the next two or three years."

"Nice." Decker raised his mug in salute. "Here's to your success. The Fleet needs more mustangs who don't play stupid officer games."

"Nothing's ever for sure, buddy, but joining the Courier Group is a lot like becoming a Pathfinder. Once you're in, you stick with it for the rest of your career. The skipper used to be an aviso chief before taking his commission. I figure in a few years, he'll be commanding an aviso flotilla somewhere as a two-and-a-half striper."

"With you as *Anke*'s master and commander."

"She'll do me fine, but the Fleet likes to shuffle aviso crews on promotion. It prevents inbreeding and makes sure we pick up enough experience sailing through any part of the Commonwealth — and beyond — on pure instinct. Those big drives on the tiny hull can sometimes muddle your navigation plot. Hyperspace physics, what little we know of them, seem to place restrictions on how skewed you can make your mass to power ratio, and these Hermes class ships are flirting with the outer limits."

"What happens when you hit those limits?"

Kallani grimaced. "We don't know, but based on the Courier Group's loss statistics over the years, it's nothing good. Avisos that vanish are never heard from again, and we carry the most powerful emergency beacons ever devised."

"Do a lot of ships vanish? Or is that classified?"

"It's classified, but we qualify for tier one danger pay. What does that tell you?"

"It tells me I hope your skipper isn't pushing the performance envelope on our account."

The chief petty officer's laugh was chillingly devoid of mirth. "Every aviso sticks to the speed limits imposed by our HQ. A skipper who tries to squeeze more from his drives will be found out and beached."

"But you're going to tell me keeping to those limits doesn't necessarily keep avisos from turning into Flying Dutchmen."

"There are things in hyperspace we can't even begin to understand." Kallani drained her mug. "And on that note, let's change the subject. You may recall we spacers are a superstitious lot."

Decker nodded once. "Understood. As a man once said, there are more things in heaven and earth, Horatio, than are dreamt of in your philosophy."

Kallani gave him a strange stare. "Say what?"

"We spooks also spend a lot of time in hyperspace on our way to and from missions. But instead of contemplating life, the universe, and everything else, I read a lot, and I'm cursed with the ability to retain trivia in industrial quantities."

Talyn slipped onto the bench beside her partner. "Actually, I'm the one suffering under the curse, since he's always sharing his fund of knowledge with a generosity that quickly turns exhausting. Worse yet, he's developed a fascination with everything pre-diaspora."

"Those who do not learn from history..." Decker intoned, one hand raised in a quasi-religious gesture.

Anke's second in command studied the Marine through narrowed eyes, then nodded. "You know, I can almost believe he's a changed man, Commander Talyn, though I'm not sure it's been for the best. Maybe I should think twice about applying for a commission."

"Did you ever think this might be the real me?" Decker asked with a mock-wounded expression on his face. "You're the one who said I was a lost soul back aboard *Musashi*. Perhaps I've found myself since then."

"I also said you still owe me twenty creds. Did you find that money along with your soul and learned to repay debts?"

Decker gave her an ironic grin as he reached into his pocket. "And I can pay you in untraceable chips issued by Naval Intelligence."

"As long as they buy me a drink in Breidablik."

**

"Now hear this. Translation to normal space in five minutes, I repeat, translation to normal space in five minutes. That is all." Lieutenant Perr's voice drew Decker back to the present from his contemplation of the madness that led to the Great Cleansing shortly before the first sublight cryo ships left an Earth ravaged by migratory strife.

"We've arrived at the Eratosthenes subspace array, I presume?" He asked Talyn, stretched out on the upper bunk, eyes closed, thoughts soaring high above the plane of the physical universe.

"The timing is right," she replied in an absent tone. "Almost to the hour, in fact."

"Meaning we're halfway there."

"Don't," she growled.

"Don't what?"

"I recognize that tone — you're about to inflict another piece of incomprehensible humor on me."

"No, but now that you mention it, what rhymes with there?"

"Death. Specifically yours. Which will ensue if you don't stop talking right now."

Decker grunted. "Be that way. What the hell is eating at you, Hera?"

Talyn let loose an exasperated sigh. "The same damn thing that's been eating at me since we found out Black Sword dug its filthy claws into the Special Operations Division. A deep and abiding need to cleanse the enemy from our midst with overwhelming violence and brutality."

"I guess killing Yang didn't do it for you, then?" He asked in a light tone.

"Not funny, Zack." She fell silent for a few moments. "Some days that need feels almost overwhelming, capable of challenging my self-control and dragging me into the darkness I've avoided so far."

"Uh..." Decker climbed to his feet and stared at her prone shape, "are you saying your inner beast is clamoring to escape?"

She turned her head and faced him with a sad smile. "Something like that. I'm worried the anger that's been simmering for months will push me into becoming the thing I've always feared. You can't understand the fury I felt at your abduction attempt, at my almost losing you to those vile, subhuman parasites."

The vehemence in her usually even tone caused Decker to take an involuntary step back. "I think you've just given me a glimpse, honey. But I know you can clamp down on the emotions, push the monsters back where they belong. Be the cold, detached intelligence operative and professional assassin who sent me unwittingly into harm's way without a single shred of remorse."

"But I don't want to suppress the emotions I've come to feel, or at least think I've come to feel and relish thanks to you. Yet I'm afraid the rage is an unavoidable counterpart."

"Aha!" His worried expression broke into a fond smile. "You do love me. I knew it."

"As much as I'm capable of loving anyone or anything. By reverting to what I was, we will lose something precious."

"Better that than you becoming someone more like the enemy." He reached out to touch her cheek with his fingertips and found an unexpected sheen of moisture. "As a commander of my acquaintance is fond of saying, the universe would be a dull place without you. And if the trade-off is the old Hera who shanghaied me on Parth when I brought Decker's Demons home from a life of slavery, then so be it. I can deal with her emotion-free self if that means the darkness within stays locked up. I'm not sure I can manage one able to make the Erinyes of ancient myth run away in fear."

"Now hear this. Translation to normal space in sixty seconds, I repeat, translation to normal space in six zero seconds. That is all."

"Trust my fellow squids to interrupt a tender moment." Talyn hoarse voice was tinged with irony. "You'd better sit, Big Boy."

"How about I join you up there?"

"Once our hosts check for messages and take us back into hyperspace. Now sit."

"Yes, sir." Decker dropped back on his bunk with a heartfelt exhalation. Life had been simpler when their existence focused on chasing down the latest Coalition scheme to destabilize the political order. Now? Faced with a network of traitors in the Fleet's own ranks and a partner losing the fight against her dark, primal urges, Decker wondered whether there could ever be a happy end to this covert war.

The warning klaxon blared out its shrill message moments before the Marine's universe went sideways while his stomach tried to escape through his nostrils. Seconds later, the intense translation nausea, worse than any he'd experienced in his life, faded away as quickly as it had surged up his throat.

Then, the sudden howl of the battle stations siren reached Decker's ears. As he sprang to his feet, instincts screaming at him to do something useful, like man the gunnery station, *Anke* shuddered as if she'd been struck by a gigantic Thor's hammer.

— TEN —

The whine of overstressed shields reverberated through the aviso's hull, punctuated by muffled curses from its bridge, whose door still stood open. Decker reached it in three long strides and stuck his head in, trying to divine who attacked them the moment they emerged. *Anke* shuddered from another direct hit and this time, warning sirens joined the whining shield generators.

"How long before the drives cycle?" Perr asked in a controlled tone.

"We can transition to FTL now if you don't mind a random jump," Kallani replied. "Otherwise, I need at least five minutes."

"The shields won't last five minutes," the petty officer manning the tactical systems interjected. "When the second bogey locks on to us, it'll be goodnight Irene."

Decker's eyes turned to the threat display and the moment its contents registered, he swore. "Those are Avalon mercenary ships — disguised, perhaps, but I've fought the bastards before and can recognize them. They're after Commander Talyn and me. And now they've opened fire, they can't afford to let us escape so we might accuse their employer of attempted piracy."

"It proves there are still traitors in our midst," Talyn murmured in Decker's ear as she came up behind him and peered over his shoulder at the display. "Someone who knew we would stop at the Eratosthenes array on our way to Scandia and warned the Coalition so it could set a trap by trusting the Courier Group's well-known navigational expertise to pinpoint where we'd drop out of FTL."

The aviso shook off another direct hit from the guns of what Decker knew to be a well-armed mercenary sloop, capable of lobbing anti-ship missiles at will. So far the captain of the nearest attacker was sticking to direct fire, hoping for an inexpensive kill. But *Anke* boasted stronger shields than he likely expected, meaning it was a matter of minutes, perhaps even seconds, before he switched tactics. And with a pair of small caliber, four-barrel calliopes as its sole ordnance, a brace of missiles was more than the aviso could absorb.

"I recommend risking a random jump, Mister Perr," Decker said. "Those sloops will have our number momentarily. We may be able to outrun them FTL, but their missiles will find us as long as we stay sublight."

"Random jumps on drives that aren't fully cycled present a much greater peril for avisos than normal starships, Major."

"And you don't want to become a Flying Dutchman. Neither do I. But we'll be space debris by the time your oversized pushers are re-tuned."

"The lead sloop just fired missiles. Impact in thirty seconds," the tactical petty officer announced. "Based on my sensor readings, if they strike, our shields will suffer a catastrophic collapse, leaving us open to a disabling salvo from their guns."

"Damn." Perr slapped his console, and the jump klaxon's mournful bleats echoed through *Anke*. "Hang on to your stomachs, folks."

Decker braced himself in the open doorway as Talyn wrapped her arms around his chest. "So much for picking up the mail."

Then, their universe went sideways for the second time in a matter of minutes. When the translation sickness faded away, Lieutenant Gallus Perr, master and commander of the aviso *Anke* turned his command chair aft and stared at the two intelligence operatives.

"What the actual fuck happened back there, Commander Talyn?" He asked in a tone pregnant with rapidly growing anger now that the immediate peril was behind them. "Unidentified ships ambushing a Fleet courier? Within sight of a naval subspace array? I've never heard of the like."

"Hardly unidentified. If Major Decker says they're Avalon Corporation mercenary sloops, then take his word for it. Among his many skills is that of starship gunnery, and as he mentioned, he's fought Avalon units before. Why ambush *Anke*? They're after the two of us. We're not just Naval Intelligence field operatives, we've also become high-value targets in recent times. Someone in the opposition's pay found out about our trip to Scandia, figured you'd drop out of FTL at the Eratosthenes array, and set up an ambush."

Perr scowled at her. "We picked you up openly at your training facility, Commander. Perhaps that was a mistake."

"Our leaving in the dead of night from a hidden strip wouldn't have made a difference," Decker replied. "They've known for a while we'd eventually make our way to Scandia. That gave them plenty of time to pre-position a few of their ships. Finding out we'd be conveyed by the Naval Courier Group sealed the deal even before you landed at Camp X. Once the powers that be ordered our transport aboard an aviso, the buggers sent a pair of sloops to the array.”

“Perhaps.” Perr sounded wholly unconvinced. “But answer me this. You keep referring to an opposition, an enemy who wants you dead. Are the Shrehari pissing about in our backyard after staying quiet for longer than I’ve been alive?”

Talyn shook her head. “The people we’re fighting are human. Many of them work within the Commonwealth or planetary governments, military and police forces, including the Fleet.”

Perr, Chief Kallani, and the tactical petty officer stared at her as if she’d grown a second head.

“You want to explain, Commander?” *Anke*’s commanding officer asked after shaking off his momentary surprise. “We’re just a bunch of regular spacers here, even if we’ve seen more of the galaxy than most.”

“I can’t say much, but in essence, there’s a large, well-connected, well-funded faction both inside and outside various governments seeking to reverse the treaties that ended the Second Migration War. They want to curtail star system independence in favor of centralized control from Earth. Since the Armed Services are sworn to uphold the constitution born of those treaties, we’re more or less in a cold civil war principally fought in the hidden realm of intelligence and special operations.”

“And somehow you and the major are important enough in this cold civil war they’d risk attacking a Fleet starship with mercenaries belonging to one of the largest private military corporations in history, which is in turn owned by one of the largest commercial conglomerates?” An ironic whistle escaped Perr’s lips. “I hope never to make enemies that determined and willing to spend a fortune so they can kill me."

"Let's just say we've done this faction a considerable amount of harm in the last while, enough to set back their plans by a considerable margin," Decker said in a conversational tone. "And we are one of the last hotshot operative teams still alive and hitting back after they almost wiped out our organization's ability to fight."

"There's also an element of revenge involved," Talyn added. "A few of the most powerful leaders in this faction feel the need to avenge themselves personally on us for things we've done to them, their families, and interests."

Perr shook his head. "Don't misunderstand, Commander, but I'm having a real hard time believing this. I've read thrillers with a more plausible plot."

Decker grinned at him. "Proving once again that truth is often stranger than fiction?"

"Factions within the Commonwealth government killing each other over who gets to control what? That's pretty damned strange, Major."

"But surprisingly common throughout human history, no matter the civilization. I can recommend a reading list that'll make you wonder how humanity ever survived to colonize this part of the galaxy."

"Thanks, but maybe I should keep my illusions — and sleep better at night." Perr frowned in thought. "Would I be wrong to think once I've dropped you off at Breidablik, these people won't make another attempt to destroy my ship?"

Talyn nodded. "I'd say it's a pretty fair assumption."

"Then I might as well figure out where this unplanned jump is taking us, so I can get back on course to Scandia."

"How long do you expect to stay on the current heading?"

Perr scratched his chin. "We don't make a big hyperspace bubble, but it's energized enough to be traceable by naval-grade sensors for a good distance. If your mercenary friends intend to pursue, I'll plan on giving us a decent margin before dropping to sublight so we can recalculate our course. Otherwise, we might end up playing Crazy Ivan and jump all over the place to shake them, and I'm not a fan of that maneuver. It's hard on hyperdrives and human psyches."

"Psyches?" Decker asked.

"Aviso dreams, Major. One of the many strange things that happen when you push against the outer edge of the power to mass ratio in hyperspace. Repeated emergency jumps make them a lot worse for some people."

"I didn't think hyperspace psychosis was a real thing."

Perr gave him a humorless smile. "It may not be in the regular Fleet, but in the Courier Group... Now if you'll excuse me, I need to figure out where *Anke* is headed, so we don't end up in a worse situation."

Once back in their cabin, Decker said, "I sense our friend Gallus Perr isn't thrilled with his passengers just now."

"We've upset his orderly world and placed his command at risk merely by being aboard. I'd say his reaction is normal."

"And what's this aviso dream?" He asked as he picked up his reader and dropped back into the lower bunk.

Talyn shrugged. "Who knows? Every part of the Navy has its stories to scare, impress, or amaze outsiders. Considering Courier Group ships spend more time FTL than any other, I suppose they've developed quirks of their own."

"So long as we reach Scandia before the turn of the century," he grumbled.

**

"Sir," a man in mud-spattered battle armor raised his hand to attract Decker's attention, "we've finally regained contact with Coulson's brigade. They've destroyed the Government Precinct's power station, which shut down the jammers plaguing us since we landed."

"Do they see the First Regiment's positions by now?"

The aide pointed at the tactical command post's holographic display. "With the jamming gone, we're pinpointing them from orbit and feeding the location to Coulson's TAC."

Decker's searched the map, wondering once more what had brought matters to this state. "Give Harkon and Rova the go-ahead to move their brigades up and complete the pincer around Geneva as per phase two of the operations plan. Maybe saner heads in the First Regiment will prevail and ask for terms. Even the idiots in command can't fail to see it's over for the government, that there's no point in dying for a lost cause."

"Shame we can't just erase the whole damn cesspool from orbit with a few pinpoint kinetic strikes."

"And repeat the sort of bloody mistakes that led to the Second Migration War? When we're here to prevent a third one by removing the rotten edifice of government before it pits the Fleet against itself?" Decker shook his head. "No. I want the Commonwealth Marines to surrender; I want every other unit on Earth and in the Home System that hasn't switched sides to surrender; I even want the SecGen, his cabinet, and the Senate to surrender. There's been enough killing."

The aide transmitted the orders, then paused as he listened to words only he could hear. "Harkon and Rova are acknowledging. Phase two of Operation Götterdämmerung is on."

Decker nodded his thanks. Having let slip the dogs of war against the Commonwealth's final redoubt, the ancient city of Geneva, he knew the fight was no longer his to control. The brigade commanders, veteran Special Forces officers, would ensure victory in a futile battle whose outcome was already known, while elsewhere on Earth, his remaining divisions were disarming and interning those who refused to renounce their loyalties. He wanted to witness the final act in person and had therefore established his tactical command post on the heights south of the city and its lake. The expeditionary corps' main command post was still in Aubagne, hundreds of kilometers away, where his deputy corps commander supervised the ongoing pacification of the planet.

He climbed up the reverse slope of the ridge and slipped into a notch between two crests covered in green, vibrant vegetation. Emerging on the other side, where an observation post fed real-time imagery to both the command posts and to the admiral in orbit, he made his way to a half-hidden ledge and studied the doomed city.

Dark columns of smoke rose from too many fires to count while distant explosions made a depressing counterpoint to the songs of nearby birds. The Palace of the Stars, seat of the Commonwealth government for centuries, still brooded in the middle of its park on the shores of the lake, untouched by artillery fire. Decker's commanders tried to preserve historical buildings if possible, which no doubt emboldened the last holdouts in their defiance.

A disembodied voice broke through Decker's contemplation of human folly, activating his communications implant. "Sir, we finally know what happened to the civilians that didn't escape before we closed in on Geneva. Coulson reports thousands of them mixed in with the First Regiment's defenses."

"Human shields?"

"It's what Coulson thinks." The aide's voice betrayed anger and contempt, sentiments Decker shared, though he'd long ago learned to keep his emotions in check.

That a regiment of the Commonwealth Marine Corps, even though it was a unit of the First Division, the much-maligned palace guard, would besmirch its honor in such a craven fashion seemed like the final insult. It was nothing less than one last 'fuck you' flung at them by a ruling class that despised its people and the Fleet.

"General Coulson is to inform the commanding officer of the First Commonwealth Regiment that we will offer no quarter to his troops if they use innocent civilians as shields. And if he won't listen, order the psyops folks to blanket every frequency with a warning that the troops will die if they don't let the non-combatants leave."

"No quarter, sir?"

"As in spit on your hands, hoist the black flag, and begin slitting throats, no quarter. If they force us into making good on the threat." Decker suddenly felt as if the weight of the universe rested on his shoulders and he suppressed a sigh. A lifetime of fighting, covertly and in the heat of battle left him with more than mere physical scars.

Part of him fancied that once Geneva fell, it would be over. He would go home, take off the uniform, and watch his grandchildren play. But Lieutenant General Zachary Thomas Decker, Officer Commanding the Third Imperial Expeditionary Corps, a strike force heavily weighted toward special operations troops, knew the end of the

Commonwealth did not mean the end of war. Empires, especially those born in violence, lived in violence.

Another column of black smoke reached for a cloudless sky where the morning sun smiled on a landscape that should inspire enchantment and not quiet resignation, let alone despair. Decker lost track of time as he stood there, absently listening to the reports from his brigade commanders while his eyes never left the mesmerizing spectacle of a city slowly crumbling under the onslaught of his Imperial Marines. He would prevail, but at what cost, not only in lives but to his soul?

Suddenly, and without warning, a brilliant flash of light filled his horizon from side to side, blanketing the city. The visor on his helmet slammed shut automatically. Instinct drove him to the ground behind a small mound of crumbling rocks. The shock wave from the antimatter explosion reached him seconds later and slammed his prone body against the mountainside, winding him even though the armor absorbed most of the energy.

"God damn it," he howled. "The fuckers blew themselves up instead of surrendering. Damn them to hell."

A hand shook his shoulder, and a soft, feminine voice cut through the noise in his head. "Zack, wake up. You're having a nightmare."

His eyes snapped open only to see the concerned expression on his partner's face. "Where…"

"Aboard the Courier Group ship *Anke*, Zack, on our way to Scandia."

"Shit." She backed away a step and allowed him to sit. "That was one dismally disturbing dream."

"Want to talk about it? You're bathed in sweat, and that haunted look in your eyes almost scares me."

"Give me a nip of the good stuff first."

Glass in hand, Decker recounted the incredibly vivid dream, ending with Geneva's destruction by a government unwilling to surrender.

"That antimatter doomsday device wiped out three of my brigades, the Commonwealth's First Regiment, and any civilians still in the city. Tens of thousands dead in a last rigid digit salute, thanks to those corrupt cockroaches in the Palace of the Stars. It was so real, so logical, everything made so much sense. It felt like no other dream. If I were prone to dramatics, I might even think it was a vision of the future. Except it was a future where the Fleet establishes the empire our Coalition enemies want for themselves. It makes no sense."

She wrapped her arm around his shoulders and squeezed. "Perhaps the same thing that allows you to sense Sisters of the Void makes you more prone to hyperspace psychosis. Meaning today's unplanned jump, with improperly cycled drives, gave you a taste of Perr's aviso dreams."

Decker drained his glass. "Probably. But it still felt so real."

"Even being a three-star general?" She asked in a droll tone. "I find that hard to believe."

He gave her a weak smile. "Oh, ye of little faith. I wouldn't be the first Marine in history to go from private to flag officer. In my case, it might be improbable, but not impossible."

"What about me? Was I in your dream?"

Decker shook his head as a sinking feeling gripped his gut. "No."

— ELEVEN —

"So," Decker reached for the coffee urn the next morning, "any idea where we are, Captain?"

The aviso's master and commander examined the bleary-eyed Marine with an inquisitive gaze. "Oh, I know where we are, but not when we are."

Perr's answer brought Zack up short. "Pardon?"

"A little Courier Group joke, Major. I can tell you where we are, not when, or I can tell you when we are, not where. It's our riff on Heisenberg's uncertainty principle. You look like death warmed over if you don't mind me saying so. Aviso dreams?"

Decker took a sip of burning hot liquid, then nodded. "Something like that, although it felt incredibly real, logical, and sequential, totally unlike anything I've experienced."

"Huh." Perr stroked his beard. "Funny. Usually, they're more of the psychedelic kind. You know, nonsense drunk on antimatter fuel. But to answer the question you meant to ask, I plan on dropping out of FTL in just under six hours. The fastest sloop ever made wouldn't be able to track us by then. Fortunately, we were pointed in Scandia's general direction when we jumped, so our trip shouldn't be lengthened by any substantial amount of time. The sooner you're in Breidablik, the better for us."

"You'll hear no arguments from me on that count. One aviso dream was more than enough."

"If it was that, Major. As I said, they're usually far from rational." Perr emptied his cup and stood. "Landlubbers grab ass from sun to sun, but a spacer's work is never done. If you'll excuse me."

Zack watched him leave through narrowed eyes, his thoughts returning once again to the vision of Geneva and three of his imperial combat brigades vaporized by an antimatter blast at an undefined moment years in the future. A future with reversed roles where the Fleet was the instrument of violent transformation rather than that of preservation.

"No need to offer a cred for your thoughts," Talyn said in a breezy tone when she entered the mess. "They're still haunting your eyes. It was just a dream, sweetheart. In this reality, wherever or whenever it is, we need to discuss a few things. For instance, do we go ashore at Breidablik with our own faces or the disguises we planned? I'm sure Gallus Perr and his crew would prefer we give the opposition concrete proof we're no longer aboard *Anke*."

"I've never been to Breidablik." Decker stared at the dregs of his coffee. "How easy would it be for us as us to vanish and reappear with fresh identities and still be able to achieve the incognito we need?"

Talyn took a juice bulb from the cooler and uncapped it. "The Scandian government runs Breidablik rather than farming it out to a private consortium like the Cimmerians do with Aquilonia. That means entry and exit protocols are more strictly enforced, and visitors are tracked." She took a sip, then shrugged. "I suppose if we head straight for *Haukka* it won't matter one way or the other."

"And what about tracking down Garrett Montero?" Decker asked. "Not to mention my daughter and former spouse?"

"One thing at a time, Zack." She slipped onto the bench beside him. "First secure *Haukka*. With her in hand, we can warn the commodore our trip aboard *Anke* was truly and well betrayed. Maybe the folks in counterintelligence we turned from Black Sword can find something useful."

"That would be a nice change from the usual," Zack grumbled. "Admiral Kruczek should shoot a few of them to give the other treasonous assholes a dose of old-time religion."

"Double agents aren't easy to manage. Besides, we don't know what's happening beyond our purview. Since the Black Sword fiasco broke wide open, Kruczek imposed a rigorous and unprecedented level of compartmentalization between the various divisions."

"Which, from the opposition's point of view isn't such a bad outcome, since they didn't completely blind us. When the right hand doesn't know what the left hand is doing, nasty things happen to the man or woman in the middle."

Talyn patted his arm. "Ours not to reason why, ours but to do and die, and all that antiquated claptrap."

"Alfred, Lord Tennyson would resent your mangling and then calling one of his most famous and noble poems claptrap. In his day that was enough to invoke the Code Duello. With flintlock pistols at twenty feet."

A delighted laugh filled the small saloon. "Trust an anachronism like you to see nobility in the commemoration of a bloody defeat brought on by miscommunication, if not outright stupidity."

Decker gave her an incredulous stare. "I'm stunned you know the basis for Tennyson's *The Charge of the Light Brigade.*"

"You're not just rubbing off in bed, Zack." She gave him a kiss on the cheek. "Although I'll never match your appetite for historical trivia."

"Do you also know what one onlooker said once it was over? Something that might apply to our own battles?"

"No."

"*C'est magnifique, mais ce n'est pas la guerre. C'est de la folie.* It is magnificent, but it is not war. It is madness."

Talyn stared at him with a touch of exasperation. "Where's my cheerful Marine? You know, the one who'll make our enemies run in fear?"

"He's wondering where this will end."

"Hopefully not with an extemporaneous recitation of the entire poem." She nudged him in the ribs. "Go work off your night sweats in the gym. If it's taken, do push-ups in our cabin until you're fun to be with again."

"Aye, aye, Commander, sir. I exist but for your pleasure." Decker slipped out from behind the mess table and intoned, with a solemn voice:

"*Cannon to right of him,*

Cannon to left of him,

Cannon in front of him, volley'd and thunder'd;

Storm'd at with shot and shell.

Boldly he rode and well, into the jaws of Death, into the mouth of Hell."

Talyn chuckled. "The charge of the one-man brigade?"

"That's what it feels like these days."

******

"We're here," Lieutenant Gallus Perr announced when the two operatives poked their heads through the bridge door. "That bright dot to the star's right is Scandia. We'll be there in under twelve hours."

"A fine bit of navigation considering where we emerged after the emergency jump from Eratosthenes," Talyn replied. "And if I'm not mistaken, our misadventure there added less than a day to the trip. Thank you."

Perr gave her a grudging nod to acknowledge the compliment. "And no trace of your mercenary friends we can find."

"They wouldn't risk anything this close to Scandia. There are too many sensors tracking in-system traffic, not to mention the milspec eyes of the 63rd Battle Group's patrol ships."

"Aye. I'll warn Breidablik that we'll need a berth for a quick touch and go — under our commercial courier registration, of course. I assume you'll be changing into new identities as well?" When he saw both operatives glance at each other, he added, "Don't worry about us. We'll return to Caledonia in a single jump, so I don't expect the folks hunting you will try the same trick twice. Besides, if they knew you were aboard *Anke*, they'll find out soon enough you've left her."

"Can I ask you to do something for us?"

"Ask away, Commander."

"Could you please check for an encrypted carrier wave on the following?" She rattled off a string of numbers.

Perr narrowed his eyes with suspicion. "An unusual frequency. What's the origin of the carrier wave — if it's there?"

"An undercover Naval Intelligence vessel. She's supposed to be docked at Breidablik, but things may have changed since we left Caledonia. Recovering her is part of our mission in this system. If the ship is no longer there, our final destination might change.”

“Worried?” Decker asked his partner.

“I’m trying to keep every possibility in mind. If someone’s tampered with her, we’ll know before landing.”

Perr gave Chief Kallani the nod. “Do it.”

A few moments later the latter said, “I’m getting something on that frequency from Scandia’s vicinity. It looks like a beacon using a variation on the standard Navy encryption protocols.”

“Can you display the data stream?”

“On the port side auxiliary screen, sir.”

Random letters, numbers, and symbols appeared, a hodgepodge that defied logic and reason.

“You can decipher that?”

“No need, Lieutenant,” Talyn replied in an absent tone, eyes parsing each line. “The alphanumerical and symbol sequence transmitted by the beacon tells me it’s our ship, that she’s still at Breidablik and that no unauthorized persons went aboard. Other than that, the signal is meaningless. Anyone trying to crack what looks like a naval code will end up with more gibberish.”

“Can’t it be spoofed?”

“Sure.” Talyn nodded once. “Anything can, but not without knowing what in that data stew is meaningful. Since I’m the one who told the ship’s AI what to say before we left Caledonia, figuring it out is almost impossible unless you’ve peeked in here.” She tapped the side of her head with a slender finger. “Even the agent who brought the ship to Breidablik has no idea what she’s transmitting. If someone moved her or breached an airlock, I wouldn’t see what I’m looking for. The ship’s orders were to scramble everything beyond any hope at reconstruction should her condition change.”

"What if your enemies changed the ship's condition before you sent your instructions?" Perr asked. "And are waiting for you?"

"That's a risk Major Decker and I must assume."

Zack snorted. "It's a given they're waiting for us in Breidablik after the ambush at Eratosthenes failed. We'll just move faster than they can and secure our ship before they're able to mount another attempt. That little beauty waiting for us isn't anywhere near as fast in FTL as *Anke*, but she carries enough armament to give those Avalon sloops a very costly bloody nose, as two of their accomplices learned. And she's faster than they are."

Perr shrugged. "It's your funeral. Once I've dropped you off at Breidablik, or an alternate location at your discretion, I've carried out my orders, and good luck."

The Marine bestowed a broad grin on the aviso's commanding officer. "We make our own luck, and so far, we've been better at it than everyone else, judging by our body count. Don't you worry."

"Oh, I'm not worried about you and the commander, Major Decker, so long as I see you off my ship without further incidents."

**

The Breidablik free port, on the surface of Scandia's only moon, shone like a rough diamond at the center of a deep crater. Its domed hub, a spacious habitat boasting an Earth-like environment complete with artificial gravity set to one standard gee, sprouted dozens upon dozens of surface spokes radiating out onto a flat plain.

These were pressurized docking arms leading to berths capable of accommodating the largest commercial starships that could land in the moon's natural one-sixth gee. Massive warehouse caverns beneath the expansive port, most beyond the artificial gravity envelope, provided transshipment facilities unmatched in the Scandia system and were among the most comprehensive in the Rim Sector.

A small, yacht-sized vessel, sitting on an outlying pad marked by a string of lights attracted Talyn's attention as *Anke* turned on its final approach path after receiving clearance to land.

"There's our baby," she murmured at Decker, who was looking over her shoulder while both stood in the open doorway to the bridge.

"It'll be a hell of a walk if those flashing markers indicate *Anke*'s berth. They couldn't have given us anything further away if they tried. Kind of suspicious considering the number of empty pads closer to *Haukka*, don't you think?"

"Nervous in the service?" Her eyes twinkled with mischief. "I don't think distance will be a factor in whether our enemies will try to pull off an abduction or assassination. Didn't you once tell me to remember the best time to ambush someone is when they're almost home and are letting their guard slip?"

Perr turned his command chair aft to face them, his expression still showing unease, if not outright disbelief at their transformation into people who resembled Major Decker and Commander Talyn merely in height and general build. Even the sober business suits they wore, reminiscent of merchant officers' uniforms seemed strange.

"Though we'll be landing in a low grav environment, I'd be happier if you were at least sitting on your bunks for the last bit. It won't be for more than a few minutes."

Talyn inclined her head. "Of course." She turned and gave her partner a playful push. "Off to the cabin."

Anke, disguised as a ComEx courier ship, settled on the pad with the lightness of a feather, proof of Perr's deft handling. A flexible gangway extruded from the docking arm's extremity and latched onto the aviso's airlock.

After perfunctory farewells from a starship commander eager to see his charges leave, Decker and Talyn stepped into the gangway's one-sixth gee, careful to keep a grip on the waist-high safety railing lest they bounce off its walls. Artificial gravity returned once they entered the docking arm itself.

Moments after the access control AI accepted their cover identities, a massive armored door slammed shut behind them and the gangway broke loose of *Anke*'s hull. The little ship lifted moments later.

"In a hurry to shake themselves loose of us," Decker muttered to his companion as they embarked on the long walk to the port's hub.

"Can you blame them?"

"I suppose not. Do we head for *Haukka* first or the harbormaster's office?"

"The latter. I'm sure they've put a lock on the docking arm's side of the gangway, pending payment of the berthing fees. Best to make our manners with the local bureaucracy first, and at the same time ask for news about Garrett's whereabouts — or rather Mattias Kenly's, as he's known in these parts."

They made their way to the harbormaster's office, a truncated pyramid dominating the entire, sprawling port complex, with no one giving them a second glance and no covert surveillance either could detect. Their anonymous appearance and innocuous behavior made them indistinguishable from anyone else hurrying through the domed habitat on the way to and from business meetings, starships, or warehouses.

A holographic AI designed to appear irritatingly androgynous greeted them with business-like courtesy at a counter reserved for ship operators' inquiries. "How may I assist?" It asked.

Talyn presented her identification. "My name is Annekka Bayle. I represent the owners of a ship currently berthed in Breidablik, named *Haukka*. My assistant, Dmitri Rauck, and I are here to take charge of *Haukka* and pay any outstanding fees." She produced another data wafer. "This confirms our orders and our authorization to assume control."

Though the AI accepted the authorization, as well as Decker's identification, it said, "My apologies, Sera Bayle, but I cannot release the ship into your custody, nor can I accept payment. Matters pertaining to *Haukka* must be handled by a deputy harbormaster. If you'll please take a seat and wait for the next available one."

"A not unexpected development." Talyn shrugged as they headed for a bank of form-fitting chairs against the far wall. "They'll want us to show them we carry the correct access codes allowing us aboard."

"And it gives them time to spread the word someone came for the ship formerly piloted by Mattias Kenly, who absented himself without warning."

"That too," she acknowledged. "If Mattias met untoward problems, those responsible will be keeping an eye out for people like us."

Beings of every description flowed through the spacious room, most speaking with AI holograms. But some, like a pair of Shrehari spacers who reminded Decker of nothing so much as the corsairs he'd fought in years past, dealt with humans in sober dark uniforms.

Almost half an hour elapsed before a pale, stern-faced woman appeared through one of the side doors and approached them with as much curiosity as caution. To

Decker's jaundiced eyes, she seemed like a perfect specimen of the Scandian bureaucrat. Eyes colder than the Great Northern Ice Sheet, lips compressed into a thin, bloodless line, smooth skin that never crinkled with laughter and no doubt a personality to match.

"Sera Bayle, Ser Rauck?" She inquired in a dull, monotonous alto.

"We are." The agents climbed to their feet.

"My name is Botilda Stigen. I'm one of Breidablik's deputy harbormasters. The AI tells me you've come to take charge of *Haukka*."

"That is correct," Talyn replied. "I trust the authorization I gave your AI is acceptable?"

"I would appreciate your following me so we can discuss the matter in private," she said, ignoring Talyn's question.

"Of course."

Stigen led them to an office dominated by a broad porthole overlooking a full quadrant of Breidablik's docking facilities, including *Haukka*'s pad. She motioned toward a pair of chairs in front of her neat, utilitarian desk before taking her own seat behind it.

"The authorization you presented certainly seems genuine. However, since the individual who registered with our office upon landing vanished without a trace, I'm sure you'll understand we're forced to use caution before releasing *Haukka* into your custody."

Talyn gracefully inclined her head. "Understandable, Sera Stigen. We are also quite worried about Mattias Kenly's welfare, as are our mutual employers. What can we do to ease your concerns?"

"The ship has resisted every attempt at entry and is demanding a specific code. We've not, as yet, forced the issue, but that time was nearing."

"I carry the appropriate codes, Sera Stigen. Perhaps I can demonstrate if you'll open a link with *Haukka*."

The assistant harbormaster studied Talyn for a few moments, then her fingers danced over a screen embedded in her desk.

"We are linked with its AI, and I've informed it representatives of its owners are here. The AI is asking for the reply to this phrase although it seems like gibberish to me." Stigen's fingers moved again, and holographic text shimmered over her desk.

"Corporate encryption. I'm sure you understand." Talyn fished a new data wafer from her tunic pocket and handed it to Stigen. "If you would transmit the contents of this chip."

The woman did so, then nodded. "It accepts your reply as a valid identifier and expects you to enter the right airlock codes."

"I carry those as well."

"In that case, I will accept payment for the overdue fees and go with you to witness the ship's AI accepting the airlock codes."

"Much appreciated, Sera Stigen. Might we inquire what Breidablik authorities know about Mattias Kenly's disappearance?"

"You might, but as it is a police matter, you must ask them. I shall inform the officer in charge you wish to speak with her."

"Thank you. May I now offer payment for the berthing fees, including the next three days in advance?" Talyn held up a payment card. "This should hold the full amount."

"Certainly." Stigen took it from Talyn's hand and held it over her embedded screen. "Precise to the last cred, Sera Bayle. A pleasure doing business with you. Shall we attend to *Haukka*?"

— TWELVE —

Botilda Stigen was already on her feet when a soft chime drew her eyes to the screen. She frowned. "My apologies. One of my people will escort you. Another matter requires my immediate attention."

A taciturn, middle-aged man wearing the dark harbormaster uniform intercepted them outside Stigen's office. In contrast to the latter's aura of cold efficiency, this one seemed to have no personality whatsoever. If it weren't for his skin's visible imperfections, Decker might easily mistake him for an android.

"I am Amund Gersman. Deputy Harbormaster Stigen has directed that I escort you to the ship called *Haukka* and witness you opening its airlock with the proper codes."

"We appreciate your courtesy," Talyn replied without the slightest trace of irony. "Please lead the way."

Gersman took them through a warren of passages that avoided the habitat and its crowded halls until they emerged from a set of back stairs and into the circular corridor anchoring the docking arms. Foot traffic seemed sparser in this area, and they soon arrived at the base of the docking arm leading to *Haukka*'s pad. It was barred by an armored door that opened at Gersman's touch. He ushered them through, then sealed the passageway off again.

"Is there a reason for this extra layer of security, Ser Gersman?" Decker asked.

"Orders."

The two operatives exchanged a brief glance.

"Let me rephrase the question. Is barring the docking arm at both ends standard policy when a ship is occupying the berth?"

"Depends on orders."

"In other words, whenever the harbormaster wants it so."

"Yes."

They reached the far end of the arm where a flexible gangway snaked out to *Haukka*'s main airlock on the other side of yet another armored door. This one too opened at Gersman's touch, and he once more ushered them through. The abrupt change from one gee to the moon's natural one-sixth took Decker by surprise, even though he expected it. They reached the airlock and he watched his partner sweet-talk the AI into accepting her as an authorized person.

Loud thunks echoed through the gangway tube once the ship accepted Talyn's code and unbarred the airlock. The massive door retracted and slid aside. Decker turned back toward Gersman, only to gaze up the barrels of large-bore needlers held by two tall, muscular, but bland-faced humans wearing dark business suits. Gersman was gone.

"No sudden movements, please." They entered the tube. "Keep your hands where we can see them."

"Who are you?" Talyn asked.

"People who've been waiting for someone to show up and unlock that fascinating ship with the doomsday device preventing unauthorized entry."

Decker glanced at his partner for a sign of her intentions but saw no indication she intended to fight back just yet.

"Why are you interested in our ship and how did you enter this docking arm?"

"I'm afraid I can't share that information." The lead intruder pointed at the open airlock with his weapon. "Climb aboard, Sera Bayle. You too, Ser Rauck. We need to discuss a few things."

"May I assume Botilda Stigen warned you we were about to board our employer's property and arranged for this intrusion while remaining at arm's length?" Talyn, with Decker close behind, stepped over the coaming and into a starship she'd last boarded on Aquilonia almost two years earlier. A full one gee tugged at her body again as the familiar mixture of lubricants, recycled air, and ozone tickled her nostrils. Lieutenant Commander Montero shouldn't have made any modifications since he retook control of *Haukka*, meaning her mental map of the vessel and its contents would conform to reality.

"You may assume whatever you wish, Sera Bayle. Please head for the saloon. And no funny moves. We'd rather avoid any acts of violence."

Once in the ship's small mess, he pointed at a bench. "Please sit against the bulkhead, Sera Bayle." Talyn complied, but when Zack aimed for a chair rather than the bench that would trap him behind a table bolted to the deck, the man shook his head. "No, Ser Rauck. Over with your colleague, please."

The second man stopped in the doorway, arms hanging loosely at his side, weapon pointing downward, though his eyes kept moving, taking in the compartment. His colleague studied the captives in silence for a moment as if trying to assess what lay behind their carefully controlled expressions.

"What is this about?" Talyn asked. "Technically, you forced your way aboard a private vessel without authorization. That is, at least, trespassing. And since you did it while threatening us with weapons, it becomes criminal trespassing. You're not members of the Scandian Police Authority, and I doubt you're private security either."

"Congratulations on your grasp of Scandian law, Sera Bayle. We are indeed neither Scandian police nor private security. But I assure you we are agents of the Commonwealth government and hold the necessary authority to board your employer's ship in pursuit of our investigation."

"Want to show us proof?" Decker asked in an unfriendly tone. "Any bozo with a gun can claim to be law enforcement. Until he shoots you that is. You gorillas don't look like Fleet and you sure as shit aren't Constabulary, so I don't understand what government agency you're supposed to represent by intimidating honest people aboard their private property."

"Your associate is rather uncouth, don't you think, Sera Bayle?"

"Perhaps. But he has a point. Who are you and what do you want?"

The man leaned back against a waist-high galley pantry and crossed his arms, gun pointing up and to one side. "As to who we are, call us Smith and Jones. It's not important which is which. I'll be Smith if that makes you feel better. We belong to a classified agency that works directly for the Secretary-General of the Commonwealth. The name wouldn't mean anything to you."

Neither Decker nor Talyn reacted, yet both came to the same conclusion. *Sécurité Spéciale.*

"Do you carry ID?" Decker asked. "Claiming to be from a hush-hush organization doesn't cut it without ID."

The man chuckled. "What is it about the word classified you don't understand? Take the fact that the harbormaster's office cooperated with us as your proof."

Decker shrugged angrily, muttering, "Fucking assholes with guns," just loud enough for their interrogator to hear.

Talyn laid a hand on his arm. "There's no point in antagonizing them, Dmitri. Let's hear what they want."

"A sensible suggestion, Sera Bayle. You claim to be employees of Universal Exports, the registered owner of this ship."

"We are employees of Universal Exports, yes."

"And you're here to take control of it?"

"Indeed. I'm a certified starship pilot, and Dmitri is a starship systems technician."

"What happened to its previous crew?"

Talyn shrugged. "We don't know. The Breidablik harbormaster informed us that Captain Kenly, the sole crew member, vanished shortly after landing, and hasn't been heard from since. My superiors are eager to avoid leaving their property unsupervised and accruing fees instead of working the star lanes, so they sent us as replacements."

The man cocked a questioning eyebrow. "Two for one?"

"After Captain Kenly's inexplicable disappearance, our employer decided to change crewing protocols," Talyn replied without missing a beat.

"And you don't know where Mattias Kenly might be?"

"Of course not. If the harbormaster put you onto us, you'll be aware we landed here less than two hours ago aboard a ComEx courier ship. Speaking to the police will be our next step after securing *Haukka*."

"I'll save you the trouble. The cops don't know either. Kenly hasn't passed a departures control check and can't be found anywhere in Breidablik."

"Let me guess, you're wondering whether he snuck back aboard *Haukka* undetected, and that's why we're talking. What do you want with Mattias Kenly, anyway?"

"I'm afraid I can't share that with you, Sera Bayle. But my agency is interested in speaking with him."

"He's not aboard this ship, I can assure you of that."

"Oh?"

"The AI would have warned us after it accepted the recognition code I gave Sera Stigen in her office. But if you're not inclined to accept my word, feel free to scan every nook and cranny to your heart's content. I'm sure a classified security agency equips its officers with military-grade sensors. That must be how you came to detect the ship's anti-intruder protection, what you called a doomsday device earlier. Funnily enough, it's only meant to appear so and isn't powerful enough to take out half of the port."

Smith didn't immediately reply. Instead, judging by his narrowed eyes, he seemed to mull over his next words.

"We will run a scan, but first, I'd like to acquaint myself with the ship's log and any other relevant information the data banks might hold."

"And intrude on legally protected commercial secrets without a warrant signed by a federal judge? I'm sorry, but I can't do that. Get a warrant, and we'll be glad to cooperate."

"Perhaps I should clarify our respective positions, Sera Bayle. My colleague and I are acting with the full authority of the SecGen's office. You must comply."

"And if we don't?"

He shook his head, and a sad smile appeared. "That would be most unfortunate, but we would enforce compliance, an experience you might not enjoy."

"What the fuck is this?" Decker demanded in a tone resonating with repressed anger. "The Commonwealth isn't a damned police state where spooks can go around threatening honest citizens at will. Why don't you leave now before things happen that we'll regret?"

"Tsk, tsk, Ser Rauck. Calm yourself." The man uncrossed his arms and pointed his needler at the Marine. "Rash acts will only result in regrets on your part. Waking up from a needler hit isn't the most pleasant thing in the universe. What we'll do is this — you and my colleague will stay here while Sera Bayle takes me to the bridge and lets me download a data dump. Once that's done, we'll do a walking scan of every deck and then leave you to carry out your duties. Simple, easy, and painless, don't you agree?"

Talyn's fingers tapped the table in a dance of indecision while her eyes avoided both captors. When Zack cleared his throat, staring defiantly at the man who'd done the talking so far, she nodded.

"Very well, then, Ser Smith. May I stand?"

The man beamed. "I thought you'd see sense in cooperating with the Commonwealth government. Please lead the way." He made a sweeping gesture toward the door with his needler, then glanced at Jones and jerked his head toward Decker.

"Keep him here."

**

With Talyn and Smith gone, Decker gazed at Jones. "So, does this classified agency pay well? I wouldn't mind looking at a job change if the pay's good. Being allowed to fuck with people seems like a nice perk as do those guns of yours."

"Shut up."

"It speaks! Will wonders never cease?" Decker bestowed a broad grin on the gorilla. "I guess you're not recruiting, then?"

Jones waved his gun in the Marine's direction. "I told you to shut up."

"That's not very nice. How about I offer you a cup of coffee while we wait on our respective bosses, so we can get better acquainted and talk about your agency's entry programs?" Decker inched his way toward the end of the bench as if preparing to stand.

"Stay right where you are, funny man."

Zack obeyed, but he was almost at the end of the table.

"I guess going to the heads for a piss is out of the question?"

"It is. Wait until we're done. Tie a knot in it or something."

"Slipknot or bowline?"

"Whatever turns you on, asshole. Now stop annoying me with your crap. Just shut up already."

Decker raised his hands in surrender, then stared over the goon's shoulder with a look of alarm on his face. Jones instinctively turned his head toward the corridor to investigate, and the Marine slipped out from behind the table. He charged at his captor with the grace and speed of a hunting cheetah.

His left hand clamped around Jones' right wrist and twisted it to one side, forcing him to release the needler while his right hand closed around the man's scrotum, fingertips digging into the fragile skin beneath the trousers. Jones gasped and bent over, left hand scrabbling for purchase on his attacker.

His fingers grasped the side of Decker's face, but the Marine gave Jones' scrotum an added twist. Then he released him and took one step back before slamming his fist on the back of the man's skull, sending him sprawling on the deck with a loud thump. Jones was out for the count.

Zack picked up the discarded needler and placed it on a nearby counter, then opened a hidden compartment behind the upper pantry, hoping the equipment storage layout remained as before. Decker's hand found the emergency kit that contained, among others, wrist and ankle restraints, as well as a choice of interrogation drugs.

He shackled the *Sécurité Spéciale* agent, then selected a knockout patch from the kit and slapped in on the side of Jones' face, ensuring he'd stay unconscious for a few more hours unless someone applied the antidote.

He stuck his head out into the corridor and listened for any sign of movement. When nothing reached his ears, he retrieved the latter's needler and silently crept up toward the bridge, gun at the ready.

The door to *Haukka*'s command center stood open, but no sounds other than the background buzz of a starship at rest came through. Decker, his back against the adjacent bulkhead, carefully edged around the door frame, weapon held high, eyes searching for his partner and the other *Sécurité Spéciale* agent.

The former sat at the pilot's console, her back to him, fingers dancing over the controls as she woke the ship from its somnolent state. The latter lay on the deck, eyes staring sightlessly at the ceiling, a trickle of blood dripping from his right ear.

When she sensed his presence, Talyn said without turning, "You took long enough. Showing trainees how to disarm someone isn't quite the same as doing so for real, is it?"

"Perhaps you need to cycle through one of my classes, darling, and refine your technique. The guy who stayed with me is merely unconscious and trussed up, not dead like this one. I didn't think it was a situation that warranted the start of a fresh body trail, at least not until we figure out what Smith and Jones were doing. They clearly didn't twig we were the fearsome duo of Talyn and Decker, wanted by Black Sword, the *Sécurité Spéciale*, and the Coalition in five dozen star systems."

"I guess the opposition has the same problems we do in coordinating activities. That's one of the inevitable consequences of segregating missions to preserve security. These gorillas probably belong to the local office while the ones after us are likely directed from their HQ on Earth. You know HQ never tells outlying detachments what it's doing."

"Half the time HQ doesn't even know what it's doing, and I'm being charitable. But that doesn't invalidate my point. We need to figure out why Smith and Jones were interested in Garrett Montero, or rather in his cover identity — as per our mission orders, remember?"

This time Talyn turned around and sighed. "Listen, Big Boy, I tried to take Smith out in a non-lethal manner, but the bugger was quicker and stronger than I expected. My reflexes took over and the next thing I knew, my dagger was slicing and dicing his brain matter via the ear canal. We'll interrogate the other one."

"And then?"

"Send him home to mother with a written apology for killing his playmate?" Talyn gave him an exasperated look. "Maybe Smith and Jones were perfectly decent human beings doing their jobs. Maybe they even intended to let us go once we'd given them what they wanted.   Not everyone in the *Sécurité Spéciale* is a psychopathic cockroach.   But as you've remarked on more than one occasion, this is a war, albeit a covert one. People die, whether in the heat of action or in cold blood. We squeeze what we can from Jones, he also meets my dagger, and we dispose of their bodies in the ship's plasma tubes during the static engine test I'll run later on."

"What happens when someone figures out they climbed aboard *Haukka* and never left?"

"Who's to say they climbed aboard? With any luck, a friendly assistant harbormaster will have turned off the surveillance network in this docking arm, to keep their visit anonymous. You know, basic fieldcraft, something the opposition is quite capable of handling. Now if you'd be so kind as to drag Smith's body to the engine room. I've already searched him." She nodded at a small pile of data wafers beside a large needler on the console in front of her.

Decker studied his partner for a few seconds before he understood she was shedding the layers of feeling built up over the years they'd been working together. The old tightly controlled, emotionless Hera was coming back. He felt a momentary pang of grief but knew it was inevitable. Trying to be something she wasn't, for his sake, placed her on a path to self-destruction. And the Fleet needed Hera Talyn. He needed her.

The Marine picked up Smith's body by the shoulders and dragged him out of the bridge and into the lift. Once on the engineering deck, he left it by the plasma tube's main access hatch. He checked the still unconscious Jones before rejoining Talyn on the bridge.

"When shall we interrogate the other one?"

She climbed to her feet and tugged her tunic into place. "Now."

— THIRTEEN —

"Where do you want to interrogate him?" Decker asked, leading the way aft to where the second goon lay snoring. "The saloon isn't exactly the best place for it."

"I assume he's been conditioned, so we'll probably be stuck using the old-fashioned way. Set him up in the cargo hold. Strap him to a chair in the middle of the deck, shine one bright light on him and leave the remainder of the compartment in darkness. I'll do the rest."

"Do you intend to try breaking his conditioning?"

"I could use the practice, but I doubt he has information worth the effort. Although I suppose, it might be educational for you to witness the technique at least once."

Decker grimaced. "No thanks. Some things are best left to the imagination."

"Your loss."

They entered the saloon and contemplated Jones' prone form.

"Did you search him?"

"No. I didn't want you to wait for me any longer than necessary." Decker knelt beside the man and rifled through his pockets. He tossed an ID wafer, a few cred chips, needler reloads, and a small, thin computer tablet on the table. "He's not been going around heavily armed. No ace in the hole or bladed weapon."

Talyn picked up the ID chip and tapped its surface. "Same as the other, whose real name was Waller Leppell. It doesn't mention the *Sécurité Spéciale* by name but identifies the bearer as an agent of the SecGen's office. This one's name is Huy Bivins."

"Genuine?"

"As far as I can tell. It has the right markers. We'll take both home with us. The documents section will love seeing recent models. Do you think you can drag him by yourself without breaking his bones, or do you need help?"

"Depends on how damaged you want him before starting. He's not particularly small and slack bodies aren't easy to handle down a flight of stairs."

"The lift goes to the cargo hold, remember?"

"Oh. Right. I forgot. You take care of the chair and the ambiance, and I'll take friend Huy." He nodded at the emergency pack on the counter. "If you want the little interrogator's field kit, it's complete except for a means to verify if he's been hardened against chemical questioning. Who knows — the *Sécurité Spéciale* could be stingy with conditioning and not waste it on low-level goons. You might not need to go medieval on him."

"Spoilsport."

"Try to restrain your glee at a chance for hands-on torture." Decker slipped his arms under the man's shoulders and straightened his back with a soft grunt. "How about you open doors for me while you decide in what order you'll yank out his toenails."

Shortly afterward, the *Sécurité Spéciale* agent was strapped to a metal chair Talyn brought up from engineering, chin in his chest, with soft snores escaping his nose. Decker slapped an antidote patch on Bivins' neck and stepped back into the shadows a pace behind the thug.

Within seconds Bivins stirred. First, his head rose, then his eyelids fluttered, but under the intensity of the light, he screwed them tightly shut again. They saw his limbs shiver as he tested his bonds in vain, then he relaxed, lower jaw working against the dryness on his tongue.

"You want to check if he's been conditioned?" Decker asked.

"It would save us time, I suppose." Talyn walked up to Bivins and backhanded him across the face. Hard. "Are you conditioned against interrogation, asshole?"

The man squinted up at her and croaked, "Fuck you, bitch."

Talyn struck him again. "I guess they don't teach you any manners in the *Sécurité Spéciale*. We can do this in a few ways. If you tell me you've been conditioned, I'll show my colleague how that can be broken. It's not pretty. If you tell me you've not been conditioned, I'll use standard drugs to loosen your tongue, and we'll enjoy a painless conversation." She paused, then continued in a more thoughtful tone. "Of course, you might tell me you've not been conditioned and hope my drugs will kill you quickly, rather than experience my interrogation skills. I've been told my ability to inflict both emotional and physical pain is beyond exquisite. What are your thoughts on the matter, Huy?"

"You can't do this," he rasped. "You don't know who you're messing with. We squash corporate drones like you all the time."

"That may well be." She took his chin in her hand and forced him to look up at her. "But it won't help you. Waller Leppell is dead, and no one's seen you come aboard this ship. Good luck to your drone squashing friends."

She saw his facial features twitch at her words and gave Zack a meaningful glance he understood at once. Talyn's assumption about the docking arm's surveillance network being switched off was correct.

"So what shall I do, Huy?" She asked, running her fingertips along his jawline and up the side of his face in a chilling mimicry of a lover's touch. "Use my drugs or my skills?" When she felt him recoil in disgust, a throaty chuckle escaped her lips. "I don't think I'm Huy's type."

Decker knew she was playacting to soften Bivins' resolve before the real interrogation began, but her ethereally malevolent tone sent a shiver up his spine, nonetheless. It evoked the memory of another intelligence officer by the name of Rika Kozlev, a truly evil woman now thankfully dead, who'd put Zack in her interrogation chair years earlier.

When Talyn started to run her fingers through Bevin's hair in a caress so creepy it made Decker wince, the *Sécurité Spéciale* man said, "I'm not conditioned, damn it. Do what you want so we can end this."

Talyn studied his face for a few moments looking for signs Bivins was lying, then she released his head and straightened her back with a moue of disappointment.

"I was barely getting started."

"Maybe the next *Sécurité Spéciale* goon we meet will need your special touch. Would you like me to do the honors?"

"No. I'll take care of my friend Huy." She gave their captive sickeningly sweet smile. "A lady has to take her pleasures when and where she can."

Decker handed her an injector which she applied against Bivins' neck. It emitted a faint hiss. Then, she stepped back and waited. When his facial muscles slackened, and he slumped in the chair, she gave Decker a nod.

He dimmed the light shining on Bivins and raised the ambient illumination. The cargo deck sank into a soft, murky ambiance which would further confuse a brain slowly succumbing to the inhibition suppressant. Talyn leaned forward and cupped the man's head in her hands. She stared into his eyes.

"How are you feeling, Huy?"

"Why would you care, bitch?"

She smiled at him. "Do you enjoy your work?"

"Yes."

"What do you enjoy most about it, Huy?"

"The power. Until you know what it's like to mess with people's lives for pay..."

"That sound nice."

Bivins giggled. "It's a blast."

"How were you planning to mess with my life?"

The man tried to shrug but shackled as he was, it turned into a brief spasm. "After you'd given us what we came for, you were slated to die. Of course, we were planning on a bit of fun first — with you in particular."

"Why kill us?"

"Because anyone able to board this ship works for opponents of the SecGen, and our job is to protect his office against enemies foreign and domestic."

"Which enemy am I supposed to be, Huy?"

"No idea. The orders didn't say. Matter of fact, the orders never say. We're just given targets. This time, we were told to find the guy who piloted this junk heap, make him give us access to his AI and then squeeze him dry. When the bugger vanished before we landed here, the boss told us to wait for whoever showed up with the right codes, then do it to them instead."

"Nice," Decker muttered from behind Bivins. Talyn gave him a brief, but stern gaze over their captive's head and he put on a suitably chastised expression.

She focused on her prisoner again. "Why the pilot and his ship?"

"Don't know. Nobody told us. We were given a job. No explanations. We're never told why. Just what." He giggled again. "But even without explanations, it's a lot of fun. Recently we did this one job with a woman on Scandia..."

Talyn speared Decker with her eyes before he could utter a sound and he raised his hands in surrender.

"Tell me about her, Huy."

"Rich old stunt. Runs one of the big Scandian companies. Don't know what she did to piss off the SecGen. But we were told to scare the living crap out of her. That was a laugh, watching the high and mighty bitch grovel. Too bad we couldn't touch her. She was cute for her age. Smelled nice too."

"Were you given any other Scandian women as targets in the last few weeks?"

"Other than the rich stunt? No." Bivins shook his head. "But she was a one-off, anyway. Waller Leppell and me, we're muscle, on account of our size and that we'll scrag anyone we're told to, even with our bare hands. We do intimidation real well. The fancy stuff is done by others, and they're nasty as hell."

Decker gave his partner a silent shrug. It was worth asking the question.

"So you don't know why your boss wanted you to seize this ship and its pilot?"

"Nope. We were to do it, then call the office. Someone else would come and take over."

Talyn continued her interrogation for another ten minutes, trying different angles to see if she could draw anything else of use from the *Sécurité Spéciale* man. However, it quickly became plain that he and his late colleague were expendable, low-grade operatives, barely different from those working as foot soldiers for organized crime syndicates.

Considering the Coalition and its *Sécurité Spéciale* minions employed groups such as the Confederacy of the Howling Stars for their dirty work that discovery didn't surprise either of the two Naval Intelligence officers.

Bivins and Leppell were no choirboys. They'd broken many laws while carrying out their orders. Enough for years, if not decades in a penal colony. But their actions were merely those of useful idiots in the service of a secretive agency doing the SecGen's bidding.

In Decker's estimation, neither Leppell, nor Bivins merited a summary, cold-blooded execution — unlike many of the *Sécurité Spéciale* agents who'd crossed Talyn's and his path. But with Leppell's body cooling in the engine room, waiting for disposal, and Bivins having undergone a professional grade interrogation, both needed to vanish. They couldn't risk anyone wondering whether Annekka Bayle and Dmitri Rauck might actually be the two Fleet agents heading the Coalition's most wanted list.

"Done?" Decker asked his partner when she fell silent.

She nodded, eyes still on their captive. "Done."

"In that case..." Decker's Pathfinder blade flashed in the low light as he pulled it from a sheath strapped to his left forearm.

He stepped forward to grasp Bivins' head with one hand while jamming the dagger into his right ear with the other, killing him almost instantly.

"There. Now you can't say I don't take my turn at doing the wet work."

"I appreciate your gesture, but since I am what I am, you should leave such matters to me. See to the welfare of your soul instead."

He gave his partner a tight, humorless grin. "I love you too, darling. And my soul's doing just fine. Let's bring this one to where his buddy is waiting and prepare everything for your static engine test."

**

"Harbormaster, this is *Haukka*," Talyn said, "We've completed our engine tests and are ready to reconnect the gangway tube."

"Acknowledged, *Haukka*. Stand by. Harbormaster, out."

She pushed away from the command console and stood. "There. Our late friends Leppell and Bivins are no more than stripped atoms, and the harbormaster's office didn't ask about them when we requested permission to disconnect from the docking arm."

"How long until they're missed, do you think?" Decker asked from the tactical station where he'd been getting reacquainted with the ship's ordnance.

"Not that long. Eventually, word will filter back to their superiors on the planet that someone's taken charge of *Haukka* and they'll wonder why their bully boys didn't step in."

"Since we still need to figure out what happened with Garrett and why the *Sécurité Spéciale* is so keen on getting their hands on him and the ship, let's hope the next operatives they send up will be a cut above basic utility-grade gorilla. Otherwise, we'll be stuck paying their Scandia field office a visit."

Talyn snorted derisively. "I can just picture you barging in with a cheesy smile to ask why they have a hard-on for an undercover Naval Intelligence ship. But to answer the question you didn't ask, no, I don't think it's connected to the disappearance of your daughter and former spouse. Besides, they could be back home already because there's no foul play involved."

"You don't really believe that last bit, do you?"

She shook her head. "No."

"What next?" Decker climbed to his feet and stretched.

"Talk to the Breidablik police about Garrett. Do a little sleuthing of our own. And if that produces nothing, fly *Haukka* to the Kollsvik spaceport. Look in on the inspector working Saga's case. Wait and see what comes crawling out of the woodwork once people realize the ship flown by Mattias Kenly, known import-export scofflaw, is under new management. Maybe even scope out the local *Sécurité Spéciale* office and see if we can do them a lot of mischief while we get a handle on their newest plans in this system."

"You're the mission commander. But before we leave, I'd like to run a full inspection of the main systems. Just because the AI let no one aboard doesn't mean there aren't problems waiting for that critical moment when we're a few dozen meters above a busy spaceport, attempting to land. I especially want to send a droid to do a full outside inspection so we can be sure no one stuck limpet mines into various nooks or crannies. That means we won't be lifting off for a while, not if we're to play detective at the same time. It's a shame your Constabulary friend isn't doing her thing in this system. Finding Garrett Montero would be right up her alley, since she already knows him in a way."

"That can't be helped. Will the AI work with you?"

"Sure. My little virtual buddy hasn't forgotten the good times we enjoyed together during the Garonne insurrection. I'm guessing you want to visit the local cop shop right away?"

"It would be wise since we're probably expected after expressing concern for Brother Mattias' welfare. It would seem strange if we didn't follow up as soon as possible."

"Right." Decker nodded once, then inspected his partner with a critical eye. "I see no bloodstains or anything else suspicious marring your fancy business suit. How about me?"

She returned the favor. "You're good as well, meaning we made two clean kills. Spending half a year behind the lines, so to speak, didn't do us much harm. Armed?"

"And dangerous. I thought I'd carry friend Bivins' needler instead of my Shrehari hand artillery, as you like to call it."

"Great minds and all that. I have Leppell's."

"We shoot and the ammo traces back to... what?"

"Not us. That's good enough. And strangely, my loads are non-lethal." Her lips twitched dismissively.

"So are mine. How did they expect to kill us?"

"We'll never know for sure. My best guess would be needlers to put us under, followed by catastrophic decompression in a secondary airlock with the bodies shoved out once the ship is well away from here."

Decker grunted. "Assholes."

"The *Sécurité Spéciale* doesn't hire nice people. Give me a moment to change the ship's access codes. Then we'll go."

— FOURTEEN —

The Scandian Police Authority's Breidablik station wasn't difficult to find. It sat at the center of the domed habitat like a spider in its web, watching through a sophisticated surveillance network which, unfortunately for Decker and Talyn, didn't extend to the port facilities.

Those were under the jealous eyes of the harbormaster's own security service, which, not infrequently, was ordered to ignore a given docking arm for a specified period, no questions asked. Free ports offered anonymity so long as the letter of the law remained intact though its spirit be grievously wounded.

A duty sergeant in Scandian blue, ensconced behind a high counter running almost the full width of the sparsely populated public lobby, looked up at Decker and Talyn when the sliding doors hissed closed behind them.

"What can I do for you?" He asked in a deep baritone that seemed to match a square, rough-hewn face framed by short red hair and an equally flamboyant, but longer beard. A true descendant of the ancient Vikings if Decker had ever seen one.

"My name is Annekka Bayle. This is Dmitri Rauck. We're employees of the Universal Exports Corporation, which owns the trader ship *Haukka*. Our superiors sent us here to take charge of said ship and inquire about our colleague Mattias Kenly's disappearance. We would appreciate a few minutes of the investigating officer's time so we might report back to our corporate headquarters on Captain Kenly's status."

The sergeant nodded once and pointed at a row of chairs set against one wall, where a dozen people of various descriptions sat in silence, eyes averted. "Please wait there while I inquire."

Less than five minutes later, a side door opened without a sound. A slender, tall woman wearing warrant officer's bars on her collar stepped out and headed straight for them.

"Sera Bayle, Ser Rauck?" When the agents stood, she continued, "I am Senior Investigator Thais Chaskiel. You are here about Mattias Kenly's disappearance?"

"We are," Talyn replied with a polite dip of the head. "He's a valued colleague and member of the Universal Exports family."

"I am charged with the case. If you will please follow me." Chaskiel gestured toward the still open side door.

She led them to an interview room that exuded all the charm of a prison cell, with uncomfortable, utilitarian furniture and a bleak decor. It reminded Talyn of nothing so much as the one she'd occupied on Aquilonia station during the Shovak murder investigation. She repressed a smile at the memory of her verbal sparring with the investigator at the time, Chief Superintendent Caelin Morrow.

Chaskiel motioned them to sit across the table from her. "Before I discuss the case with you, might I see identification that proves you are employed by Universal Exports?"

"Certainly."

Both agents handed over their fake credentials. The Scandian examined them with great care, her wrist-mounted sensor acting as a scanner, before handing them back without comment.

"I can't tell you much about this case. The harbormaster's office contacted us after Captain Kenly stopped responding to communications and his ship's AI advised them he was not aboard and had not been for several days. It also informed the harbormaster that Kenly had placed *Haukka* on lockdown, meaning no one could board without the proper authorization codes.

"The harbormaster's security office has a video of him leaving the ship three days before they raised concern about his inexplicable absence. That was the last piece of visual evidence found anywhere in Breidablik. He has not passed through any departure control gates, used his payment codes to make purchases or used his credentials for any other purpose. Our inquiries didn't find witnesses who encountered Captain Kenly since the day he left his ship."

"May I ask about the investigation's current status?"

"Certainly, Sera Bayle. We posted a 'be on the lookout' bulletin in public areas; the surveillance networks, both ours and the harbormaster's are programmed to raise the alarm if Captain Kenly is spotted; finally, our police informers are keeping an eye out for your colleague. We cannot do more at this point. Besides, if Captain Kenly disappeared of his own volition, no crime has been committed."

"Is there any way a body can leave this moon without passing through official channels?" Decker asked.

Chaskiel nodded. "There are many ways, Ser Rauck, as I'm sure you can imagine. None of them are legal, of course, but anyone using them is not concerned with legality."

"Meaning Mattias Kenly could have been shanghaied and smuggled aboard a departing starship or shuttle undetected?"

"Sadly, yes," Chaskiel acknowledged. "No surveillance system is foolproof."

"And if you make it foolproof the universe will come up with a better fool."

The Scandian warrant officer gave Decker a pained smile. "No doubt."

"Do people vanish without a trace often? If so, it must be bad for business."

"No more often than in any other free port along the Rim, Sera Bayle, or on Scandia itself for that matter. Most of these disappearances are likely voluntary, to escape obligations, enemies, or even the law. Or to set out on adventures. Unlike some places, we do not suffer from an organized crime problem, so involuntary disappearances should be rare."

"No organized crime activity?" Decker asked with a skeptical smile. "Not even in the warehouse district? You're fortunate. In my experience the crooked buggers always wiggle their way in, more often than not right under the local cops' noses."

"And yet it is so in Breidablik. Is there anything else the Scandian Police Authority can do to help you?"

**

"Wasn't that special," Decker grumbled once they were back out on Breidablik's promenade, a broad avenue that cut through the middle of the habitat. "If the cops looking for Saga show the same amount of concern, I might as well find her myself."

"Don't borrow trouble ahead of time, Zack. You can't blame Chaskiel. There are only so many avenues of inquiry open to the police. It looks like she explored the available ones. If Garrett went to ground voluntarily, no one will find him. And if the opposition picked him up, then chances are we'll be putting another memorial star on the wall back at HQ."

"Now who's borrowing trouble?" He smirked at his companion. "Perhaps Garrett was nice enough to leave us clues. He'll have expected the boss to dispatch a retrieval team for *Haukka* at the least, if not you and I in person. Although since you reached out to him about Saga and Ingrid, our showing up shouldn't be a total surprise."

They retraced their steps to the docks in silence, dodging other pedestrians, their eyes everywhere, looking for signs of surveillance or a tail. Once in their docking arm, Talyn said, "If our friend left us clues, we may simply not have asked the right question yet or looked in the right spot. He's one of us, so he'll know how to hide something only we can find."

"The AI? As in feeding it a code that unlocks a hidden layer of data?"

"Perhaps. It would be a logical place to stash a message."

"How do we figure out the magic password?"

She glanced up at a small, inconspicuous blister hiding a hemispheric video sensor on the docking arm's ceiling. "We should ask Chaskiel for a copy of the sequence showing him leaving *Haukka* the day he went walkabout. The man always could speak volumes with the smallest gestures."

"Ah, yes." Decker nodded. "I heard he was handy with his fingers. Reminds me of someone else I know." He nudged his partner and leered.

"There's plenty of work waiting for us before we can take a break," she warned.

"An hour or two of rest and recreation might jog the old brain cells."

"First the video. I'll call Senior Investigator Chaskiel when we're aboard."

**

"If the AI's hiding something, it's not letting on," Decker said once Talyn cut the communications link with Chaskiel. "I can't tell whether that's because Garrett didn't leave us an Easter egg in the data banks or my scintillating personality's not enough to pierce through the security layers."

"Let's hope the video shows us more. It should arrive at any moment."

"Excellent. I so love a cooperative cop."

"I think our dear senior investigator was a little embarrassed by the paucity of news she could share with us."

"Professional pride is a useful thing in the wrong hands. And yours can be so wrong sometimes…"

"I'm sure they can, Big Boy. Now back to work. Garrett didn't march off into the sunset without leaving something behind."

"Incoming data packet from the Scandian Police Authority," a soft, disembodied alto announced.

"The AI has relearned how to speak?" Talyn gave Decker a suspicious glare. "I thought I told you my voice wasn't an acceptable template for its audio subroutine."

"First, that didn't sound like you anymore. Garrett obviously fine-tuned its programming." Decker ignored her snort of disbelief. "And second, I want to make sure we miss nothing by restricting communications to the odd chime and text displays. *Haukka*'s AI might hold the key to finding out why Garrett walked away from his assignment."

"You hope." She allowed herself an exasperated sigh. "But if I find the audio getting on my nerves, we return to the status quo ante, understood?"

"Aye, aye, sir." Decker tossed off a facetious salute. "Shall we see what that data packet might be?"

"It is a video sequence showing Captain Kenly walking through the docking arm toward the hub," the AI answered without prompting.

Talyn squeezed the bridge of her nose, exhaled and muttered in an irritated tone, "So it begins." Then, louder, "Play the video on the main display."

They watched Mattias Kenly, master of the trader *Haukka* emerge from the gangway tube and stride through the arm at a steady, if unhurried pace, seemingly a man heading out to do business. He wore the sort of dark, utilitarian clothes preferred by spacers — trousers tucked into boots, collarless shirt, jacket loose enough to hide a sidearm and equipped with enough pockets to carry a small arsenal. His long, gray-flecked chestnut hair was gathered in a queue at the nape of the neck. A neatly trimmed and groomed beard, more silver than brown, framed a strong chin beneath intense, watchful eyes.

"The earring's a nice touch. If I didn't know ahead of time he's Lieutenant Commander Montero, of the Special Intelligence Operations Division, I'd take him for a real smuggler. It is Garrett, right?"

She nodded. "If it isn't, someone's gone to great trouble replicating his cover identity." After the sequence ended, Talyn asked, "Did you spot anything?"

"Other than the fact he looked like a tax avoidance specialist whose latest batch of contraband is about to be seized and sold at auction? No. Let's replay it in slow motion."

The moving images froze and then faded at the end of the second repetition, this time at one-third speed.

Talyn said, "If Garrett left us a message or any sort of clue, it wasn't something meant to be seen in this video."

"Perhaps he thought it too risky, in case the opposition got wise and set about deciphering whatever he wanted to communicate. There's no telling who can access the port's surveillance network."

"True. But you were right — he didn't seem completely footloose and fancy-free, even though he kept it from showing too much."

"And we're no wiser than before. The answer is aboard *Haukka*. If Garrett was concerned with security, then it's the only place in the whole damn system where he could be reasonably sure the bad guys wouldn't find it."

"Or rather, where he could be reasonably sure someone from Special Operations and only Special Operations would find it." Talyn stood and nodded toward the open door. "While we let our minds work on the problem, why don't we run that full survey you mentioned? I'll monitor the droid inspecting our hull from the outside while you go deck by deck on the inside. Who knows — you might stumble across something useful."

"Why do I inherit an oversized share of the survey while you sit on your delightful butt to watch a machine look for limpet mines?"

"Because you're an oversized lummox who's overly interested in my delightful derriere."

**

"Zack." Talyn's voice echoed through the engineering compartment. "Find the nearest display. The droid found something tucked away under the port nacelle pylon it says isn't part of the most recent specs it carries in memory."

"Shit."

Decker reached out and stroked the main panel's screen. It came to life with a feed from the small inspection robot clinging to *Haukka*'s hull. A targeting reticle was centered on a small blister that almost seemed part of the ship, something a casual surveyor might miss. It was as scarred and stained by atmospheric re-entries as its surroundings were, but the droid obligingly highlighted a faint seam between the bump and the hull.

"What do you think?"

"My first guess would be a subspace tracking beacon. It doesn't look big enough for an explosive device able to penetrate the hull, let alone damage the pylon. At least not in a vacuum."

"Master Gunner's opinion?"

"Yep."

"What should we do?"

"*We* won't do anything about it right now. *I* will finish inspecting the lower deck and engineering spaces while you keep the droid running. Then I'll hand the inside survey over to you while I suit up and go out with my tools. If it's a beacon, we may want to leave it right there for now, so as not to alert whoever planted the thing we're on to them."

"Do you think Garrett would modify the ship and not note it in the specs?"

"Sure, but changing stuff and not taking notes eventually leads to a shipload of problems so I won't use that as my first premise. Remember our *Sécurité Spéciale* friends had plenty of time to tag *Haukka* between Garrett leaving and our arrival."

"Without the AI taking note?"

"It might not if port inspection droids are crawling around the pad, as I'm sure they regularly do to verify that berthed ships are properly secured. I'm willing to bet the harbormaster sent out a swarm after Garrett walked away. But until I examine the blister in person, all we know is that the engineering droid doesn't remember it."

Half an hour later, a pressure-suited Decker climbed out of the port side secondary airlock and attached his harness to the patiently waiting engineering droid that would carry him to the mysterious blister. Walking on the hull using his suit's magnetic soles would be awkward in the moon's one-sixth gee gravity since his target was on the ship's underside. It was best to hang off the droid which could move several times Decker's weight while its centipede-like traction belts adhered to *Haukka*.

He made the robot stop less than a meter from the object and scanned it with a high-powered military-grade unit. After digesting the results, Decker reached out and ran his hand over the seam he'd seen via the video feed. He stopped when the tactile sensors built into the glove's fingertips alerted him to a small depression on the side facing the pylon.

Talyn, who'd been watching via his helmet camera feed asked, "What is it?"

"Can I ask the starship pilot version of you a hypothetical question?"

"Of course."

"What happens if an explosive charge, one that's not powerful enough to breach the hull, explodes inside our hyperspace bubble when we're FTL? I know hyperspace torpedoes force a ship back to sublight speeds, but they're designed to disrupt the bubble by blowing against its outer edges. I'm talking a nasty bang inside our own little pocket universe."

She was silent for a few moments, then said, "No one actually knows, but it can't be good. If I recall correctly, the Navy carried out tests long ago to see what would happen if a ship suffered from internal explosions while FTL. The test drones they used were never found."

"So they could be roaming through hyperspace for eternity, each stuck in its own permanent bubble?" Decker asked.

"Or they've been wrecked during a catastrophic translation back to sublight.

"In other words, there's probably no good outcome."

"Doesn't seem like it. What do you intend?"

Decker chewed on the inside of his cheek for a moment, then exhaled noisily.

"Assume my scans correctly identified it as a mine, find a way to defeat any anti-lift device and remove it. If I try to pry the damned thing off just like that, I doubt you'll find enough left of me to fill a small envelope. Or we put the ship on automatic, get off, and let the AI fly it into Scandia's sun."

"Why would someone use such a device?"

"No idea. Mind you, to the casual and even not so casual eye, it looks like a normal hull patch. Something with enough punch to break us open would look exactly like what it was, even to the dumbest space cadet. However, if our culprit knows about the Navy experiments, he'll think it was worth a try."

"But the *Sécurité Spéciale* or whoever has put them onto *Haukka* want the ship and its data banks intact," Talyn protested. "Not turning into space debris or a mythical Flying Dutchman."

"I know. It doesn't make much sense. Unless..." Decker paused. "You've worked with Garrett before. Is he a big sideways thinker?"

"About as twisty as most of us."

"Check the ship's log and tell me if he inspected the hull in the days between landing here and going walkabout."

"You think *he* planted that limpet?"

"It's no stranger than thinking the *Sécurité Spéciale* did so."

"What about third parties? People Garrett offended in his undercover role?"

"Check the log," Decker repeated.

After almost a minute of silence, Talyn's voice rang out again.

"Garrett took an inspection tour in a pressure suit a few hours before he was last seen in the docking arm." A pause, then, "It's not really an explosive device, is it, Zack?"

"Nope. Just something cunningly disguised as a mine. Garrett wouldn't booby-trap his own ship. Not if he plans on lifting off in a hurry."

"Then what's the point?"

"Points — plural. Or so I figure." Decker ran his finger along the seam between the supposed patch and the hull. "If the ship is stolen and the thief surveys it before hauling ass into the badlands, he'll think he has a real problem on his hands. Besides, civilians like the *Sécurité Spéciale* goons might not know offhand how much explosive you need to punch a hole through the hull and think this is a huge problem."

"Plausible, if not necessarily probable, but okay — a decoy to mess with the bad guys. What else?"

"Where would you hide something that only your equally twisted colleagues from the netherworld of black ops should find?"

"A hull patch pretending to be a limpet mine?"

"Precisely." He chuckled, pleased with himself. "Does that sound like Garrett?"

"It does. But how will you get confirmation?"

"Simple. If it's what I believe, I need is a code of some sort." He paused. "A recognition code that can be given to whatever is hidden inside the hull patch without using a keyboard, touchscreen, optical sensor, or another direct interface."

"And an arm you can afford to lose if things go wrong. Would it respond to a radio transmission?"

"Possibly, but if you're trying to hide something in plain sight, you might want to use a method that can't be picked up by a receiver aimed at your location. I have an idea..."

— FIFTEEN —

"You're crazy, you know that?"

"Look who's talking," Decker replied after removing his pressure suit helmet. The squat, boxy engineering droid carrying the hull patch waited patiently inside the now re-pressurized airlock for orders.

"What if your assumptions were wrong?"

"The little fella over there would be gone," he nodded toward the droid, "and we'd face a long conversation with the harbormaster. But my assumptions were correct. We'll likely find he uses that droid to help set and remove the fake patch, then wipes its memory, hence the alert when it came upon a feature not in the specs. And that's probably by design, so people like us investigate. I can't wait to unpack the thing and see how Garrett did it."

"And what in the big, wide galaxy made you think of playing 'Silver and Green' at it. Or at least having the droid latch on and send electromagnetic pulses that would sound like 'Silver and Green' if passed through a speaker?"

"It's the Naval Intelligence branch's march, isn't it?" He gave her a satisfied smile. "Once I decided Garrett planted the hull patch himself, I had to decide how he'd disarm the thing. Not that it was actually armed in the first place, but you know what I mean — make the threatening appearance of a mine with anti-lift disappear and release the magnetic seal holding it to the hull. His method was bound to be something others from our spook shop might figure out. I'm willing to bet he programmed it for a few different pieces of music."

"And what if it your attempt didn't work?"

"Then I'd still be running through the repertoire. Now how about I look at what our missing friend hid." He turned to the droid. "Go to cargo hold number one."

"Why there?" Talyn asked as they followed the droid toward the lift.

"Easier to contain problems and if necessary, eject the patch. I still need to account for the zero point one percent possibility I missed something, or that Garrett added another layer of security I can't see."

"Should I don a pressure suit?"

"No, because I'm doing this alone as well. Someone still needs to finish the mission and find the missing people."

An urgent chime forestalled Talyn's response, and the AI's voice came over the ship's public address system.

"A human male at the main airlock is attempting to gain entry. He has entered an invalid access code."

"Shit. The *Sécurité Spéciale* again?"

Talyn held up her hand. "Perhaps not. Give us a visual."

A holographic image of the gangway immediately outside the airlock materialized in the center of the passage. It showed the familiar shape of a powerfully built man in his forties, with long hair gathered in a queue and a thin beard around his full mouth. His clothes were those typical of a spacer, including a jacket loose enough to conceal a spacer's arsenal.

"That has to be Garrett," Decker said. "Back from his unannounced excursion."

"A face different enough to fool police sensors, but not too different. I presume he entered the access code used by Captain Mattias Kenly?"

"Yes," the AI replied.

"It'd be nice if you mentioned it right away," Decker grumbled.

"My apologies."

"How about we go to the airlock and confirm it is Garrett instead of a *Sécurité Spéciale* puke in disguise?"

"Are you armed?" Talyn patted the needler on her hip.

"No."

"Then we'll stop by our quarters for your gun. I don't want to run through the recognition sequence out in the open where we can be seen. Our friend knocking on the door will need to come in. That means I want you able to shoot if anything goes wrong."

"Agreed."

The AI spoke once more. "The human male at the airlock has asked to speak with the ship's captain."

"Ah, he finally figured out there's been a change in management," Decker said.

"And is hoping it's a friendly face."

Once the Marine was armed and standing by the airlock, needler at the ready, Talyn ordered the AI to open. The muted clang of mechanical locking bars withdrawing was followed by a soft groan as the heavy outer door pulled inward, then slid to one side, revealing the flexible gangway tube and its sole occupant. The latter's eyes widened slightly when he saw Talyn and Decker, weapons aimed at the center of his chest.

"Please step in," Talyn said in a soft tone.

The man complied, his gaze never leaving her face, even when the airlock's outer door closed again with a solid thunk.

"I was praying it was you who took over my ship."

The man raised his right hand to waist level, then his fingers began a frantic dance.

Talyn nodded, raised her own hand, and answered in kind before glancing over her shoulder at Zack. "I don't know if you caught that, but it's Garrett Montero, and he's not under duress."

"Good to see you again, Hera." A broad smile lit up Montero's solemn expression. Then, he turned his eyes on the Marine. "And you must be the notorious Zack Decker, ravisher of everything that's noble in our sordid trade. I heard a lot about you."

"Likewise." Decker lowered his gun.

"I was hoping to be back before someone called Universal Exports for overdue berthing fees, but I was waylaid. However, it's just as well you're here. Serious problems are brewing on Scandia, problems that are more in your area of expertise than mine."

"We arrived earlier today aboard a Courier Group aviso, but intended to take *Haukka* planetside in another twenty-four to forty-eight hours," Talyn said.

Montero nodded. "It's what I would do in your place. Does the pressure suit mean you were doing a hull survey, Zack?"

"I removed your improvised safe with the help of the engineering droid. We were trying to figure out why you disappeared."

"That didn't take long. I guess my unorthodox solution isn't as good as I thought."

"Among other things, the big guy is a born improviser. He can pretty much figure out most puzzles in less time than you'd believe. This was child's play."

Decker whistled a few bars from 'Silver and Green,' then winked at Montero.

"Cute.　Considering half of the intelligence branch couldn't whistle it to save their lives, your musical choice would easily stump the *Sécurité Spéciale* and its various pets, let alone pirates and other scum."

The latter inclined his head.　"Nicely done, good sir. Your reputation does not lie."

"Neither does yours."

Talyn speared both men with a suspicious glance, wondering whether this was the start of a mutual admiration society.

Montero pointed at Zack.　"May I suggest you take that tin suit off?　Then we can grab a coffee and discuss what caused me to be absent without authorization for so long. I'm afraid we must move quickly if we want to avert a disaster in this system."

******

"Your message to be on the lookout for Saga Lagman caught me shortly after I returned from a trip into the Protectorate Zone.　I was chasing down reports that supposed Shrehari corsairs were actually undercover units from the Imperial Deep Space Fleet."　Montero cradled a coffee mug in hands that rivaled Decker's for size and callouses.　"Why are we interested in her?　I'm asking because my story involves her mother to some extent."

Talyn, sitting across from him in the saloon, nodded at Decker.　"She's Zack's daughter."

A fleeting expression of surprise crossed Montero's face.　"Am I right that Zack was therefore involved at one time with Saga Lagman's mother, Ingrid Lagman?"

"It's been two decades, but yeah, we were married for five years and a bit.　She couldn't take my long absences on patrol with the 902nd Pathfinders and left me to return home."

"You know who Ingrid Lagman is nowadays, right?"

"The worried mother of someone who dropped out of circulation, and who might be missing too," Talyn said. "Other than that? No."

"I'm surprised you didn't research her before setting out for Scandia. How much do you know about local politics?"

"Not a lot," Talyn confessed. "This system has been quiet for so long, and we always find plenty of other problems to keep us busy."

"That calm is wholly deceptive. The Scandians are so proud of what they think is an exceptionally enlightened society they'll do anything to hide what is fast becoming a bitter cultural war between two competing visions of Scandia. Visions represented by the two major political parties, the People's Alliance on one side and the Reform League on the other."

"Planetary politics can turn nasty." Decker shrugged. "What's this to do with my kid's disappearance?"

Montero raised a placating hand. "It may be related. You need to understand what's brewing.

"Fair enough."

"Four years ago, the Reform League finally won a majority of parliamentary seats and for the first time in sixty years, formed a government. Needless to say, after three generations of unchallenged People's Alliance rule, it didn't please the powerful and influential folks who underwrote the Alliance for so long. The Reform League wasn't supposed to win elections anymore. A large part of that stemmed from Alliance policy in recent times of supporting unrestricted immigration, which they hoped would create a large, mostly urban voting bloc loyal to its generous social policies.

"Except the Scandian-born and those immigrants who came here for the opportunity to colonize new areas of the planet, grew tired of shouldering the increasingly heavy financial burden. Tired enough, in fact, that the Reform League, once decried as un-Scandian by the chattering classes, became a viable alternative, and is now the ruling party. And it looks like they'll hold on to that parliamentary majority in the next elections. A lot of people are happy with what they're doing, especially by overturning the more contentious and expensive Alliance policies that turned what was once a high trust society into something a lot less pleasant."

"Not a new story." Decker drained his mug. "Political parties throughout history have tried to dissolve the people and elect another so they might retain power."

"For sure, but the degree of polarization I saw is stunning. People were unhappy with the People's Alliance for years, but openly supporting the Reform League could, at one time, turn you into a social outcast. So they stifled their thoughts and pretended to be as virtuous as their neighbors. Then, a preference cascade started with regional elections six years ago, where many previously unknown Reform League candidates won seats in the various town, city, and provincial councils. Suddenly, supporting a party other than the sainted, visionary, and benevolent Alliance wasn't quite as evil as propaganda made it out to be."

"You don't seem to be a fan of this People's Alliance," Talyn remarked.

"They've turned parts of the planet into no-go zones where the worst exports from the Core Worlds live out lives of indolence punctuated by mindless violence. But they reliably vote Alliance in such large numbers you just know something isn't right. You don't hear about this, and the people voting for those insane policies don't suffer the consequences — yet. More importantly for us stalwart Naval Intelligence snoops, I've picked up enough signs to make me conclude the People's Alliance party fell under the sway of our Coalition friends years ago."

"And with forecasts showing the Reform League will stay in power for another full term, I can see there's trouble brewing," Decker said. "If Scandia, considered one of the most stable systems in the Rim Sector, falls into political disorder, it'll be a signal to the others that maybe a little more Commonwealth weight behind their planetary administrations might be a good thing. And since the Coalition is backing the People's Alliance, we can be sure that whatever will happen won't be good."

Montero tapped the side of his nose with an extended index finger.

"Exactly. That was by way of a thumbnail sketch, so you know what's happening beneath the deceptively calm surface.   A lot of folks woke up a few years ago and noticed they were being fleeced by their government for purely political ends and fed loads of propaganda in return. They won't stand for a return to that situation. But they're not, with a few exceptions, part of the elite, the movers and shakers who occupy the upper strata of Scandian society. And the latter will do what they can to make sure the Reform League is ousted by means fair or foul, and, if they can manage it, destroyed.

"Now, to answer your question what this mess has to do with your daughter. Ingrid Lagman is a long-standing confidante of the woman behind the Reform League success, Alisa Berneiser. She's their number two who, for various reasons, does not sit in the parliament, preferring to work behind the scenes while the party's number one, Dasco Dahlstein, occupies the prime minister's residence."

Decker snorted in disbelief. "Somehow, I remember Ingrid as an avid People's Alliance supporter. She was always raving about how Scandia would show the other star systems what it means to give everyone a chance at living on a pristine, unspoiled world. She was a true believer that one."

"And yet she underwent a conversion since then," Montero replied. "So if someone abducted your daughter and her mother has gone incommunicado, then I'd say there's a better than even chance it's related to the coming political battle for Scandia's soul and future."

"Why involve me — us?"

Talyn shrugged. "Opportunity? Perhaps Ingrid reached out to you because she understood the stakes and thought a Fleet officer, someone who's not even remotely connected to the Scandian governmental apparatus, might be able to help."

"Which isn't an outlandish idea," Montero said. "The societal fractures, perforce, run through the police, the security agency, and the National Guard. And I daresay, we might find they touch the Scandia Regiment too, even though it's a Commonwealth Army unit and should, by law, be insulated from planetary politics. What I don't understand is why we — Naval Intelligence — know nothing about this."

"That's easy to explain. It was probably Black Sword's doing. Considering how deeply they infiltrated us, it's a given they recruited members in the Political Analysis Section, which deals with this sort of thing. People yet to be found and purged. They'd be in a perfect position to suppress the truth so we don't meddle."

Decker's hand reached for the pantry and extracted a trio of beer bulbs. He held them up and glanced at both of his colleagues in turn. When they nodded, he slid two bulbs across the table and uncapped the third. He took a mouthful and swallowed. "What does this mean?"

"That's why I'm glad you two are here. I'm a hunter-gatherer of information and doer of specialized deeds. As I said, the events unfolding on Scandia, big and small, seem more in line with your talents, not least if the rumors are true. Apparently, a good chunk of the Scandian National Guard would support the People's Alliance's call to oust the current government on trumped-up grounds. After all, its senior officers came up the ranks during Alliance rule and would support its policies as a matter of course, in the pursuit of a successful career."

"A constitutional coup d'état?" Talyn sounded dubious. "Here? Where does the governor general stand? She has the final say for dissolving a government, no?"

Montero's laughter was as cold as interstellar space. "Viveca Nygaard is a creature of the previous administration and chummy with the SecGen, whom she represents with commendable enthusiasm, more so than most governors general in the Rim Sector. Where do you think she'll stand if they do it with sufficiently plausible deniability?"

"Did you gather this intelligence during your walkabout?" Decker asked.

"Not all of it. I picked up a fair bit in the year I've been operating out of this system, without necessarily smelling anything more than normal planetary politics. When your cover is that of a suspected smuggler, you tend to hang out with shady figures who know what's really happening behind the polite facade of Scandian society. A lot of the customs and excise scofflaws around here, believe it or not, consider themselves patriots, and therefore Reform League supporters. They give me an earful every time I mention politics."

"Patriotic crooks. Will wonders never cease?"

"The People's Alliance insiders are much worse crooks, trust me. But back to your last question. I found out about Ingrid Lagman's connections recently. It appears to be a closely held thing."

"But not closely enough, if an Alliance bastard took my daughter to put the screws on the government through Ingrid. Though why involve me?"

"We don't know it's the case," Talyn interjected. "Let's stick to the evidence. Go on, Garrett."

"The rumors of senior police, security, and National Guard officers supporting the Alliance's return to power are also new developments. I fear things are moving at an ever faster pace and that the Alliance might not wait for next year's elections. Word on the street is the government's ready to call a parliamentary vote to enact laws that would significantly weaken any political party's ability to stay in power for generations. As you might guess, it will be popular with a majority of voters, but not the Alliance. What's beyond dispute is that the situation has noticeably deteriorated in the year I've been working out of this system."

"Any idea why the *Sécurité Spéciale* is after you and *Haukka*?" Decker asked. "Is it related to what's happening planetside?"

"I didn't know they were after me and the ship. What's up?" When Talyn finished telling Montero about the late Waller Leppell and his equally deceased partner Huy Bivins, he took on a thoughtful expression. "Perhaps that explains what happened in Hamar. I had a little misadventure that resulted in delaying my return to

Breidablik until today. Unidentified parties were asking too many questions for comfort about one Captain Mattias Kenly. They've stopped doing so, but the police might wonder who killed them."

"How did you leave Breidablik with no one having a clue?" Decker asked. "You know you're listed as a missing person, right?"

Montero winked at him. "Friends in low places. There are channels the harbormaster and police don't control. Access to them is one of the many benefits of my cover as a suspected smuggler. Well, that and my ability to swap identities at will. But enough about my fabulous secret agent skills. What will we do?"

"About?" Talyn asked. "The main reason Zack and I came was to secure *Haukka* and find you. Done and done."

"I meant about stopping the Coalition from throwing Scandia into political chaos so they can put their stooges back in power. And finding Zack's daughter, naturally, since her disappearance and the coming crisis are probably related because of her mother."

"First, we prepare a report back to the commodore." Talyn's tone was that of a commanding officer issuing orders. "To let him know you're alive and well, and that the pride of the Special Operations Division's very own private Navy is still in safe hands. Said report will be accompanied by an assessment of the current situation on Scandia, which you will draft up the moment we're done here. Once everything is ready, we will lift off to move away from prying eyes and ears, then hook into this system's naval subspace relay directly and transmit the lot to Caledonia. We will wait for fresh orders while gathering what additional intelligence we can. Any questions?" She eyed Montero and Decker in turn.

"One addendum to the message packet for the commodore," Decker said. "We need a few direct action troops from the Special Forces Regiment, stat. I would prefer a full squadron. If he can send them aboard a Q-ship along with their own gunboats, so much the better, in case we find the best course of action is dropping in on Coalition garbage from above.

"If not, then send the squadron aboard the fastest transport available. We'll need serious backup if we're to be useful. I can feel it in my bones. And even bare-assed, a squadron without a Q-ship as an operating base is light years ahead of no backup, period. If they need a cover story, it's the same as I proposed before, cold weather training with the local unit."

"Why not ask for Fleet Pathfinders? I daresay they can be here a lot faster," Talyn replied.

"Because Fleet Pathfinders like my old outfit are built to punch a very precise and deadly hole into anyone who falls afoul of the Commonwealth, as you might recall from our first operation together. The boys and girls from the 1st Special Forces Regiment, on the other hand, have the training to deal with the sort of situation that seems to be brewing in this system. And they're trained to work with regular units like the Scandia Regiment if needed. Especially if Garrett is right and a few of them are paying local politics too much attention. There's nothing like a troop of special operators to give rifle companies added backbone. If I thought the commodore might listen, I'd ask for a full battalion instead of just one squadron, but I doubt that would fly."

"Very well. We'll add that to the message packet." Talyn climbed to her feet. "Zack and I need to finish surveying the ship, and you have an analysis to write for the boss, Garrett."

"What about the fake hull patch?" Decker asked. "The poor engineering droid is sitting in the middle of the cargo hold with it, waiting patiently."

Talyn nodded and turned to Montero. "Is there anything inside your improvised safe that needs immediate attention?"

He shook his head. "No. And if we're about to run an intelligence operation on Scandia, it's just as well you brought it in. That's where I keep money and other untraceable financial instruments."

— SIXTEEN —

"In what universe is that a good idea?" Talyn demanded after Decker explained his plan during breakfast one morning. Almost a week had passed since *Haukka* lifted off and settled into a high orbit around Scandia where they could keep a discreet but direct link with the naval subspace relay.

The message packet with Montero's assessment and the request for reinforcements from the 1st Special Forces Regiment had reached Caledonia, care of Commodore Ulrich's office, days earlier and they were waiting for a reply long in coming.

"In the universe where we act according to our talents. You and Garrett are the professionals, trained to trawl through government garbage heaps for state secrets. I'm a grunt who works for snoops. Why don't you pros develop Garrett's threat assessment while I put contingency plans into place? Plans we'll need if the opposition pulls a fast one and turns Scandia, the Rim Sector's paragon of peace and progressivism, into the next planetary civil war.

"There are plenty of folks who won't stand for a constitutional coup. And therefore, they will pull their great-granddaddies' guns from the closet in the basement. Remember what happened to the Shrehari when they tried to take Scandia? Because the idiots in the People's Alliance and their Coalition backers sure as hell don't if they expect those who voted for the Reform League to accept an illegal change of government. They're the ones who remember the war and know how to use the weapons their forebears turned on the boneheads. I've seen it before. You spend years thinking the worst will never happen until suddenly, the shooting starts."

The three operatives had spent most of their time in discussion about the Scandia situation when they weren't analyzing every bit of information they could scrape off the star system's info net. While Talyn was inclined to take a more nuanced view, the Marine's fears conjured a scenario that dwarfed the worst colonial war either she or Montero could imagine.

"I still don't think you going around as Major Zachary Thomas Decker, a liaison officer from the Joint Special Operations Command, is worth the risk. Especially if Garrett and I aren't around to watch your back."

"And if I show up on the Scandia Regiment's doorstep as Dmitri Rauck or anyone other than myself, I'll never so much as make it through the main gate. Since it's the only Commonwealth Armed Services ground unit in the system, I see no options unless we want to wait until everything goes sideways. Or just let events happen and then hope the Senate will see its way to vote on authorizing intervention by the Fleet — after a lot of blood is spilled." He gave his partner a mulish stare she knew only too well. "Besides, more than a few people in the unit will remember me from the last time the 902nd dropped in on them for cold climate training. That'll help us."

"Not to mention regimental headquarters are in Kollsvik, where your daughter lives, or at least lived before she vanished, giving you ample opportunity to glance over the Police Authority's shoulder and offer impertinent advice. Did you think about the possibility some of the regiment's senior officers might be Black Sword?"

"So what? As we've found out, their cell structure is a tough nut to crack because they're heavily compartmentalized and only pass on essential information.   Chances are the local Black Sword bastards, if there are any, didn't hear about the target on my back yet. And even if they did, I doubt they'd chance discovery by acting after the Grand Admiral ordered that no quarter be given to traitors."

"Your points are valid."   Talyn exhaled noisily. "Considering you've survived things that would kill most men, and have a stubborn streak to match, I suppose my choices are limited."

"Limited? No. Nonexistent is the word you're looking for. This is how it has to be. I'll travel to Kollsvik from Hamar as Dmitri Rauck. But when I'm there, the man of a thousand faces needs to wear his own. Shame I can't show up in full Marine rig, but liaison officers from JSOC usually travel in civilian anyhow. My credentials will serve as a uniform."

"And what will you show them to prove you're on orders?" Garrett asked. "I can't see the regiment's CO entertaining a random major who claims to work for JSOC but appears to be suffering from a case of acute conspiracy theory disease."

Decker jerked a thumb at his partner. "Hera's an expert forger. That's why she was the commodore's first choice as chief of staff after Manfred Yang talked himself into a fatal traffic accident. Or we might receive real orders from the boss. If I've figured this approach out on my own, I'm sure he has as well."

"Or he could send orders forbidding you to do it," Talyn pointed out. "I'll wait until we hear back before spending time on documents to support an idea I don't like."

"Be that way. But I'll write out what I want those forged orders to say anyway."

"Is he always like this?"

She sighed and shook her head. "No. Sometimes he's worse. Zack will never be a proper intelligence officer."

"That's why Commodore Ulrich keeps me around. I think of solutions that would never occur to you guys."

"And as I've learned, most of them involve loud detonations of some sort."

"Of course. Every problem can be solved by the judicious use of high explosives or an overloaded fuel cell." Decker grinned at Montero, who smiled back, shaking his head.

"Your reputation definitely doesn't lie."

**

The AI's eerily Talyn-like voice pulled Decker from a pleasant dream involving innumerable, faceless Coalition grandees kneeling by an endless row of juluk pits squirming with awful insectoid creatures ready to inflict indescribable pain.

"An encrypted subspace message from headquarters has arrived, bearing Commodore Ulrich's signature."

"About bloody time. Is everyone on holidays back home or did they forget how subspace radio works?" He nudged his half-awake partner, who was stretched out beside him on the master cabin's broad bunk. "Rise and shine, sweetheart. HQ remembered we exist."

"So I heard. And we will discuss shutting off the AI's voice subroutine once more."

"You may be the mission's senior officer, but it's still Garrett's ship." Decker rolled off the bunk and onto his feet.

"It's been my ship since we climbed aboard after reaching Breidablik. Check the log if you don't believe me. Those codes I fed it make the change of command official." Talyn climbed out of bed at a more sedate speed and stretched. "I've merely been exercising my privilege as mission commander and allowed him to be the acting captain."

"Which explains why we're using the owner's cabin and not one of the crew compartments." He pulled on his trousers and stepped into his boots.

"Garrett graciously took the first officer's quarters. He knows when to bow out."

When they entered the bridge, Montero, who was slumped in the command chair, glanced over his shoulder and smiled. "I was wondering whether I should send the engineering droid with a crowbar, in case separating you from each other or the bunk proved to be beyond the AI's dulcet tones."

"Having it show up with two cups of coffee would do the trick," Decker replied.

Montero touched the control screen embedded in the chair's arm. "You can use the commo station to decrypt the boss' love note, Hera. It looks to be pretty short."

A few minutes later, Talyn turned away from the console and grimaced. "You were right about it being a brief missive. All the commodore said, other than acknowledging our assessment of the Scandia situation was 'proceed at your discretion.' I take that as permission to act if we see an opportunity. He's probably worried someone might intercept his orders and bring proof to the SecGen and Senate that the Fleet is interfering in the affairs of sovereign star systems."

"No mention of my request for Special Forces backup?" Talyn shook her head. "Not a single word."

"Damn."

"The commodore would need to clear your request with Admiral Kruczek before sending it to the Commander, Joint Special Operations Command," Talyn replied. "And maybe the Chief felt that, in turn, it needed the Grand Admiral's blessing, which wasn't forthcoming. Sending a Special Forces unit to a sovereign star system experiencing political upheaval, even if done under the guise of a training visit with the local Commonwealth Armed Services unit, is risky. It wouldn't surprise me if the Chief or the Grand Admiral decided it wasn't a risk worth taking. The repercussions that might stem from public perception of the Fleet taking sides without Senate sanction, let alone without being asked by a legitimate star system government, could be far-reaching. We can interfere in minor colonies such as Garonne and maintain plausible deniability. Here? Not so much."

"Why did we not discuss this before we added my request for backup to our report? I might have couched it in different terms."

"I was expecting more defined mission parameters, including whether our brief was merely to observe and report rather than engage in direct action, not for the commodore to tell me we should proceed at my discretion. He knows giving us free rein means we'll do more than intelligence gathering, especially since he's well aware of your proclivities."

"Which ones?" Montero asked with a mischievous grin. "The tendency to blow things up on general principle?"

Talyn ignored him and asked Decker, "Does this change your plans about the Scandia Regiment? There's not much point in pretending to be a liaison officer if there's no incoming Marine unit. Never mind we have no orders to offer the current government military aid in case the People's Alliance and its supporters try a coup d'état."

"I'll figure something out," he growled. "There's no way I'll allow those Coalition fuckers to mess this place up. What do you think will happen once the bastards figure they can pick and choose star system governments to suit their schemes?"

"I didn't mean we do nothing, Zack," she replied in a more gentle tone. "And if you still want to try co-opting the Scandia Regiment by yourself, I won't object. But perhaps we should give our options more thought before landing in Hamar."

"What other options? I'm sure the current prime minister knows his government's under threat. He's been draining the People's Alliance swamp for almost four years and has faced just about every obstruction possible. I'm also convinced he's well aware that changing laws to prevent another fifty years of Alliance rule will trigger the most serious response to date. And yet, he's going ahead with it, even though his senior civil servants, generals, and police commissioners are Alliance creatures. What can we do, other than give him Fleet backing through the only unit available?"

"Zack's not wrong," Montero interjected. "Until you've been there, you can't appreciate how volatile things are. Just keep in mind the Scandia Regiment's members aren't as apolitical as the average Marines. Most of them were born here and have extensive family connections on both sides of the political divide."

"Though I'll bet a majority aren't Alliance supporters," Decker said.

"True. But it only takes a few to sabotage anything you might undertake. That's why you were hoping for your Fort Arnhem buddies to stiffen the ranks, no?"

"I'll figure something out." Decker glanced at his partner. "Can you forge those orders for me now? There's no need to change anything. The way things are moving, by the time the regiment's commanding officer figures out there aren't any special operators from Caledonia coming, it'll be too late."

"Give me a few hours," she replied in a resigned tone. "Meanwhile, please ask traffic control for a landing slot, Garrett. And trash the Mattias Kenly identity along with his face. The *Sécurité Spéciale* obviously decided Kenly was a person of interest. That means he stays among the disappeared. Sorry."

Montero winced. "A lot of time and effort creating a new me flushed away."

"Maybe it's time you chose another occupation than smuggler as your cover, Garrett, or took a shore billet until things smooth over."

"Please don't pull me from the field."

"That'll be the commodore's call to make," she said with finality.

Decker snorted. "Based on your recommendation." He gave Montero a commiserating smile. "Garrett, my friend, you need to understand something. Even though Hera's back in the wild with her inner assassin free to kill, she's still in many ways Commodore Ulrich's executive officer, the one whispering in his ear. We serve at her pleasure as much as at his. And since she's told you to find a new name and face, can I offer a barely used set I no longer need? We're roughly the same size and build."

Talyn's eyes shifted from one to the other.

"That's not a bad idea, Zack. Annekka Bayle and Dmitri Rauck sightseeing in Hamar won't attract much notice since both entered Scandian jurisdiction legally on their employer's business. Mattias Kenly, however, is officially missing and unofficially on the *Sécurité Spéciale*'s wanted list. That only leaves the matter of getting you off *Haukka* and on your way to Kollsvik unseen."

"I seem to recall this tub has a shuttle. Why don't you fly me to the Kollsvik spaceport where I can enter Scandian jurisdiction legally as my own self?"

"With the name Zack Decker showing up in the immigration records and triggering alarms? I think not. And it wouldn't take long for an enterprising individual to trace the shuttle back to *Haukka*, no matter how much we try to hide its provenance. No, you're coming to Hamar with us. We'll smuggle you off the ship somehow — as one of your spare cover identities, needless to say. You can become the infamous Major Decker once you're in Kollsvik."

Zack knew by her tone she would brook no further discussion. "Aye, aye, sir."

"I'll tap one of my contacts working the Hamar spaceport for help," Montero said.

"Why would the contact help Dmitri Rauck?" Talyn asked.

"Because I took the precaution of warning my more reliable acquaintances that friends might show up and identify themselves with a specific set of code words. It's not an uncommon thing in those circles."

"Well then." Decker rubbed his hands together with glee. "What are we waiting for? Let's swap faces, forge my orders, and land this puppy."

**

"You a friend of Matt Kenly too?" The heavy-set Scandian stevedore appointed as Zack's native guide asked as he led the latter away from *Haukka*'s landing pad. He aimed them at a dense warehouse cluster on the edge of a tarmac big enough for an entire battle fleet. The wild blond hair and a shaggy beard framing a sharply angled face gave him the fearsome appearance of his distant ancestors, but his lilting, slightly accented Anglic sounded incongruous to the Marine's ears.

"More like a friend of a friend." Decker wore his dark spacer's clothes for the occasion, to better blend in with the rough men and women working the cargo-handling end of Hamar's spaceport. The Shrehari blaster he preferred as his sidearm sat comfortably in its shoulder holster while his dagger rested in its forearm sheath. The large-bore needler taken from the *Sécurité Spéciale* goon was in his backpack, concealed beneath a change of clothes appropriate for a Marine Corps liaison officer in mufti.

"So you don't know Matt Kenly?" They reached a row of grimy hangars tall enough for starships of *Haukka*'s size and slipped into a narrow alley. "Shame."

"Why is it a shame?"

"He's a good man to know."

This late in the afternoon, they met few people in the rabbit warren of lanes separating the warehouse clusters. Anyone other than Decker would soon lose his orientation, and the Marine suspected it might be on purpose. He was an outsider, enjoying access to the spaceport's unguarded, hidden egress points solely because 'Dmitri Rauck,' as Garrett Montero now styled himself, had spoken those magic words identifying himself as someone in Mattias Kenly's confidence.

They reached a building that seemed in even worse shape than its neighbors and the stevedore pulled the door open, inviting Decker to enter the unlit warehouse ahead of him.

Something in the man's eyes and gestures seemed false, but the Marine stepped through anyway, right hand reaching for his blaster. He sensed the stevedore move behind him and shifted to one side with blinding speed. The Scandian stumbled past him, clearly taken by surprise. Zack whipped his blaster out as his guide shouted something in Scandian, and a half-dozen men who'd been hiding behind old crates rose up, needlers and scatter guns at the ready.

"Surrender, and we won't hurt you," one of them, an older man with a face lined by decades of criminality, yelled in a rumbling, thickly accented Anglic that seemed to rise from the very gates of hell. "There's no need for you to die."

"He claims he doesn't know Mattias Kenly," Decker's erstwhile guide said.

"Shame," The other man replied, parroting the stevedore's earlier comment. "But I'm sure they'll want to decide that for themselves." He pointed the barrel of his weapon at the Marine. "Drop that miniature artillery piece you're holding and come along nicely. You wouldn't like the pain my riot gun can inflict. My loads aren't fatal, but you'll wish they were. We're paid to bring you in alive, but no one said the word intact."

"Whose dirty work are you supposed to be doing?"

Decker ran his eyes over each of them, noting their stance, the way they held their weapons, the expression on their faces and the degree of confidence in their gaze. He decided these men were adept at waylaying travelers. He saw no fear, no nervousness, and most importantly, no spark of conscience. Born thugs. The sort who'd do the *Sécurité Spéciale*'s bidding without question provided the price was right. But he could sense an undercurrent of confusion, thanks to his own visible lack of concern at the situation. The other goons threw their boss sideways glances, looking for cues. They likely weren't used to prey that didn't immediately surrender.

"You'll find out soon enough," the leader said. "Now drop that damned gun. I won't tell you again."

Instead of replying, Decker stroked the blaster's trigger. It coughed once. A black, smoking hole appeared in the middle of the man's chest. His face contorted into a mask of outrage before he crumpled to his feet. But the Marine didn't waste time admiring his handiwork.

The large, alien weapon spoke five more times in rapid succession, until only the stevedore who'd led him to this trap remained standing, a look of pure astonishment transforming his rough features. Decker gave him a good long look up his blaster's barrel before speaking.

"I should kill you too," he said in a hard voice devoid of emotion. "For betraying the smuggler's guild if not for leading me into a trap. But I'm willing to deal. Tell me who hired you, then help me off this spaceport. After that, keep your mouth shut and your head down, and you might live."

An unearthly gasp interrupted Decker, and the Marine spotted a hand reaching for a discarded needler out of the corner of his eyes. He swung his gun at the prone man and fired two shots. The hand jerked once and stopped moving.

He turned his weapon back on the stevedore, whose terrified gaze was darting everywhere as if looking for an escape. Then, the man's eyes rolled back, and he crumpled to the ground in a dead faint.

"Fucking amateurs," Decker muttered in disgust. A quick check confirmed that the rest of the ambush party, save for his guide, was dead. Their weapons, though old, were serviceable but carried only non-lethal rounds.

He pulled out the communicator hidden in his jacket's inner pocket and switched it on.

"Rookie Trooper to Mother Goose."

A few seconds passed, then an anonymous female voice, which he knew to be Talyn's, but masked, replied, "Mother Goose here."

"The guide led me into an ambush. Our friends are still looking for Matt and thought I could help. The ambush party was low-quality muscle for hire, six of them, and now gone to whatever hell accepts useless garbage. The guide is alive but fainted from fright."

"Acknowledged. Any changes to the mission parameters?"

"No. But watch yourselves. Don't trust the smuggler's guild around here. They've been bought off."

"Understood. What about the guide?"

"I'm nowhere near the back door to this place. Once he's taken me there, I'll set him loose."

"Terminate him. We can't afford anyone running to our friends. Better they're faced with a mystery." When Decker didn't respond at once, Talyn said, "That wasn't a suggestion, Rookie Trooper."

"Acknowledged."

"Was there anything else?"

"No."

"Mother Goose, out."

Decker leaned over the stevedore and backhanded him across the face.

"Wake up, asshole."

The man's eyes fluttered open, then widened when they stared up the barrel of Zack's weapon again.

"I need to know who hired you and where I can find the nearest exit."

A faint noise from above reached Decker's ears, and the stevedore's head exploded in a pink mist.

— SEVENTEEN —

Reflexes took over, and Decker dropped back toward the dubious shelter offered by the open door, weapon held high, while his eyes searched the warehouse's dark upper recesses for the shooter.

He expected a second round from what he figured was a rail gun, but saw nothing more than a small, native, eight-legged critter scamper across the cracked concrete, stop for a moment beside each of the bodies before vanishing into the gloom, clearly uninterested by human flesh.

When nothing else happened, Decker decided the stevedore's killing came under the heading of cleanup job, to make sure no one could trace the abortive attempt to its sponsors. Kudos to the *Sécurité Spéciale*, if this was their handiwork, for covering every eventuality. He called *Haukka* to inform Talyn of this latest development.

"Strange that the cleaner didn't try taking you out as well," she said once he finished speaking. "You're a loose end too."

"Could be he or she was there to kill the goons if they failed, especially since I claimed not to know Mattias Kenly. Or they figured that my death would raise too many uncomfortable questions, not least among the local smuggler's guild, while the rat pack that tried to jump me was expendable. Now to find my own way through the spaceport's security perimeter."

"That shouldn't be hard for an old-time recon trooper. Just avoid increasing the body count. Mother Goose, out."

Decker left the doorway's shadow and stepped back into the alley, looking for anything that could guide him to the nearest potential exit, but in vain. The surrounding warehouses shrunk his horizon to only a few dozen meters. Using the sun and his mind's eye view of the spaceport map, he set off in what was the right direction, though without knowing whether it would lead him to one of the exits preferred by shady operators.

After finding himself in a few blind alleys and having to reverse course, he finally emerged on the perimeter road running along the high wall that separated the spaceport from Hamar's less savory outskirts. The workers he met along the way paid him little attention, and he wasn't inclined to ask anyone about the best place to cross the wall unnoticed. He turned right on the perimeter road, figuring the further he went from the spaceport terminal proper, the more likely he was to find his exit.

Decker finally came around a corner and saw a stream of humans, most wearing faded dockworkers' clothes, heading for a gate recessed into the wall. He'd caught the late afternoon shift change as planned before his guide's betrayal. A few gave him curious glances as he joined the queue to pass through the security checkpoint, but most seemed lost in their own tired thoughts.

A finger tapped his arm as he neared the gate and a rough, but distinctly female voice said, "You aren't passing through security like that, cully."

Decker glanced over his shoulder and into a face prematurely aged by hard work and even harder living.

Deeply set dark eyes beneath a shock of tight, curly gray hair stared back at him without hostility.

"Why do you say that?"

"You're not working the spaceport, that's clear because you look like a spacer, not a wharf rat. This here checkpoint is for dockworkers only. If you don't show the proper ID, that security AI over there will whistle up spaceport police. Then your troubles really start."

Decker nodded his thanks. "Appreciate the warning, and you're right. I'm fresh off a starship, but my native guide didn't show up, so I'm trying to find my way."

The woman frowned for a moment, as if assessing her options, then stepped out of line and jerked her chin to one side, telling him to follow suit. She led him into a nearby alley between two buildings and stopped.

"Who fixed a guide for you?"

"Friends in the import-export business."

A knowing smile twisted thin lips. "Okay. I understand. Hope your friends didn't pay the guide up front."

"No idea."

A raspy chuckle escaped her throat. "No honor among thieves, eh? Mind you, there's been strange doings lately in some corners of this dump."

"Offworlders playing fast and loose with the locals?"

"Something like that." She studied the Marine for a few moments, the intentness of her gaze betraying a sharp mind behind the tired expression. "If you're carrying cash, I can be your guide."

"What'll it cost?"

"Five hundred cred." She smiled again, this time with a hint of irony. "Make it seven-fifty for my no names, no pack drill guarantee."

"Meaning?"

"Meaning I can always use a little extra money to finance my lifestyle, and you look like a man who knows his way around the sort of weapons you don't see legally in civilian hands. Like I said, seven hundred and fifty buys you a safe exit and my silence."

"Do you often accost strangers and offer them services for money?" Decker reached into his pocket for a handful of cred chips.

The woman cackled with glee. "Sure. And I offer a whole range of services for money when it comes to big, strong guys with bedroom eyes."

Decker held out five one-hundred cred chips. "I only need a native guide. Here's the down payment. You'll see the remaining two-fifty when I'm on the other side of that wall."

"Deal." She snatched the chips and made them vanish with a single gesture. "Come on."

The chances she was another *Sécurité Spéciale* plant were low, but he nonetheless followed her with heightened caution, hand hovering near his holstered gun throughout. After almost ten minutes navigating through a straightforward set of alleys, they re-emerged on the perimeter road, this time near a gate large enough to admit standard-sized container flatbeds.

She nodded at a person-sized door cut through the wall hard up against the vehicle opening.

"The security AI in charge of that one won't let you in without the right credentials but doesn't particularly care who's passing through, as long as at least one person can show the right ID. The story is that an interested party with a lot of juice in these parts paid plenty so a systems engineer messed with its programming."

"How do you know about this back door?"

"I said no names, no pack drill, cully. Remember?"

Decker raised his hand, palm facing her, in a gesture of apology. "Sorry."

"Let's do it."

Once they were through, Zack gave her the rest of the money. "With my thanks. Just answer this. Why did you help a stranger like me? It wasn't just the chance for extra creds."

She studied him again with those dark, knowing eyes. "Let's just say I did a hitch in the Corps long ago and can spot a fellow Marine and leave it at that." She pointed at a busy roadway skirting the spaceport a mere hundred meters in front of them. "You'll find transport into town over there. I need to go back and exit through the regular dockworkers' gate. Good luck with whatever you're doing."

Then, she turned on her heels and passed through security again, leaving him to stare at the closed door in wonder. The galaxy was a big place, but the Commonwealth Marine Corps remained a small family.

**

"Zack made it off the spaceport without further incident," Talyn announced when Montero entered *Haukka*'s bridge with a cup of coffee in each hand.

"Good. No hue and cry about seven dead goons?"

Talyn accepted the proffered mug and shook her head. "No. And I doubt we'll hear anything. But you and I need to talk about the *Sécurité Spéciale*'s newfound fascination with Mattias Kenly." She motioned for him to sit at the tactical station. "Is there anything you didn't mention in your reports?"

"No. I've been racking my brain since we left Breidablik trying to see if I did anything in recent weeks to attract their attention."

"I've been wondering whether this is somehow related to the Aquilonia operation," Talyn said before taking a sip of the bitter brew.

Montero shrugged. "Anything is possible, I suppose, but I was exceedingly careful in building the Kenly identity. Even *Haukka* can't be traced back to her earlier incarnation in anything other than generalities. There are literally thousands of starships her size and general configuration in the Rim Sector alone. Okay, perhaps none with such powerful drives, but she doesn't really stand out. I'd think it more likely someone with access to my cover at HQ is in the opposition's pay. You said this Black Sword cabal has its tentacles in every corner of the Fleet."

"We ruthlessly sanitized the Special Operations Division after finding out about Manfred Yang, and anyone who joined since has not been given access to anything about current field operations, let alone details on deep cover agents like you. Few people are aware Mattias Kenly is Lieutenant Commander Garrett Montero, Naval Intelligence. And every officer who knows has received the most thorough vetting in our history, *including* Commodore Ulrich. He insisted, as a matter of fact, to set the example."

"It's academic at this point, no matter the reasons for their interest. Kenly is gone, and *Haukka*'s been recovered by Annekka Bayle and Dmitri Rauck, of Universal Exports, the ship's registered owner."

"Which means they'll look at us now since two of theirs vanished in Breidablik while waiting to nab Kenly, and someone unknown to them we offloaded here massacred six of their hirelings in a matter of seconds. I don't think we can afford to let the ship sit in Hamar while we snoop around."

"What do you propose?"

"As I already mentioned, I think your days playing smuggler along the Rim are over. The opposition has you in their sights. It could well be that they've linked the Kenly identity back to your previous one and are looking for answers after their schemes collapsed on Aquilonia. We might never know, but welcome to the exclusive club of those with targets on their backs."

Montero gave her an ironic bow. "Honored."

"I've therefore concluded we need to follow Zack's example and come in from the cold, so to speak. The starship known as *Haukka*, and its passengers, Annekka Bayle and Dmitri Rauck, will lift within the hour and sail for the hyperlimit, ostensibly headed for home. There we will make a short jump to vanish from traffic control sensors. Once we're just another lump of metal in deep space, *Haukka* will resume her true identity as the Commonwealth Starship *Phoenix*, but assigned to JSOC, and not the Special Intelligence Operations Division. Please tell me you kept the proper transponder and registration decals hidden away somewhere."

"I did."

"Good. When we've turned her back into *Phoenix*, you and I become naval officers again, not Talyn and Montero obviously, but whatever we can come up with identity-wise on short notice. Then, we return to Scandia as if newly arrived in the system and land at the Commonwealth Armed Services Arctic Training Center, where the ship will be more secure than anywhere else on the planet. I'll draw up orders from JSOC to cover everything. From there, we return to Hamar under new cover identities and figure out what's brewing."

"I'll miss the carefree life of a rogue." Montero gave Talyn a wistful smile. "However, I know you're right."

"And I'm also your commanding officer, meaning you have no choice, but thanks for seeing the light. Once we're done in this system, I'll recommend *Phoenix* go into dry-dock for a refit that includes cosmetic changes so the *Sécurité Spéciale* can't link her back to *Haukka*."

"What about me?"

"Perhaps a stint at Camp X training the next generation of deep cover operatives might be a good idea."

Montero groaned theatrically. "I thought they outlawed cruel and unusual punishment long ago."

"Not in the Special Operations Division. Just ask Zack."

**

Decker finally reached the Hamar river docks shortly before sunset after jumping on and off several of the city's automated busses to blur his trail and check for anyone interested in him. Simply because the mysterious assassin who killed the stevedore left without taking a shot at him didn't mean his or her employers had lost interest. The lightning-fast way he'd dispatched the ambush party would raise even more questions since a random smuggler or courier rarely shoots like a professional gunman.

He stood for a while in the shadow of a silent container crane, watching *Munin*, a huge, beetle-like cargo skimmer, as it finished loading. The ungainly looking craft connected Hamar with Kollsvik on an overnight run, using the surface of the icy Torne River as its highway. It wasn't the fastest means to reach his destination, but it was the one with the least questions asked.

Because passengers were a way of filling unused cabin space and generating added profit at little extra expense, the price of a trip upriver was reasonable enough to attract those with more wanderlust than ready funds. Or those wanting to avoid the identity controls found around air and rail travel but without the means of buying their own conveyances. People such as Zack Decker, who was still wearing the throwaway identity he'd assumed upon giving Dmitri Rauck's face and credentials to Garrett Montero.

After a last glance at the surrounding dockyard, he headed for *Munin*'s gangway, creds in hand, to rent a bunk, or even a corner of the saloon if none were available. A sailor, whose hair and beard were only slightly less unkempt than those of the man who'd led him into the ambush, watched Decker approach without showing the slightest spark of curiosity.

"Any room for another traveler?" The Marine asked when he came within earshot.

The man spat into the water between *Munin*'s curved hull and the quay, then nodded. "Pusser's mate at the top of the ramp will see you right."

"Thanks."

Decker trudged up the incline, inquisitive eyes darting everywhere. The salt tang of the Torne estuary tickled his nostrils, but thankfully no strong, fishy odors seemed to emanate from his ride.

A leathery-faced woman intercepted him the moment he set foot aboard *Munin*. "Looking for a berth?"

"Yes, to Kollsvik."

"You showed up just in time. We're casting off in ten minutes." She quoted him a price, which he paid without dickering, and pointed at a door marked 'Passengers' in several human languages. "First cabin on the left. Take whatever empty bunk you want. Stay away from places marked 'Crew Only' and stick to this deck. There's food and drink for purchase in the saloon. Don't drink yourself stupid because you won't like our brig. Any questions?"

Decker shook his head. "No."

Two of the eight bunks in the cabin were occupied, the stowage compartments beneath them closed and locked. Decker took an empty one near the door and checked it for cleanliness. Then, he shoved his backpack into the attached locker and slammed it shut after making sure its biometric lock would recognize his hand print.

Decker found the saloon a few doors down and stuck his head in for a quick glance. Twenty humans, most nursing a drink, were scattered around the compartment. A few conversed in low tones, but many just sat silently, lost in their own thoughts. None attracted his attention, nor did anyone so much as stare at him after a quick first glance.

Unwilling to join such a melancholy group just yet, Decker went out again onto the single open deck girding *Munin* like a sideways canyon. He wandered aft for a dozen paces before finding a suitable spot to lean against the raining. His eyes roamed over a quay bathed in artificial light now that Scandia's sun had set. A few small, furry, native creatures scurried about on their eight legs, darting between crates that lay abandoned to the elements, their markings almost washed away.

The distant thunder of a starship lifting off drew his eyes upward to a sky glowing with Hamar's lights. Moments later, he saw the brilliant glow of thrusters against the star-speckled horizon and felt a brief longing for his partner. Then, the sound of hurrying feet reached his ears. He tensed up, eyes searching the shadows.

A tall, lean figure emerged from the darkness between two warehouses and headed for the gangway with a determined gait. Under the quay's sharp illumination, the figure turned into a woman with long dark hair and the narrow face of an endurance athlete. Carrying a backpack not dissimilar from his, she also wore the dark, practical clothes favored by spacers and wharf rats all over the Commonwealth.

After a brief exchange with the sailor at the foot of the gangway, she boarded, paid, listened to the purser's mate, and then entered the passenger section. Moments later, the sailor trudged up the ramp, and it retracted into *Munin*'s hull. Mooring lines followed suit and, to the soft vibration of its drives, the transport moved away from shore, its bow pointed upriver where the Great Northern Ice Sheet gave birth to the Torne, close to his destination.

Already, he fancied he could feel the cold wind coming off the continent-sized glacier, but that was merely a result of *Munin* picking up speed as it left Hamar's bright lights behind. After a last glance at the city, he headed for the saloon and a non-alcoholic drink to make a more extended study of his fellow travelers.

A quick glance into his shared cabin along the way showed the last minute passenger by the bunk next to his, storing her bag. Up close, her features seemed harder and more intensely etched by life, her dark eyes colder and more watchful. He gave her a polite nod in passing, a gesture she didn't return.

The same morose tableau greeted him upon entering *Munin*'s passenger saloon, virtually unchanged from earlier. He bought a juice and a sandwich from the catering machine and took a corner table from where he could watch his fellow travelers without being obvious about it. The latecomer entered shortly after that and headed for the dispenser.

Drink in hand, she turned toward Zack, and their eyes met. He felt a strange jolt of recognition even though she was a complete stranger. But as she headed for an unoccupied chair near his corner table and sat with effortless grace, he understood his reaction. The woman moved like a predator. He recognized another hunter, someone trained in the art of death. And that made him wonder about her presence aboard, especially arriving at the very last minute. There were no coincidences in his line of business.

She caught Decker looking at her and leaned toward him. "Do we know each other?" Her voice was low, with a rough edge, as if she had damaged vocal chords.

"Not in this incarnation. I'd remember someone like you."

"Oh?" She cocked a sardonic eyebrow. "Should I be flattered? Or should I ask what someone like me is supposed to mean?"

"Ask me no questions, and I'll tell you no lies."

The woman chuckled throatily. "Fair enough. I'm Mariel Lazarre, by the way."

"Harry Devine. Pleasure. What brings you aboard this tub at the last minute?"

"As a man I just met said, ask me no questions, and I'll tell no lies."

"Touché." He drained his juice bulb and grimaced. "Good thing it's only an overnighter. Otherwise, the catering around here would trigger a mutiny."

"Not a booze hound, Harry Devine?"

"I prefer to keep my head clear when I'm traveling. That way I lessen the risk of getting my ass lost in the wilderness, or my pocket picked."

"Voice of experience?"

"You know it. As the saying goes, to become old and wise, you must first be young and stupid. I see you're not partaking either."

"I've woken up in the wrong bed often enough in my younger days."

"Funny how that happens. My bed's been the wrong one often enough."

"I'll bet." The look she gave him would have shriveled a lesser man. "What do you do for a living, Harry Devine?"

"I solve problems."

"Funny that. I also solve problems."

"You any good at it?" Decker gave her speculative gaze.

"My solutions are permanent."

"I'll bet."

Lazarre's thin lips twisted into a faint, mocking smile. "Somehow, I get the feeling you're the sort to prefer permanent solutions as well."

"I'm not much for do-overs. Maybe we should compare notes."

"And I'm not much for idle shop talk." She drained her coffee bulb and stood. "Enjoy your evening, Harry Devine."

Decker watched her leave the saloon through narrowed eyes, wondering what, if anything, that little interchange might mean? Mariel Lazarre wasn't an ordinary person, to be sure. And she'd pegged him as someone like her, someone who didn't fit with the other passengers in the saloon.

Yet she didn't hum with that *Sécurité Spéciale* vibe. The SecGen's private security and intelligence agency preferred operatives who blended with their surroundings, not someone who exuded such a strong, feral aura, even if it was something only Decker could sense. She was too memorable.

He finished his sandwich and tossed its wrapping and the empty juice bulb into the recycler before leaving the other passengers to their morose contemplation of life. A brief glance into the cabin showed Lazarre wasn't in her bunk. Perhaps she was enjoying the fresh air, though considering *Munin*'s speed, it would probably feel more like a fresh gale.

With nothing better to do, Decker stepped out and was pleased to find that the craft's strange beetle shape kept the wind well away from the open deck. With nothing more than faint illumination to guide the unwary, his night vision took over. He made out the last, fading glow of Hamar behind them as *Munin* entered a bend in the river.   Here and there on the heights bordering the Torne, tiny lights, the evidence of human habitation, dotted the black horizon.

He glanced up at the cloudless heavens and felt once more that familiar awe at seeing the Milky Way's river of stars with its black cosmic dust eddies. It was one of the few astral sights familiar to all human worlds, something that linked them together despite the political fractures pushing them apart.

With his eyes adjusting to the shadows, he caught sight of a slender, long-haired silhouette further aft, leaning against the railing. She gave no sign she'd seen him, but Decker knew Lazarre sensed his presence. He turned toward the bow and strolled away, nostrils breathing in the chill night air, but not without feeling her eyes on his back.

— EIGHTEEN —

Munin pulled into the Kollsvik docks shortly after sunrise. A smaller version of those serving Hamar, they also sat at the foot of a steep incline. Like the capital, Scandia's second largest city was built on high ground to prepare for the day the planet's current ice age ended and the resulting melt-off flooded much of the lowlands.

Since no one knew when and how that might happen, or whether it might happen at all, the Scandian obsession with keeping settlements well above current shorelines was considered a tad eccentric by offworlders.

Decker and the other passengers, Mariel Lazarre included, poured off *Munin* the moment its gangway touched the quay. Though he wouldn't be able to see the three-kilometer thick continental glacier looming on the far horizon until he climbed out of the Torne's riverbed, Decker fancied he could feel its chilly presence, nonetheless.

Were it not for the incredibly rich ore seams immediately below the surface in this area, the first Scandians would never have bothered building a city so close to the Great Northern, as the locals called it. With human presence on the planet a mere blip in the current glaciation's timeline, the colonists didn't know whether the ice cap might still advance instead of retreating.

He studied the scars left on the canyon-like walls by the first horizontal mining shafts as he followed the others to the waiting ground transport. Those seams were long played out, but beyond the city limits, ore extraction still powered the local economy.

Decker had not exchanged words with Lazarre since the previous evening. By the time he climbed out of his bunk, she was already out on the deck, watching Kollsvik grow in the distance.

Her demeanor screamed 'leave me alone,' a wish he gladly granted. Usually, he found women with a dangerous edge attractive — Hera Talyn being a prime example. But something about Lazarre's aura kept him at a distance. Maybe he was developing a sixth sense like the one wielded by Sisters of the Void. Or his instincts were hypersensitive after the events of the last year.

Decker rode the bus up and out of the river canyon, then left it at the first stop where traveler's hotels jostled for space with bars and diners catering to the local wharf rats. He felt Lazarre's eyes tracking him again as he walked to the nearest inn, a sensation that continued until the bus turned a corner and vanished from view.

The innkeeper didn't blink an eye when Decker dropped a few cred chips on his counter and booked a room only until noon. That gave him a few hours to eat breakfast, shower, nap, and then turn back into a major of Marines before heading across town to Fort Hardrada, home station of the Commonwealth Army's Scandia Regiment.

The temptation to contact the police and inquire about his missing daughter remained strong, but until he was safely ensconced at Hardrada, it would be inadvisable to broadcast his presence in Kollsvik. Decker didn't check in with *Haukka* for the same reason even if his communicator could encrypt transmissions and the chance of a message being intercepted was vanishingly small.

He did, however, call for a taxi shortly after eleven and left a bored innkeeper to wonder why the man who just left didn't resemble the one who'd rented room sixteen for a few hours.

The automated taxi's AI, fortunately, wasn't programmed for idle chatter. Or it was programmed to recognize when a fare wasn't the type to enjoy it. Decker's trip through Kollsvik, therefore, took place in silence, leaving him free to renew his acquaintance with a town he'd last seen years ago. It was, if anything, messier than he remembered, a result of rapid expansion with insufficient controls.

They skirted an area that used to house workers back in the day — miners, refinery operators, and the other trades necessary to turn ore-bearing rock into refined metals. Now, it was a grim, ill-tended slum full of idlers, people lazing about in the middle of a workday.

The sight was a raw testament to the social fractures lurking beneath Scandia's pseudo-progressive veneer. No wonder folks like the workers who'd moved on to other parts of Kollsvik, rather than live among the perpetually unemployed, switched their political loyalties to the previously marginalized Reform League.

The taxi passed within sight of Jökul University's somber granite buildings, where his daughter had been preparing to defend her doctoral dissertation before she vanished. It gave way to suburbs where the low-density housing allowed Decker his first glimpse of the brooding ice wall filling the northern horizon. Even though its leading edge was over two hundred kilometers away, the sheer thickness of the continental glacier made it seem perilously near. He'd stood on it, long ago and gazed back at a Kollsvik so tiny in the distance it was hard to make out with the naked eye.

Increasingly sparse suburbs finally gave way to an open countryside that quickly turned to Scandian taiga, the planet's version of boreal forest, not much different from Earth's. A sign announced the turnoff to Fort Hardrada, but the installation's defensive berms were still hidden by the trees. Only a few communications arrays sticking up above the dense greenery betrayed its location. Decker's taxi slowed and took the side road, its passage noted by an undisguised access control sensor that would warn the security detail at the main gate.

They emerged from a curtain of trees and into the vast, cleared space surrounding the fort that gave its defenders unobstructed fields of fire, should anyone be so bold as to try a ground attack. A large sign stood to one side of the main gate, announcing this was the home of the Scandia Regiment, one of the Commonwealth Army's most famous units. The sign sported the regiment's emblem, a loping timber wolf superimposed on a stylized snowflake, and something no other Army unit could boast of: a naval anchor etched into the snowflake's bottom lobe.

During the previous century's Shrehari War, the Scandia Regiment earned the signal honor of providing a reinforced company to serve as Marines aboard one of the Navy's special operations starships. That unusual relationship with Decker's own part of the Armed Services continued to this day, which was why he felt approaching the regiment's commanding officer, Colonel Salminen, was worth the risk.

The taxi made its way through a concrete-lined chicane until it came to a halt in front of a thick slab seamlessly blocking the entrance. Two armed soldiers in battledress uniform, a private and a corporal, emerged from a smaller door cut into the main gate while Decker climbed out of the taxi, bag in hand.

"Can we help you, sir?" The corporal asked.

"I certainly hope so. My name is Zack Decker. I'm a Marine Corps major with the Joint Special Operations Command, here on orders. I would appreciate a moment of Colonel Salminen's time." He fished his identification — for once the real deal — from his business jacket's inner pocket and held it out for the corporal's scanner. "Or if the colonel's not available, that of the deputy commanding officer."

"Thank you, sir," the noncom replied after verifying the ID's authenticity. "Please wait here while I contact regimental HQ."

He stepped back through the gate while his number two watched Decker with dull eyes, only to return a few moments later.

"If you'll dismiss your taxi, sir, the duty runner will take you to the HQ building where the adjutant is waiting."

Decker inclined his head. "Thank you, Corporal." He turned to the automated vehicle and waved it away, having paid for the ride in advance. The taxi backed out of the chicane and sped off. The passenger it brought to his destination was no longer its concern.

Fort Hardrada seemed unchanged since Zack last visited as a troop leader in the 902nd. It was a modern version of an ancient Roman *castra*, with the tents replaced by two-story buildings. They were laid out in orderly rows along broad avenues crossing each other at perfect ninety-degree angles.

Home to regimental headquarters, one of the four rifle battalions as well as the artillery, aviation, cavalry, and service support battalions, it also had its own airfield and extensive underground storage facilities. The latter were proof against anything less than a direct kinetic strike from orbit. The remaining three rifle battalions occupied bases dispersed around Scandia's single inhabited continent, near other major settlements. Hamar itself was protected by the Scandian National Guard, which answered solely to the planetary government.

A large parade square lined with flagpoles fronted the regimental headquarters building. Though on a regular working day, it served principally as parking for personal ground cars, since most officers and noncoms lived in Kollsvik. Here and there, Decker saw troops in formation moving about, some wearing armor, most in regular battledress. A broad swath of taiga adjoining the fort itself was a military reservation where much of the training up to company level happened.

The duty runner's utility skimmer came to a smooth halt in front of stairs leading to the main entrance. Decker climbed out and swung his backpack over one shoulder. He'd know soon enough if his plan would work. The doors opened at his approach, admitting him into a spacious lobby with an imposing staircase taking up most of the back wall.

A mosaic of the regimental crest in various shades of granite occupied the center of the gleaming floor, while a century's worth of images, awards, pennants, and other relics hung from every wall. But one item held pride of place — the blackened, mangled remains of an imperial standard taken when the Scandia Regiment, fighting alongside the 10th Marines, stopped the Shrehari invasion force in its tracks over seventy years ago, and forced it to withdraw. They were among the few to do so with success during the entire war, and the regiment still celebrated the anniversary of the standard's capture.

A stern-faced captain in rifle green garrison uniform came down the stairs, the sound of her footsteps pulling Decker's eyes away from the trophy. She wore the weathered features of a long-service soldier beneath short silver hair. The Marine pegged her as a mustang like himself, a former senior noncom commissioned from the ranks. Perhaps she was even a veteran of the Corps, doing a hitch before transferring to the Army and a more sedentary career on her home planet.

"Major Decker?"

"Yes."

"I'm Laila Rantanen, the regimental adjutant. Welcome. I understand you're here under orders from the Joint Special Operations Command?"

"Indeed. I would appreciate a few minutes of Colonel Salminen's time."

Rantanen inclined her head. "Certainly, sir. The colonel is expecting you. If you'll follow me."

She led him up and past more display cases with relics of the war that gave the Scandia Regiment its most prized battle honors. At the top of the stairs, a smaller lobby with a settee group around a low table fronted a row of offices, each with a sign above the door announcing the occupant. Rantanen led him to the open one marked 'Commanding Officer' and knocked on the door frame.

"Major Decker, from JSOC." She pronounced the acronym jay-sock.

"Please enter, Major," A deep resonant voice replied.

Rantanen moved to one side and motioned at Decker to go ahead. He complied, executing a precise parade ground halt a regulation three paces in front of Colonel Salminen's desk.

It, and the rest of the furniture, as well as the decorations, spoke of great reverence for military traditions. Salminen himself was an athletic, muscular man in his late fifties, with salt and pepper hair and a thin, silvery beard. He examined Zack with intelligent dark eyes that missed little though his face was expressionless.

"At ease, Major." Salminen came around his desk and offered Decker a strong hand calloused by a lifetime of soldiering. "And welcome to the Scandia Regiment. Would I be wrong in assuming this isn't your first visit with us? My regimental sergeant major knows a Command Sergeant Zachary Decker, from the 902nd Marine Pathfinders who left a lasting impression on the regimental sergeants' mess."

A faint smile of embarrassment twisted Zack's lips. "That was entirely by accident, sir."

"Which often happens when vodka and tall tales are involved." He pointed at a chair grouping in one corner. "Please sit. Can I offer you coffee, tea, or something stronger, perhaps, if you promise not to leave a lasting impression in my office?"

"Coffee will be fine, sir. Black."

Salminen nodded at his adjutant, who vanished. "I don't recall running across you back when Regimental Sergeant Major Gulliksen says the 902nd last visited. But I was the executive officer of the 3rd Battalion in Vaasa back then."

"Did you say, Gulliksen, as in Niels Gulliksen, sir?"

"Yes."

Decker chuckled. "Glad to see Niels earned himself a regimental sergeant major's cane. He was my troop's native guide during our arctic warfare refresher training. By the way, sir, he was the one plying us with the homemade stuff you folks call vodka that evening, so part of the blame is his."

"You two can reminisce tonight if you like. He lives in the senior command noncoms' quarters. I assume you'll want to stay in our temporary accommodations?"

"I'd appreciate a bunk anywhere in Fort Hardrada, Colonel. And I'm not particularly picky."

"We don't see many visitors, so I'll ask them to put you up in something more fitting to your rank and length of service."

Decker noticed a portrait on one wall, of an Army officer in rifle green, wearing a major's oak leaves and four-pointed star, with a humongous battleship as a backdrop.

"Pardon me for asking, sir, but is that Tatiana Salminen, who was the first to command a Scandia Regiment company aboard Admiral Dunmoore's Q-ship?"

"It is indeed. She and her soldiers fought a rather unusual war, but they did us proud. And turned us into the only Army unit with an anchor on its insignia and colors."

"Any relationship?"

Colonel Salminen nodded. "My great-aunt. She's still alive and living in Vaasa, though she only comes up here once a year these days due to the vicissitudes of old age, and then only for the regimental birthday celebrations. You'll find another portrait of her in the rogues' gallery downstairs. She was commanding officer at the turn of the century."

Captain Rantanen returned with two steaming mugs, then left them alone to talk behind closed doors.

"So," Salminen said after swallowing a healthy sip, "what does JSOC want? The message we received yesterday warning us of your arrival was rather short on details, including when you'd show up on our doorstep. I'm surprised you followed up so quickly."

Decker struggled to hide his surprise at the Army officer's words. Had Commodore Ulrich figured out his plans based on the request for a squadron from the Special Forces Regiment and quietly greased the skids? Or did Talyn somehow forge a transmission from Fleet HQ?

"I'm traveling incognito due to operational security reasons, sir. That made my arrival date difficult to estimate since I didn't take conventional transportation means. JSOC probably waited until the last minute to warn you, for security reasons."

"Understood. I've been around long enough to know there's always a security angle with you secret squirrels. But if you don't mind me saying so, JSOC showing up on Scandia right now, what with the political atmosphere souring like never before in our history, seems a tad rash, if not provocative. Or has the Senate decreed that the Fleet may, for once, show its muscle ahead of time to prevent a repeat of the Garonne and Marengo disasters, and hasn't made it public knowledge?"

Decker, surprised by Salminen's accurate and clear-eyed view of the situation, didn't immediately reply.

The colonel noticed Zack's hesitation and chuckled.

"Come now, Major. Every Army CO and I daresay every National Guard commander along the Rim has become highly sensitive to the fact that the sector's planetary and colonial governments are becoming increasingly unstable and prone to accidental or manufactured crises. Last year's electoral meltdown on Cimmeria and rumors about the colonial administration essentially collapsing on Mission at around the same time were just more grist for the mill. Both were once considered the most boringly stable anywhere."

"As was Scandia, sir."

"As was Scandia, indeed. That status as boringly stable came to an end when the People's Alliance was ousted in a free and fair vote. Although the Scandian political establishment, under considerable pressure from leading business and financial personalities, has kept the growing social fissures hidden. I doubt there's much time left before the mask falls off and things turn ugly. We Scandians are usually of a 'go along to get along' temperament, but we also have an internal switch that turns us into berserkers given enough provocation. And if you know Norse history, you'll be aware that berserkers can cause untold bloodshed."

"When you say we Scandians, you mean your regiment included?"

A bitter laugh escaped Salminen's throat.

"Sadly. Although the Commonwealth Army lives under the same strictures as you Marines and our Navy siblings, meaning we're not allowed to vote or otherwise take part in planetary politics, my people are mostly natives of this world. That means they form opinions even if they don't express them. I dread the day things might crack wide open because none of us know what will happen, how the soldiers of this regiment will react. Not everyone will be able to follow the oath of service ahead of everything else. It's human nature. So you'll understand why I'm leery of offworld troops showing up just now. It might send the wrong signal and perhaps even precipitate events. At least some of my folks might think our own commanders on Caledonia don't trust them to obey orders."

Decker sipped his coffee so he could buy time and think while he studied the Army officer. Finally, feeling more than a bit reckless, he asked, "Does the name Black Sword mean anything to you?"

Salminen shrugged. "No. Is it a classified special operations designator?"

"Something like that." Decker's gut instinct told him the Scandian was telling the truth. He displayed none of the telltales associated with lying, especially about something as momentous as treason against Grand Admiral Kowalski's legacy. "It's not important."

"No doubt," Salminen murmured, clearly skeptical. He continued in a normal voice, "If I were a gambling man, I'd wager you just pulled a quick test on me, Major. I should be irked, but there's clearly something bothering you, so I'll chalk it up to sound operational reasons."

"Thank you, sir." Talyn would be annoyed that her forged orders would go to waste, but he knew playing it straight with Salminen was his sole alternative. "Colonel, before going to the heart of my reason for being here, I'd like to mention that I was on both Garonne and Marengo during their respective troubles, and saw the bloody messes they'd become."

Salminen interrupted Decker with a bark of amusement.

"I knew it. The way the rebellion on Garonne ended, with a decapitation shot that took out the entire colonial administration in one night, could only be due to JSOC intervention. You sneaky bastards. Too bad both the Marengo rebels and the colonial administration there learned from that fiasco, making Marengo a much tougher nut to crack."

"Colonel, what I'm about to say next must absolutely stay between us. At least for the moment." When Salminen agreed with a nod, Decker took a deep breath, then said, "I'm here to prevent a bigger, bloodier version of what we've already witnessed in this sector. We've uncovered intelligence leading us to believe the People's Alliance, helped by offworld interests keen on disrupting legitimate governance here and in other systems, will attempt a coup d'état. It aims to overthrow the current administration before it can enact legislation to prevent another half century of single-party rule. We believe elements within the National Guard, the Security Agency, and the Police Authority will support such an attempt. I'm sure you can see what this means for civil peace in the Scandia system."

Salminen contemplated Decker in silence before exhaling noisily.

"I don't know what frightens me more. That I'm not even the slightest bit surprised by your words? Or that I believe Scandians can actually contemplate destroying what we've worked so hard to build on this planet over matters of political advantage?"

"So you believe me, sir?"

"Of course I bloody believe you, Major Decker," Salminen replied in a vehement tone that took Decker aback. "Apart from a hitch in the Corps as a youngling, I've served the Commonwealth here, on Scandia, my home. I can see what's happening, if not always with clear eyes, and I can acknowledge unpleasant facts. But I'd be lying if I didn't admit you've just laid bare the sum of my fears. And those of many around here. Biggest among them is the fear we'll be forced to watch our home tear itself apart because the Senate, pusillanimous as ever, refuses to intervene before things go to hell. There's always someone with deep pockets profiting from disaster."

"In that case, sir, may I lay out what we think might happen, and what can be done?"

"Of course you may. Spit it out, man. That's why you're here, isn't it? And without the Senate even knowing, I'll wager. Just like Garonne."

— NINETEEN —

"Shall we make our manners with the 63rd Battle Group?" Montero asked once *Phoenix* dropped out of FTL on Scandia's hyperlimit after her round-trip away from prying eyes.

"Even though I don't like placing myself in a situation where a bored flag officer might decide to exercise his or her prerogative, I suppose we should. Call it taking out an insurance policy in case we need to intimidate someone on the ground or God forbid, need actual fire support from orbit. Let them know we'll be landing at the Arctic Training Center."

"I'll link us."

Talyn felt a little strange at Montero occupying the station Decker manned during their last tour aboard the converted yacht. Hopefully, her regular partner was getting somewhere with the CO of the Scandia Regiment after avoiding any further unfortunate encounters on his way to Kollsvik.

"That was surprisingly easy," Montero said a few minutes later. "The flagship accepted our JSOC codes, sent back a hearty welcome, and advised it will clear us with Scandian traffic control as well as let the training center know we're coming."

"How kind of them. I always thought the regular Navy wasn't a big fan of our sort — or more precisely the sort

202

we claim to be. Perhaps they're just happy we intend to land straightaway and not bother anyone."

"Or HQ greased the skids somehow. Commodore Ulrich has a history of Machiavellian sneakiness when it comes to helping his operatives in the field. Especially when his orders are of the 'proceed at your own discretion' variety."

Talyn snorted. "I think the commodore can teach good old Niccolo Machiavelli a thing or two in matters of sheer deviousness. If this is indeed his handiwork, then I hope he did the same for Zack." She climbed to her feet. "I've put the ship on automatic. The AI will accept traffic control instructions when those come in. Otherwise, there's little for us to do until we reach Scandia, and I want to finish a book before we go haring off after plotters and wannabe putschists."

"And I'll climb back aboard my hobbyhorse and parse the most recent news from Scandia to see how things stand." He swept an open hand over his console screen to call up the main feed and began reading.

A few moments later, Talyn heard him curse, and she returned to the bridge. "What?"

"They've announced the date when parliament will vote on the bill changing various bits of legislation that allowed the People's Alliance to rule for so long. Apparently, the governor general is now saying she doesn't support such a radical change and might refuse to sign the bill into law, which will trigger a crisis for sure. I don't understand how Nygaard thinks she can thwart parliament. The damn position is mostly ceremonial, not executive, but she still has what they call residual powers. Although refusing to sign off on a bill voted into force by elected officials, so long as it doesn't violate the constitution, isn't one of them. Trust me, I checked after discovering Scandia's unreported problems."

"It's about creating instability and defining the battle space. Delegitimizing the government's agenda is a big part of ousting the Reform League and paving the way for the People's Alliance's return to power."

Montero exhaled with gusto. "Of course. And as per the constitution, the governor general is Commander-in-Chief of the Scandian National Guard, and Commissioner-in-Chief of the Police Authority."

"Right, and with the governor general playing for the opposition, that constitutional safeguard against abuse of power by elected officials may become a weapon in the hands of traitors. When is the vote anyway?"

"Friday of next week. Dahlstein doesn't want to drag things out, and since he appears to have the support from two-thirds of parliament, ensuring it can only be reversed by another two-thirds majority vote, why wait? If we don't figure out what's going on and how we can stop the worst from happening, Scandia might experience its bloodiest incident since the Shrehari invasion."

"Not to mention what will happen in other star systems along the Rim if the Coalition engineers a successful coup against the legitimate planetary government here. Every world in this sector might experience its bloodiest days in over seven decades."

**

When Decker fell silent, Salminen sat back in his chair, eyes on a regimental memento decorating the wall in front of him, lost in thought.

"You're an interesting man." He turned his gaze back to the Marine. "You walk into my office and blithely propose we defy the Senate by sticking our heavily armed noses into Scandian affairs. Never mind doing so means an excellent chance of facing a court-martial and an unpleasant stay in a military prison on Parth. And that's even if we pull off an operation requiring exquisite timing. But I'll admit you definitely live up to the Marine Corps' Special Forces motto."

"*Audeamus* — we dare," Decker quoted with a smile. "I might be a bit of an outlier in that respect, sir. No one's ever accused me of being overly cautious. Quite the contrary."

"Next you'll tell me you planned and executed the decapitation strike on Garonne."

"Planned, sir. The rebels carried it out. I was just another grunt during the operation."

Salminen guffawed. "So you're *not* a one-man army, and reasonably modest as well. Good to know." His expression turned serious once more. "I need to digest this, Major, then speak with a few of my close advisers, though I'll make sure to keep certain details unmentioned for now. Something this momentous deserves plenty of sober second thought, especially since we'll only get one chance. If we miss our window of opportunity, the outcry will reach Earth. We might even make things immensely worse for Scandia. Until I've sounded out my people, I'm not in a position to help you or JSOC."

Decker inclined his head by way of acknowledgment, knowing Salminen's reaction to his proposal was better than expected.

"Of course, sir. If I might impose on your hospitality and perhaps sign out a staff skimmer, I'd like to deal with a personal matter that may or may not be related to the general situation on Scandia."

The colonel cocked a questioning eyebrow. "Oh?"

"I was once married to a lovely Scandian lady. Together we produced a child, a daughter. When my daughter was five years old, my spouse decided she couldn't spend her life waiting for me to return from dangerous missions and came home. I've not seen either in twenty years until I received notice shortly before JSOC sent me here that my daughter, a doctoral candidate at Jökul University, has gone missing."

"And you want to speak with the police investigators handling the matter. Understood. As I said, we'll set you up in the transient quarters for as long as you're here, and I'll ask my adjutant arrange for a car."

"Thank you, sir."

Salminen waved his words away. "We take our hospitality duties seriously, especially with old comrades. Niels Gulliksen speaks highly of you. That's everything I need to know. He's one of the advisers I'll be consulting, by the way, so feel free to discuss matters with him when you renew your acquaintance. Now you said your daughter's disappearance might be related to the general situation..."

"Aye. My daughter's name is Saga Lagman."

"As in Ingrid Lagman? That family?"

"Ingrid was my spouse, half a lifetime ago."

Salminen winced. "You know she's reputed to be a close confidante of the Reform League's number two, right? Alisa Berneiser, the woman who many think is the real driver behind the party's agenda, a sort of *éminence grise* advising Prime Minister Dahlstein and his cabinet."

"So I was told. Hence, my fear that Saga vanishing is related to the looming power struggle. To make matters worse, last I heard from the police investigator, he's not been able to speak with Ingrid for a while either, though she'd not been reported as missing when I left Caledonia."

"I see." Salminen rubbed his beard. "Would you like me to put in a word with the Kollsvik District Police Director? He and I gravitate in the same social circles and occasionally share a bottle of vodka."

"If you think it might help me obtain more from the police than a boilerplate brushoff, I'd be grateful."

"Then I'll speak with him. If this is related to everything else, I daresay we're better off finding out as much as possible. Do you know the name of the investigating officer?"

"An Inspector Jakob Harms."

Salminen stood. "I'll do that right now while my adjutant takes you to the dining hall for lunch."

**

Captain Rantanen was regaling Decker with stories of her time in the 11th Marines, confirming she'd not only been a noncom but also served twenty years in the Corps, when Colonel Salminen entered the dining hall. By the frown etched on his forehead, he was a worried, if not an unhappy man. As soon as he spotted his adjutant and their guest, he made a beeline for their table.

Salminen took one of the unused chairs and sat. "I'm afraid my conversation with Police Director Verschoor was rather puzzling, Major Decker."

"Sir?"

"At first, we exchanged the usual pleasantries, and he seemed normal enough. But when I told him Saga Lagman's father, a Marine officer, was in Kollsvik on Fleet business and wanted to speak with the detective investigating her disappearance, Verschoor became rather distant and abrupt. He told me that his detectives could not discuss ongoing cases with members of the public, including biological relatives. When the Police Authority has something to announce, they will contact you. And then he begged off, citing urgent business. I've never seen him behave in this manner."

Decker smirked. "Don't call us, we'll call you. Nice example of public relations. Anything about Ingrid Lagman?"

"I wasn't able to ask before Verschoor cut the link, but I imagine his answer would have been similar."

"Maybe I should just sweet-talk my way into the detectives' bullpen downtown and buttonhole Inspector Harms."

Rantanen shook her head. "Bad idea, Major. The Police Authority has a pretty uptight culture. You could almost say it is old Scandian in some ways. They don't take well to sweet talkers who've been told no already, especially offworlders."

"They were happy enough to pass along basic information about the case via subspace radio. Inspector Harms even asked if I'd heard from Ingrid lately. I wonder what changed to make me *persona non grata*."

"The fact you're here and not dozens of light years away?" Rantanen suggested in a semi-facetious tone. "On the other hand, our police, though humorless, is competent by any standard, more so than many forces I've seen when I was in the Corps. They'll eventually sort this out, sir."

"That's as it may be, Laila," Salminen said in a distracted tone. "But Verschoor's behavior makes me wonder." He gave Decker a meaningful glance.

The Marine returned a half shrug meant to convey uncertainty. "Are you grabbing a sandwich, Colonel? I'll pour myself another coffee and keep you company."

"I suppose I should." He turned to his adjutant again. "Call the command team together for a fifteen hundred hour briefing. Outlying battalion COs can join via scrambled comlink — no need to fly in. And thanks for entertaining our guest, Laila."

"My pleasure. The major and I spent time in the same star systems and know the Corps' more colorful characters." The adjutant stood. "Major, if you'll pop by my office afterward, someone will show you to the transient officers' quarters."

Salminen quickly returned from the buffet line with a full tray and handed Zack a mug of coffee. Then, after a glance around to make sure no one could overhear, he said, "Before leaving my office, I caught a newscast with the latest from Hamar. Parliament will vote on the new legislation next Friday. If you're right, we have until then to make up our minds and prepare. It's not much."

"No, sir. It isn't. Do you think Police Director Verschoor's unusual behavior when you brought up my daughter's case might be germane to what's brewing?"

"I don't know. That sort of question is probably more in your area of expertise, but considering who her mother is... Damn, I wish this wasn't happening."

Before Decker could reply, a voice boomed across the now almost empty dining hall.

"There he is, large as life, and twice as respectable." The Marine looked up to see a big man in dusty battledress, with a face so fierce beneath short blond hair it would even frighten his Viking ancestors, cross the room toward them. "And looking no better in person than he did on the guard post's video pickup, although someone with a sense of humor made him an officer."

A big grin spread across Decker's face, and he stood.

"Niels Gulliksen, you old bastard. Still unwashed and uncouth."

The two men embraced.

"I was out watching the junior NCO course go through its paces when you dragged your ass to our doorstep, hence the less than presentable suit. When I heard you were coming for a visit, I made sure the folks at the gate would call me once they warned the colonel. You here after so many years, I figured it wasn't for an arctic warfare refresher, so I cut my inspection tour short."

Gulliksen gave his commanding officer a quick, almost imperceptible nod. Decker saw a spark of relief in Salminen's eyes and realized the latter was waiting for his regimental sergeant major to offer final proof of Zack's identity.

"Major Decker is indeed after something much different, RSM."

"Let me guess." Gulliksen followed Decker's lead and sat. "Fleet HQ is getting nervous at the political situation here. No other reason for JSOC to send a liaison officer just now, and at such short notice."

Decker tapped the side of his nose with an extended finger.

"Your CO and I discussed my mission before lunch."

"I'll be speaking with the command team at fifteen hundred today," Salminen said, glancing at his timepiece. "Meaning in just over an hour. If you want to take Major Decker to a quiet corner of the sergeant's mess for another coffee and a chat, feel free."

Gulliksen gave the Marine a curious glance. "I surely will. Let me grab a bite to go."

Salminen's communicator buzzed, and he raised a restraining hand.

"CO."

"Rantanen here, sir. The Arctic Training Center just called to let us know the 63ʳᵈ Battle Group's flagship advised them a Navy vessel by the name *Phoenix* is inbound and has requested permission to land."

"Let me guess — the flagship didn't bother copying us and went straight to the ATC. Again." A look of annoyance crossed Salminen's face. He glanced at Zack. "Our Navy siblings think the normal military courtesies aren't required around here, such as informing me that my Arctic Training Center's landing strip will be occupied for who knows how long. Laila, what organization does this ship belong to and why is it landing at the ATC instead of a regular spaceport?"

"The what is apparently JSOC," Rantanen replied. "The why is unknown."

Salminen's eyes turned to Decker again. "Friends of yours, Major? Reinforcements, perhaps. A few Special Forces troops?"

"Friends of mine, yes. But there are only two officers aboard." Upon hearing the familiar name *Phoenix* Decker concluded Talyn and Montero couldn't afford to stay in Hamar or land at any other civilian installation after seeing proof of treachery from within the smuggler's guild. And if the ship wore its official name, it was likely the two operatives aboard now carried naval officer identities.

"Why are they here?"

"Recon, sir. I imagine they want to stash *Phoenix* at the ATC to keep it safe from folks with evil intent. She's not particularly big. More of an oversized yacht with kick-ass engines and a corvette's worth of ordnance."

"A true special operations ship, then."

"Yep."

"Is there anything you suggest we do, other than allow your friends to land and make sure no one tries to sabotage this *Phoenix* while she's on the ground?"

"I believe they'll want to reach Hamar incognito, sir. If they've been monitoring the news feeds, they'll know we're running out of time and need more intelligence about the situation."

Salminen nodded. "We can help them reach the capital unnoticed, but it might take a bit of doing. The ATC isn't exactly near any civilian transportation nodes."

Gulliksen pointed at his chest. "I'll take care of it with the training center's sergeant major, sir. He's used to organizing sightseeing trips for visiting senior noncoms, if you get my drift."

"I probably don't want to, RSM, but thanks — the job of moving Major Decker's recon buddies to Hamar is yours."

"Consider it done." The regimental sergeant major climbed to his feet. "With the colonel's permission?"

"See you at fifteen hundred, Mister Gulliksen."

"C'mon, *Major* Decker. Let's see if you spontaneously combust the moment you enter the sergeant's mess. We have an hour to catch up."

**

"Heck of a tale, Zack."

Gulliksen shook his head once Decker finished relating the reason he was here and the matter of his daughter's disappearance. They were ensconced in the regimental sergeant major's private nook in one corner of the sergeant's mess, where no one could overhear them. The remains of a hasty lunch and several empty coffee cups sat on the table between them.

"The colonel will decide what's what, but I can tell you some of the battalion commanders won't want to make a move without written approval from Caledonia. They'll not support risking our reputation on the say-so of a JSOC secret squirrel. I'm willing to bet the S-2 will be equally skittish."

"And you?"

"I'm the colonel's man. If he decides we can't stand idly by, then we won't. It'll be an interesting command briefing for sure."

"Too bad I can't watch. My life is short on entertainment these days."

"Stuff like this is family only, buddy."

"I know."

"But maybe I can help you find out more about your kid."

Decker gave his friend a quizzical look. "How?"

"Ever heard of the Shield Wall Bar?"

"No."

"It's an unofficial watering hole for local law enforcement people, but the National Guard and us Army pukes are welcome too. I'm sure they won't mind a jarhead in mufti. Mainly noncoms hang out there, but I know a few detective sergeants well enough for friendly questions over a beer or three."

"I'll buy however many rounds it takes."

Gulliksen gave Decker a wolfish smile. "That goes without saying, *Major*, sir."

"If I weren't the soul of generosity, I'd point out that regimental sergeants major and the commissioned sort of major draw the same pay."

"True, but I'm not entitled to the fancy bonuses you JSOC squirrels get just for being super ninjas."

Decker grinned at his friend. "And if I weren't a paragon of modesty, I'd point out we earn the damn bonuses."

"Perhaps." Gulliksen shook his head. "Man alive, I still can't believe you're a damned senior officer after they gave you the boot when you were a command noncom."

"It's a strange universe, with strange gods watching over fools and drunks. And I qualify on both counts."

"Still overflowing with modesty, eh?" Gulliksen glanced at the ancient clock on the fireplace mantel. "Time for the colonel's briefing. We'll talk about going into town afterward."

"We can talk about it on the way to the HQ building. I still need to see the adjutant about my quarters."

— TWENTY —

Gulliksen pulled up to the transient officers' quarters in a slick, sporty skimmer. Its gull-wing passenger door opened, allowing Decker to drop into a seat more appropriate for the cockpit of an orbital fighter.

"Nice." He looked around the compartment. "Must be worth a fortune."

"On what else am I supposed to spend my pay? Can't let the junior noncoms corner the fancy car market, right?"

The door closed and Gulliksen, wearing civilian garb, gunned the drives.

"How was the briefing?"

"Ever sat in the middle of a family dustup about money? That's nothing compared to what I lived through this afternoon."

"And?"

"And the colonel wants everyone to think about matters for twenty-four hours, then he'll speak to each battalion commander and the main staff officers individually. What happens after that? No idea. In other news, I set things up with Torsten Ellingboe, the ATC's top kick. The moment your folks land, they'll be taken to Hamar incognito."

Decker could sense his friend's natural reticence at discussing regimental matters in detail with an outsider.

He' would have to wait until Salminen made his decision rather than ask Gulliksen too many questions.

"Thanks, Niels. I owe you a big one."

"Just do me a favor in return. Try not to get any of my people killed with your mad schemes, okay?"

"I hope that by doing something rather than stand idly by until the esteemed members of the Commonwealth Senate pull their thumbs out of their fat bums, I'll prevent deaths."

"Yeah, I know." Gulliksen exhaled. "I just never thought I'd see the day when Scandia became one of those far off places where people solve political squabbles with guns and boots up the backside."

"Even in those far off places, folks figured it wouldn't happen until the day it did. Problems accumulate over a long time while few see what's happening, except the assholes who profit from the disorder. And they add fuel to the fire so gradually no one notices the decline until suddenly everything goes to shit. Then, people die. In job lots. Just once, I'd like to be a few steps ahead of the chaos merchants rather than show up when the bloodshed's already well underway. I'm tired of cleaning up politicians' messes, Niels. So fucking tired."

"I hear you. One hitch in the Corps was enough for me. I don't understand how you're still doing it thirty plus years later."

"What else am I supposed to do? I've made so many friends by now that retirement somewhere in the Shrehari Empire is the only way to avoid an assassin's knife."

"At least there you'll be close to the source of your favorite tipple."

Decker snorted. "Sure. Make the idea seem appealing."

The security detail waved them through Fort Hardrada's main gate. Soon Gulliksen's skimmer was crossing the suburban belt as they headed for the heart of Scandia's northernmost city. One that would be a subtropical paradise were the planet not in the throes of an ice age.

Just before Kollsvik proper swallowed them, Decker spied the last of the setting sun's rays bouncing off the continent-sized glacier's leading edge, far to the north. By the time Gulliksen pulled into a downtown parking slot, full night was upon them.

The two friends walked up a softly lit street, crossing paths with office workers hurrying home or looking for a pint and a meal. They soon came upon a garish sign hanging a few meters over the imitation cobblestone sidewalk — four medieval shields overlapping each other horizontally. Their destination.

A gust of warm air, laden with the heady aromas of fermented drinks and abundant food, and underscored by the buzz of two dozen low-key conversations greeted them as they entered. The pub, paneled in pale blond wood, furnished with imitation oak tables and chairs, and decorated with relics of a time when the shield wall was a regular battlefield tactic, gave Decker an immediate sense of coziness, or *hygge* in Scandian.

Never mind the relics came from a knickknack factory in Hamar. Or the wood came from native varieties, not far away Earth. It felt right. He could see why the local police, whose headquarters was one street over, used this place as their watering hole.

As Gulliksen led him to a vacant corner table, the soldier waved and nodded at several uniformed cops, as well as patrons wearing civilian clothes but with those unmistakable bumps under the arm betraying the presence of handguns. Decker noticed, however, that his friend exchanged no greetings with the handful of

National Guard noncoms slamming down beers as if they were dying of thirst. Moments after taking chairs that faced the room, a squat serving droid, the first modern item he'd seen since walking in, approached them with two foaming glasses of ale.

"I guess you are a regular in these parts." Decker accepted one of them while Gulliksen took the other. "Drinks arriving before you've even warmed your seat."

"It's a tough life. But when they asked for volunteers to live it, I stepped up so I could prove myself." He raised his drink. "And this is one of the best beers on the planet, brewed right here in Kollsvik with meltwater from the Great Northern. Skoal."

"Skoal." They took a healthy sip and Decker smacked his lips. "Not bad. Not bad at all. So what's the deal with the National Guard kiddos over there? A few of them gave you the death stare."

Gulliksen chuckled. "Yeah, they don't like me much, that's for sure. Used to be we'd train with the Guard regularly, attend each other's ceremonies and social functions, that sort of thing. But lately, they've turned standoffish. Not sure what happened, but we're pretty much living separate lives these days."

He paused and gave his friend a thoughtful frown.

"I guess this could be part of that decline no one really notices until things go to shit you talked about in the car. But anyway, one day, oh it was almost a year ago, I was in town on business, in uniform. I ran into a few of those charming creatures acting like asses when they were out looking for lunch. They're full-timers with the local Guard unit, by the way, and sometimes it's not because they love the military life but because they can't find a civilian job.

"When you consider there's no shortage of work in this area, you have to wonder, right? So I did what comes naturally to any sergeant major. I jacked them up right there and then, after which I engaged in a rather terse conversation with their unit's top kick. Let's just say my intervention didn't help improve our relationship. A few years back, we called it professional courtesy between sergeants major. Now?" Gulliksen shrugged. "It's more likely to trigger a vendetta."

"Did the beginning of this chill between you guys and the local soldiery coincide with the People's Alliance being ousted from power?"

Gulliksen thought for a moment, then nodded. "You know, it never occurred to me. That could well be. Most of the Scandian National Guard, outside the Hamar Brigade, is part-time, and many of the more senior part-timers are pretty close to the Alliance, even if they can't officially play politics. Heck, the Guard's current chief of staff was appointed by the last Alliance government in large part because he's buddies with the party's chairman-for-life."

"What a surprise." Decker took another sip of beer. "Most National Guards and militias engage in unnatural relationships with the dominant political forces on their home planets. That's why the Commonwealth has an Army on top of a Marine Corps. Anyway, not to change the subject, but how will I find something useful on my daughter's case? Walk over to the friendliest looking detective and say, hi, I'm Niels Gulliksen's drinking buddy and Saga Lagman's Dad. Can you tell me about the investigation into her disappearance?"

"Nothing quite so awkward. Watch and learn."

Gulliksen's fingers stroked the small screen embedded in the tabletop. Shortly after that, a serving droid trundled up to a table where a man in mussed civilian clothes was staring into the dregs of his drink.

"That's Senior Detective Sergeant Lars Calbach, one of the most experienced investigators in the Kollsvik division, and the least friendly, by the way. But he's plugged into the big cases run out of the divisional major crimes office. He and I share a few mutual interests."

"Hard booze and soft women?"

"Good beer and classical opera, among others."

"Opera?" Decker stared at his friend with an air of astonishment that was only half feigned. "And here I thought your idea of culture was yogurt for breakfast."

"Go fuck yourself, jarhead," Gulliksen replied with a good-natured smile. "You won't understand true beauty until you've experienced some of the greatest performances live on stage." He glanced at the detective. "Look sharp, Zack. Lars Calbach just gave me the old what the hell do you want glance after picking up the beer you bought him. And here he comes."

Decker watched the tall, lanky Scandian cop weave his way, a fresh drink in hand, through the labyrinth of tables on steady legs, his hooded eyes boring into them. As he came near, the Marine saw a face etched by years of dealing with the worst humanity could muster. Calbach looked to be in his mid-fifties, but with eyes that had seen a century's worth of misery.

"To what do I owe this free drink, Niels?" The detective dropped into a vacant chair. "Did the vice squad nab one of your troopers again?"

"Meet an old friend of mine who's in town on business — Zack Decker." Gulliksen nodded toward the Marine. "Zack, this is Lars Calbach, who knows where the Police Authority buries its bodies."

Calbach gave Zack a curious stare. "You're new around here, right? First time in Kollsvik?"

"No, but it's been a while since my last visit."

"What business brings you here?"

"Checking out the Arctic Training Center ahead of my unit's arrival for a refresher."

"So you're a Marine, then? We don't see many offworld Army outfits."

"I am."

"And you're willing to hang around with this reprobate?" Calbach pointed at Gulliksen.

"It's part of a Marine Corps outreach effort to give disfavored soldiers a fresh start in life."

Calbach's brief outburst of laughter sounded halfway between a croak and a strangled bark.

"Finally, a grunt with a sophisticated sense of humor." He took a big gulp of his beer. "Since Niels rarely introduces me to his friends, and then only when he's after something, I suppose you're the reason for this chilled freebie."

"Zack has family living here. One of them became a missing person case. Only, when Zack tried to find out where things stood, your brass gave him the cold shoulder."

"I don't remember a case on someone named Decker. Who's the investigator?"

"An Inspector Harms and the missing person is my daughter Saga Lagman."

Calbach's eyes widened for a brief moment. "You're related to the Lagmans?"

"Ingrid Lagman was my spouse twenty years ago. We split up, and she came home to Scandia with our girl."

"That explains the cold shoulder." A pensive expression brought the lines on Calbach's face into sharper focus. The detective took another gulp of his beer and sighed. "Your daughter's case turned political in so many ways after the first couple of days I'm not surprised the higher-ups put an embargo on details. How much do you know about Scandian politics, Zack?"

"I'm aware Ingrid whispers advice into the ear of the Reform League's number two and I realize Scandia's well on its way to a crisis involving the two main political parties. That's about it."

"It's more than most people know." Calbach's tone held an undercurrent of bitterness. "Too many folks spend their lives ignoring the reality that Scandia's not the progressive paradise our leaders keep touting. I don't know where Harms is at with the investigation, but he's no dummy. If anyone can find her, Harms and his team will. But they'll be under intense scrutiny and even worse pressure. I'll see what I can find out, but it's the sort of case that'll be heavily compartmentalized. In the meantime, I strongly suggest you don't try to speak with anyone else in the Police Authority about this. Otherwise, you might become a person of interest on general principles."

Decker was about to reply when the Shield Wall's door opened to admit a familiar figure. She still moved like a predator on the hunt, but her wardrobe was of a much higher quality than what she'd worn aboard the river transport. He looked away before her eyes could meet his. Though he didn't resemble the man she'd spoken to the day before, Decker knew she might recognize him nonetheless, if he seemed too curious.

"The tall, dark-haired party that just walked in... Does either of you recognize her?"

Calbach turned to glance over his shoulder, then grimaced. "Yep. She's bad news, that one. The name's Mariel Lazarre. She works for the Scandia Security Intelligence Agency, which is full of bad news. Scurrilous folks might even accuse the SSIA of being in the People's Alliance's pocket."

"What's Lazarre doing here?"

"You mean here in the Shield Wall or here in Kollsvik?"

"Both."

"Lazarre's based out of the agency's Kollsvik office. We see her a lot at the central police station, hobnobbing with the brass. She's a liaison officer, but I always get a weird vibe from her, something that doesn't fit."

"What kind of weird vibe?"

Calbach looked up at Zack. "The kind I've sensed from a few of the worst murderers I've arrested. What's your interest?"

"I ran across Lazarre on my way up from Hamar. Like you, I picked up a strange aura. I'm surprised to see her in a pub frequented by us uniformed types."

"She has friends — read informants — in the police and Guard, and I daresay in your outfit as well, Niels. This is a good place to meet without being obvious. Everyone's used to seeing Lazarre from time to time. Heck, a few wouldn't mind getting to know her better."

Gulliksen snorted. "People with a death wish. And just for the record, if I hear any of my soldiers gave her the time of day, they're spending the next six months on guard duty at the ATC. She may be able to flash a warrant card at your lot or the guardsmen, Lars, but federal troops are out of bounds to her sort."

The detective drained his beer glass and placed it on the table. "I wouldn't be surprised to find Lazarre's keeping a close eye on the investigation into your daughter's disappearance, Zack. It's a case that would fascinate her agency. She could be responsible for shutting you out. The SSIA doesn't like to share with offworlders."

Decker watched Lazarre join a round-faced man wearing well-tailored civilian clothes at the long, brass bar. "Why would an SSIA agent take a slow river transport like *Munin* to travel from Hamar to Kollsvik instead of the regular shuttle?"

"Is that where you met her?" Gulliksen asked.

"Yeah. I wanted to take in the sights."

Calbach's chuckle seemed almost macabre. "Why would Mariel Lazarre slum aboard *Munin*? Not a clue. Did you count how many passengers stepped off compared to how many came aboard? Hear any suspicious splashes in the middle of the night?"

The Marine raised a questioning eyebrow. "Is the SSIA in the hit job business?"

"I think they might prefer the term cleanup business, but I'm not about to ask." Calbach climbed to his feet. "I'll give Niels a call tomorrow, but don't hold your breath. Especially if Lazarre and company are interested in the case. A pleasure to meet you, Zack. Enjoy the rest of your evening, gentlemen."

Gulliksen glanced at Decker. "Want to go grab a bite at the Ice Dragon?"

"Is the food there still good?"

"Better."

"I'm in."

As he was following Gulliksen out into the night, Decker felt eyes on his back. He instinctively knew whose they were without having to turn and look. Mariel Lazarre had identified him as the professional who traveled aboard *Munin* as Harry Devine.

And she would soon find out he was really Major Zack Decker, Commonwealth Marine Corps. How long after that until she discovered he was not only a Naval Intelligence officer but also on the *Sécurité Spéciale*'s hit list would depend on whether the SSIA was in bed with the SecGen's thugs.

**

"Wow. That is seriously impressive." Garrett Montero stepped out of *Phoenix*'s shadow, eyes on the massive ice sheet's leading edge sparkling in the early morning sunshine. It seemed almost close enough to touch. He unconsciously sank deeper into his jacket when a gust of cold air flowing off the glacier tugged at his hair.

"Zack says standing on top of it and looking down is even more impressive." Talyn's eyes shifted to a pair of soldiers in white, cold weather battledress, emerging from one of the structures abutting the landing strip.

"No doubt, but it's not something I'm overly keen to experience. Knowing the Army, they'd probably make me climb up on foot instead of offering a ride in a warm, comfortable thopter. Anyone who thinks arctic combat training is fun has to own a twisted sense of humor."

"You can always ask." She nodded at the approaching men. "I think that's our welcoming party. If you're ready, hand control over to the AI and close her up."

The taller of the two, a jovial-looking major with a flowing mustache, tossed off a salute when he and the sergeant major at his side reached *Phoenix*.

"I'm Henning Bruhns, the Arctic Training Center's commanding officer, and this is Torsten Ellingboe, my top kick. Welcome. Regimental HQ warned us you would need a way to reach Hamar incognito. Sergeant Major Ellingboe has set everything up. You can leave at your convenience."

Talyn and Montero, both still wearing faces that weren't their own, glanced at each other, understanding this was Decker's doing. It meant he'd reached the Scandia Regiment without problems and obtained at least partial cooperation from its colonel.

"That's very kind of you," Talyn replied. "Please excuse me if my first officer and I withhold our names for now. Operational security."

"Understood. If your transponder code is enough identification for the 63rd Battle Group's flagship, we need nothing else. Besides, HQ also advised us you were traveling under JSOC orders and working with the JSOC liaison officer currently at Fort Hardrada. Does your ship need anything?"

She shook her head. "No. We've secured her and left the AI to stand watch. It'll make sure no one tampers with *Phoenix* and will deploy defensive ordnance if necessary. As a result, I would suggest advising your people to keep away."

"Of course. How long will you be gone?"

"Hopefully no more than a week."

"Will you need transportation back to the ATC when you've completed your mission in Hamar?"

"No. We'll find our own way, or arrange for our liaison officer to help us."

Bruhns nodded toward the buildings. "Shall we?"

"Please. And if possible, we'd like to leave for Hamar right away."

"Both a car and a driver are standing by," Sergeant Major Ellingboe said. "You'll be on your way in a few minutes."

"Thank you. If I could ask for one more favor — could you inform the JSOC liaison officer at Fort Hardrada of our arrival at the ATC and subsequent departure for Hamar?"

"Certainly," Bruhns replied. "I intended to report back in any case."

They walked through what served as a reception building for personnel landing at the ATC's airfield and emerged on the other side, where a dusty, slightly battered, and distinctly ancient aircar waited. Its driver, a wiry man in his seventies, with white hair and an equally white beard, climbed out.

"Meet Harold Nyland," Ellingboe said. "Harold spent forty years in the Regiment and still does us the odd favor in his retirement, such as running sightseeing trips for visiting troops."

Talyn inclined her head at the veteran. "A pleasure. I'm afraid my colleague and I can't give you our names."

"No problems, ma'am." Nyland's voice was surprisingly deep and strong. "Torsten mentioned you were traveling under orders. I'm ready to leave whenever you are."

"Now would be good."

Nyland reached in, and the doors on the passenger side opened silently to reveal a clean, comfortable interior capable of seating a dozen humans.

"Climb aboard. I assume those little knapsacks are your only luggage."

"Correct." Talyn turned to Bruhn and Ellingboe. "Once again, thank you for your help and your courtesy."

"Our pleasure," the major replied. "We Commonwealth warriors need to stick together. Enjoy your trip."

The aircar lifted off smoothly, and Nyland pointed its nose due south.

"It'll take about five hours to reach Hamar's outskirts, ma'am. Where precisely would you like me to drop you off?"

She glanced at Montero who said, "How about the Christiana transit station?"

"No problems, sir. Good choice."

They left the confines of the Arctic Training Center for the open tundra which was carpeted with hardy native vegetation that made up in color what it lacked in height.

"I imagine you're Scandian bred and born, Ser Nyland?" Montero asked. "If you've served in the Scandia Regiment for four decades."

"That I am, sir. And please, call me Harold. As the old joke goes, Ser Nyland was my father, God rest his soul."

"If you don't mind me asking, what's your take on the current political situation?"

Nyland's laugh was devoid of humor. "You mean the idiots fighting for who gets to screw the rest of us over? Bugger 'em, if you'll pardon my Anglic."

"So you're not a fan of either party?"

"Well." Nyland scratched his beard. "If you forced me to pick sides, it sure as hell wouldn't be the People's Alliance. We saw what they've done to this planet. The other lot hasn't messed things up. Yet. But they will. Everyone does. Politicians might be honest on their first day in parliament. But give the bastards a few years in power, and they'll do anything to keep it, slimy tricks included. That's why governments are like dirty diapers — you need to change them regularly otherwise you'll choke on the stench. And phew, did the Alliance ever stink when they were turfed."

"So you're in favor of the legislation Prime Minister Dahlstein is putting before parliament next Friday?"

"If it helps make sure we can change the gang of thieves in charge every few years and keep offworld riffraff from coming here to suck us honest citizens dry? You bet, *min herr*."

Montero glanced at Talyn.

"Do you figure the Alliance will let that pass?"

"They'd better not try anything nasty because a lot of people on this planet won't sit still and let the Alliance fuck us over again. Not this time, *min herr*. Not this time."

Then, as if embarrassed by his outburst in front of two strangers, even if they were from the Fleet, Nyland fell silent for the rest of the trip.

— TWENTY-ONE —

"There's nothing like leading a patrol through the muck in unpowered armor to separate the kids from the grownups, is there?" Decker smiled as the memories of his own, long ago junior NCO course came flooding back. He stood with Gulliksen on a hill overlooking a swampy section of Fort Hardrada's training area, happy to be out in the fresh air, enjoying the sight of basic soldiering for a change.

The regimental sergeant major had arranged for Decker to draw an issue of battledress and armor from the supply stores that morning. And with nothing better to do until Colonel Salminen came to a decision or the Police Authority improved its public relations policies, he'd accompanied Gulliksen while the latter resumed his inspection tour.

"You forget the freezer up north. It'll make the candidates remember this phase of their training with fondness. I seem to recall a certain Pathfinder troop leader who couldn't stop telling everyone the only use for ice was to chill drinks."

"It was true then, and it's still true now. The only thing that's changed is the quality of my drinks."

"What? You've found something worse tasting than that Shrehari swill?"

"If you insist on being an asshole, you dumb pongo, then the question should be you've found something worse tasting than that Shrehari swill, *sir*."

Gulliksen gave him the rigid digit salute. "I see no rank insignia on your tin suit. Since you don't want to go around looking like a major because of secret squirrel nonsense, you can shove your 'sir' where the sun don't shine."

"Does your mother know you talk to people like that?"

"Who do you think I learned it from? Folks who find me intimidating would melt if they met her. She'd make an awesome RSM." Gulliksen tilted his helmeted head to one side. "Hang on. I'm getting a call. It could be Lars Calbach with news."

"Nope," the RSM said a few moments later. "That was the colonel's office. It seems the guy investigating your daughter's disappearance will speak with you after all. They expect you downtown at fifteen hundred hours."

"Maybe common sense has finally made an appearance."

"That would be the day. I'll drive you back to the fort and see you're given an unmarked staff car. We wouldn't want anyone to find out you're a JSOC live action role player."

"And just because you're doing that for me, I'll overlook the insubordinate editorial comment this one time."

"There's plenty more where that came from."

"No doubt." Decker nodded toward the combat car waiting at the foot of the hillock, hidden from trainee eyes. "Shall we? I'd like to change and grab a bite before heading into Kollsvik."

"Might as well, before the cops change their minds again."

**

Decker parked his small, four-person Army skimmer in a visitor's slot behind the Police Authority's district headquarters building, a utilitarian gray cube with black windows, fronted by a stand of flagpoles. He pulled his blaster from its shoulder holster and dropped it into the vehicle's lockbox.

Cop shops doors were usually surrounded by sensors, and the Shrehari blaster would trigger them. After a moment of hesitation, the dagger strapped to his forearm joined his gun. Then, Decker climbed out of the car and made sure it was locked with his own biometric signature.

He entered the building via the main door and approached a copper-topped counter beneath a sign reading 'Reception.' As he came near, the hologram of a life-sized androgynous human materialized behind it.

"May I help you?"

"My name is Zachary Decker. I'm here to speak with Inspector Harms."

"Confirmed. Please wait for a member of staff."

Zack paced the reception area instead of taking a seat, surprised at being the only human present until he remembered that street policing was carried out via local substations scattered around Kollsvik and the surrounding settlements. Citizens, other than those summoned here, wouldn't visit the district HQ. His inner clock ticked over to fifteen hundred hours and as if on cue, a door whispered open. A short, stocky man in a severe suit, with a severe haircut, and a face hewn from granite, stepped through.

"Mister Decker? I'm Sergeant Wallings, from Inspector Harms' team. If you'll please follow me."

"Certainly."

Wallings led him along a quiet, tastefully decorated corridor with closed doors on either side, then down a stairwell that seemed to plunge deep into Scandia's crust. They got off at the second landing, well beneath the street surface, where the floor and walls were bare, in stark contrast to those of the main level. The doors, except for one, were also closed, and the sounds muted. Wallings gestured at Zack to enter. The moment he walked over the threshold, Decker understood this was an interrogation room, not an inspector's office.

"Sit." Wallings pointed at the single chair on the far side of a metal table. He left, closing the door behind him.

Decker examined the room with practiced eyes, spotting the video and sensor pickups, and wondered why he was brought here. He didn't wait long for an answer.

The door opened again, and Mariel Lazarre entered, alone. She wore a predatory expression and clothes that would not seem out of place in an interstellar corporation's executive suite.

She stopped short of the table, beyond Zack's reach, crossed her arms, and studied him through narrow feline eyes. "Zachary Decker. Or is it Harry Devine? Which is the real name, the true identity?" Her voice was a mocking purr.

"I'm here to meet Inspector Jakob Harms on a matter concerning a blood relative," Decker replied in a calm tone. "Since you're obviously not Inspector Harms, could you please tell me what this is in aid of?"

"As your drinking friends probably told you last night, I'm an officer of the Scandian Security Intelligence Agency. One of our responsibilities is to find individuals or groups inimical to Scandia and, in cooperation with the Police Authority, make sure they pose no danger to this world.”

“Good for you. But as the Police Authority probably mentioned, I’m a serving Commonwealth Marine Corps officer, and therefore beyond the jurisdiction of planetary security intelligence organizations. If the Scandian government has issues with me, it’s free to contact the flag officer responsible for this sector.”

“True, yet you’re within the jurisdiction of the Scandian Police Authority if they suspect you’ve committed a civilian crime. At least until the Armed Services extradite you for prosecution through military channels.”

“Asking about the investigation into my daughter’s disappearance is a crime?”

“No.” A hungry smile tugged up the corners of her lips. “Of course not. Don’t be ridiculous. However, your presence here is problematic for several reasons.”

Decker cocked an eyebrow and gave her a sardonic grin. “I have that effect on a lot of worlds I visit. It’s a rare talent. What’s irking you Scandians in particular?”

“For one, I can’t find a record of you passing through a proper port of entry. In effect, you’re on Scandia illegally.”

The Marine shrugged. “A minor oversight stemming from legitimate military reasons. I’m sure it can be fixed without further ado since this probably happens often with Commonwealth Armed Services personnel traveling directly from orbit to a federal installation such as Fort Hardrada.” Or the Arctic Training Center, he thought, but why give Lazarre ideas.

“Yet you didn’t travel directly from orbit to Fort Hardrada, did you? I’m curious — why take *Munin* upriver while hiding your real identity?”

“Did I?”

"Come now, Mister Decker. You and I traded words in the transport's saloon. You even remarked that you'd remember someone like me. Did you forget already? I'm crushed."

"Sorry. I can't please everyone. In fact, I've been told often enough that my abilities lie in the other direction. But if Inspector Harms won't show up, there's no point in me waiting." He climbed to his feet.

"Sit." A wicked needler materialized in her hand. "You're staying here for the moment. As I was saying, your presence on this planet has not been cleared through Scandian immigration officials. That's a security matter. On top of that, you were traveling on Scandia under a false identity, which is a criminal matter. Petty? Sure. But it's enough for me to order you detained. Who knows? Perhaps you might even be able to help the Hamar police with their investigation of seven murders in the spaceport warehouse district a few days ago. A professional job if they've ever seen one."

"No idea what you're talking about. I never set foot in the spaceport." Either the cops connected Harry Devine with the failed ambush and published a 'be on the lookout' that made its way to the SSIA, or Mariel Lazarre and her agency were playing footsie with the *Sécurité Spéciale.*

"So you admit to landing on Scandia without passing through an authorized port of entry."

Decker sighed. "To repeat myself, since I'm a federal officer, you're overreaching. Either let me go free, or use that damn popgun and make yourself subject to Commonwealth jurisdiction for assault on an Armed Services officer traveling under orders. This conversation has run its course and face it, honey, you're not interesting, or particularly memorable."

"I could just make you disappear, *honey*. You wouldn't be my first."

"No doubt. But I've run across your type before. It didn't end well for any of them."

"Talk is cheap."

The Marine contemplated her with a bored expression. "And doing anything other than letting me walk out of here will be extremely expensive as well as truly painful."

Something about his confident tone gave Lazarre pause. Decker noticed a slight tightening of the skin around her eyes as she examined him.

"You didn't think I'd walk in here without taking elementary precautions, did you?"

"Such as?"

A cruel smile twisted his lips. "I really shouldn't ruin the surprise, but I have friends watching my back. Well-armed friends. Besides, the skimmer I came in is booby-trapped. If I don't disarm it, the resulting explosion will shred the back half of this building. That should do wonders for Police Authority cooperation with the SSIA."

That air of uncertainty flashed across her eyes once again. But before she could reply, the door opened, and two gorilla-sized thugs in dark suits entered. Decker knew just by looking they were *Sécurité Spéciale*. Both stared at him with those telltale dead fish eyes.

"Thank you for holding him," the older of the two said. "We caught the last bit and can confirm his skimmer isn't booby-trapped. We scanned it. But I'd recommend against forcing the doors. Leave it for the Army to recover."

"And his supposed friends?"

The man shrugged. "That's your lookout, Sera Lazarre, but Decker is a well-known bullshit artist. If his car's not rigged to blow, then I doubt he has Army snipers on the rooftops."

"What'll happen to him now?"

The man glanced at Zack. "We take him to our field office. After that? I don't know. My superiors asked me to convey their thanks for helping us. Major Decker is apparently a hard man to catch."

"But catching a hard man is a good thing, right?" Decker winked at Lazarre. "Too bad you're helping these mental defectives. They're not the kind you can trust."

She pointedly ignored him. "You came in through the underground garage, I hope?"

"We did."

"Good. It would be a shame if someone noticed you taking Decker away after the trouble I went through to make sure no one saw him."

The Marine snorted. "What about the reception AI and Sergeant Wallings?"

Lazarre gave him a contemptuous look. "Please. I took actual precautions. The AI has already been wiped, and Wallings is one of my officers, not a cop. Besides, there never was an appointment with Inspector Harms. He's not even aware you're in the building. In fact, none of the Police Authority's officers know. They were merely ordered to cooperate with an SSIA rendition."

"What about my daughter?"

She shrugged dismissively. "Not my concern. I was tasked to help take you in when you showed up in Kollsvik."

"So our meeting aboard *Munin* wasn't entirely coincidental?"

"No, it wasn't. I didn't know then you were the Zack Decker our *Sécurité Spéciale* friends wanted to capture; merely that you came off a ship they were watching and attracted their attention with your gunplay at the spaceport. Too bad you visited the Shield Wall to enlist that idiot Calbach last night. It allowed me to figure out Devine and Decker were the same man. You didn't try very hard with the disguise."

"I didn't expect the local secret police to be playing nice with the SecGen's goons, which is a major failing on my part."

"And it'll be your last," the lead *Sécurité Spéciale* operative said. "Stand so I can cuff you. Try anything stupid, and you'll enter a universe of unimaginable pain. My colleague has you covered."

Decker glanced at the second man, who was pointing an electroshock gun at his midriff. They were serious about taking him alive even though they had to know he was conditioned against interrogation. Or perhaps they finally had their own Hera Talyn, an interrogator who possessed that near-mythical combination of skill and soullessness to break conditioning without killing a prisoner.

Seeing no way out of the trap, Decker slowly climbed to his feet and raised his hands. Best to cooperate and save his strength for a chance at escaping later on. The first goon, careful to stay out of his partner's line of fire, came around the table and expertly cuffed Zack's hands behind his back. Then, he slapped a muzzling patch over the Marine's mouth before frisking him. In short order, he relieved Zack of his communicator, ID, and money.

"As I thought. He left his weapons in the car, like a good, law-abiding citizen visiting the police. If you'd please walk ahead of us, Sera Lazarre, and make sure our way to the garage remains clear."

"Certainly." The SSIA officer gave Zack a last, expressionless glance, then left the room.

Boxed in between the two operatives, with the electroshock gun pressed into the small of his back, Decker followed Lazarre down the corridor and through an airlock-type vestibule that gave onto the station's underground garage. There, they bundled him into the sealed-off rear compartment of an unmarked aircar and shackled him to a seat before driving away.

Decker felt the aircar lift the moment it cleared the ramp leading into the courtyard where he'd left his borrowed skimmer — and his weapons. He mentally cursed himself for failing to confirm the invitation to speak with Harms was genuine after the previous day's refusal.

But he'd let his concern for Saga's welfare override his instincts as a covert warrior. And now he would pay the price of his imprudence. One thing was certain. Talyn would never let him forget this sorry episode. It was almost worth falling on his sword to avoid her reproachful stare. Almost.

**

After what seemed like an eternity stuck in the darkened compartment, Decker felt the aircar slow and veer as if lining up for a landing. Unless they'd spent the last few hours spinning in circles, he was a long way from Kollsvik.

Then his stomach lurched as the vehicle abruptly shed its forward motion and dropped vertically before coming to a full stop. After a few moments, the rear compartment's door opened, and one of the goons reached in to release his shackles while the other kept careful aim on his head with the electroshock gun.

When Decker's legs were free, both stepped back. "End of the line. Get out."

With no viable alternatives in sight, he complied. As soon as his feet touched solid ground, the Marine stretched his limbs as best he could, even though his hands remained manacled. They were in a courtyard surrounded by interconnected, two-story, flat-roofed buildings on every side. Polarized windows pierced the walls at regular intervals as did doors on the ground level. Night had fallen, but his surroundings were bathed in soft illumination thanks to a constellation of light globes hanging from wrought iron arms cleverly forged to look like stylized dragons.

The air felt warmer, and his nostrils picked up a faint tang of salt, indicating they were somewhere near the Equatorial Ocean, on the southern edge of the continent. If so, the aircar had made good time.

The lead thug wrapped a large hand around Decker's bulging biceps and steered him toward the closest door. It opened on a brightly lit corridor with bare white walls and widely spaced, closed doors. They stopped in front of an open lift cab and shoved him in.

"Don't try anything, Decker. This cab is monitored. At the slightest hint of your doing something stupid, it'll be flooded with knockout gas."

Zack nodded his understanding. With no visible indicators or control panel, he couldn't figure how many levels the lift dropped before disgorging them into an underground corridor in every respect identical to the one on the surface.

A door stood open, and the *Sécurité Spéciale* agent holding his arm directed him toward what turned out to be a three meter by three meter cell with the bare necessities: metal cot without mattress or blankets, toilet, and sink. The walls, as white as the corridor outside, were smooth and featureless, amplifying the ceiling fixture's brilliant glare.

The agent, still covered by his partner's gun, tore off the muzzle patch and removed Decker's wrist manacles, then backed out of the cell. Its door slammed shut, leaving the Marine to contemplate his predicament. He still wore his own clothes rather than a prisoner's garb. It meant they were confident he carried nothing with which to fabricate a means of resistance, let alone escape.

Besides, they would watch him at all times. What he didn't know was why they'd brought him here. Since the Coalition wanted Decker dead, the care they'd shown in taking him alive did not augur well.

He stretched out on the cot and immediately winced. It was not only hard but cold. That meant getting more than fifteen or twenty minutes of sleep in one go would be impossible, never mind the lighting.

Keeping a prisoner awake and uncomfortable to soften him for interrogation was an old trick. And because he'd been conditioned, it meant the weaker he became, the easier it would be for his system to shut itself down permanently under questioning. But his captors would know that, which made him wonder what lay in store.

Fortunately, he was still an infantryman at heart, able to take brief naps anytime and anywhere. He found the least uncomfortable position and quickly fell into a light sleep.

— TWENTY-TWO —

Zack's eyes fluttered open when he heard the door to his cell sliding aside. A quick check with his internal clock told him it was still the middle of the night.

So far, his jailers had not subjected him to unpleasantness aimed at weakening a subject's resistance, such as random bursts of loud, brain-rattling sounds, rancid, vomit-inducing odors, or strobing lights guaranteed to trigger fits. An uncomfortable, always lit cell seemed to be the worst of it.

The lead goon from earlier entered, manacles in hand, while the other one stood outside, electroshock gun aimed at Decker's head. "Stand."

Decker sat up and slowly climbed to his feet, working the kinks out of his stiff muscles while staring at his captors.

"Hands."

When Decker stuck out his arms, wrists touching, the man cuffed them together.

They took him to the end of the corridor and into an interrogation room little different from the one in the Kollsvik Police Authority building. The *Sécurité Spéciale* man pushed Zack into a metal chair bolted to the floor and shackled his ankles to its legs, then both left without another word.

He examined his surroundings and decided the wall in front of him was at least in part a one-way window or a display panel. Or both. It was subtly different from its other, blindingly white, siblings. Decker was no stranger to the wrong side of an interrogation table, notably facing the late and unlamented Rika Kozlev on Garonne, during the insurgency.

But this place felt like a professionally designed dungeon compared to Kozlev's chamber of horrors. Of course, she'd been a sociopath, and although the *Sécurité Spéciale* recruited people with maladapted personalities, they rarely hired her type.

With nothing to do but wait, Decker fell into a meditative trance. He let his thoughts wander where they pleased until the door opened again, admitting a man and a woman.

They wore the dark business suits that seemed to be a *Sécurité Spéciale* uniform, at least in this star system, but were otherwise surprisingly different. He appeared old, dried out, with a fringe of gray hair around a shiny dome. Dark, emotionless eyes stared out at Decker from either side of a hooked nose dominating a face that was all angles with no softness in sight. The man reminded Zack of pictures he'd seen depicting what was termed a hanging judge in the days before humanity's faster-than-light diaspora.

She, on the other hand, appeared young, or at least younger than her colleague, with soft, unmarred skin, a blond pixie haircut, and bright green eyes that seemed to exude malicious enjoyment at seeing him so powerless. Her refined features, from the pert nose through the full lips, to the high, sensual cheekbones, seemed almost sculpted, though Decker could see no clues hinting at facial reconstruction.

They sat across from him, on the opposite side of the bare steel table and studied their captive with the intensity of praying mantises eying their next meal.

"Major Zachary Thomas Decker," the man finally said in a strong baritone that belied his appearance. "You've been quite a pain in the ass for many of the Commonwealth's most powerful people."

Zack smirked. "Like my pappy used to say, a man needs to go with his strengths."

"Ah yes, a pain in the ass with a questionable sense of humor and a colorful career. But one of nature's ultimate survivors. It's a shame you insist on fighting the flow of history. You could do so much to help the Commonwealth evolve into its next incarnation by joining forces with the visionaries who will make it happen."

"I think the word you're looking for is *de*volve. Besides, if you know so much about me, then you'll be aware I believe people are judged by the company they keep and my standards are pretty high."

The woman snorted with derision. "You? Standards? You're a borderline alcoholic who'll fuck anything that stands still. At least when you're not brawling, killing, or otherwise acting like a barbarian from a bygone age."

Zack blew a kiss at her. "I think you're cute too, darling. Want to stand still for me?"

Her features twisted into a mask of disgust. "I'm not some cheap twisted creature like your usual sort of degenerate."

"Ooh." Decker winced. "I can think of at least one highly functioning psychopath who'd take grave exception to your mischaracterization of my intimate friends. And she pushes the concept of retribution to a whole new level. Excruciating pain hardly describes it."

"Speaking of Commander Talyn." The man raised his hand to stop their back-and-forth, even though Decker knew they had carefully scripted this interview. "Where is she?"

"Your guess is as good as mine."

The woman glanced at the small tablet she'd pulled from a tunic pocket shortly after sitting. "It appears he's telling the truth."

A lie detector? Decker repressed a smile. Special Operations Division agents were trained to control their physical reactions so they could tell the most outrageous lies and still fool anyone or anything. She saw something in his eyes because a sly smile tugged at her mouth.

"We are aware of your abilities, Major."

Thanks in no small part to that damned bastard Manny Yang, Decker thought.

"And our newest tools let us make allowances for them."

"I don't think your newest tools can break my conditioning against interrogation."

"Perhaps. But we're also aware it's possible to do so," the man smoothly interjected. "Commander Talyn is supposed to be one of the few capable of such a feat."

"With a mortality rate that would make Satan blanch."

"No doubt." He inclined his head. "But we're not here to interrogate you, Major. We can still count on friends in the right places to feed us the intelligence our movement needs."

"Black Sword traitors."

"Patriots, Major. Men and women of vision who realize Grand Admiral Kowalski's legacy has become an anchor holding humanity back from the destiny it deserves."

"If you don't want what I carry in my head, then why the hell am I here instead of lying in a ditch with my brains scattered across the highway?"

A thin smile appeared. "You're here because we wish to enlist you and Commander Talyn."

Decker eyed him with incredulity and laughed. "That's rich. I figured you clowns weren't right in the head, but wow! You want Hera and me to betray our oaths? Get bent, you moron."

"After the damage you've done," the man continued, ignoring Zack's outburst, "we should execute both of you. But it's proved very costly and so far impossible to achieve. As I said, you're one of nature's ultimate survivors, and so is Commander Talyn. Then there's the Black Sword purge at Fleet HQ, thanks to your intervention, leaving us in dire need of well-placed collaborators who can act on our behalf. I can't think of a better way to find those collaborators than convince Naval Intelligence's best, most dangerous operatives to join our cause and align themselves with the right side of history?"

"The only well-placed thing you're getting from Hera or me is a third eye above that beak you call a nose. And if you didn't have your head up your butt, you'd know garbage like what your Coalition is peddling has always been on the *wrong* side of history."

"Ah yes." He smiled again. "You're fascinated by the past, aren't you, Major?"

"He who doesn't learn from it will repeat every damn mistake committed by rats such as you across the ages."

The woman shook her head. "I don't think that's precisely what Santayana said. Your ability to spout quotes from men wiser than you seems overrated."

"Any fool can spout platitudes. A sage understands their meaning well enough to paraphrase."

She sneered. "You're full of it, Decker."

"And if you play your cards right, you can be full of Decker too." He turned back to the older man. "Okay, buddy. Amuse me. Tell me how you will convince us to switch sides and go full Black Sword on Naval Intelligence's ass."

"In due course. Now, back to Commander Talyn. Where is she?"

"No idea."

"Is Commander Talyn on Scandia?"

"No idea."

The woman's lips twitched as she glanced down. "He's unsure, though not outright lying." When Decker turned eyes of stone on her, she laughed softly. "As I told you, our tools can make allowances for your particular idiosyncrasies. I'll wager Talyn's in this star system. He doesn't know for sure whether she's on Scandia, however."

"Meaning she has a shuttle or starship at her disposal." The man nodded. "Does she have a starship at her disposal, Major Decker?"

"No idea." Decker's expression remained stoic though he felt inward pleasure at hearing evidence the *Sécurité Spéciale* had not yet connected Talyn with *Phoenix*, or *Haukka* as they thought the little transport was named.

"Unsure, if not quite lying again." She speared him with a skeptical glare. "Decker knows more than he's willing to admit. He's just playing fast and loose with the truth in his own mind."

"Perhaps a bit of motivation is in order..." The man stroked his chin as he contemplated the Marine with eyes that exuded the warmth of an iceberg on a liquid methane ocean. "It's a given you can contact Commander Talyn if necessary, yes?"

He pulled Zack's communicator from a tunic pocket and studied it for a moment. "With this, maybe? Experienced operatives such as yourselves would arrange for a way to stay in touch. Perhaps we'll receive a call from her at any moment. Yet I'm puzzled. Why was Talyn not watching your back? What is she up to by herself?"

"That's something I don't want to contemplate." Decker grinned. "If you know what I mean."

"What did Mariel Lazarre tell us?"

The woman kept her stare on Zack. "She told us Major Decker traveled alone up the Torne River aboard the transport skimmer *Munin*, wearing a different face and calling himself Harry Devine. Apparently, this Devine was a man who did not pass through a proper port of entry upon landing on Scandia since there's no immigration record of his arrival. Interestingly, however, he was seen exiting the Hamar spaceport shortly after a mass shooting in an abandoned warehouse area known to be used by criminals. And we're aware how good Major Decker is with weapons."

"Did you get into an altercation with the local smuggler's guild after they brought you to Scandia unseen, Major?" The man asked. "That's hardly the way to keep your cover intact."

Decker shrugged, puzzled by the question since he believed the ambush was set at the *Sécurité Spéciale*'s behest as part of their effort to trace Mattias Kenly. Of course, the guild itself might be looking for Garrett Montero's now-vanished alter ego.

Or was it a case of the Scandian field office keeping its local operations from the prying eyes of HQ hotshots, which the two specimens in front of him would be. Either explanation meant they weren't aware *Phoenix*, or as she was then, *Haukka*, belonged to Naval Intelligence.

Decker was glad to see the opposition still suffered from plenty of blind spots the Fleet could exploit.

"You know how terminal greed can sometimes result in mercy killings."

"How did Commander Talyn travel to Scandia?"

"I would assume it was via starship since instantaneous molecular transportation hasn't left the realm of fantasy yet."

"Why didn't she travel with you?"

"I'm in this star system on family business. Hera has no family here, or elsewhere. At least not any she'd acknowledge, or more to the point, family that would acknowledge her."

"Ah yes, your daughter. We finally come to her." The man nodded. "Unfortunately, we've run out of time for today. Besides, without Commander Talyn joining us, we're at a bit of a standstill. We shall continue this fascinating conversation at our next meeting." The two *Sécurité Spéciale* agents stood as if by common accord. "I would tell you to enjoy our hospitality, but as you've seen so far, we don't offer much beyond the bare necessities."

Then, they left him alone in the room, debating whether they'd ended the interview at this exact point so he'd stew a little longer wondering about Saga's welfare and her role in this mess. The two goons showed up soon after and led him back to his cell.

**

"Why would Decker simply vanish?" Colonel Salminen asked after Regimental Sergeant Major Gulliksen finished telling him about the abandoned skimmer by the police station and Inspector Harms' insistence he never made an appointment to speak with Zack.

"Your guess is as good as mine, sir. The station's reception AI has no record of him showing up but we found his personal weapons stowed in the car's secure bin, that Shrehari blaster he favors and his Pathfinder dagger. I've put them in the HQ armory for safekeeping. If you ask me, whoever is behind the coup d'état he wants to prevent lured him into a trap."

"Supposed coup d'état, RSM."

"You've been listening to the news, sir. With the fresh accusations hurled at the Reform League government in the last few days, it's obvious someone's trying to foment a crisis in Hamar, and the noise is only getting worse. I'm convinced Zack was really on to something. And now, he's disappeared without a trace." Gulliksen frowned in thought. "You know, if I were a betting man, I'd wager that snake Lazarre was involved in his disappearance."

"The SSIA interested in Decker?" Salminen rubbed his cheek, then nodded. "It would fit with your buddy's doomsday scenario. The buggers were always too cozy with the Alliance."

"That's because the damned Alliance created the SSIA in the first place."

"But would Lazarre and company dare abduct a Commonwealth Armed Services officer?"

"If there's a coup coming, and they found out he was trying to prevent it, sure. In a heartbeat. They're about as political as any security service can be."

Salminen grimaced. "Then Mariel Lazarre might already have sent Decker to join his ancestors if rumors about her proclivities are correct."

"I doubt that, sir."

"Why?"

"A gut feeling. If I can make a suggestion. Why don't we try speaking to the AI controlling that ship sitting on the ATC's tarmac, the one that brought Zack's JSOC colleagues to Scandia? It might be able to contact them and let them know he's gone missing."

"I suppose it's worth a try."

"In that case, how about I go to the ATC with Zack's side arms and show them to the ship's AI as our bona fides?"

Salminen let out a soft snort. "I can just see you standing in the snow, holding up a gun and a knife, trying to attract the AI's attention. But I get your point. You may leave at once."

"Yes, sir. Thank you. What about the trouble brewing in Hamar?"

The Scandia Regiment's commanding officer sighed. "I can't do more than play it by ear, RSM. There's too much resistance in the command group at the idea of a proactive stance. And just between you and me, I wouldn't be surprised if some of them are wondering where their loyalties lie, thanks to family ties. And family ties are, I suppose, what lured Major Decker into a trap. Considering he's a JSOC professional, it proves their potency. Now off with you. I need to think about how we prepare without looking like we're doing it. When you ask the AI to call Decker's colleagues, tell it to find out whether they can give us an updated reconnaissance report."

"Will do, sir." Gulliksen sprang up and snapped to attention before turning on his heel, leaving Salminen to stare at his famous great-aunt's portrait. Back in her day, senior Scandia Regiment officers never doubted where their loyalties lay. Another change that could be traced back to the People's Alliance's decades of quasi-dynastic rule. Or as many would say, misrule.

**

Talyn's roving eyes froze for a second when she felt the communicator in her tunic's inner breast pocket vibrate softly. Montero, sitting opposite her in one of the pubs favored by soldiers of the Scandian National Guard's Hamar Brigade, noticed the hesitation and cocked a questioning eyebrow.

"She's calling."

Montero nodded his understanding. 'She' could only be *Phoenix*. And that meant news important enough to justify breaking radio silence. Even encrypted, a comlink could be traced.

"We should drink up and go elsewhere."

Talyn nodded. "And come back later."

They finished their beers and walked out into the early evening without a backward glance, heading for a nearby park where the sight lines were open and the traffic density such that they wouldn't be overheard. They found a quiet bench and sat. Talyn pulled out her communicator while Montero kept an eye on the surroundings. She read the dense text on its small screen and sighed.

"A Scandia Regiment soldier by the name Niels Gulliksen showed up at the ATC with Zack's blaster and dagger, claiming Zack vanished after being called to a meeting with the police about his daughter. The police deny he entered the station, let alone that they summoned him. The Army found the staff skimmer Zack borrowed to travel from Fort Hardrada to Kollsvik abandoned in the police station parking lot, with Zack's weapons aboard. Gulliksen, who's the regimental sergeant major and another of my partner's endless supply of old buddies, figures the Scandia Security Intelligence Agency is involved."

"Working hand in glove with the *Sécurité Spéciale*, no doubt. Those two organizations must share the same DNA if rumors are true."

"Probably, which means my dear partner, bless his paternal soul, was lured into the trap we knew waited in Kollsvik, and is now sitting in some dank cell."

"Why not just kill him?"

"They want me as well, and he's *my* bait."

"Do you think it's related to our current mission?"

"Perhaps, but the fact we're here, acting at my discretion is the product of chance rather than design. Using Zack's daughter to lure us out into the open, that's clearly by design."

"What do you intend?"

"I would look to the needs of the many if I could be sure Zack's mission to the Scandia Regiment succeeded before he was abducted. He's capable of taking his chances until we've seen whether the Alliance will make good on the rumors and try to seize power, triggering what we fear. But since I can't tell without calling Colonel Salminen, which I don't want to do yet, and there are several days left before the vote in parliament, we need to figure out where he is."

Montero chuckled. "A tall order. Scandia's a big place, and we can't tap into the local authorities for help. The cops will treat his disappearance with the same bureaucratic zeal as his daughter's. And it's been how long now?"

"I can narrow it down. But I might tip our hand to the opposition."

"Meaning?"

"We split up.   Continue the recon until you've exhausted every possibility, then rejoin *Phoenix* and at the very least report back to HQ. If you decide there's an imminent threat, you can contact the CO of the Scandia Regiment at your discretion, in case Zack set the groundwork. Otherwise, lift off and wait for orders."

"And you?"

"I will pull my partner's ass out of the fire. You may not be aware of this, but we formally met for the first time while I was doing just that. Of course, back then, I was mostly responsible for putting him in harm's way."

"Sounds romantic."

"Only if you're into serious kink."

"What's your way to find Zack's location?"

"Order the ship to ping his communicator via Scandia's satellite constellation. Of course, whoever has it will notice and prepare accordingly, but at least they won't be able to trace it back easily, and if they manage, it'll only be to *Phoenix*."

"And if Zack tossed his communicator or lost it?"

"Then I drop the disguise, report to the nearest immigration port of entry as Hera Talyn and wait for the opposition to find me."

Montero made a face. "That sounds like a last-ditch option."

"Things often turn out that way for Zack and me, yet we're still alive and adding to the *Sécurité Spéciale*'s body count with monotonous regularity."

"Until the day you aren't."

"Which isn't today." She stood and glanced at the nearest transit stop. "Take care, Garrett. Don't be foolish or reckless. I'll ping Zack's communicator once I'm well away from here, just in case. If I find its location, you may assume I'll head there."

"Do me a favor and take your own advice on not acting foolishly or with recklessness, Hera. And tell the ship to call me once you've freed your favorite Marine."

"No promises."

— TWENTY-THREE —

Out of sheer devilment more than anything else, Talyn stood in the shadow of Scandia's brilliantly lit parliament when she ordered *Phoenix*'s AI to ping her partner's communicator. While waiting for a reply, she studied the seemingly endless swirl of activity around the imposing stone buildings at a time when most citizens were enjoying their evening.

It was probably the result of two days spent listening to people all over town, but Talyn fancied she could sense an undercurrent of crisis, if not yet chaos, flow through every bright window and every open door. She could even see it in the hurried steps of those still toiling within.

The question of whether that political discord would turn sour still hung over their heads unanswered. Talyn wanted to check the National Guard's mood tonight, but that was now a job for Garrett Montero and his field operative's instinct.

The AI finally reported that it received a return signal from Zack's communicator. But from an unexpected location — a private manor just outside Vaasa on the extreme south coast, about as distant as one could be from Kollsvik and still stay on this continent. Zack's communicator reported no longer being in her partner's hands, but subject to intense hostile electronic scrutiny instead.

It was as she feared. The price of tracking the device was giving herself and quite possibly *Phoenix* away. Whoever held Zack would now expect her. She ordered the AI to inform Montero and then, after a last glance at the parliamentary precinct, Talyn retraced her steps to the transit station for a ride to Hamar's maglev depot. Her best bet at traveling, and more importantly arriving unnoticed was stowing away on an overnight freight to Vaasa.

**

After several uncomfortable hours in his cell, Decker once again found himself in the same interview room as before, staring at a blank wall, waiting for Chrome Dome and the Evil Pixie, as he'd dubbed his interrogators. Once again, they let him stew for over an hour, shackled to the chair, before entering.

Where Decker felt tired, sore, and unwashed, they seemed fresh, rested, though wearing the same clothes as before, or exact copies. Maybe *Sécurité Spéciale* operatives had closets full of identical suits.

They studied him in silence for a while, then Chrome Dome pulled out Zack's communicator and placed it on the table.

"Someone or something pinged this a few hours ago. As far as we can tell, the signal came from Scandia's satellite constellation. It bounced around the planet a few times to mask its origin. Your communicator returned an almost identical ping, but with what appears to be more data than what it received. We traced that to a ship sitting on the tarmac at the Army's Arctic Training Center — a Navy vessel by the name *Phoenix*. But unfortunately no further. Could Commander Talyn be looking for you?"

Decker shrugged. "With my luck, it was probably someone looking to sell me the latest in virtual bondage equipment. Or term life insurance."

"Hilarious." Evil Pixie gave him one of her patented stares. "If that was Talyn, she must know you've gone walkabout. And now she knows where you are and is likely coming. We won't have to search for her."

"When we last conversed," Chrome Dome said, "we'd reached the subject of your daughter, Saga Lagman. Such a pretty name, Saga, if you don't mind me saying so. A pretty young woman too."

"That's because she takes after her mother, not me, thank God."

"I daresay a certain type of woman finds you handsome enough, Major. Your reputation in that area is quite remarkable as well."

Decker winked at Evil Pixie. "And I hear no complaints. Now, what's your interest in Saga?"

"She's a fascinating person." Chrome Dome gave Zack a thin, cold smile. "Not because of who she is, but what she is. It's almost too perfect for words. Saga Lagman is not only the daughter of the biggest thorn in our side. She's also the daughter of Alisa Berneiser's closest friend and confidante. Imagine that — Alisa Berneiser, reputedly the real force behind the current government. But not for long as I understand."

The Marine knew Chrome Dome was trying to goad him by dragging this out, but he wasn't about to give the *Sécurité Spéciale* officer any satisfaction.

"That's what I like about you folks, always willing to state the obvious, so the retarded ones in your ranks understand." He glanced at Evil Pixie. "I guess that makes you the cretin in this scenario, sweetheart."

"Come now, Major, there's no call to insult my colleague, not if we'll be working together soon."

"Get to the point. Your gorillas interrupted a perfectly good wet dream. I'd like to see if I can pick things up where they left off." Decker gave Evil Pixie a leer. "Don't worry, darling. It didn't involve you. I prefer actual human beings."

Chrome Dome sighed theatrically. "If we could stop the badinage and return to business. I'm pleased to tell you Saga Lagman is alive and well, and though she's being detained, her living conditions are quite comfortable. Before you ask, no one has so much as touched her. We want to bring you over to our side, not trigger a destructive vendetta."

"Where is she?"

"Where is not important. So long as you understand that we hold her." He waved his hand at an unseen flunky behind the opaque window made up to look like a wall.

The image of a plush living room shimmered into existence and Decker took a deep, calming breath. His daughter was sitting on a white sofa, legs tucked under, reading an old-fashioned printed book that might even be an antique. Her pose, the look of intense concentration on her face, the frown she'd inherited from her mother, everything screamed genuine.

"This is a direct, real-time feed from the place she's being kept. As you can see, her conditions are somewhat better than yours. But then, she's a non-combatant, not a hardened warrior like her father." When Decker didn't speak, Chrome Dome said, "Won't you ask me why we abducted Saga?"

"Why should I? You'll tell me whether or not I want to know. Your sort can never quite shut up. Reason number one thousand two hundred and fifty-five why you won't find me enlisting in your army of darkness."

Another thin smile. "Oh, I think you will, Major Decker. You're a survivor. And yes, it's the real thing, not a sim."

"Show me proof."

"Please." Chrome Dome shook his head with an air of exasperation. "We both know you wouldn't accept any proof short of a DNA analysis performed under your own control with your own equipment. But I can give you the chance to speak with the delightful Saga and see if her memories coincide with yours. That's something no one can fake."

"Unless you brain-drained her and fed the results to a sim or an imposter."

The man looked pained.

"You can't be serious, Major? A brain-drain means she's under our control, and if she's under our control, we've achieved the aim. No need for something messy and potentially fatal. I thought you possessed a better grasp of logic."

Decker, privately annoyed with himself at having fallen for such an obvious mistake, stared emotionlessly at his interrogators. "What do you want from me?"

Chrome Dome inclined his head by way of acknowledging the Marine's first step toward cooperation. "First, we need you to believe the young woman you're watching is Saga Lagman. Once we're in agreement about her identity, we can discuss you joining our cause."

"Give it your best shot. I'm what you might call a captive audience."

"Funny you should word it that way. I'm about to free your mind." Chrome Dome waved his hand again and moments later a silent *Sécurité Spéciale* gorilla, judging by his dark suit, entered the interrogation room carrying a stiff bag. He placed it on the table, then withdrew. "Did you ever experience true mind-to-mind communications?"

"Why?"

"We ran a project a few years ago, one that unfortunately ended rather abruptly, to tap into the human brain's unused abilities. But before the project's demise, we reached the point of transforming mind probes into neural gateways allowing the wearer to directly access virtual reality environments where people can interact unheard, unseen, and with no physical contact."

As Chrome Dome spoke, Decker realized the project in question was the one he'd interrupted by killing the rogue Sister of the Void called Anca and rescuing neurological specialist Elyce Sakal.

"If your contraption is the mutated child of a mind probe I'll pass. Mind probes score a perfect one-hundred percent kill rate on people conditioned against interrogation."

The man tut-tutted with the sad expression of a schoolmaster watching his prized pupil fail a test.

"Another disappointing lapse in logic, Major. I wouldn't propose to use our VR facilities if this mutated child, as you call it, could in any way harm you. As I keep repeating, we want you to work with us, and you're of no use dead. This will allow you and Saga to commune unhindered while still preserving the anonymity of her whereabouts."

Decker chuckled. "And at the same time introduce some sort of brainwashing to make me change sides, something my conditioning won't detect as a hostile intrusion that would trigger instant death?"

"You give us too much credit. We've yet to perfect a means of influencing loyalty through direct neural stimulus. Someone who doesn't wish to be influenced will be even more resistant to pressure applied directly via the neural network than through traditional means. I won't waste my time trying to determine whether you might be an exception."

"But you will peep into this virtual reality while Saga and I catch up on the last twenty years."

Chrome Dome nodded. "Of course."

"Why not just let us talk over a regular comlink?"

"Because a mind-to-mind conversation in a virtual environment allows something not possible in regular conversation. You're able to sense raw emotions, a great way of detecting falsehood."

"Useful for interrogation."

"Sadly, no. We cannot force a mind to interact with the virtual environment. It must be voluntary. But we're working on the question."

"Just so you know, my conditioning will kick in if you try to interrogate me after I've voluntarily accepted to play your virtual game."

"That goes without saying, Major. We ran extensive tests using live subjects and know what is and isn't possible. Right now, I need you to accept we hold your daughter. Once you've cleared that hurdle, we will continue this conversation."

Chrome Dome nodded at his colleague, who climbed to her feet and picked up the equipment case. She came around the table and produced a metallic headband which she fitted around his skull.

"Close your eyes and try to relax. If you fight it, Saga won't be able to connect." Evil Pixie nodded at the display where he saw his daughter being fitted with an identical headband.

She did something with her tablet, and Decker's universe went sideways.

******

Decker found himself in a room very much like the one he'd seen on the display moments earlier, but everything seemed slightly askew, slightly wrong as if seen through the lens of a dream. The room became a disorganized mess of pixels in his peripheral vision, though when he turned his head, everything that seemed to dissolve took on a solid appearance while what seemed solid was now dissolving in his peripheral vision.

The tall, slender shape of a long-haired blond woman materialized on a sofa that shimmered as if at the bottom of a shallow sea. She stared at him for a fraction of a second. Then she metamorphosed into a five-year-old girl, the same girl he'd held in his arms for the last time twenty years earlier, including the partially healed gash on her left cheek. Decker had been saying his goodbyes to Ingrid and Saga before embarking on the deployment that ended his marriage and estranged him from the only people he'd ever loved.

"Daddy?" A tentative, high-pitched voice asked. Decker felt a strange wave of uncertainty, mixed with incomprehension and fear waft over him. It took a moment or two before he understood it to be the manifestation of his daughter's emotions, laid bare by the neural connection.

"Yes, Punkie, it's me." Punkie, the private nickname given a bright, loving child by a doting father who always seemed to be off on deployment. Did Saga manifest as a five-year-old because of his memories or because of hers? He glanced at himself and saw nothing other than the clothes he was wearing in real life.

As if the nickname nobody else ever used or even knew about was a magic incantation, Saga's VR image turned back into her adult self.

"What's happening? Why are we in a virtual environment? Where are you? Where am I?" Her aura of fear strengthened, and he felt an unaccountable desire to take her in his arms and protect her from the monsters under the bed, just like he did so long ago. But Decker pushed back the surge of fatherly emotions that threatened to overwhelm the dispassionate field agent he needed to be.

"I'll answer those questions in due time, Punkie. Right now, I need to ask you a few things. Do you remember your imaginary vorpal bunny, the one whose existence we kept just between us?"

"Yes." Her image nodded, the gesture seeming somewhat skewed by the virtual environment's anomalies. "Mister Froufrou. I used to blame him whenever I did something that displeased you."

"Do you remember when we used to sit out in the backyard after dark and look at the stars, just you and me?"

"Like it was yesterday." A gentle aura of joy shoved the fear and uncertainty aside, and it felt so achingly familiar he could picture a happy little girl lying in the grass beside him pointing up at the night sky. "You told me about the constellations visible from old Earth, and the stories behind them. And you made up constellations of your own to amuse me. Like the Giant Grampster and the Tipsy Clown Fisher."

Decker's heart suddenly felt like it would tear itself apart. Those were memories only he and Saga shared. His former spouse didn't approve of him filling her head with playful, lighthearted nonsense back then. And speaking of nonsense, one last question should confirm his instinctual conviction this really was his daughter. Or at least her VR avatar.

"Do you remember your favorite bedtime story, the one we kept a secret from your mother?"

Sadness filled the space around her. "Of course. I haven't heard it since the night before you left for the last time, but I'll always remember. Grampster Grumpy and the Big Bang."

The Marine felt tears welling up in his eyes. He'd invented that story when Saga was two and told it with regular variations almost every night he was home, and every time, she would giggle herself to sleep thanks to Grumpy's hilarious misadventures.

"It really is me, daddy."

"I know."

The moment his thoughts formulated those words, she dematerialized along with the virtual living room. He found himself alone, in a dark, formless place. For a few seconds, something akin to the feathery mind fingers of a Sister of the Void touched his thoughts Or more specifically, the fingers of a long-dead, psychopathic Sister with the ability to kill by projecting her neural energy into another's consciousness. Then, Decker's universe tilted again, and he was facing Chrome Dome once more, with Evil Pixie hovering beyond his field of vision as she removed the headband.

The Marine briefly wondered whether the strange sensation was an artifact of memories resurfacing because of the VR link before Chrome Dome asked, "Convinced?"

"Where is she?"

"A safe space, where she'll stay."

"Now what?"

Chrome Dome's tight-lipped smile came back for an encore. "Now we talk about you working for us, Major Decker."

"I told you that wouldn't happen."

"Funny how you still don't understand that failure to cooperate will entail consequences for Saga."

"What sort of consequences?"

"There's a thriving slave trade in the Protectorate, as you might know, being what passes for a Naval Intelligence officer these days. I'm sure you can figure out the rest yourself."

Decker's impassive gaze turned into a murderous stare. "Mark my words, you sleazy little fuck, I will kill you one day. Probably sooner than you expect." He turned his eyes on Evil Pixie. "You too, honey, and the rest of your evil lot. You've read my dossier, you know I will do so with absolutely no remorse."

"Perhaps, Major. But I doubt it. You're not like Hera Talyn, even though you pretend to be a cold-blooded assassin. Abandoning your daughter to a life of slavery on an alien world, to suffer every indignity one can possibly think of just isn't part of your moral makeup. You've hunted slavers and know what happens to humans out there once they fall into the wrong hands."

"And you've just joined the ranks of the walking dead, asshole. It's not a question of if, but when," Decker growled in a last burst of defiance. But he knew a show of cooperation so he could free Saga was the only choice. "Now tell me what you want."

"I'm sure you're familiar with the political situation on Scandia, and what may happen within the next week."

"Yeah. So what?"

"We want you to help us precipitate the looming constitutional crisis and make sure the Reform League is ousted, never to come near the levers of power again."

Decker cocked a mocking eyebrow, his disdainful expression hiding the rage burning deep within. "Is that all, my prince?"

"There is one more thing. Commander Talyn's considerable skills as an assassin are essential to this endeavor." He produced Zack's communicator. "Convince her to join you."

"Otherwise?"

"Otherwise, your lovely daughter will enjoy a taste of what life as an alien's property can be like." Chrome Dome gestured at the display behind him, showing a bewildered Saga still sitting on the sofa, the book abandoned, eyes on a pair of armed thugs staring at her. "They won't inflict permanent damage. At least not physically. And since she carries at least in part your DNA, she should also share your mental toughness to make it through the ordeal."

"Unshackle my hands and give me the damn communicator."

"We will do even better, Major. Now that you understand the price your daughter will pay if you don't become a wholehearted member of our team, we will release you from confinement. You'll be taken to an officer's suite, where you may refresh yourself and put on a change of clothes. Then, we will contact the delightful Hera Talyn from our command center. She should be in Vaasa by now, even if she took the slowest means of transportation available, short of walking."

"Just like that, I go from prisoner to *Sécurité Spéciale* operative?"

"You'd be surprised how many we've recruited using similar incentives." His habitual and to Decker increasingly annoying smile turned cruel. "We'll release your daughter once you've accomplished what we want, but by then, your deeds will ensure loyalty to the *Sécurité Spéciale.* Betraying us to your former Naval Intelligence superiors after that will not only end with your death by summary execution at their hands but guarantee a one-way ticket on a slaver's starship for the lovely Saga.

"Oh, you'll go back to Caledonia and your intelligence jobs once the Scandia mission is over, but with orders to further the Coalition's work. Orders that will help transform our chaotic, inefficient, and unruly Commonwealth into an empire capable of taking its rightful place in the galaxy. Of course, anything less than full cooperation until you've committed yourself to our cause by showing complete and utter submission will result in immediate death for Talyn and yourself, and a life of horror for Saga."

Chrome Dome made another of his hand gestures, and Decker's usual guards entered. Except this time, they removed both ankle and wrist restraints, then led him not back to his cell but to the lift.

— TWENTY-FOUR —

The communicator's gentle buzz took Talyn by surprise and she mentally cursed. Any call now could only mean bad news. Both Montero and *Phoenix* remained under radio silence, and Zack — he was presumably somewhere in that suspiciously large and well-defended compound barely visible above the treetops on the other side of Vaasa Bay.

She glanced around the small, almost empty cafe overlooking a steep, cliff-like shoreline, then pulled the device from her pocket. One look at its screen confirmed the call was from Zack, or more likely, from whoever held him. Considering they probably noticed *Phoenix*'s ping, her partner's captors must figure she'd be on the way to Vaasa, if not already there. This was the overture to negotiations.

She accepted the call. "Yes."

"Hey, honey, it's your Big Boy." The code Decker used told Talyn he was under coercion but cooperating for now and needed her to play along.

"Talk to me, lover." *Message understood. I will comply.*

"I've found Saga. The folks taking care of her made me an irresistible proposition. I need you at my side to help. Going along to get along can't be avoided."

A brief frown flashed across Talyn's face as she tried to divine the meaning behind Zack's words. Were Coalition henchmen holding a gun at Saga Lagman's head and forcing the Marine to do their bidding by threatening her?

"What do you want me to do?"

"Where are you?"

"In Vaasa. I presume they're holding you somewhere around here."

"Holding is no longer the right word. I've made new friends and climbed on a new bandwagon. They'd like you to join me in an endeavor that will further the Commonwealth's interests. Besides, Saga would very much appreciate your helping me because it would also help her."

Now Talyn understood. The opposition was using Zack's daughter to force his cooperation, and if she didn't go along, Saga would pay the price.

"You know I'd watch your back anywhere, anytime, and for any reason. Lay it out."

Talyn thought she heard relief in Zack's voice when he replied. "Take a taxi to a place called Saemund Manor, it's on the opposite side of Vaasa Bay from the town proper. I'll meet you at the gate."

"Will do. Until then."

"Until then."

Talyn debated whether to warn Montero about the latest developments. But after a last glance across the bay, she decided it would be better to leave no hint, faint as it might be, that another Naval Intelligence officer was operating on Scandia. Someone still needed freedom of action to help prevent Friday's suspected putsch.

She finished her coffee and left the terrace in search of a taxi.

**

The taxi dropped Talyn in front of a wrought iron gate that pierced a wall protected by sensors and what Talyn suspected were remote weapons stations. Decker chose that moment to come through the manor's front door. He wasn't alone. The man at his side, although thinner, older, and weaker looking than the Marine, was surrounded by an invisible, yet deadly nimbus she recognized as a kindred to her own.

He was another soulless human, capable of anything to further whatever cause he served. And in this case, the cause was that of the Coalition and its ambitions, since he was evidently *Sécurité Spéciale*, one of the SecGen's henchmen. A senior one if her instincts were correct. To see her partner at ease with such a man, and wearing a similar dark business suit, made her feel even colder inside.

What price did they put on Saga's life? His loyalty, which she thought to be inviolable? No, she couldn't believe he would give up that which defined his very being — the deeply held sense of honor that made him Zachary Thomas Decker, Commonwealth Marine Corps. Her partner was playing a long game.

Decker smiled and raised his hand in greeting. "You took your time."

The gate slid aside silently, and Talyn stepped through, eyes never leaving the Marine and his shadow.

"Welcome, Commander Talyn," the latter said, with a brief bow of the head. "I am Spaeth, although Major Decker no doubt has several other, likely unflattering names for me. As you might surmise, I'm an officer in the *Sécurité Spéciale*, the organization you and he have just joined."

"How does that work?" She asked with a sardonic smile. "I don't recall volunteering for the SecGen's Own Scumbags."

Spaeth shook his head in mock exasperation. "Try to be polite, Commander. If you'll follow us, Major Decker will explain the situation. Once you understand your and his position, we can discuss the mission for which we've recruited you."

She glanced at Zack who returned a nod so faint, anyone else might miss it. But the expression in his eyes told her he was dead serious about cooperating with the *Sécurité Spéciale*. At least on the surface.

As Spaeth led them into the manor, he glanced over his shoulder at Talyn. "I assume you're armed, Commander. We won't take your weapons but please do nothing regrettable until you understand the situation."

"So you're saying I *can* do something regrettable once I know?" She smirked at him.

"I see you share Major Decker's questionable sense of humor."

"The big guy rubs off on me."

"In more ways than one," Zack added.

"What is this place, Ser Spaeth?" She asked.

"Saemund Manor belongs to the Scandian Security Intelligence Agency, which has temporarily turned it over to us. They use the manor mostly as a training institution. But its underground facilities have been turned into a black site not much different from the ones Naval Intelligence operates on Caledonia and elsewhere."

"Charming."

"I can show you around if you wish, but we'll be working in the institutional part of the manor, above ground. Major Decker can tell you about the black site beneath our feet."

Talyn looked around as they walked down a long corridor pierced by numbered doors on either side. Here and there, the odd bit of decoration on the walls provided a modicum of color. "The place looks very pedestrian."

"But it has excellent amenities for people such as you or me." Spaeth stopped at an open door and waved them through. "Major Decker has much to tell you. I shall return when he's done."

"You'll be listening?"

Spaeth inclined his bald head. "Of course. Trust is a dirty word in our business, don't you think?"

"Trust has its place, provided one verifies."

"Perhaps." Then, Spaeth vanished into the hallway, and the door to the small conference room slid shut with a soft sigh.

"So..." Talyn slowly walked around the oval, imitation wood table, examining her surroundings. "We work for the *Sécurité Spéciale* now, do we? You'll need to explain because I feel like I've stepped through the looking glass and might meet a giant rodent at any moment. Switching loyalties at my age isn't as easy as it might be for a youngster such as yourself."

Decker pointed at two adjoining chairs. "Why don't we sit? This will take a while to explain."

**

Talyn studied her partner's face when he finished telling her about his abduction, meeting Saga in a virtual reality environment and Spaeth's threat to sell his daughter into slavery.

"You're sure it was her?"

"A father can tell, Hera. There's no way they could fake it."

"I can think of a few ways, but they involve things that might kill her. What if she's already dead, or a mind probe vegetable?"

"Do you expect me to take that chance?" Decker's fingers touched the back of her left hand in what looked like a caress, but was, in fact, a tactile language taught to Special Operations agents.

We play along to gain time, find out where she is.

Talyn placed her right hand over Decker's.

And help overthrow the government?

"No, I don't, Zack."

What if we're tools to be discarded afterward? She tapped. *Or worse, means to compromise the Fleet?*

"As a wise man said, where there's life, there's hope. Saga's only hope is for us to switch sides."

We can fuck up the overthrow and still look like we're cooperating.

"You understand that once we've compromised ourselves by helping the *Sécurité Spéciale*, there's no way back. We'll be following in Manfred Yang's footsteps."

Decker chuckled. "Actually, we'll be doing one better. You and I will work directly with the SecGen's minions rather than a cabal of deluded officers led astray by the Coalition."

"And if I say no?"

"Our new friends will deal with you while I carry out the mission. I won't let you do anything that'll end up with Saga as some alien bastard's flesh doll deep inside the Protectorate Zone."

"I could kill you right here and now before Spaeth's gorillas can intervene."

If saving her means chaos, she must be sacrificed.

Talyn held her partner's stare until Decker nodded his grudging acceptance. "But we've been a team for too long, Zack. Let's see where this takes us. In other words, I'm with you."

We'll sort these assholes out.

Talyn gave him a final caress. *I hope you're right.*

Spaeth chose that moment to return. He gave them an ironic smile. "I'm glad to see you're intimate enough to hold hands. That means my extra motivation will be as effective as I've hoped."

Decker gave him a dangerous glare. "What do you mean?"

"I believe you'll work with us to save your daughter from a fate worse than death, Major, but Commander Talyn has no such motivation. She couldn't care for Saga Lagman's fate if she tried. It's just not in her. Your fate on the other hand..." Spaeth turned his eyes on Talyn. "Believe me when I tell you this. Should you fail to follow our orders, Major Decker's daughter will be sold into slavery, and he will die."

"How do you propose to kill him, considering every attempt on his life so far ended in failure?"

"When Major Decker communed with the lovely Saga in the VR environment, we planted something akin to a mental bomb in his subconscious. Given the proper instructions, it will kill him by tricking his brain into believing it was under chemical interrogation. You can guess what happens once his conditioning kicks in." He paused for effect before continuing. "The human psyche is a powerful thing, Commander. You'll find that contrary to Naval Intelligence, the *Sécurité Spéciale* has not shied away from weaponizing it. As I was telling Major Decker, we ran a very promising project a few years ago. It produced enough results before its abrupt end to give our scientists a way of using virtual reality as a control mechanism."

Talyn snorted in disbelief to hide a sinking feeling in her gut as she connected Spaeth's words with Doctor Sakal's research, interrupted only when Decker rescued her from Coalition servitude. "I find that very hard to believe." When she glanced at her partner only to see understanding dawn in his eyes, the sick feeling solidified into an indigestible knot.

Decker now knew beyond any doubt the meaning of that brief mind touch after meeting his daughter in the VR environment.

"I don't find it hard to believe because I felt it happen without knowing what that was."

Spaeth's smile broadened. "Good. We won't waste time with a demonstration that can be extremely distressing. Now we're on the same page, we can move forward. Time is of the essence. We hoped to see you on our team well before today, but you've been incredibly hard to catch. I was wondering whether you cared for your biological daughter, Major Decker."

"We rarely respond to invitations delivered via illegal means, Spaeth," Zack replied. "Though I wonder if you clowns know legality from a tear in the fabric of space."

"*You* clowns?" Spaeth's tone was deliberately mocking. "Surely you mean *we* clowns, only don't mistake appearance for reality. We do things for the betterment of humanity that are beyond anything Naval Intelligence, and the Fleet as a whole can contemplate. Or perhaps even comprehend."

"Such as weaponizing the human psyche against its will."

Spaeth inclined his head. "Just so."

"How is that for the betterment of humanity?"

"Come now, Commander. Surely an experienced operative such as yourself understands that it is not the act itself but the results that count."

"One can't make an omelet without breaking eggs, or suborn a Marine officer and his partner without kidnapping and threatening a young woman's future."

"See, you understand." Spaeth gestured toward the door. "Shall we repair to the briefing room and introduce you to your mission? As I mentioned, time is fleeting, and I'm sure the major's daughter would like to resume her doctoral studies."

******

The briefing room was empty save for Evil Pixie, whose real name was Trulock. *Sécurité Spéciale* officers didn't seem to have first names or at least none they'd admit owning. Perhaps the SecGen didn't pay them enough to afford one. They took seats around a conference table while Trulock switched on a wall-sized display.

"In four days," Spaeth began, "the Scandian government, under the leadership of Prime Minister Dasco Dahlstein of the Reform League, will ask parliament to hold a vote enacting new legislation. And word is Dahlstein can count on the minor parties to give him more than the required two-thirds approval, thereby enshrining the new law as an amendment to the Scandian constitution. It will disrupt the long-standing balance of power in this star system. The ripples will be felt throughout the Rim Sector if not across human space.

"For many reasons, most of which you can probably guess, the SecGen and his administration wish to prevent Prime Minister Dahlstein from carrying out his intent. For the greater good of the Commonwealth, of course. Dahlstein has rebuffed representations made by the Commonwealth High Commissioner to Scandia and the

Scandian Governor General. This leaves us no options other than to remove his government."

"You remember that direct interference in star system affairs by Earth precipitated humanity's last civil war in which billions died, right? That the intra-human peace we've enjoyed since is based on respect for star system sovereignty?"

"Of course, Major. But in this case, a sizable part of the population, including the most important citizens, believe Dahlstein cannot be allowed to continue destroying what previous governments built over the last few decades."

Decker exhaled noisily. "Sizable does not mean a majority, Spaeth. I daresay the majority is happy at the respite from years of People's Alliance corruption and misrule, and is equally pleased with the prospect of never having to live through another multi-generation political dynasty."

"But that majority does not include those with the most stake in Scandia and its interests, be it here or elsewhere in the Rim Sector. I'm talking about the civil society and business leaders whose endeavors give this planet its high standard of living, something Dahlstein and his people are imperiling by their appeal to the blind prejudices of an unenlightened citizenry. In any case, I don't intend to debate planetary politics with you. Earth gave us a job and an explanation why this is necessary. I'm sure you're familiar with Alfred Lord Tennyson and his most famous poem."

Decker nodded. "Ours not to reason why."

"Consider it one of the *Sécurité Spéciale*'s unofficial mottoes. May I continue?"

"Sure. It's your mission briefing."

Spaeth touched controls embedded in the table's surface, and a man's image materialized on the display.

Lean, hard-faced, and dapper, he wore his blond, almost white hair in what Marines called a high and tight.

"Prime Minister Dasco Dahlstein."

The image of a woman joined Dahlstein's. She was handsome, well-coiffed with long platinum tresses. Although appearing somewhat older than the prime minister, she shared his elegance and steely look of determination.

"Alisa Berneiser, the Reform League's number two and many say the true power behind the prime ministerial chair. This pair represents the greatest threat to Commonwealth interests in the Rim Sector. They're widely reviled among those who still see Scandia as a progressive star system in sync with Earth's vision. Your mission will be to assassinate them this Friday, immediately before the parliamentary vote, thereby clearing the way for a national government of salvation under the leadership of the People's Alliance. The Alliance will be called on to do so by Governor General Viveca Nygaard, who also shares Earth's vision, and form a new cabinet with emergency powers until fresh elections can be held under the existing laws."

"So basically, our job is to precipitate a putsch against the duly elected government."

"That's the mission Earth has given us. I happen to share the opinion it's the only way we can prevent further rifts between restive star systems and the Commonwealth government. An example to encourage others if you like." Spaeth nodded at the display. "Commander Talyn, your target is Dahlstein, the more difficult of the two since he enjoys the protection of a special unit from the Scandian Police Authority. Major Decker, you're to assassinate Berneiser, who I understand is a good friend of Ingrid Lagman, Saga's mother. That gives you a way to move in without attracting undue attention. You have four days to prepare and deploy. Dahlstein and Berneiser must be dead by ten in the morning, Hamar time, on Friday."

"What if we're ready before Friday?"

"Then you will wait. Your actions are merely the trigger to set off a much larger sequence of events we've meticulously planned, events that depend on precise timing to avoid any unnecessary bloodshed and destruction."

"Such as the National Guard securing the parliamentary precinct, no doubt. In case the deaths of the planet's two leading political figures throws their party membership into disarray."

Another thin smile twisted Spaeth's lips. "Precisely. I'm glad to see you're getting into the spirit of things. You'll be granted access to the armory for whatever weapons and equipment you might wish, and of course the intelligence we've collected on both targets. Trulock will be at your disposal throughout the mission. Consider her your aide. And if you try to play us false, she'll be your executioner. She has access to the levers that trigger punishment for non-compliance."

Trulock gave Decker a hungry smile which he returned with a blown kiss and a leer.

Spaeth climbed to his feet. "If you need to speak with me, I'll be around until tomorrow morning. After that, I'm expected in Hamar. Don't disappoint us. You can expect a bright future working within our organization. The only alternative open to you is a painful death knowing an innocent will spend her life treated like an animal."

"Well." Decker rubbed his hands together with mock glee. "I'm convinced. Let's pour starship fuel over Scandia and light it up bright enough our sainted SecGen on Earth will see the extent of his power when he gazes at the night sky over Geneva."

"Wrong hemisphere, honey," Talyn replied. "He must be in the land of your distant ancestors to see us torch this world and wait a long time for visible light waves to reach Earth. We're better off sending him pictures via subspace radio."

"How about you two comedians start preparing? We don't enjoy the luxury of time and failure will guarantee a bleak future for Saga Lagman, not to mention the end of your lives."

Decker gave his partner a look of exasperation. "Did you notice our new colleagues are masters at the fine art of being killjoys?"

TWENTY-FIVE

"Gimme another shot and a beer, Tolo." A stout man bellied up to the bar beside Montero. His short hair, leathery face, and long-distance squint marked him as a career noncom, like many in this pub. It, and the one he visited with Talyn before she left to find her partner, seemed to serve as an annex to the Hamar Brigade's sergeants' mess. "Every time I think about the damn parade practice they laid on for Friday I get thirsty all over again."

"You guys celebrating something, or are your officers getting bored?" Montero asked.

The noncom sized him up, eyes lingering on the tall glass of amber ale in the agent's hand. "What's it to you, stranger?"

Montero gave the man a crooked smile. "Twenty years in the Commonwealth Army before I cashed out and set myself up as an independent trader. I've lived through plenty of officer nonsense back in the day."

"You were a noncom?"

"Sergeant first class, infantry, Cimmeria Regiment. The name's Dmitri Rauck." Montero drained his glass and caught the bartender's eye. "Give me a shot and a beer as well. Put his on my tab."

"That's mighty nice of you, Dmitri. I'm Johan Eltham, Hamar Brigade, Scandian National Guard. I'm a company quartermaster sergeant. What brings you here?" Eltham studied Montero with the gimlet eye of an old soldier who believes he can spot bullshit in a microsecond.

"I'm here for a bit of intercourse and intoxication after a successful run into the Protectorate. A few days doing nothing useful and then it's off again on my next contract."

"Good pay?" Eltham picked up the shot glass and downed it, then sighed.

"Better than the Army." Montero imitated the Scandian, though he almost choked on the high octane aquavit. "And no bored officers with the urge to parade their troops up and down the damn square."

"Sounds like good work." Eltham took a healthy sip of his beer. "But me, I'm a homebody. Can't see my ass riding starships across the damned galaxy, so I'll put up with her nibs starting the rehearsals a few weeks early."

"Rehearsals for a special ceremony?"

"You could say that. Once a year, the entire Hamar Brigade marches through the streets to exercise its Freedom of the City, with bands, regimental colors, full dress uniforms — the whole bit. Except this time, we'll be doing a mounted tour and taking our combat cars on parade. I suppose it was the mayor's idea to juice up the pizzazz in an election year. And what the mayor wants, her nibs the brigade commander dishes out, if you know what I mean. And just for fun, we're starting rehearsals so damn early we'll be practiced out by the time the main event rolls around in six weeks. At least we'll be rehearsing in battledress until the last two or three runs next month."

"Better you than me." Montero drained his beer and gestured at the bartender to serve another round.

"Maybe I'll watch your brigade go through its paces, see if I miss my days in a green suit."

"I can think of better ways to waste your time." Fresh shot and beer glasses appeared before them. "Thank you kindly, Dmitri Rauck. Skoal."

"Skoal." This time Montero swallowed the fiery liquid without problems. "By Friday I figure I'll be done with I&I."

"I don't see how that's possible, but hey, none of my business. You want to watch us prance around, we go from the barracks up Mannerheim Boulevard past parliament to city hall and then back home via Helsingborg Avenue. They told us to be on the parade square for nine-thirty, so by the time everyone gets their asses in gear, we'll be through the main gate at ten." Something caught Eltham's attention, and he said, "Thanks for the drinks, my friend. Next time we're both in here, it'll be my turn."

Montero watched the Scandian noncom amble off to join a group of newly arrived drinkers, then climbed to his feet and left the pub. Company Quartermaster Sergeant Johan Eltham had just given him the last piece of the puzzle and confirmed the rumors he'd picked up over the previous two days. That the National Guard's Hamar Brigade would happen to parade past the parliamentary precinct on Friday, weeks early was no coincidence. And they would do so in battledress while riding their combat cars.

In his estimation as a veteran intelligence operative, the degree of confidence Scandia was a few days away from a coup d'état topped eighty percent. The only thing that might stop the National Guard from backing a government ouster by force of arms was the Scandia Regiment. And without orders, its commanding officer couldn't be blamed for staying on the sidelines.

Federal intervention into the affairs of sovereign star systems without Commonwealth Senate sanction entailed far-reaching political consequences, not to mention personal consequences for those who presumed to usurp the Senate's authority. But Montero nevertheless felt an obligation to try warning Colonel Salminen of the imminent danger, whether or not Decker's groundwork would allow him through Fort Hardrada's main gate, let alone into Salminen's office.

He booked a seat on the following morning's first suborbital shuttle to Kollsvik. Then, ensconced in his dingy hotel room, Montero drafted an update to his last intelligence report, which he sent to *Phoenix* for onward transmission via secure Fleet subspace radio. With only four days left, and counting the time it would take for his report to reach Caledonia, there was nothing HQ could do any more to influence the situation. He could only hope Talyn found Decker before things went pear-shaped. Then he could turn everything over to agents better versed than he was in the fine art of overthrowing governments and therefore how to prevent such an occurrence.

**

Talyn declined the offer of a private suite and joined Decker in his after a long day studying their targets' habits and habitats. They made little conversation while preparing for bed, but once the lights were out and both beneath the covers of the suite's single bed, she grasped his left wrist with her right hand and tapped out words.

We can't assassinate those two. If people find out Fleet officers did it, things will turn ugly fast. In fact, I bet that's the plan. Blame the Fleet. It plays into their hands.

Decker, in turn, grasped her wrist.

Sure. But we find my daughter first. Once she's safe, we wipe out these assholes.

And the booby trap in your head? I don't want to lose you.

He grinned at her in the darkness.

They don't know what I can do if I put my mind to it.

You can disarm?

I can try.

And if you fail?

Then you're free to act.

Be careful.

Always.

Decker released her wrist to signal the silent conversation was over and turned onto his back, eyes closed. "Good night, Hera."

"Good night, Zack. Try to keep the nightmares away." He understood she meant the dreadful prospect of a violent death triggered by his own brain.

"You and everyone else keep forgetting that I am the nightmare."

He soon fell into a meditative trance, the sort taught to agents as a fallback when held captive or placed under duress. It allowed him to separate his thoughts from his being's physical shell. The mental IED planted by Spaeth's infernal virtual reality setup would likely sit somewhere on the threshold between his subconscious and conscious mind. It needed to hide from him while remaining alert to the external stimulus that would set it off and kill him.

Spaeth and his *Sécurité Spéciale* researchers might have continued the work started by Doctor Sakal, now living under Fleet protection and a new identity, and the rogue Sister of the Void, Anca. However, they weren't aware of his own sensitivity to mind-meddling.

No one was, besides Hera Talyn, Commodore Kos Ulrich, and an exile on Parth's Desolation Island condemned to die there after a life of privation. And, as he reminded himself, a pair of secluded Sisters of the Void on Garonne, though they didn't know his identity, unlike the other three. Fortunately, he'd convinced his partner and his commanding officer to keep the knowledge closely held. In light of Manfred Yang's treason, that caution seemed almost prescient.

Once he felt an eerie sense of detachment from his inner self, Decker turned back and contemplated the amorphous construct representing both his conscious and unconscious mind. Memories clamored for his attention, as did worries, not least about Saga's fate.

Murderous rage at Spaeth and the *Sécurité Spéciale* tried to shove its way through the fog of emotions hindering his vision. Gently, one by one, he pushed them away to free a path leading him to the darker corners of his self, where long-suppressed parts of his personality still lived. His self-destructive temper crouched in one corner, eying him with suspicion while in another he found the unbridled appetites that dragged him into a semi-alcoholic stupor long ago.

Unexpectedly, Decker came face-to-face with a kernel of pain, the remnant of his near-death experience in a juluk pit on a world far away. The juluk, venomous, biting insects native to that planet, had been unleashed on his body at the order of alien slave masters as a means to break his spirit and turn him into a docile, loyal janissary. But without success.

Now, in retrospect, Decker understood that the juluk venom and its effect on his nervous system were at the root of his ability to sense intrusions into his mind. He didn't know about the talent until his first encounter with a Sister of the Void after freeing himself from bondage. Whether it was there, but dormant before his excruciating experience with juluk would remain a mystery. However, Decker's lifelong, instinctive suspicion of the Void Sisterhood might be a good indication.

He punted the kernel back into the past, knowing it would never plague him again. Then Decker gently examined the outer edges of his conscious mind where it vanished into something both less and more than the sum of who he was. His search was akin to that of a doctor palpating his patient, looking for an elusive cancerous nodule hidden beneath the skin.

Then, his mind's eye stumbled across something self-contained, silent and brooding. It existed within him but wasn't part of his thoughts or memories. The closest analogy Decker could visualize was a mental black hole, absorbing his neural energy and emitting nothing in return. As he watched the thing, he sensed it growing, pulsating, gathering strength, waiting until it was time to burst and kill its host.

Touching the intruder's edges and feeling the malevolence trapped within, Decker realized the question wasn't whether Spaeth or Trulock would eventually trigger it. Instead, it was a matter of when the mind killer would strike unprompted once its power reached a critical mass. The *Sécurité Spéciale* didn't intend to keep him alive after he'd done their bidding and assassinated Berneiser.

He gingerly probed around the seething nodule, looking for an opening, something that would allow him to sever it from his being. But in vain. Though seemingly crude, especially compared to Sister Anca's intrusions when she'd probed Decker's mind, it nonetheless felt solidly attached.

Decker would die within a few days, shortly after the putsch, becoming a Fleet assassin's corpse to be displayed as proof of the military's illegal interference in star system politics. That Talyn was doomed to a similar fate, if not through similar means, seemed beyond question. And what of Saga?

The Marine slowly swam up from the depths of his meditative trance and once more found himself in a darkened bedroom with Talyn at his side. He felt exhausted. After listening to his partner's breathing rhythm for a few seconds, Decker realized she was awake and watching him. He grasped her wrist and tapped with his fingers.

No can do. The booby trap is solidly attached. Will try again when I'm rested. But I figure it's on a timer in addition to a command detonator. Whether or not I cooperate, I won't survive past Friday.

She returned the grip.

A dead Marine to incriminate the Fleet.

Yes. And if they programmed me to die, the bastards will kill you as well. Sorry for getting us into this mess.

Didn't you tell me where there's life, there's hope? We have four days to figure it out and stop the coup. And inform the boss about our enemies' new weapon. That discovery alone makes this worthwhile.

You think we'll find my kid before it's too late?

She smiled at him. *Hell, yeah.*

**

Montero, still traveling as Dmitri Rauck, rented a ground car at the Kollsvik spaceport shortly after landing aboard the morning's first suborbital run from Hamar. Rauck's name and ID didn't raise any alarms when he booked his flight, or when he let the rental company's AI scan Rauck's payment card.

He stopped at the side of the road leading out of Kollsvik, just before reaching the Fort Hardrada turnoff, and transformed himself back into Lieutenant Commander Garrett Montero, minus a Navy uniform. Though he tucked the disguise and false credentials into his overnight bag's secret compartment, Montero understood Rauck was condemned to vanish just like his other cover identities.

The sergeant in charge of Hardrada's main gate security made him park the rental car in the visitor's lot, after subjecting it to a thorough scan. Then, two soldiers from the guard detail escorted Montero across the fort to the regimental headquarters building and Captain Rantanen's office. Though a naval officer who was not particularly familiar with the Army's peacetime routine, he nonetheless decided that Hardrada was imbued with a heightened sense of purpose.

It was especially noticeable in the number of troops, armed and armored, moving about with energy, and in the distant sounds of mock warfare emanating from the training area beyond the fort's defensive walls. He fervently hoped the unexpected level of activity stemmed from Decker convincing Colonel Salminen the Fleet couldn't let offworld interests throw Scandia, and thereby the Rim Sector, into political turmoil.

Montero managed only a quick glance at the captured Shrehari standard in its display case as the senior of the two soldiers, a corporal, led him through the HQ lobby and up the winding stairs. There, the noncom aimed them at an open door marked 'Adjutant.' He rapped his knuckles on the wood frame. "Lieutenant Commander Montero, sir."

"Please send him in, Corporal. You can return to your duties."

He stamped to attention. "Yes, sir." Then, he pivoted on his heels and left.

Upon entering the spacious office, Montero caught sight of a middle-aged, stern-faced captain with the weary lines of a veteran soldier beneath short silver hair. She rose from behind a cluttered desk and waved him toward an empty chair, her expression carefully neutral.

"I'm Laila Rantanen, sir. May I assume you're one of the two Navy officers from JSOC who came off the ship currently sitting on our ATC's tarmac?"

"Correct, Captain. I'm also a colleague of Major Zack Decker, who I believe passed through Hardrada a few days ago."

"Passed through is right, sir. One night and then he vanished."

"Your regimental sergeant major was kind enough to warn us via *Phoenix*'s AI. My CO, Commander Talyn, is looking for Major Decker as we speak. We believe he was abducted by enemies of the Commonwealth and is being held in Vaasa."

Rantanen's eyebrows crept up her forehead. "Really?"

"Was Major Decker able to brief Colonel Salminen before his disappearance?"

She nodded with a guarded look in her eyes. "He was."

"Then you'll know about our suspicions offworlders are working with elements in the People's Alliance and the Scandia security forces to overthrow Prime Minister Dahlstein's government ahead of Friday's parliamentary vote."

"Yes."

"These same offworlders seized Major Decker to prevent him and thereby JSOC from intervening via your regiment, or so my CO, and I believe."

"Would his daughter's disappearance play a role in that, Lieutenant Commander?"

"We believe she was used as bait."

"Even though Saga Lagman disappeared quite sometime before Decker showed up?" A booming voice behind Montero asked. "I'm Vaino Salminen, by the way."

Montero stood and came to attention. "Pleasure, sir. Garrett Montero. And to answer your question, that remains a mystery. Saga Lagman's situation might not be directly connected but used opportunistically to waylay Zack. Perhaps we'll know more once Commander Talyn finds him."

"Apparently he's in Vaasa," Rantanen said.

"Any idea where?" He glanced at Montero. "It's my hometown. Our 3rd Battalion is based there."

"I can give you the coordinates of Commander Talyn's search target, sir."

"Pass them to Laila and let's see what we're facing." Salminen took the other chair in front of his adjutant's desk and motioned at Montero to sit.

A minute or so later, the satellite image of a large, walled-in compound at the steep shoreline's edge appeared on Rantanen's office display. Salminen nodded, frowning. "Bad news, Lieutenant Commander. That belongs to the Scandian Security Intelligence Agency. The run a training center there and if rumors are true, a black site beneath it."

"Which would fit, since your regimental sergeant major said he believed the SSIA was involved in Zack's abduction."

"Yes. A nasty piece of work by the name Mariel Lazarre. But why would the SSIA do this?"

"We believe they're working with or on behalf of an agency controlled by the Secretary-General's office on Earth, an organization with a similar mandate to the SSIA's, only Commonwealth-wide. Its operatives turn being vile into a virtue. And among other ugly habits, the agency in question likes to target JSOC and intelligence officers, with the likes of Zack Decker sitting high on their list."

"Since you showed up on our doorstep, am I right to assume you're looking for help?"

"Actually, sir, unless Commander Talyn asks for backup, I'll let her handle Decker's situation. What I'm here about is the planned coup d'état."

"Supposed coup d'état."

"Sir, I've spent the last few days in Hamar, ferreting out whatever I could from whoever I could, including the National Guard. Something will happen on Friday morning. My experience with political unrest in this sector screams putsch. Let me explain." While Montero spoke, Salminen kept a guarded, almost skeptical expression until the agent relayed his conversation with Sergeant Johan Eltham about the Hamar Brigade's unusual parade rehearsal. At that point, the colonel's face turned grim.

"We always sent a delegation to witness the Freedom of the City ceremonies, as one does, I suppose. But I've never heard them practice six weeks early, and they've never, in my lifetime, done it mounted in combat cars. Even cavalry units exercise their Freedom of the City on foot."

"And just before parliament is scheduled to hold that controversial vote," Rantanen added. "The National

Guard leadership is too politically savvy for it to be a coincidence or an example of lousy planning. If you want my opinion, Colonel, I think that clinches it. Major Decker is right."

Salminen grunted. "I've always believed Decker was onto something. That's never been my problem." He looked at Montero. "Nevertheless, thank you for coming here with the latest intelligence."

"Am I right to think your regiment is at a heightened state of vigilance, sir? I got that impression when I dove up from the main gate just now."

"So far, everyone but a few of my closest staff think I'm putting the unit through an unplanned and unexpected deployment exercise. We do those from time to time. Often we even leave Hardrada and the other forts for battle training elsewhere on the planet. The reason I'm putting the regiment through its paces under the guise of training is due to dissension within my command staff. A few are shy of acting in the absence of orders to the point I can't risk planning an intervention as such, lest word gets out and we become a factor in precipitating this crisis. So I improvised."

Montero nodded in agreement. "A wise course of action, sir."

"Of course, your news that the Guard intends to deploy under cover of a parade practice just put an uncomfortable veneer of realism on my so-called exercise. It means I must now figure out ways we can put ourselves between them and parliament without causing massive bloodshed, and their using combat cars worries me. While I can send a fully equipped infantry battalion to Hamar in a matter of hours using my organic aviation assets, getting my own armored vehicles there will take time.

"Pre-positioning them at such short notice might well alert the Guard since we always warn them ahead of time whenever we leave the confines of our military reservations. Let's hope the Guard's commanders will be wise enough to hold fire while the politicians sort this mess out." Salminen sighed. "Unfortunately, the National Guard's chief of staff, Kristoffer Karlsen, and the commander of the Hamar Brigade, Ula Brand, are People's Alliance creatures through and through. They know their stars won't be worth a timber wolf's droppings if they fail their patrons."

"On the other hand," Rantanen said, "they and most of the senior officers enjoy little respect among the rank and file, if the Guard's noncom grapevine isn't spinning tales. Brand might find her soldiers reluctant to go up against Commonwealth troops, especially under leaders they don't particularly trust."

"While we might find ours reluctant to open fire on compatriots in Guard uniforms. Let's pray we can stare them down long enough for the moment of greatest danger to pass with no ammo expenditure." Salminen gave Montero a rueful smile. "That's one of the Army's biggest weaknesses — serving the Commonwealth's interests on our homeworlds. We always worry about what would happen if they come into violent disagreement with Earth."

"I think in this case, sir, you will serve Scandia's interests as a sovereign star system by acting, even if doing so clashes with what Earth might prefer."

"That's the sole reason I'm actually contemplating putting my regiment and my career on the line."

"I wouldn't be surprised if you find Fleet HQ supporting an intervention. It knows of the situation. Our team, meaning Commander Talyn, Major Decker, and I, were ordered to proceed at our discretion, which is JSOC speak for take whatever action necessary to protect the most lives."

"I won't count on it, but thanks for the encouragement." He climbed to his feet with a weariness that spoke of his worries. "Laila will take care of getting you settled in, assuming, of course, you plan to see this through with us."

"Thank you, sir, and yes, I intend to stay and act as your JSOC liaison and intelligence analyst. I can also move at least a full company's worth of armored troops faster than any of your aviation assets aboard *Phoenix*. Or turn her into the sort of close air support that'll make even the bravest run for cover. There's nothing quite like a starship doing a low altitude pass over enemy positions with its gun turrets deployed to increase the value of toilet paper futures."

Salminen chuckled. "I'm beginning to like you, Garrett Montero."

— TWENTY-SIX —

Trulock watched Decker and Talyn with a faintly mocking smile as they filed into the briefing room after a silent breakfast taken under the dull stares of the two goons who'd captured Zack. "I trust your night was restful. Today's schedule will be grueling so we can make up for lost time."

"It was adequate."

"Really?" The mocking smile grew. "We detected heightened brain activity in both of you shortly after lights out. In your case, Major, it was off the charts and didn't settle for hours. What were you doing, I wonder? Searching for the little control mechanism we planted in your thoughts? Don't bother. You won't find it, never mind purge it. Just remember that one step out of line means you die in agony and your daughter... Well, you know what will happen to her. But don't hold back if you feel the urge to disobey. Your death and her sale into slavery would be entertaining to watch."

Out of reflex, Decker took a quick look into himself and spotted the malignant pustule almost immediately. Once seen by his mind's eye, it could not be unseen. He gave Trulock a lazy grin. "If you say so."

"I do, and I'm never wrong about these things. So far, I've maintained a perfect score."

"In what? Getting it right or killing people?"

"Both." She nodded at the main display. "Now that you've digested the information about your targets, we'll discuss how you're to carry out the mission."

Talyn shook her head. "That's not how it works, Trulock. Assassins are free to choose their own way of doing the job, provided they stay within mission parameters. We will develop our own plans."

"There's no time, Commander. This happens in seventy-two hours, give or take, and we've already done the legwork to figure out our best course of action. That's the one you'll be taking since we can't afford to let you run another recon of the targets and sites." When Talyn opened her mouth to respond, Trulock said, "Remember what's lurking in your partner's brain and the consequences of non-cooperation."

Talyn inclined her head by way of acknowledgment though her tone carried an acerbic edge. "Since it's the only brain he has, please go ahead and tell us how we're to kill Scandia's prime minister and his most important backer."

"Thank you so much for understanding your lack of options. Constant arguments quickly become tiresome. The mission, or rather the two missions are actually quite simple." Trulock explained the plans she and Spaeth had drawn up in precise detail, using images and holo-projections to make sure there would be no misunderstandings.

Decker and Talyn digested the information in silence for several minutes. Then the Marine said, "Since you expect this to work, I guess you have people inside the SSIA and the Scandian Police Authority. Folks who won't do their jobs properly."

"Just so, Major. Who they are and what they do isn't important for your purposes. It suffices that you know security around the prime minister and Alisa Berneiser will be compromised sufficiently to permit the assassinations."

"I'm not clear on how you expect the extraction to work once we're done," Talyn said. "You seem to assume everything will proceed as per plan and we're guaranteed to slip away before law enforcement shows up, which rarely happens in the real world."

"Again, Commander, we have people in the right places to ensure you not only find your targets but escape afterward."

"And that includes the Berneiser household?" Decker asked. "I can see how I'll get in using my relation to Ingrid and Saga. But that place is a fortress. Once the alarm is raised, it turns into a doorless cube, and I'm a sitting duck for the Police Authority's Special Branch shooters."

"The plan allows ample time to leave before our people on the inside raise the alarm."

Talyn cocked a skeptical eyebrow at the *Sécurité Spéciale* officer. "My partner and I don't appear to share your sanguine view of the matter."

"Because you don't understand the full picture. Trust me, we don't want you to be caught."

No, you want us to die, Decker thought, convinced more than ever they were to become damning evidence against the Fleet. But will that be before or after the targets are dead?

Trulock stood. "If there are no further questions, we'll start rehearsing. The SSIA has a comprehensive simulator setup here, and we've programmed it to replicate the conditions you can expect on Friday in every detail. Killing in this sim doesn't give you the same rush as in real life, but it's a close second."

**

"Why don't I introduce you to the regimental S-2, Major Hanson Trostorf, since you wish to help with intelligence analysis?" Rantanen suggested after Colonel Salminen retreated back into his office so he could mull over Montero's news.

"Absolutely. I've never witnessed the inner workings of an Army all-sources intelligence center."

"Then you're about to receive an education. The S-2 activated his ASIC when the colonel ordered our deployment exercise yesterday." She stood and came around her desk. "And he's very particular about doing things correctly as per doctrine. But please no mention of us taking action in Hamar. Major Trostorf is one of those sitting on the fence, with strong leanings toward non-intervention. As far as he and his staff are concerned, we're merely carrying out a bit of unplanned training, to shake the regiment from its garrison torpor."

"Does this so-called exercise include the outlying battalions, such as the one in Vaasa?"

"Certainly." Rantanen led him down the massive stairs, past the captured Shrehari battle standard, and into one of the building's extensive wings. "Were you wondering whether it might help Major Decker and your commanding officer?"

"If it comes to that, perhaps. I'm trying to cover every eventuality, in case Commander Talyn is unable to retrieve Zack on her own, or is taken by the enemy herself."

"I see. Then maybe our training exercise should include plans to capture the SSIA training center in Vaasa under the pretext it's been seized by insurgents. You'll not find the CO of the 3rd Battalion averse to such a thing, nor to actually carrying it out. We don't much like the SSIA. The feeling is mutual. As federal troops, we're beyond their jurisdiction, and they bitterly resent the notion. I'll introduce you to the S-3, Lieutenant Colonel Birgit Carstens, later today so you can discuss the idea."

"I'm grateful to you and your colonel for receiving me in this manner. Many units aren't as kind to a JSOC liaison officer appearing out of nowhere."

Rantanen's laugh was as humorless as it was sharp.

"Scandia has been quiet since the end of the Shrehari War. Other than the odd company or battalion group deployments on offworld missions to support the Marines, we do little more than train, or help the Scandian government when a natural disaster overwhelms civilian services and the National Guard. This could well turn out to be the first time the Scandia Regiment sees real action as a whole in over seventy years even if we're hoping it doesn't turn bloody. Right now, I'd say although he seems to carry the regiment's worries on his shoulders, Colonel Salminen is secretly having the time of his life."

"Not so I could tell."

"We Scandians, especially Suomalainen like the colonel and me, tend to keep our emotions under tight control and seem the same to outsiders whether we're deeply depressed or overjoyed."

Montero's step faltered when he felt his communicator vibrate.

"One moment please, Captain. I believe my ship is calling. Perhaps it has news of Commander Talyn and Major Decker." He fished the device from his tunic's inner pocket and glanced at the screen. "Well hot damn!"

"What is it?"

"Can we find a quiet spot where no one will overhear?"

"Certainly." Rantanen led him to a small conference room off a side corridor. "It's soundproofed and swept for listening devices on a weekly basis. Should I leave you?"

"No. I think you should hear this so you can report back to your colonel." He dropped into a chair and waited until the adjutant closed the door and sat. "*Phoenix* is transmitting a signal from orbit. It appears the Commonwealth Starship *Sorcerer* has arrived with a contingent from the 1st Marine Special Forces Regiment. They want to speak with either Commander Talyn or Major Decker. By the way, *Sorcerer* is a special operations Q-ship — a warship disguised as a civilian transport."

"I've been aboard one of those during my hitch in the Corps. Savoyard class, right?"

Montero nodded. "We were wondering if our reinforcements would arrive on time." Or at all, he thought. "But it seems Fleet Command was able to cut through the bureaucratic bullshit for once." He brushed his thumb across the communicator's controls. "Lieutenant Commander Garrett Montero here."

"This is *Sorcerer*. We are on a secure, encrypted connection. What is your designator, sir?" An anonymous male voice replied.

Montero gave Rantanen a quick glance. "Close your ears, Captain." Then, "Topkapi gamma five nine alpha two bravo zeta."

A moment of silence. "Designator accepted, Topkapi. We're looking for Rookie Trooper or Dark Fury."

"Both are unavoidably detained right now, with emphasis on detained."

"Is there anything H Troop, 1st Special Forces Regiment can do to help with that?" Another male voice asked.

"We've worked with both of them before, which is probably why JSOC tapped us for this mission."

"And you are?"

"Command Sergeant QD Vinn, sir. I'm the troop leader. They didn't tell me much when they bundled us aboard *Sorcerer* for a trip to the Scandia system. But if it's at Decker's request, then I guess we're here to help him save the galaxy again."

Montero chuckled. "Perhaps not the entire galaxy, but a small corner. What's your strength?"

"Forty, myself included. We have two armed dropships and the gear necessary for a combat jump from low orbit, including spares for Decker and Talyn. We're full up on ammo and supplies as well."

"I'm with the Scandia Regiment at Fort Hardrada. They've been brought in on our mission. So what I'd like to do is set up a conference call involving you, your command team, *Sorcerer*'s captain, and whoever he wants present as well as the Scandia Regiment's CO and his folks. The comlink we're on right now is being relayed via my ship, but for this, we'll set up a direct connection via the Hardrada signals facilities."

Montero glanced at Rantanen, who gave him a thumbs up. "Give me an hour to prepare everything, sir."

"You hear that, Sergeant?"

"Yep. One hour. We'll be waiting."

"Excellent. Glad you're here. Decker will be even happier that his own tribe is rallying to the cause. Once we pull him out of the opposition's clutches."

"Again?" Vinn chuckled. "That seems to be the story of his life."

Montero cut the link and sat back in his seat with a smile. "I'm suddenly feeling much better about this."

"I'll take you to meet the S-2. You can talk while I organize the conference call."

**

Sorcerer's captain, a Navy commander wearing a merchant officer's uniform and insignia, like the rest of his command team, let out a low whistle once Montero finished speaking.

"You intelligence folks don't do things by half. Now I understand why they ordered me to reach Scandia as fast as possible, with no concern for the wear and tear on my ship's drives. We set a record, by the way. But the old girl lost a few years of useful life in the bargain. Only an aviso can do better. But if you don't mind me saying so, shoving the Fleet's nose into planetary affairs without Senate sanction is beyond risky, though I suppose that's why you're entitled to spook-level bonus pay."

The moment Salminen heard the word 'intelligence,' he speared Montero with a cold stare. The agent gave him an apologetic shrug.

"My colleagues and I belong to Naval Intelligence, sir, that's true, but we're from a division which spends its life working with JSOC. We're not what you would call sneak and peek agents."

"They're the sort who drag JSOC units into the worst trouble spots," Commander Len Pirillo said with a dry chuckle. "Garrett's lot are good at finding and sorting out bad situations before they turn into complete and utter chaos. And they often do it with a bang."

"That's the impression I got from Major Decker."

"Speaking of which," Vinn, who wore unmarked, mercenary-style battledress, said, "I suggest we put a recon team on the ground near his communicator's last known location. It, and what *Sorcerer*'s sensors manage to pick up should give us a good idea if he and Commander Talyn are in fact there, and what we might do to help.”

“Can you reach Vaasa from orbit without detection? I mean other than jumping?”

“Sure, Colonel. I propose having one of *Sorcerer*’s unmarked shuttles land the team at your 3rd Battalion’s garrison — Fort Lothbrok, correct?”

Salminen nodded. “Correct.”

“From there, they’ll move out and case the SSIA training academy without the enemy knowing. Depending on what they find, we can reconvene and discuss options. If that’s okay with you, Commander Montero.”

“Of course, provided Colonel Salminen agrees.”

“I agree, and I’ll do you one better, Sergeant. We’ll arrange anonymous ground transport and anything else you need.” Salminen glanced at his operations officer, who nodded.

“Thank you, sir. Operating with friendlies already in place always makes things easier.” Vinn’s dark eyes switched to Montero. “About the suspected putsch, what do you expect from H Troop, Commander? Surely we weren’t sent here on an emergency basis just to rescue Major Decker, and possibly Commander Talyn.”

Montero gave the noncom an embarrassed smile. “That would actually be Zack’s area of expertise. He’s the one who asked for you, and he’s the one with experience in carrying out dirty tricks against planetary governments, or in this case, preventing them.”

“I see. So to find the answer, we need to retrieve his wayward ass. Just another day in the life of the Special Forces Regiment, I guess.”

"How soon can you put a recon team on the ground in Vaasa?"

Vinn turned to Pirillo. "Sir?"

"By the time your people sort themselves out, the shuttle will be ready to launch."

"In five minutes, then?" Vinn's mischievous grin brought a smile to Salminen's careworn face.

"Four, if you want."

"You're making this too easy, sir."

Salminen shook his head at the lighthearted banter. "We'll let Fort Lothbrok know to expect your people within the next two hours."

"Thank you, sir. Staff Sergeant Carrie Paulus will lead the recon team. They'll be in civilian getup, with weapons and gear hidden on their persons and in their packs. Sergeant Paulus will identify herself to whoever greets the shuttle. Two ground cars would be excellent, but if you can only provide one, that'll work as long as it carries eight people."

"I'm sure we'll manage two. There are enterprising noncoms in the 3rd Battalion who run a sideline selling used cars. Their fleet magically turns into rentals whenever visiting troops land in Vaasa. In your case, they'll be glad to waive the fees."

"We'll pay for any breakage, sir. It's in the budget."

"I'm sure my entrepreneurs will be relieved to hear that."

**

Decker tossed the sim gear aside and shoved his way through the emergency door out into Saemund Manor's inner courtyard. Although his sweat-streaked face showed no emotions, Talyn could read the thunder in his eyes when she joined him to bask in the afternoon sunshine.

"Wasn't that special?" He glanced at her right hand. When she did the same, his fingers danced.

Did you notice how the escape part of the simulation keeps feeling like an afterthought? Like they didn't bother entirely formulating it? We're meant to die.

Agreed. I doubt they intend to let your kid go either.

Yeah. We bust out, find Saga, and nuke this place.

Once you disarm the bomb in your head.

If I can't, you bust out. Warn the targets. See that their security is vetted. The bastards may have a backup plan.

Decker saw the usual two goons step through one of the manor's doors and stroll around the inner perimeter, keeping an eye on their charges.

How many tangos are we facing?

Those two, the woman. I saw two more earlier, so at least five. Probably a few more to handle surveillance.

Good odds for us.

Until the woman triggers your IED.

So I kill her before she can. One hand around the neck and squeeze.

At that moment, the woman in question, Trulock, stuck her head out.

"Break's over, people. Let's do this again. Until you're sure of every bit, every reflex so you could do it half-sloshed, the simulator's your best friend."

"Choking her to death would be too kind," Talyn muttered. "She gives psychopaths a bad name."

"You just don't like her style."

"I hate the pixie haircut, especially on an intelligence officer."

"What's that?" Trulock gave them a strange look.

"Hera was just saying she'd love to know the name of your hair stylist."

"I'll introduce her after she kills Dahlstein, for which she still needs plenty of practice."

Decker wrapped his hand around Talyn's arm and tapped his fingers.

I know how you will die, or at least fail. Simulator imprint, so your reaction time is slowed when things go differently.

"Probably," she whispered.

Two dead Fleet assassins. The Senate will go ballistic.

That night, after lights out, Decker plunged back into the recesses of his mind and studied the thing that would kill him in three days if he didn't find a solution. And as before, his searching and probing proved to be in vain. Mentally exhausted, sleep overtook him the moment he came out of the meditative trance. But rest proved elusive.

**

"Ready, General?"

An aide-de-camp, a Marine colonel in full dress uniform, his right shoulder awash with knotted gold cords, came out of nowhere to join Decker in the otherwise empty antechamber.

It, like the rest of the palace, was once occupied by the Wyvern Governor General. But that worthy voluntarily vacated the premises when the newly formed empire decided on Wyvern as capital to replace Earth, which now had the status of a colony under an imperial administrator.

Decker took one last glance at his reflection in the full-length mirror standing to one side of large double doors. His black uniform didn't lack for gold adornments either, though they were a flag officer's ornate cuff, collar, and trouser piping, suitable for of a lieutenant general of Imperial Marines.

A five-pointed star he recognized as the Medal of Honor, humanity's highest award for valor, hung on a dark blue and silver ribbon around his neck. Decker's other decorations and awards crowded his left breast, beneath Pathfinder wings embroidered with too many combat stars to count, while a sheathed sword hung at his left hip.

He still wore the insignia of the Third Imperial Expeditionary Corps on his right upper sleeve even though the formation was stood down after Earth's pacification and its divisions scattered to other duty stations. All, that is, except one. It would permanently reside on Earth.

However, its garrison was nothing more than a monument to the memory of those who died when the last remnants of the Commonwealth detonated an antimatter device to obliterate their dying capital. Establishing the sacred site and supervising the monument's construction were among Decker's last acts before boarding a starship and leaving Earth to its fate.

Other corps commanders, in other star systems, were still busy imposing the empire's will, but the Commonwealth died on that fateful day in Geneva, with no hope of resurrection. Yet he knew the rats that prospered beneath the previous regime's rotten edifice already scurried about, finding new ways of rebuilding their wealth and reclaiming their influence.

The Coalition might have died along with its plans and ambitions when the Fleet set about to preserve humanity by destroying the sick, tottering edifice of a state inexorably sliding toward another destructive civil war.

But many of its members remained at large, even now worming their way into the new power structure.

At least the murderous *Sécurité Spéciale* had followed its forbear, the Special Security Bureau, into oblivion, and the Imperial Senate would not tolerate any new agencies reporting solely to the ruler. Matters concerning intelligence and security now belonged exclusively to the Imperial Constabulary and the Fleet.

"I'm about as ready as I'll ever be, Colonel." Decker knew the summons to court was in honor of his seizing and pacifying the cradle of humanity, thereby humbling it before the galaxy. That punishment, harsh though it might seem, was necessary to quash the sort of hubris that almost always led to a civilization's violent destruction and the extinction of entire populations.

Yet Decker wanted no more honors. On the contrary. He hungered for a chance to hand the emperor his resignation and slip into obscurity but knew permission to retire would be denied for as long as he remained sound of body and mind. The Marine grasped his sword's sheath in his left hand, momentarily soothed by the cold metal, then squared his shoulders.

"Lead on."

The massive doors made of dark, carved wood slid aside at the aide's gesture, opening onto a throne room lined with men and women in every variety of uniform.

"Lieutenant General Zachary Thomas Decker, Imperial Marine Corps."

At the far end of the polished marble floor, facing him, stood a man wearing a simple Marine's black tunic. It was without rank insignia or adornments other than the medals he'd earned beneath a set of gold combat Pathfinder wings. The flags of every star system and every branch of the services hung from the wall behind him, framing the new silver galaxy banner now uniting the human species.

Decker took a deep breath and then marched at a slow parade pace toward his liege. He felt the eyes of his peers, the admirals, generals and chief constables who swore the oath of fealty to an empire whose genesis he still couldn't quite understand, follow him. When he neared the man selected as ruler by those same flag officers now standing in attendance, Decker realized he couldn't make out his face, even though everyone else's was clear enough.

He stamped to a perfect halt three paces in front the throne and raised his right hand to his brow in salute.

"Lieutenant General Decker reporting to His Majesty as ordered."

Then, the emperor, his retinue, and the throne room dissolved. He found himself in complete darkness, save for a baleful, pulsating *thing* that seemed on the verge of absorbing everything he was and might become.

Decker woke with a start, and when he turned his head toward Talyn, who was lying at his side, he saw her watch him intently in the room's dim light.

"Bad dream? You were talking, but I couldn't understand a word you said." She reached out to touch his brow. "And you're soaked in sweat."

"Remember that dream on the way here, the one with a strange future?"

"Sure. How could I forget your foray into soothsaying?"

"I just experienced part two." He described what he'd seen, conscious that his recollection of every little detail seemed more than unusual.

"We can't blame hyperspace psychosis this time. So you could see everyone's face clearly, but not the emperor's? That's strange."

"No kidding. There were even a few familiar ones in the crowd, proving I'm not the only reprobate who makes good in an alternate future."

She ran the back of her fingers over his cheek. "Was I among them this time?"

"I don't know."

The sadness in Zack's voice was enough to send an unaccustomed chill down her spine.

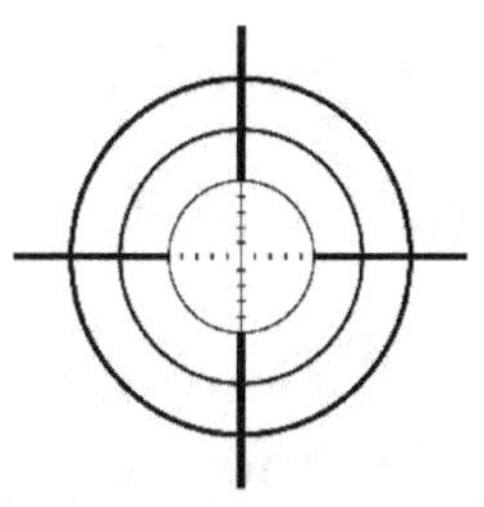

— TWENTY-SEVEN —

"Another rough night, Major? Your brain wave activity scans were off the charts again, but this time in two separate spikes. One shortly after you went to bed, the other around three in the morning." Decker ignored Trulock, sitting at the head of the oval table in Saemund Manor's main briefing room and headed for the sideboard where a coffee urn waited. "What was that about?"

"You're the one who fucked with my mind. Why don't you tell me?" He kept his back to the *Sécurité Spéciale* officer while pouring. Then, mug in hand, he wandered to one of the windows overlooking the grassy strip between the manor proper and the high perimeter wall.

"I don't know what goes on in your head, thankfully."

"Then why bother scanning my brain wave activity?"

Trulock made a moue. "It's merely a part of our overall monitoring. We wouldn't want anything to befall our star assassins."

"Not before they do the deed, right?"

"What do you mean?"

"Zack means he doesn't trust you. Neither do I."

"Fortunately, we need not run on trust, my dear Commander. It's so old-fashioned. If you haven't figured it out yet, the *Sécurité Spéciale* operates on incentives, where everyone has something dear to lose by not acting as desired. Conversely, the rewards for enthusiastic compliance with orders can sate the most rapacious souls.”

“Sounds charming.” Talyn joined her partner by the window. “Speaking as someone who apparently has no soul herself.”

Decker, oblivious to the exchange, was studying the tree line beyond the wall through narrowed eyes, unsure whether his mind was playing new tricks on him. Then, when another gust of wind ruffled the distant trees, he saw it again. A few old rags caught in the branches.

Except seen from the manor, they seemed to mark the four points of an elongated diamond shape, just like marker lights at the center of a drop zone. If it was what he thought, he should see similar signals elsewhere around the manor. Perhaps even from the side facing Vaasa Bay, though the steep, almost cliff-like shoreline would hide anything close in.

The Marine drained his coffee and turned to face Trulock. “I think that before we start on today’s never-ending rehearsals, I’ll take a walk around the grounds and clear my mind. You know how it is when you experience more than one brain wave activity spike per night.”

Trulock gave him a suspicious stare. “Fifteen minutes, Major. No more. I’ll use the time to review Commander Talyn’s performance yesterday.”

Zack tossed off a mock salute, then ambled down the hallway and out through the front door, trailed by his inevitable shadows, the goons he’d finally nicknamed Frick and Frack. They stayed at a respectable distance while he strolled along a gravel path bordered by rock garden style flowerbeds.

He stopped to gaze through the main gate’s iron grille and sure enough, one of the trees bordering a farmer’s field on the other side of the main road, bore a familiar marking.   This one, made from broken branches, resembled a crude arrowhead — another common drop zone marker.

The Marine took a deep breath to still his growing excitement and resumed his walk, eyes now looking over the wall bordering the property's other side. Once might be a coincidence, twice could be wishful thinking. But then he saw the third sign, a small, elongated strip of plastic caught in the upper branches of a dead tree, looking like a drop zone wind direction indicator.

What were the odds he'd see three innocuous marks on the landscape, put there by chance, that would appear so achingly familiar to any Pathfinder? Decker searched his memory to see if he noticed any of them before and came up with a blank. His gut instinct told him they were fresh, placed there overnight.

Nothing caught his eye when he reached the rear of the property, but it was more challenging to leave inconspicuous signs over water. Whoever placed the improvised drop zone markers was watching the manor, even if it was only from a ship in orbit, and would see him. But Decker had to leave an acknowledgment, something that told the watchers he'd received their message, without tipping off Frick and Frack.

He found a wooden bench overlooking the bay and slumped into it until his shoulders were level with the edge of the backrest. Then, he turned his face up at the blue morning sky and stretched his arms above the crown of his head until his hands met, forming a large circle. Anyone watching the manor from orbit with naval-grade sensors couldn't fail to notice the exaggerated grin on his face or the two-armed version of the jumper's signal for 'I'm okay.'

His heart felt lighter when he rejoined Talyn and Trulock in the briefing room though he kept the resurgence of hope well hidden behind a stoic facade. Unless he was gravely mistaken, Commodore Ulrich didn't merely smooth his way into Fort Hardrada. He also convinced Admiral Kruczek, and through him, the flag officer commanding JSOC, to authorize the deployment of Special Forces operators to Scandia. God only knew how fast they traveled.

Garrett Montero must be responsible for dispatching them to his last known location the moment they arrived. Hopefully, they'd come aboard a Q-ship which was even now scanning Saemund Manor with its powerful sensors. If only he could disarm that damn IED in his brain, they would make short work of the *Sécurité Spéciale* contingent and find his daughter before hell broke loose on Friday.

Later, during a break in the morning's simulation runs, Decker took Talyn out to the courtyard for a breather and via touch language let her know they were no longer alone, that the cavalry was here. And that he'd given them what he hoped they would understand as both an acknowledgment and as a signal to wait.

**

"Decker knows my folks are in Vaasa, watching him." Vinn called up an image from *Sorcerer*'s sensors showing Zack on the bench, smiling as he made the okay sign. "If that's not a signal, then he's suffered a stroke or something equally debilitating. Besides, Sergeant Paulus has video footage of him examining two of the three sign and surmises he saw the first from inside. His promenade around the grounds was for no other reason. She's convinced of that."

"What about Talyn?" Montero and Regimental Sergeant Major Gulliksen, who'd appointed himself the Scandia Regiment's liaison with Vinn, were in the latter's office. His main display was linked to the Q-ship via a secure, encrypted channel.

Another image flashed on the screen, this time of the manor's inner courtyard. "We took this ten minutes ago. Although it's impossible to be a hundred percent certain, I'd say the woman beside Decker is Talyn. She fits her description. You can see them holding hands."

Gulliksen chuckled. "Cute."

"That's the point, RSM," Montero replied with a tolerant smile. "Everyone thinks they're whispering sweet nothings at each other, but in reality, they're communicating via touch. It means that while they may enjoy the run of the place, they're still in hostile territory."

"Precisely. We watched these two men," a fresh image appeared, "follow Zack around during his inspection of the perimeter. They were also in the courtyard with him and Commander Talyn."

Montero nodded. "Minders. If those are our usual opponents, they want something from Hera and Zack, otherwise, why keep them alive and allow them to wander around in the fresh air?"

The Special Forces noncom grimaced. "Considering what we think might happen the day after tomorrow, I'm sure it's not something designed to help keep Scandia quiet, sir."

"No, it's not. What sort of signal would you expect from Zack if he was calling for an extraction?"

"Hard to say. Now he knows we're watching, there are a lot of possibilities, but I'm sure we'll recognize the signal when he makes it."

Montero rubbed his chin. "No doubt. We should stay alert to the possibility he and Talyn are playing a deeper game and won't want us to intervene until they're ready."

"I'd say that was a given. A shit-eating grin and the okay sign are clearly meant to tell us they're good for now. If he were looking for an immediate rescue, we'd have seen something else."

"Right. Keep up the surveillance but be ready to move at a moment's notice. In my experience the deeper the game, the more urgent the emergency extraction."

"True, sir. But we'll still need about an hour to reach them from orbit unless Sergeant Paulus takes on the door-knocking job with her seven troopers. There can't be much more than eight or nine tangos on the target, and the moment she knocks, Zack and Commander Talyn will become troopers nine and ten, meaning the odds will be in our favor."

"As much as I hate doing this to you, Sergeant, I hereby give you full discretion as the senior JSOC ground forces commander for rescuing our people. I'm quite obviously out of my depth."

"No sweat, sir. It wouldn't be the first time." Vinn grinned. "Besides, freeing Zack is enough incentive. Once freed, he becomes the senior JSOC ground forces commander, and I'm off the hook." His expression turned serious again. "Did you get any ideas about what we can contribute on Friday if things go as you fear, sir?"

"The best I can think of, and Colonel Salminen agrees, is for you to act as a mobile reserve, prepared to home in on anyone who looks like they're ready for bloodshed. Your dropships are the fastest atmospheric craft available, and your troopers are the most used to dealing with incipient insurrections."

"Works for me, sir."

"You mean until Major Decker is back in charge, right?"

"I wouldn't want it any other way, though I figure he was probably thinking along those lines, anyway. Well, that and us tackling the putsch alone if the Scandia Regiment didn't join in. With all due respect, RSM."

Gulliksen waved Vinn's apology away. "It was a fair and necessary consideration, Sergeant. Zack couldn't guess whether our colonel would defy the Senate and act without orders. I daresay some I've known wouldn't give him the time of day, let alone the support of an entire Army regiment. But our Vaino is a true scion of the Salminen family. He'll make his great-aunt Tatiana proud. Unfortunately, not everyone agrees, so we need to take care. Both between now and Friday, and on Friday itself."

"Roger that, RSM."

******

"I wish we had more time to prepare," Trulock said as Decker and Talyn came out of their respective simulators after another long day of training. "But you're leaving Saemund Manor tomorrow for safe houses near your respective targets."

"Safe houses, plural? You mean Hera and I are splitting up?"

"Of course. What were you expecting, Major?"

"That we'd be together until shortly before show time."

"Sorry to disappoint. But we'll make sure you're reunited once the mission is over."

Did the Marine detect a hint of mockery in Trulock's eyes?

"As long as it's not reunited in death."

"Pros like you shouldn't have difficulties getting away unscathed," Trulock said over her shoulder as she led them back to the briefing room. "This is Scandia, where they've never seen a political assassination. The police and SSIA won't know how to react."

Decker grabbed Talyn's wrist.

We need to move before we're separated and taken away from our watching friends. Otherwise, our chances to make it out of this alive will suck.

She jerked her chin toward his head, silently asking about the mind bomb.

I grab the woman before she can trigger it and then call in the cavalry to help us deal with the goons. No other choice. I die today, or I die in forty-eight hours. We do this, you get a chance to escape and stop them. Wait for my signal.

Talyn gave her partner a reluctant nod because she knew he was right. They must deprive the *Sécurité Spéciale* of its designated assassins and if they were right about their chances of escape afterward, its designated fall guys. The latter role could cause the Fleet untold damage, which was the point of drafting them as unwilling agents for the SecGen's office. Any competent gun for hire could kill Prime Minister Dahlstein and Alisa Berneiser. The simulations bore that out.

Once back in the briefing room, Decker returned to the window. The rags he'd seen hanging in a rough diamond shape that morning now formed a downward pointing arrowhead. He took it to mean whoever was out there wanted him to know they would answer a call for help.

"That's strange," he said leaning forward as if scrutinizing something outside. "Should this be happening?"

"What?" Trulock joined him by the window, a frown marring her smooth forehead.

Unseen and unheard by the *Sécurité Spéciale* officer, Talyn slipped in behind her, knowing Decker had given the word.

The Marine glanced back to make sure his partner was in place, then seized Trulock's right wrist and twisted her arm back with a painful jerk. The moment Talyn saw her partner's move, she did the same with Trulock's left arm.

They forced the SecGen's operative forward until her head slammed into the armored window pane, then down onto her knees. A sharp blow to the temple, courtesy of Decker's fist, knocked her out.

"That was almost too easy," he said, searching his mind for evidence the IED was about to kill him.

"Tess Trulock became complacent, nothing more." Talyn glanced around the briefing room for something they could use as restraints. "She believed we'd place your continued survival over our duty, which speaks volumes about the *Sécurité Spéciale*'s corporate ethos, if you ask me."

Decker frisked the unconscious women and retrieved a wicked-looking needler from a concealed shoulder holster as well as a small, but powerful communicator. He felt Trulock stir and gave her another rap on the head. The sudden clamor of an alarm siren brought both agents up short.

"Too easy, eh?" Talyn gave him a crooked grin. "Delayed reaction by the stooge manning the security console is a more likely explanation. It would help if you could summon the cavalry, considering we have one weapon between the two of us."

Decker held up Trulock's communicator. "Working on it." He was reaching for the unconscious woman's hand so he could open the biometric lock on the device when movement at the edge of the tree line beyond the perimeter caught his eye. The alarm must be audible outdoors and whoever seeded the surroundings with Pathfinder symbols took it for the signal to move. "Never mind. The cavalry is on its way."

"As are the goons." Talyn pulled her head back inside the room. "Gun."

Decker tossed the needler at her. She caught it in a fluid movement and was shooting at unseen targets in the corridor before he could blink.

"We need to reach the control center and make sure our *Sécurité Spéciale* comrades don't aim the remote weapons stations at our special ops comrades. A comrade on comrade shooting isn't done in polite society."

Talyn fired again. "Tell that to the idiots keeping us penned in."

"There are always one or two morons who don't get the message."

After finding nothing suitable to restrain Trulock, Decker ended up pulling her jacket down to her elbows, immobilizing her arms, and her pants to her ankles so she couldn't easily kick or run.

"Let me try."

He hauled Trulock up by the armpits and held her in front of him like a shield, then joined Talyn by the hallway door. "Hey Frick and Frack, it's your favorite Marine. Your boss is with me, you know, the woman able to kill you with a single gesture. I'm coming out, but if you shoot, you'll hit Trulock instead. That won't be a career-enhancing move. Here, let me give you a taste."

Decker stuck the unconscious woman's upper torso through the doorway, one hand holding the back of her shirt, the other her surprisingly solid underwear waistband. "Place your guns on the floor and back away. Cooperate, and everyone gets out of this alive."

"What if we don't care about Trulock?" Frick — or was it Frack — shouted back.

"Then she'll do something decent for once and take incoming rounds for yours truly."

Decker glanced at Talyn who nodded, then he stepped out into the corridor, most of his bulk hidden by the *Sécurité Spéciale* officer. Taking advantage of the momentary confusion created by Zack's appearance, Talyn came through the door behind him and stitched the thugs with a dozen well-placed shots. They crumpled to the floor, victims of darts coated with a fast-acting knockout drug. A second alarm joined the first one.

"Intrusion threat detected. Unidentified, armed humans approaching the perimeter. Intrusion threat detected. Unidentified, armed humans approaching the perimeter."

"I hope your cavalry has zeroed in on the manor's defenses. We may not reach the control center in time."

"Don't worry about them." Decker leaned Trulock against a wall. She slid to the floor while he relieved Frick and Frack of their weapons. "Worry about finding something that'll tell us where they've stashed Saga before Spaeth gets wise to the situation."

"That something is probably snoring beside you right now."

"She'll be conditioned." Decker checked one of the needlers and tucked it into his waistband. He tossed the other one at Talyn. "Since you have two hands."

"So? Did you intend for little Miss Pixie to survive this? Of course not." Talyn picked up the extra weapon and pointed it toward the stairwell at the near end of the corridor. "But we should still secure the control center. I can't question her in the heat of battle. Plus she needs to recover from your sweet caresses."

"Right." Decker picked Trulock up and slung her over his shoulder without a shred of gentleness. "And maybe we can ask her to remove the silent killer in my brain, while we're at it."

"Yeah, I'm not letting her near any VR equipment." Once at the stairwell door, she carefully pulled it aside and tried to listen over the alarm siren. "Where are the other gorillas, I wonder?"

"They probably don't know whether to face inward or outward and are having a merry dance right now." Instinct suddenly clawed at Decker's gut. He turned around, hand reaching for the captured needler.

One of the other *Sécurité Spéciale* enforcers burst through the door at the far end. The Marine shot twice, both needles hitting the man in the face. As the goon crumpled to the ground, his partner stumbled over him. Decker's next two shots missed. The ones after that didn't.

"That's four on the floor." When he pivoted back toward his partner, he saw she'd already gone into Saemund Manor's bowels. "And one playing potato sack over my shoulder."

Just as Decker entered the stairwell, a muted thump reached his ears, and he smiled. The first remote weapons station destroyed. Then a wave of dizziness washed over him. He clutched at the safety rail, almost losing his grip on Trulock.

It passed as quickly as it had come on, but one glance inward with his mind's eye showed the malevolence in his brain splitting open. He took the stairs on shaky legs. As he emerged on the first of several underground levels, where the control center was located, a more violent onslaught of dizziness threatened to knock him over. He dropped Trulock and leaned against the wall, fighting for self-control.

"Hera."

Talyn's head popped out of a nearby side passage. When she saw him, her face turned into a mask of fear.

"Someone's triggered the damn thing." His breathing became shallow, and he swallowed convulsively. "My conditioning has triggered terminal anaphylactic shock. Just like they taught us in training."

"Meaning Trulock's not the only one with her finger on the controls." She seemed torn between coming to her partner's aid, which could only be palliative and very brief, and finishing the job of seizing Saemund Manor.

"Go." Decker slumped to his knees beside the unconscious *Sécurité Spéciale* officer. "Destroy the bastards."

"Hang on, Marine."

He raised a feeble hand in acknowledgment, but she was already gone. Then, his throat swelled shut, and everything turned dark. Decker's last conscious thought was of his daughter and her fate now that he could no longer come to her rescue.

— TWENTY-EIGHT —

Disjointed pictures, like those a madman might string together haphazardly hoping to create an artistic installation, passed before Decker's eyes. He always expected a recap of his life in the moments before it ended. But instead, the Marine saw images culled from his dreams of the future, from the experiments Doctor Sakal and Sister Anca performed on him, from nights with Hera Talyn. Many that made no sense whatsoever.

As the visions flew by at a dizzying rate, he tried to see beyond them and find the ugliness that triggered his body's self-destruct mechanism. Decker wanted one last glimpse of it before the energy some might call a soul separated from his physical remains and merged with the universe, lost to place and time.

A burst of willpower broke the picture procession into a million shards that spun off in every direction until nothing but darkness remained. Yet it wasn't darkness so much as the absence of everything.

Even the mental bomb, the *Sécurité Spéciale*'s IED, wasn't there anymore. It dematerialized along with the procession of memories, visions, and nonsense, destroyed by the neural flare he'd called into being. Zack's essence, the spark that gave his body life, was the only thing that remained.

He began to chuckle as he finally understood the nature of what had lurked at the edge of his consciousness since the VR experience. That chuckle quickly turned into a roaring laugh, but one that remained strangely silent.

Decker heard a tortured gasp, then felt himself spiraling out of the nothingness and back into his body. His eyes fluttered open. The first thing he saw was Trulock's unlovely, unconscious face hear his.

"You tried to trick me good," he murmured through a tortured throat. "But it wasn't good enough. Not after that damned rogue Sister made me her private experiment."

Decker didn't know how long he'd been out, but someone silenced the alarm siren and the intruder alert. Either Talyn or the cavalry now held the manor, or their attempt had failed. He heard footsteps coming from the side corridor where he last saw his partner and tried to push himself up.

When she came around the corner, her eyes widened at the sight of his weak smile and his struggle to sit. She closed the distance between them in a single bound and knelt at his side so she could cradle Decker's head in her lap.

"What's happening in that thick skull of yours?" Her voice seemed hoarse with emotion.

"Nothing," he whispered. "As usual."

"Didn't something trigger that bomb they planted in your thoughts?"

"Yeah. The control center crew probably had orders to add the self-destruct command to the alarm siren if it looked like we were about to take over or escape. But it was a damp squib." A tortured laugh escaped his lips.

"What do you mean?"

"The bastards were bluffing. They planted a suggestion that would make me experience what I'd believe were the symptoms of conditioning self-destruct, but it wasn't strong enough to force my body's shutdown."

"You mean there's no such thing as a mental IED?"

"Nope. Only a mental firecracker meant to simulate an IED, a suggestion unable to overcome my survival instincts. The way I figure it, if either of us disobeyed, they'd trigger the suggestion, let me taste what I thought was incipient death, then shut it off again before I found out it couldn't actually kill me. And on Friday, turn it on to incapacitate me while the Scandian Police or their cleaning crew finishes me off."

"You don't know how relieved I am, both for you, and to know the *Sécurité Spéciale* didn't develop a magical thought control weapon."

Feeling his strength return, Decker finally sat. "People who don't share my familiarity with the damned mind-meddlers might still fall for the suggestion, and weaker minds could even shut off completely, but I doubt it can kill." He paused, then said, "I suppose they would have given a demonstration if I didn't acknowledge that I sensed them plant the suggestion. In a way, I helped Spaeth and Trulock perpetuate their fraud. If I'd forced them to run a demo, we might have figured it out early on and acted accordingly."

"At least you're alive."

"Yep, but I won't hide the fact it scared the crap out of me. Speaking of which, how's the battle?"

"One downed goon in the control center."

"That makes five enforcers — I caught two more after you took the stairs. There is at least another matched pair somewhere."

"I didn't spot them, but I switched the remote weapons off and unlocked the gate. The last thing I saw was your buddies infiltrating the compound. They'll take care of any stragglers."

"Then, there's Trulock." She glanced at the *Sécurité Spéciale* officer. "Who seems to be coming out of her Decker-induced slumber."

"Shall I administer a fresh dose?"

"No." Talyn climbed to her feet. "We need to start on her interrogation now, in case Spaeth or whoever is holding your daughter tries to check in and finds the inmates are now running their asylum. Can you stand?"

Decker ran a quick check of his nerve endings and nodded. "Everything seems functional." Using the wall as support, he rose and shook himself. "That felt damned real, though."

A disembodied voice rose from Talyn's tunic pocket. "Rookie Trooper, Rookie Trooper, this is Pegasus Bravo, come in, over."

She gave her partner a surprised glance. "I found your communicator in the control center. The duty officer was probably monitoring it in case someone else tried a locating ping, or as in this case, direct contact." Talyn handed him the device.

"Pegasus Bravo, this is Rookie Trooper. If you're the nice people who've been redecorating trees with mystical symbols birthed in the fires of Fort Arnhem, welcome. We've downed six tangos with non-lethal rounds, but expect there's at least a few more."

"Roger that. We see two on the roof."

"Remote weapons are disabled, in case you were preparing to fire a few bunker-busters, so you're free to enter Saemund Manor at your own discretion. Dark Fury and I are on the first basement level, by the control center. We need to carry out an urgent field interrogation. Friendlies are being held at another location, currently unknown."

"Understood. Try not to fire on any of us when we come near. Pegasus Bravo, out."

Talyn gave Decker a questioning glance. "Pegasus Bravo? Does that mean your old drinking buddies from the Pegasus Club?"

"I think you mean *our* old drinking buddies, my dear NILO. I'm sure they'll be familiar faces, folks who've worked with us before. Even Commodore Ulrich wouldn't be cruel enough to make newbies endure the Talyn and Decker show on such short notice." He nudged a half-awake Trulock with the tip of his foot. "Where do we take this fine example of humanity's worst?"

An unpleasant smile twisted Talyn's lips as she met Trulock's half-panicked gaze. "There's a fully equipped interrogation suite down the hall. It's been a while since I broke someone's conditioning but I remember it being rather interesting. For the interrogator that is."

"Wha-what's happening?" Trulock asked as she came to, her eyes shifting from Decker to his partner.

"You've suffered a cruel reversal of fate, my dear. And now we'll enjoy a nice conversation about where we can find Saga Lagman. Zack is rather worried about her being in the hands of incompetent bumblers like you."

Trulock struggled to sit up, hampered by clothes turned into emergency restraints. "You won't get away with this. Reinforcements will be on the way."

"Funny how that works." Decker smirked at the downed *Sécurité Spéciale* officer. "Our reinforcements are already here, so good luck to yours. Now, this can go in one of two ways." He flexed his fingers, then formed a fist. "Either I give you another digital anesthetic, which will make your current headache seem like a tantric orgasm, or you walk to the interrogation room on your own."

"My trousers are around my ankles."

"So do the shuffle, but move your scrawny ass, darling." When she didn't answer, Decker bent over, grabbed Trulock under the armpits and hauled her up. When she refused to follow Talyn, the Marine grabbed her left ear and twisted hard enough to elicit a gasp of agony. "Just a word of warning. I have no inhibitions against inflicting pain on someone who uses my daughter as a hostage, especially after threats to sell her off as a slave. So you'd best come along nicely before I rearrange your face with my bare fingers."

Unable to resist and with tears streaming from her eyes, Trulock complied. Once in the interrogation suite, Decker shoved her into a chair. Then he clasped restraints over her forearms, ankles, and around her neck, while Talyn browsed through equipment drawers filled with neatly stored tools, from the medieval to the most sophisticated surgery implements. A shout from the corridor drew his attention.

"Rookie Trooper, it's Pegasus Bravo." This time, Decker recognized the voice, and he grinned at his partner. "My drinking buddies from the Pegasus Club indeed."

He stepped out of the suite. "Carrie Paulus, as I live and breathe. Did you lose a bet to end up here?"

"Believe it or not, Major, QD volunteered H Troop the moment word came from JSOC that a special operations spook called Zack Decker needed some muscle, stat."

The Marine's face lit up with a smile. "All of H Troop is here?"

"Yep. We made a crossing from Caledonia in record time aboard *Sorcerer*, which is playing civilian freighter for this mission. My team's the only one dirtside right now. We were detailed to watch this place, but when the alarm went off, I figured you pulled the plug, so I came in without waiting for QD and the others to join us."

"You did right, Carrie." Decker clasped the stocky brunette's shoulder. "It wasn't exactly a planned breakout. I experienced a *carpe diem* moment and acted on my whim. Tomorrow would have been too late for several reasons."

"Where's the commander?"

"She's getting comfortable with a prisoner who has information we urgently need."

Paulus made a face. "Will that be like what you pulled in Sanctum last year?"

"Worse. This one's conditioned against interrogation."

"I don't really want to know. In any case, the target is secure. Six tangos down, alive and tied up."

"There's a seventh in the control center."

"My team sergeant is taking care of it. Our sensors spotted no one else. Kind of reckless, only eight to guard the likes of you and the commander, sir."

"They counted on blackmail as a force-multiplier. Two kinds, one of which failed. The other one concerns my daughter, who they've kidnapped and are holding somewhere else on Scandia. If I don't behave, the bastards expect her to fetch a good price on some Protectorate slave market."

"Shit. I guess that means we're off on another rescue operation after this one's done."

"You guess right."

"I'll warn QD."

"Warn him and your folks to keep an eye out for enemy reinforcements headed this way as well. There's no telling whether our tangos sent a warning their asshole buddies."

"Roger that, sir."

A pained gasp came through the open interrogation suite door. Paulus winced. "I'll be off now if you don't mind. Some things are best left to the imagination. Oh, and before I forget, we brought full sets of jump gear for you and the commander."

"I'll let her know. She'll be thrilled."

"Sergeant Major Bayliss asked us to remind you that refresher time was coming up fast. One combat drop would take care of that. Unless the commander would rather do the full five practice jumps to keep her NILO wings current." Another moan reached their ears. "I'll be upstairs if you need me, sir."

"Maybe I'll join you and chat with QD about how things are around here."

"Lieutenant Commander Montero already took care of that." She tossed off a mock salute and hurried toward the stairwell.

Decker turned back to the interrogation suite, ignoring a fresh cry of terror. He steeled himself for the unique experience of watching Talyn do what few could stomach — breaking another agent's conditioning against interrogation while keeping her alive long enough to answer questions. But the moment he entered the room, Decker froze.

Talyn looked up at him and shook her head. "Go hang out with your buddies. There's nothing for you here."

He obeyed with the alacrity of someone who's seen too much. Decker never again wanted to witness the sort of horror he saw in Trulock's eyes for as long as he lived. How Talyn could inflict it in such a short time remained a question best left unanswered.

Decker found Paulus on the manor's roof with a surface to orbit radio. "Hang on Pegasus, Rookie Trooper is here. He can tell you himself." She handed him the device. "We're audio only, and I didn't have time to explain about your daughter being held hostage."

"How are you, buddy? Pegasus Bravo tells me you volunteered for this gig."

"After last year's taste of adventure, things were getting a bit dull on the old farm. Since we know how you and your boss work, it was a no-brainer. Now, what's this Pegasus Bravo said about another rescue op?"

"The opposition kidnapped my daughter and used her to lure me into a trap. After that, my daughter's future became conditional on my cooperating with their scheme. I play ball, she's let loose afterward. I don't, and she's on her way to a slave market deep inside the Protectorate. Mind you, once I found out they planned to kill me anyway after this Friday's events are over, I figured they wouldn't release her. We're trying to find my daughter's location right now."

"What did they want from you?"

"How secure is this link, Pegasus?"

"It's not rated Top Secret Special Designation."

"Then let's just say the opposition wanted my CO and me to carry out actions severely inimical to our objectives, and to peace and good order. Pegasus Bravo tells me you've been briefed by my wingman. Imagine the havoc we could create while under enemy control."

"Gotcha, Rookie Trooper. We can pick everyone up the moment you get coordinates for the next target and then mount any sort of op you want. Our rides aren't flying team colors but are otherwise fully functional if you catch my meaning."

"Even better. Can you send one now and tell it to fly a waiting pattern over the Vaasa area? I expect that by the time we're ready to leave, we'll be in a hurry."

"Sure. You want the pickup at your current location or where we dropped off Pegasus Bravo?"

"To this location. Warn our friends in green once we're done talking, will you? Just in case we need extra firepower as a backstop."

"Done and done. Glad to be working for you again, Rookie Trooper."

"Glutton for punishment?"

"You know it."

"If home base got around to sending anyone, I'm glad it was you and your mob, Pegasus."

******

Decker and Paulus spent two hours talking quietly about happenings back at Fort Arnhem while scanning the manor's surroundings, alert to any *Sécurité Spéciale* rescue team before Talyn joined them on the roof.

"You seem green around the gills, Hera. Feeling nauseous?"

Talyn folded her legs and sat beside him with a weary sigh. "Trulock was one tough customer."

"Does your use of the past tense mean she's dead?"

"She would never have survived my attempt at breaking her conditioning, anyway. And she died hard, harder than most I put to the question. If I don't do this sort of work ever again, it won't be too soon. There's a limit to what I can stomach."

"Putting a lie to your frequent assertion of living without a soul."

"Even psychopaths acknowledge boundaries they don't like crossing. Or at least most of them do. But I got what we need." She handed him a data chip. "I looked the location up in the manor's database. It's a villa by the name Vyborg that resembles nothing so much as a small fortress built on the tip of the Ostrobothnian Peninsula, about two thousand kilometers west of here.”

“Who owns the place?”

“You’ll love this — a local subsidiary of our favorite conglomerate, ComCorp.”

“Hence the fortress look. It must be another corporate hideaway hardened against attack, like Amali’s old place on Nabhka. A fat lot of good it did him against the desert nomads.”

“That’s what it looks like, minus the easy overland access, with desert storms replaced by the maritime variety.”

“Did Trulock pass on anything else of importance?”

“With the time available, I stuck to getting Saga’s location. The more questions a conditioned prisoner doesn’t want to answer, the longer it takes to break through and the greater the chances he or she will die before talking. And it gets untidy...” She exhaled slowly. “Speaking of which, I’d suggest placing the interrogation suite out of bounds to your people, Sergeant Paulus, even those who were with us in Sanctum. On the other hand, when Trulock’s people find her, they’ll understand loud and clear what it costs to mess with Naval Intelligence.”

“There won’t be time to sightsee anyhow.” Decker nodded at Paulus. “Call our battle taxi. The manor’s previous occupants used the inner courtyard. It should be big enough for a standard shuttle or dropship.”

“Did you want us to do a little demolition before leaving, sir? A few grams of high explosive in the control center, maybe?”

“Sure. Why not? I ended up here thanks to an SSIA officer, so it’s only fair they suffer blowback.”

Paulus gave him a sly grin. “We carry enough of the good stuff to turn a lot of this into very bouncy rubble.”

Decker climbed to his feet with a humorless laugh. "Why punish a perfectly good building for the misdeeds of its occupants? I subscribe to the notion of making the enemy suffer rather than committing wanton vandalism."

Talyn smirked up at her partner. "You could have fooled me. I seem to recall one of your favorite sayings is something about solving every problem with the judicious application of high explosives."

"The operative word being judicious, my dear Commander." He stuck out his hand to help her stand. "Besides, we might need every bit of high explosives our friends brought with them for more practical purposes between now and Friday. You mentioned a fortified villa. Waste not, want not." A faint thud reached their ears, followed by vibrations coursing through the manor's flat roof. Decker gave Paulus an amused glance. "You rigged it before asking, didn't you?"

"I figured the major would stay true to his predilections." She tilted her head back and scanned the late afternoon sky. "I can hear the bugger but damned if I can see him."

"Stealth coating is a wondrous thing, Sergeant."

"Yeah, especially when it doesn't rub off during atmospheric re-entry. That shuttle must be straight out of refit."

"It's not from the regimental aircraft pool?"

"Nope. They didn't give us time to organize our own. The shuttles and gunships are *Sorcerer*'s, but we've been assured the pilots are qualified to drop jumpers."

"I certainly hope so, because it seems to me the best way into that fortified villa is from above."

Paulus gave Decker a big grin. "Ooh-fucking-rah, Major." Then she nodded toward the inner courtyard.

"Time to join the rest of my team. Our pilot won't want to stay on the ground any longer than necessary, even if *Sorcerer*'s in the right position to give top cover from orbit, which she may not be at the moment."

"Once we're aboard, I want to send our target's location topside so the ship can scan and QD can plan. We need to rescue my daughter before the bastards discover Hera and I are in the wind and move her. Which means before first light tomorrow at the latest."

— TWENTY-NINE —

"Don't misunderstand this, Major, but the question needs to be asked, if only for the record." Commander Len Pirillo, *Sorcerer*'s captain, tapped his fingers on the conference room table as if to emphasize the importance of his intervention. "Isn't rescuing a kidnap victim something for the Scandian Police Authority? It's a criminal matter, beyond our jurisdiction. If the government was inclined to ask us for help, sure, but what we're contemplating violates this star system's sovereignty."

Decker, seated across from him in *Sorcerer*'s conference room, nodded. "It's a fair question, sir. And for the record, we've determined the kidnapping and detention of Saga Lagman was a political act perpetrated by offworld interests planning to destabilize the Scandian government, and not a criminal act. That these offworld interests are tied to the Secretary-General of the Commonwealth makes it a federal matter that demands our involvement because we may thereby prevent a violation of this star system's sovereignty."

"So noted, Major. Thanks for understanding. Unlike you spooks, we JSOC minions still need to account for niceties like the rule of law, if only in the abstract so our admirals and generals can lie to the Senate with a clear conscience. That being said, I can turn one of my shuttles into an improvised wild weasel and solve your last two thousand meters problem by blanketing the target area with full-spectrum white noise. It'll blind any sensors capable of detecting your jumpers during their final approach. By the time they realize it's not a natural phenomenon, you'll be on the ground."

"Or so we hope." QD Vinn gave a half shrug. "It's better they suspect something is wrong but not see what, than actually spot us on final. I'll take the offer, Captain."

"Done. Would you like me to move *Sorcerer* into a geosynchronous orbit so we can keep station above the target?"

Vinn glanced at Decker who shook his head. "Too much distance for the dropships and the wild weasel. We can't afford to waste time in transit or risk showing up on someone's sensors. Besides, if we need your guns or a kinetic strike from above, it means the mission failed. Once we launch, we're on our own."

"We?" Pirillo gave Decker a quizzical look. "You're jumping with Sergeant Vinn's troop?"

Talyn's laugh was entirely devoid of humor. "My partner wouldn't miss it for the riches of the galaxy. He has this Pavlovian reflex when it comes to stepping off a perfectly good shuttle in low orbit."

Zack gave her his most self-satisfied grin. "And I'll need my favorite NILO to help coordinate our operation with the Navy."

"I thought you said calling for fire support would mean failure."

"There's more to being a Naval Intelligence liaison officer than calling on big guns in orbit, as you might recall. Besides, that one jump will let you avoid a full annual refresher at Fort Arnhem just to keep the qualification current." When she gave him a dirty look, he laughed. "You scowl and yet deep inside, you love stepping out the door with us crazy Marines. Otherwise, you'd have turned in your wings long ago. The Fleet's not hurting for NILOs, not even Special Operations Command. Besides, I want you to meet my daughter."

"And how will we not be in Sergeant Vinn's way once we're there? I thought you said it was his mission."

"By staying out of H Troop's line of fire and doing our job as gatherers of useful intelligence. You called it a ComCorp redoubt. We're bound to find plenty of data that might interest the folks back home."

Talyn gave QD a significant glance. "Comments?"

"I never refuse an extra pair of trained shooters, Commander. Especially when one of them not only outranks me and has been jumping out of serviceable shuttles for longer than anyone else in H Troop, but is also our kidnapping victim's father."

She snorted. "Discretion is always the better part of valor, isn't it?"

"For staying on Zack's good side? Always, Commander."

"If there's nothing else," Decker said to forestall any further kibitzing from his partner, who always put on a show of reluctance before jumping, "I suggest we break up and let QD's people prepare. Hera and I need to speak with Lieutenant Commander Montero and update him on our plans. I'd also like to find out what, if anything, the Scandia Regiment's CO intends for Friday."

"One last thing, Major."

"Yes, sir?"

"If you don't want the ship in geosynchronous, what would you say to a stealth satellite instead? Something to watch the area on a continuous basis and give you a real-time view? We'll reconfigure one of our recon drones."

"Absolutely."

"I'll see that it's prepped right away and launched when ready."

**

"Has the *Sécurité Spéciale* lost its ever-loving mind?" Montero's face was a mask of disbelief. "How the hell did those clowns expect to frame you as assassins responsible for destabilizing an entire star system?"

Talyn shrugged. "Information spin. A lie will spread across the galaxy before the truth pulls on its boots. There are plenty of news agencies in the Commonwealth who would be happy to spread calumnies about the Armed Services, most of them owned by Coalition members. The resulting damage to our reputation would be hard if not impossible to repair. Risky, sure, but that sort of payoff, not to mention a formerly stable star system in disarray and back under a Coalition-aligned, corrupt government, probably seemed irresistible."

"Do you think there's a backup assassination plan? Or was that solely meant to implicate the Fleet?"

"No idea, but if you ask me," Decker said, "I don't think the putschists need Dahlstein and Berneiser dead to carry out their coup. Our part in this was to help spice up the bigger picture."

Montero rubbed his jaw with one hand as he considered the matter. "I'm wondering whether it might be prudent to warn both they could be targeted. If the SSIA and the Police Authority's Special Branch are compromised, Dahlstein and Berneiser may effectively be unprotected."

"No." Talyn shook her head. "At least not yet. Word might filter back to the *Sécurité Spéciale*. If it does, they'll know for sure we didn't simply abscond or are lying low to put as much distance as possible between the

Fleet and Scandian politics. Let's discuss the matter again once we've taken away their last bit of leverage by retrieving Zack's daughter."

"When is it happening?"

"In about eight hours, shortly before dawn hits the Ostrobothnian Peninsula."

"That's not much time to prepare."

The Marine made a dismissive hand gesture.

"Between *Sorcerer*'s sensor suite peeling back Vyborg's secrets one layer at a time, and a troop of Special Forces operators used to pulling off rescues in the worst conditions, it'll be enough. Once they find out we've trashed their setup in Vaasa and buggered off, Spaeth, the head bastard, may develop enough paranoia to move Saga before Friday's main event. Besides, even though I didn't see what shape Trulock was in after Hera finished with her, if I were Spaeth, I'd wonder whether just maybe she broke before dying."

Talyn exhaled noisily. "Like as not, he'll wonder once he sees her. Spaeth didn't strike me as a beginner in this business."

"How's the mood in Hardrada?" Decker asked.

"Weird is probably the aptest description. Colonel Salminen has been running an impromptu field training exercise, ostensibly to shake out the cobwebs, but soldiers being soldiers, they can sense something is up. Since the brewing political storm in Hamar is blanketing the news, you can imagine the quiet conversations they're having around a cup of coffee."

"Are you seeing splits? People taking for one side or another? Rumors?"

Montero shook his head. "Nothing overt. If you're asking whether we can rely on the Scandia Regiment to deploy in good order on Friday morning, I'd say yes, provided Salminen doesn't change his mind. If you're asking whether they'll aim their weapons at fellow Scandians from the National Guard or police services, a few might refuse. As to opening fire…"

"That's why H Troop is here. The Scandian Regiment's job is to convince the Guard they'd best stay in their barracks until parliament has voted. If we need to encourage them with something more than a bit of brawn and a few strong words, QD Vinn's people will do it."

"Which will ease Salminen's worries."

"It won't because we're not telling him," Talyn said. "If people are hurt, I'd rather we keep plausible deniability so we can blame the plotters."

"Turnabout being fair play and so forth." Montero nodded. "Okay. Keep in mind Salminen might bow out at the last minute and stay home. I doubt it, but no one would blame him if he got cold feet at the last minute."

"Then we'll simply bluff. But one thing at a time."

"Aye." Montero raised a clenched fist. "I hope you give them hell. In the meantime, I'll send a love note to the boss and let him know the *Sécurité Spéciale* found a way to plant suggestions via virtual reality immersion. He'll be thrilled."

"We'll talk again once we're back from the Vyborg raid," Talyn said. "*Sorcerer*, out."

Decker pushed himself away from the table. "Time to join QD and draw our kit. We should take part in the battle simulation, to make sure we still know how to keep out of the way."

"Or we could stay aboard and let the true pros run with it."

"Not a chance, honey. I long to be free as a bird and smash into the fuckers like a big, iron core asteroid."

"My longings aren't quite so earth-shattering."

Decker pointed at the door. "Sure. You prefer toe-curling, but you're still coming."

"I know. But if I didn't complain you'd think something was wrong."

******

"Hello again, jumpers, this is the flight deck. For your continued comfort and safety during the next leg of our sightseeing trip, please seal your suits and go to portable air. I need to depressurize economy class so I can open the ramp and toss you peasants out."

A few subdued chuckles greeted the Navy pilot's lighthearted tone. Sergeant Benji Trimble, appointed jumpmaster for the occasion, stood, walked aft and turned to face the other jumpers. H Troop was split in half, two teams per dropship, with Vinn aboard Loki Alpha and the two intelligence officers aboard Loki Bravo.

Trimble raised an armored hand to his open helmet visor and shouted, "Seal suits."

Twenty-two hands slammed helmets shut.

He placed his hand on his throat and said, over the troop push, "Cut to portable air."

Decker shut the intake valve on his battle armor. When a green telltale appeared on his helmet's heads-up display, he took a deep breath. The air passing over his tongue had that familiar metallic taste which confirmed his suit was telling the truth.

"Sound off for breathing check."

The jumpers closest to the front of the compartment on either side raised their right hands. "Okay." Then, the next pair did the same, as did the pair after that, until it was Decker and Talyn's turn, as first on the port and starboard sticks, respectively. They would lead their chalk out of the dropship.

"Flight deck, this is your cabin crew. Our passengers are on canned air. You can depressurize and open the panoramic window at your leisure."

Moments later, a red telltale appeared on Decker's display, confirming external pressure no longer sustained human life.

"Sound off for suit integrity."

The same sequence of raised hands and okays flowed from the front to the back, confirming everyone's armor remained tightly sealed.

"Flight deck, suit integrity confirmed."

"Roger that. We are green light minus five minutes. Upper winds are as per jump briefing. Surface winds near the target are erratic but still within safety limits."

The news about the surface winds didn't surprise Decker or anyone else aboard. A storm was brewing out to sea, on the other side of the Ostrobothnian Peninsula, and its most extended tendrils were bound to reach land before sunrise.

He stared at his partner, sitting across the aisle from him, her face hidden by the visor, hands joined over the small, elongated chest container that would protect her carbine during their free-fall descent in the upper atmosphere. She, like the rest, sat on a larger bag containing ammunition, explosives, first aid kits, water, and ration bars. It was attached to the tightly packed kite-parachute container on her back.

Studying Talyn reminded Decker once more how fully equipped jumpers took on a disquieting, insect-like appearance that brought to mind the day she'd rescued the Marine from a horrible death. One he faced because of her actions though it was something best left unmentioned. Most of the time.

"Green light minus two minutes. Opening panoramic window."

The compartment went dark soon afterward, but since the jumpers knew what was coming, none of them switched on their visor's night vision feed. Then, the dropship's aft bulkhead slowly transformed into a ramp, giving Decker and the others a breathtaking view of Scandia's nighttime surface, one hundred kilometers below. Here and there, small light clusters betrayed the presence of settlements, with a larger patch to the north where Hamar's inhabitants slumbered, and a lesser one aft, along the shores of Vaasa Bay. At this altitude, they could see the terminator heralding dawn brighten the atmosphere's curved edge as it chased them to their target.

"Green light in one minute."

"GET UP."

As one, the jumpers climbed to their feet and faced aft in two orderly lines. The seats they occupied folded back into the dropship's bulkheads.

"STAND BY."

Decker and Talyn shuffled out onto the ramp until they stood a bare hand span from its edge, followed by the rest of their respective sticks. The view never failed to give the Marine shivers of awe. Pathfinders called it staring at infinity.

Talyn privately called it one of the most terrifying moments of her life.

Try as he might Decker couldn't see the other dropship, let alone the shuttle reconfigured as a wild weasel. It was already flying in a waiting pattern over the open ocean near the target but below its sensor horizon.

A green dot began flashing on Decker's heads-up display as a voice shouted in his ears, "GO, GO, GO."

He and Talyn flung themselves into the void, followed closely by the others in their sticks, with the jumpmaster exiting last. A targeting diagram took over one part of his display with telemetry giving him airspeed, altitude, and time and distance to the target.

Another diagram, showing one dot per jumper, confirmed the forty-two who made up H Troop's two chalks were coming together in a single formation. From now on, they were under electronic silence and would appear to most sensors as small meteorites, or a flock of birds, depending on altitude.

******

As it so often did, the moment to deploy his kite-parachute came upon him almost by surprise, even though he'd been able to see the lights marking Vyborg Manor, their target, for several minutes already. He felt a sharp jerk signaling the end of the free-fall portion of their flight and raised his hands to grab the chute's control lines. His targeting diagram now changed to show a three-dimensional view of the formation, each little jumper symbol topped by the representation of an open canopy.

A quick count confirmed that even though he and Talyn exited the dropship first, as a courtesy to give them the best view, they now flew at the rear of the formation and would be among the last to land. The wild weasel should already be in position above them, blanketing the target's sensors, but since they remained under electronic silence, Decker took the assumption on faith.

The dark outlines of the fortified manor finally swam into view. *Sorcerer*'s scans from orbit didn't show sentries on the walls or flat roofs, but without observing the inhabitants' routine over a full twenty-four-hour period, it remained a risk. So his eyes searched for any hint of movement, or any irregular shape that might betray a watcher. Or a sign they'd been detected, and the enemy was preparing to open fire.

These were a jumper's most vulnerable moments. He let out an audible sigh of relief when the lead troopers landed on the main building's roof without problems after navigating through erratic wind gusts. Their chutes vanished, pulled back into the hard, protective shells while carbines appeared in their hands.

An unexpected burst of wind sent Decker sideways and off his planned track. For a heart-stopping moment, it seemed as if he would catch the building's crenelated corner. He pulled on his control cords to correct his course, eyes looking for an alternative landing spot if he missed the roof. Another gust pushed him up and almost stopped his forward movement.

He barely had time to watch the rest of H Troop land in the courtyard before the roof's edge came at him with what seemed like breakneck speed. He flared his chute to kill most of the remaining momentum. Then, when he felt his feet touch a hard surface, he took a few steps to absorb the rest, praying he wouldn't slip and fall off the roof.

The chute retrieval mechanism kicked in as he pulled out his weapon and fell into a crouch, looking for his partner. Vinn's operators were already on the move, communicating with hand signals, several taking up covering positions while others made for their assigned entry points — the doors and windows they'd identified from the orbital scans.

An armored shape appeared by his side. Talyn. He gave her the okay sign, then pointed toward a door that led off the roof and into Vyborg's central building, where several shadowy figures worked at getting in without setting off alarms.

Saga Lagman was presumably being held in this part of the manor, rather than one of the smaller structures clustered around it, which was one of the reasons why he and Talyn landed on that particular roof.

Decker was beginning to fret when the door finally gave way without raising a ruckus. The door-kicker team vanished inside. He tapped Talyn on the shoulder and rose from his crouch, senses alert, then made his way toward the stairwell's dark, gaping mouth.

No sooner was he inside than the banshee-like wail of a siren pierced the pre-dawn stillness. Decker cursed under his breath but kept moving, carbine held at the ready.

"Contact," an anonymous voice said over the troop radio. "Four armed tangos exiting the building designated Victor Three."

Victor Three was the outbuilding they'd tagged most likely to be barracks for the guards.

"You are weapons free," Vinn responded. With the alarm already triggered, there was no point in holding back.

"Roger." A pause. "The tangos are down. I repeat all four tangos are down."

"Shots fired inside Victor One," another voice announced. Decker figured it belonged to the team that had entered ahead of him because he'd seen the telltale flash of plasma rounds briefly illuminating the stairwell.

"Bravo team, you're clear to enter Victor One."

Vinn's words barely faded before Decker heard a dull thump, signaling that Bravo team, in the courtyard, had blown the keep's main door wide open.

"We're in."

With the building's occupants now caught between two groups of armored and highly skilled troops, the room to room fight should become a foregone conclusion. But there was always someone who didn't understand further resistance was futile.

"We've found her," one of Vinn's men reported. "Ground floor, northeast corner room. But there's a problem. One of the tangos is using her as a shield and has his gun screwed in her ear. A second tango is covering him and keeping us away. Both are wearing civilian pattern armor. They appear to be headed for stairs leading below ground. Probably the passage we detected."

Decker made as if to see for himself when Talyn's hand caught his shoulder. "Let them work it out, Zack. They're the experts at hostage rescue."

He shook her off and took the stairs at a slower pace even though his instincts roared at him to hurry before the *Sécurité Spéciale* thugs could take his daughter through an escape route they hadn't detected.

Vinn came back on the push. "Charlie team, enter Victor Three, find the underground passage, and block the way. Terminate any tangos still in Victor Three."

"Roger."

Decker finally reached the ground floor corridor and found Sergeant Paulus, leading Bravo team, pressed against the wall by an open doorway. Two of her troopers were in nearby firing positions, weapons aimed at the opening. When she saw him, she pointed over her shoulder. "In there."

"Who are the tangos?"

"No idea, but they're twitchy as hell. Any normal goon would read the situation and surrender in exchange for letting your daughter go."

The troop push came to life again. "Victor Three clear. Two more tangos down. Entering the underground passage."

"If we read the scans correctly," Paulus said, "Benji will come up their asses at any moment."

"Let me go talk to the tangos."

"Are you sure?"

"If anyone should take a risk right now, it's me." Decker's tone brooked no reply. When he glanced at Talyn, now standing at the foot of the stairs, waiting, he expected to see signs of disapproval. But instead, she closed the distance between them.

"I'll be your winger, you stubborn git. Maybe I can get a clean shot."

"Break, break, break," an unfamiliar, distant sounding voice overrode H Troop's radio chatter. "This is Loki One, Pegasus. Unidentified ground units headed in your direction. Arrival in about twenty minutes."

Loki One, the lead dropship, was flying a figure eight pattern over the Ostrobothnian Peninsula with its twin and *Sorcerer*'s wild weasel.

"This is Pegasus Niner," Vinn replied. "Describe the contact."

"Twelve skimmers on the target's MSR, approximately sixty kilometers north of your location, moving fast. I make them out to be standard military pattern troop transports."

"Markings?"

"None visible from my location."

"Keep them under observation and update us every few minutes, Loki One."

"Wilco. Loki One, out."

"Probably National Guard," Decker said in the ensuing silence. "Our siblings in green would warn us if they sent reinforcements unbidden. Or our colleague up north would stop them."

"It likely means they know we've escaped and are worried Trulock gave up Saga's location before she died."

Decker swore. "We can't afford to let the Guard find us. If the buggers figure out Marine Special Forces are operating on Scandia, it could make the next twenty-four hours even more uncomfortable for everyone. Time to finish off two idiots who think holding my girl at gunpoint is a good idea."

He stepped into the doorway, carbine at his shoulder, and stared at the tableau over open sights. Right into his daughter's terrified eyes.

— THIRTY —

"Not another step, asshole," the man holding Saga as his human shield snarled from behind a closed, but transparent helmet visor. His buddy, halfway down a flight of stairs leading into the basement kept his gun trained on Zack.

"You kill her and then what? Did you think it out? She dies and so do you, exactly three seconds later. As does your equally moronic friend. There's only one way out that won't end with three more dead bodies. That's if you surrender. Let her go and drop your guns. I promise we'll let you live."

"I can't do that."

"Why not?"

"If I let her go, Jack and me, we'll both die in agony. Better we take our chances with you."

Decker noticed a distinct tremor in the man's voice. An ugly thought reared its head. "What's your name?"

"Lou. Lou Dryden."

"Tell me, Lou, did someone plant a mind bomb in your head? A guy called Spaeth or his sidekick, an annoying woman with a pixie haircut named Trulock?"

"How — how did you know?"

"They tried it on me. It doesn't actually work. You'll think it does, but once the damn thing peters out, you're still alive and kicking."

"Bullshit. Spaeth gave us a taste of what would happen if we failed. It was the worst thing I've ever experienced."

The second goon nodded in agreement.

"Me too," Decker replied. "But I'm here, right? And Trulock, she's dead. So will Spaeth be when I catch up with him."

"So how did you beat it?"

"Told myself it wasn't real and let the fucking thing pass through, just like a terrible kidney stone you didn't know about."

"Shit." The second man, who heard one of Benji's troopers in the tunnel, turned and fired into the stairwell. "There's company coming up our six. The big guy is just bullshitting to keep us distracted."

"Blow them up, Jack." Dryden's crazed expression gained an edge of suicidal determination. "Blow the whole place up. Let's take everyone with us."

"No, wait! I'm not telling you stories." Jack fired another burst into the stairwell. "The suggestion they planted in your head can't kill you, not if you want to live."

A carbine coughed near Decker's right ear. Lou Dryden's helmet visor acquired a small, smoking hole in its center. As did his face. The hand holding a gun to Saga Lagman's ear fell away as the man crumpled to the ground, dead.

But before Talyn could switch her aim to Lou's buddy Jack, the latter picked up the large grenade cluster at his feet and lobbed it at the Marines coming up behind him. Her second shot punched through his low-grade helmet, but it was too late.

Decker lunged at his daughter, to place himself between her and the explosion, while Talyn called out a warning over the troop push. He barely found time to enfold her in his arms, place his hands over her ears and turn his back on the stairs before the cluster detonated.

Shrapnel and chunks of concrete blew up the stairwell like a geyser of death, slamming Jack's body against the far wall. The debris struck Zack's armor like hail on a tin roof while the sound and pressure of the detonation washed over them. But he stayed on his feet and kept the worst of it from hitting Saga.

A voice over the radio called out, "Pegasus, this is Charlie leader. Man down, I repeat, man down. The tunnel is collapsing. We're extracting via Victor Three." But neither Decker nor Talyn heard it.

The latter, shaken but unhurt, hurried to her partner's side as he raised his helmet's visor and examined his daughter with eyes that were moister than usual. She raised hers as well.

"Hello, Saga. My name is Hera Talyn. I'm a good friend of your father's." She nudged Zack. "Say something, you big lummox."

Decker was forced to clear his throat before he could speak. Even then his voice was husky with emotion. "Hi, Punkie."

"You came for me." Tears welled out of the corners of her eyes.

"The entire Shrehari marine force couldn't keep me away." Decker released Saga and stepped back. "Are you hurt?"

Her brief giggle barely went over the line into hysterical. "Just bruised from your suit's bear hug, Dad."

Decker saw a brief vision of the little girl he remembered and smiled. "You don't know how happy that makes me."

"I hate to interrupt your family reunion," Vinn said over the push, "but we need to scram before the approaching unknowns are close enough to see us. The Lokis are inbound. I want everyone in the courtyard now. Charlie team has two casualties, one walking, one not, and will load first. Move out."

"Are you okay to walk, Punkie?"

Saga nodded. "I'd crawl out if it means getting away from this place and those cretins."

"Did they harm you?"

"No. They weren't allowed to touch me." Her tone held more than a hint of contempt. "And they wouldn't dare disobey their boss, an evil old gargoyle who gave me the creeps. But the bastards sure enjoyed disrobing me with their eyes and spying on me when I was showering. The women as much as the men."

They joined Paulus' team in the hallway and left Victor One, Vyborg Manor's central keep, through the ruined front door.

"Where's your mother?" Decker asked.

"You don't know?" A fresh upwelling of tears shimmered in the courtyard's faint light.

"No."

"She's spying on Aunt Alisa for my kidnappers. They told her if she didn't do it, they'd hurt me."

"Aunt Alisa? You mean Alisa Berneiser? The Reform League's number two?"

Saga nodded. "They plan to make mother betray Aunt Alisa."

Decker glanced at Talyn behind his daughter's head and grimaced. "I think our night's not quite over yet."

"Yes, it is." She gestured toward the east where a hint of pink-tinged the far horizon. "But the day is young. We need to regroup aboard *Sorcerer* and plan our next move. Visiting Aunt Alisa with a Special Forces troop might not be the way to do it."

"What is *Sorcerer*, Dad?"

"A Navy ship up in orbit. It carried these fine Marines here from Caledonia so we could save you from cockroaches who want me dead."

"Really? I find that hard to believe."

"Okay, help find you and help me prevent the People's Alliance from carrying out a putsch tomorrow."

"Ah." The young woman nodded. "That makes a lot more sense. When I was still a girl, I always fancied you'd become some sort of big wheel in the Corps, and that's why we never heard from you. But I didn't think you were big enough to get me rescued by the Corps' Special Forces. I mean big enough rank-wise. Not physically. Though you seem smaller from what I remember. But that's probably a matter of perspective. Mine being from a greater height nowadays." Saga realized her uncontrolled chatter betrayed an edge of hysteria and she took a deep breath before turning to Talyn. "Mom never mentioned you. Hera, right?"

"Hera Talyn. I'm a Navy commander. Your father and I work together."

A knowing smirk tugged at Saga's lips. "Work? Is that what your generation calls it? How quaint."

Talyn chuckled. "She's your daughter, Zack, no doubt about it — she displays a questionable sense of humor at the most inappropriate time."

"I'm rather proud of my sense of humor, Commander."

"So is your father. About his, I mean. Though I'm sure he's equally proud of yours."

As the soft whine of the approaching dropships reached their ears, the push came to life once more.

"Hi there, this is your friendly wild weasel calling. A trio of stealth recon drones is inbound from the north, flying nap of the earth. They're almost around the last bend.

"Crap. That's exactly what we don't want. The National Guard seeing us pull out aboard unmarked shuttles. They'll spot us for Fleet right away." Decker looked around until he found Vinn examining the Charlie team casualties. He switched his suit's radio to 'send.' "Pegasus, this is Rookie Trooper. We need to take out those drones the moment they're within range."

Vinn raised his arm in acknowledgment, then fired off terse orders, sending a sniper squad with long-barreled plasma rifles up the nearest staircase leading to the top of the wall. There, they found firing positions facing north and settled in.

Moments later, dark shapes blotted out the sky over the courtyard as the whine of thrusters became ever louder, then a sharp gust of displaced air blanketed them.

Decker, still watching the snipers, saw three shots streak downrange. Then, all three operators rose to their feet and jogged down the stairs to rejoin H Troop.

He turned back toward the courtyard in time to watch the shuttles land, their stealth coated hulls indistinct, if not outright blurred against the dark background. Aft ramps dropped, and two troopers carrying a third with another helping a limping comrade climbed aboard Loki Two.

Vinn waved Talyn, Decker, and Saga aboard, then ordered the rest of H Troop to follow suit. They were off the ground and away before the National Guard column up the road even realized they'd lost their recon drones to enemy fire rather than a triple malfunction.

**

When a grim-faced QD Vinn entered *Sorcerer*'s mess deck, everyone present — H Troop as well as Decker,

Talyn and Saga stared at him, knowing he was about to announce the worst.

"Folks, I'm really sorry to say Reg didn't make it. The ship's doc tried her best, but even if we'd put him in stasis right there and then, it wouldn't have been enough." Vinn's news elicited a round of muttered curses. "But Yanni will be fine. A few days in sickbay and she'll be kicking doors with the rest of us. Because we're still on mission status, the wake will wait, but Captain Pirillo is making sure regimental HQ finds out as soon as possible so they can notify Reg's family."

Decker closed his eyes and shook his head in what seemed like an unaccustomed display of self-recrimination and grief. Vinn came over to their table and dropped into a vacant chair with a deep sigh.

"You never get used to losing one, even though we work the most dangerous jobs in the Corps."

"Reg? The Reg Dannik who was with us during the Sanctum operation?"

Vinn nodded. "Yeah. He was one the real good guys. Bright, keen, fearless. Benji says Reg caught the grenade cluster and hugged it so he'd absorb most of the shock." Moisture collected in the corners of his eyes. "Reg took it for the team, Zack. Benji figures without Reg, he'd have lost half of his troopers. Suicidal, brave idiot."

Decker closed his eyes, took a deep breath, and exhaled. "Tell Benji to write the story of what happened in his own words. I'll turn it into a proper citation and walk the damn thing right up to the Commandant myself. I'll fucking sit on him until he signs off on a Cross of Valor at a minimum. It's the least I can do after putting Reg into a position where he felt the need to sacrifice himself."

"Shit, Zack. It's not your fault. We know what we're signing up for when we transfer to Special Forces — the chance at an anonymous death in a forgotten rat hole because of yet another moronic, cowardly politician's mistake."

"There won't be anything anonymous about it, QD. Unless Reg's will forbids it, he's getting a funeral with full military honors. Hell, I'll even make sure the Commandant pins that Cross of Valor to his casket before he goes in the ground. Ask Captain Pirillo to warn the regiment they'd better prepare, or I'll know the reason why once I'm back at Fort Arnhem."

Saga stared at her father, trying to comprehend the storm of barely contained emotions brewing inside this big, confident, self-contained Marine. Talyn correctly interpreted the young woman's expression and patted her on the hand, murmuring, "Your Dad is one of the good guys too. He always takes a comrade's death very hard, especially when he feels guilty about his part in it."

A soft sob escaped Saga's lips as she leaned over to whisper in Talyn's ear. "Another thing I've inherited from him."

"That means you're a good person, just like your father, honey. And I've yet to meet a better officer or a better man."

Decker raised his mug. "Godspeed, Lance Corporal Reginald Dannik." Then he drained it and stood. "The war's not over, folks. We need to speak with Garrett. He's best placed to find Ingrid."

"Why not call Aunt Alisa's place from here?"

"Because we can't afford to leave traces of Fleet involvement, Punkie. It's bad enough that the National Guard will find Vyborg Manor sacked, its sentries killed, and their own recon drones downed by ground fire. Better that Garrett — that's Lieutenant Commander

Garrett Montero, one of our colleagues who's in Kollsvik right now — lets your mother know you're safe."

Saga's eyes narrowed. "Kollsvik? You mean Fort Hardrada, don't you? Is that what you're planning? To use the Scandia Regiment as backstop tomorrow? How interesting."

Decker's amused chuckle drained some of the sadness from his eyes. "Not only did you inherit my questionable sense of humor, but you also appear to have my head for tactics. That's exactly where Garrett is, working with the Scandia Regiment to prepare a counter-coup."

"Well then, what are we waiting for?" Saga slipped out of the booth. "Let's talk to Lieutenant Commander Montero so he can tell mom to stop spying for those Alliance bastards."

**

"Pleasure to meet you, Sera Lagman." Montero inclined his head after Decker introduced them over the video link between *Sorcerer* and Hardrada's classified communications room. A mischievous smile played on his lips. "Zack was right. Your looks do come from your mother."

"Unfortunately, she's inherited other things from Zack."

"Let's put my failings aside for now," Decker growled, "and move along. As you can see, we've rescued Saga, but H Troop incurred two casualties, one of them fatal."

"Fuck!"

"A young lance corporal who took a grenade cluster to the chest so he could shield the rest of his team. Our *Sécurité Spéciale* friend Spaeth has been planting suggestions in other minds than mine, including those of the hired guns holding Saga. The last two preferred to go out in a blaze of glory rather than release my daughter and surrender because they feared Spaeth would trigger the mind IED and make them die in agony. Spaeth needs to be found and terminated."

Montero nodded. "Understood. I'll put out feelers and see if we can track him."

"But first, I want you to contact Alisa Berneiser. Saga's mother is supposed to be with her. Spaeth has been forcing her to spy on Berneiser and the Reform League as a condition for Saga's continued welfare." When Montero's eyes widened, Decker nodded. "Kidnapping my daughter gave them a twofer. Another reason Spaeth needs to be taken out of circulation permanently."

"Do I tell Sera Berneiser or Saga's mother about what we expect will happen tomorrow? Warn them?"

Talyn shook her head. "No. You can let Ingrid Lagman know Zack rescued Saga and is keeping her in a safe place for a few days until her abductors can be brought to justice. But nothing more. It's bad enough already that the National Guard found traces of our raid on Vyborg. Stopping the putsch with minimal bloodshed tomorrow will depend on our keeping the element of surprise. If anyone guesses the Fleet is preparing to step in, things could spin out of control. Captain Pirillo says the chatter on military frequencies planetside is already way up since we lifted."

"Understood. Where can I find Alisa Berneiser? She's not at her primary residence. I already checked."

Saga grimaced. "I only know about her home."

"If it helps," Decker said, "I'll give you a description of what I saw in the simulator. That might narrow the possibilities."

"Go ahead."

Once Zack fell silent, Montero said, "I'll run a search through the Scandia Regiment's satellite imagery database using those parameters, starting with Hamar's immediate surroundings. On a related note, can I take a brief video sequence of you and your daughter together? Maybe Saga might speak to her mother. You know, as proof I'm not a lunatic."

"Good idea." Decker turned his head to make sure the bulkhead behind him was free of anything that might betray the fact they were aboard a Navy starship. Satisfied, he glanced at Talyn. "Let's keep you out of the frame. I'd rather Ingrid not wonder who my lady friend is."

"Mom will guess pretty quickly."

"What? That she's a Naval Intelligence officer?"

Saga gave her father an exasperated look. "Let's just record the message for mom so Lieutenant Commander Montero can do his thing."

"Whenever you're ready."

Decker and his daughter exchanged looks, then the former nodded. "Now."

"Go ahead."

"Hi Ingrid, as you can see I received your message about Saga's disappearance and found her a few hours ago."

"Hi, Mom!"

"I also know why she was taken — to blackmail both of us. You to betray your friends and me to betray my oath. That's now over. Saga is safe with me in an undisclosed location until the rest of the people responsible are arrested or otherwise put out of circulation. Perhaps another day or two. Then, you and Saga will be reunited. Please stay where you are for now and refuse any communication with the blackmailers. The man who gave you this message or I will let you know when it's safe again."

"Mom, Dad is right. Sit tight with Aunt Alisa for a few days more. I'm in the most secure place possible, surrounded by people who'll protect me. Dad still has work to do before I can come home, but he's a man with a plan."

"Talk to you soon, Ingrid."

"Later, Mom."

"And cut." Montero smiled. "That was kind of cute. A father-daughter act."

"Spare me the editorial comments. Find Ingrid, will you?"

The spy tossed off a salute. "Aye, aye, sir."

"Let Colonel Salminen know I need to speak with him later today so we can confirm plans."

"You intend to land H Troop in Hamar?"

"Of course. Why waste their talents by making them spectators to what will be the shortest government overthrow attempt since the Beer Hall Putsch back in the dark ages?"

"Why indeed? Will do. Was there anything else?"

"No."

"Hardrada, out."

Montero's image faded away, replaced by *Sorcerer*'s unit crest.

"You seem pretty confident you can stop the Alliance from disrupting tomorrow's vote and triggering a crisis, Dad."

Talyn jerked her thumb at Decker. "This guy planned and organized the overthrow of a corrupt colonial administration.   If anyone around here can stop someone else from doing the same, it would be your father."

"It takes a putschist to stop a putschist?" Mischief twinkled in deep blue eyes. "I think I'll look up which colony underwent an unplanned change of government in recent years."

"No names, no pack drill, Punkie."

"With your sort of friends? No kidding."

"I suggest we take a few hours of rest. You most of all, Zack."

Decker winked at his daughter. "Better do what Hera says. She's my commanding officer as well as my friend."

**

"Let me see if I'm clear on what you're proposing, Major. You'll infiltrate your Special Forces troop into Hamar overnight to cover the Hamar Brigade's barracks, the Scandian Police Authority's metropolitan station, and the SSIA HQ? That's a lot for only forty Marines."

"Thirty-eight, sir. We took two casualties in Vyborg. One fatal."

Salminen winced in sympathy. "Please pass the Scandia Regiment's condolences to his comrades."

"Will do, sir. Thank you. And to answer your question, one team each for the police and SSIA, to observe and if necessary, interdict; and two teams on the barracks, one for recon, and one for direct action. The latter will be our ace in the hole, in case General Brand calls our bluff. I'm counting on your presence to deter any rash action by the junior ranks."

"You intend to shoot the Guard's senior people?"

"A few key ones, like Brand, should she make the mistake of riding out at the head of her formation, which is what I expect. Better one political brigadier general dies than forty privates who didn't ask to be there. Especially if they're yours."

"You're very cold-blooded about this, Major, if you don't mind me saying so."

"The offworlders behind this crisis are thoroughly vile people, and it rubs off on those flocking to their cause. Once this is over, I'd suggest that Prime Minister Dahlstein purge the senior ranks of every single Scandian institution, but since I'm just a simple Marine, I doubt he'll give me the time of day."

"There's nothing simple about you, but I don't disagree with the notion of cleaning up the Guard, the police, and especially the SSIA." He paused. "I won't hide the fact that those of us who know this isn't another training exercise but an actual, unsanctioned deployment, have butterflies in our stomachs."

"So you've decided to act?"

"Yes. If I stood by and watched Scandia go up in flames, I would never forgive myself. A reinforced battle group built around the 1st Battalion will fly out after dark tonight and land in a hide close to Hamar where it will wait for your signal. I will go with them. My cavalry battalion is already on its way to Hamar, split up into small packets, so it doesn't attract attention. The remaining infantry battalions will deploy at first light tomorrow and contain the National Guard units in Vaasa, Kristiansund, and Manarfell. My second in command will form a quick reaction force from the support battalions to contain the Kollsvik Guard units."

"That sounds like an eminently practical deployment, sir. Two battalions in Hamar, along with my special operators will suffice."

Salminen gave him a crooked grin. "I'm glad you approve. Now I have to wait for H Hour with my guts twisted into knots. And not just because of the operation itself, but because of apprehension at how folks in the regiment will react once they realize we're not playing war games."

"It would worry me more if you didn't feel trepidation, Colonel. There's an old adage among Pathfinders that someone who no longer feels fear before a jump will inevitably make deadly mistakes born of overconfidence."

"Do you always worry before every jump?"

"I'm like a cat at a dog convention every single time. The same will happen to me between now and when we stand along Mannerheim Boulevard in downtown Hamar, blocking traffic. But just as those butterflies vanish once the green light goes on, they'll take a powder the moment the barracks gate opens."

"Glad to hear even men who've seen more than their fair share of war still react like those of us with a rather sedate lifestyle."

"It never gets easier. On the contrary."

"I hear you. If there's nothing else, I'd like to spend a bit of time in prayer before we move out."

"Put in a good word for me, if you would, sir, even though I'm a compulsive sinner, or perhaps precisely because I'm a compulsive sinner. We'll need every bit of help we can get tomorrow."

"Of course. Until then. Hardrada, out."

Decker slumped in his chair, feeling drained even though he managed five hours of sleep after speaking with Garrett. The latter still hadn't reported back. Salminen could only confirm Montero left the fort earlier in a borrowed aircar, sure he'd found the right villa.

With Spaeth unaccounted for and aware Decker and Talyn were free to strike at will, the Marine worried he might act against Berneiser, and therefore also Ingrid, either by himself, or through his hired guns.

He glanced at the time. QD would be gathering his people for the mission briefing shortly. He had to join them, and not only because tomorrow's operation was his brainchild.

Stopping the attempted coup might involve an entirely different use of force, legally speaking, from that authorized during a hostage rescue, especially since tomorrow's intervention was unauthorized. And that meant presenting the rules of engagement personally so that the final responsibility for any directed kills fell on him alone.

Then, he needed to speak with *Sorcerer*'s supply chief and see if the ship's fabricator could make him a Marine officer's black service dress uniform with all the silver trimmings.

— THIRTY-ONE —

Decker found Hamar abuzz with speculation, rumors, and gossip the next morning, all of it tinged with fear. He'd flown from *Sorcerer* to Fort Lothbrok with H Troop, where disguised aircars from the Scandia Regiment's 3rd Battalion ferried them to the capital under cover of night.

As per Salminen's plan, the battalion itself remained in Vaasa to keep an eye on the local Guard unit, made up of part-timers activated for a three day training weekend the previous evening. It was a pattern repeated in other garrison towns across the continent — Guard units unexpectedly called up, not knowing the Scandia Regiment already had them in its sights.

Somewhere to the north, hidden in rough terrain as yet almost entirely untouched by human colonists, Colonel Salminen waited with his battalion group and its gunships. Meanwhile, the cavalry battalion was moving through Hamar's outskirts via back roads in small, platoon-sized groups, still undetected by the Guard.

The Marine, inconspicuous with his uniform hidden beneath a drab civilian overcoat and his beret tucked in a pocket, strolled along Mannerheim Boulevard. He'd observed the activity around parliament for clues that things were indeed coming to a head.

Though his instincts had missed the mark before, he was convinced a sense of impending doom cloaked that solemn stone building. It was as if the Reform League government knew its time in office would abruptly end that morning but remained determined to play its hand until the final card.

As he neared the Hamar Brigade's extensive barracks complex, he surreptitiously scanned the surroundings for QD Vinn's two teams. The Special Forces operators, unlike Zack, wore civilian clothes over light armor and carried their weapons concealed in bags. He spotted no familiar faces and saw no human shapes where they shouldn't be, but was sure they were tracking him.

On the other hand, Decker knew someone from H Troop was watching the barracks because he heard a steady stream of updates via the audio bug in his right ear. The brigade was mustering its combat cars in columns on the parade ground. Meanwhile, armed soldiers in battledress scurried about, driven by harried noncoms under pressure from officers who didn't seem to be in full control of the situation.

Decker wasn't surprised. Few if any of the Guard's soldiers would know they weren't actually forming up for a parade practice. They would be even more confused once their quartermaster stores issued ammunition.

A string of police aircars passed overhead as if patrolling the length of Mannerheim Boulevard. And when Decker stopped in front of an information pillar, he saw a clip showing the grim-faced leader of the People's Alliance, Rollo Ilsberg, leaving the Scandian Governor General's residence.

The text banner beneath said something about Ilsberg and Governor General Nygaard discussing the government's legally questionable vote, giving rise to the possibility Nygaard might obtain enough justification in using her reserve powers to dissolve parliament. And it was feared that the government might use unconstitutional means to resist such an order. Even the news feeds on Scandia were in the opposition's pockets. The Coalition and its minions had prepared the political battlefield with care.

Decker watched a string of official ground cars, surrounded by police units speed up the boulevard. Prime Minister Dahlstein headed for parliament? Or was that Ilsberg, who could already feel his buttocks back in the prime ministerial seat? When a second string passed him minutes later, he figured the main characters in this morality play were about to walk on stage.

There would be an impassioned speech, accusations and then a declaration from Nygaard to be delivered by Brigadier General Ula Brand at her masters' orders. He checked the time, then raised his hand to scratch the top of his head.

Almost at once a voice in his ear said, *"Fuse lit. I repeat, fuse lit."* It confirmed that the trooper detailed to watch Zack saw the hand signal ordering Vinn to call in the Scandia Regiment.

**

"Major Decker just passed the word, Colonel."

Salminen, aboard a gunship outfitted as a tactical command post, glanced at his regimental sergeant major. The butterflies in his stomach, after plaguing him all night, suddenly vanished.

Gulliksen gave him a nod. The RSM's eyes held the steely edge of a man convinced they were about to do the right thing, and now that it was upon them, Salminen discovered he shared the feeling.

"Where's the cavalry battalion?"

"Nearing the parliamentary precinct at this moment, sir," the command post operator, a career noncom replied. "They've not yet been challenged by the Guard or the police."

Salminen took a deep breath, knowing he stood on the banks of his own Rubicon. However, unlike Julius Caesar on that fateful day almost twenty-six centuries ago, he wanted to save a government, not overthrow it.

He gave his RSM a tight grin. "I believe it's traditional to declare *alea iacta est* at a moment such as this."

Then he switched his radio to the strike group's command frequency. "Launch."

Within seconds, the first gunships lifted out the primeval forest north of Hamar and aimed their noses at the nearby capital.

Salminen caught a glimpse of parliament's tall clock tower in the distance before his flying command post veered to join the other aircraft streaming toward Mannerheim Boulevard, where Scandia's destiny would be decided.

**

Decker shrugged off the overcoat and folded it neatly into a square which he dropped on a nearby cafe table, then retrieved a sky blue beret from his tunic pocket and placed it on his head. More than one passerby threw him a puzzled glance, wondering why a Commonwealth Marine Corps major in silver-trimmed black dress uniform suddenly appeared in their midst.

If they recognized the uniform at all. It was a given that few could identify the insignia of the 9th Marine Regiment Decker wore on his collar tabs and headdress, or know the jump wings with combat stars marked him as a veteran of frontier skirmishes. The holstered Shrehari blaster at his hip drew more attention than anything else.

"The guppies have just drawn ammo and are loading up." Decker repressed a smile at the watcher's use of the pejorative for National Guard soldiers. *"The head guppy's climbing aboard a command car."*

He'd been right. Brigadier General Brand would lead her brigade from the head of the column, expecting to share in the greater glory of executing the governor general's orders in person. The fact it would make the Guard even less popular among Scandian citizens who voted for the Reform League likely didn't bother her. With the Alliance in power again, who could tell how far her career might go?

"Hakkapeliitta Air inbound. Hakkapeliitta Land approaching the target." Not the most imaginative code name for Colonel Salminen's strike groups, but the Scandian picked it for sentimental reasons. Decker wasn't about to deprive him of that pleasure. Not after he'd put his career on the line to save his native world from a potential civil war.

Decker raised his hand in acknowledgment. The airmobile battalion would arrive within minutes.

"I see movement at the cop shop," a new voice said. *"It looks like every car they own is heading out on patrol."*

The Scandian Police Authority getting into place ahead of expected trouble once Dahlstein and his cabinet were overthrown? Mannerheim Boulevard seemed eerily quiet all of a sudden as if the city was holding its breath. Decker looked left and right, then crossed the four lanes to where a short, tree-lined road leading from the barracks' main gate met it.

"The head guppy's car is at the front of the assemblage. She's standing in the turret, like the other crew

commanders." They clearly weren't expecting any opposition, let alone be shot at. Otherwise, they wouldn't stick their heads out. That arrogance played to Decker's advantage.

"Target acquired." A fresh voice, belonging to Vinn's best sniper, joined the troop push.

The barracks' main gate opened, and General Brand's car came through at the speed of a walking man. Decker, to the sound of an aviation battalion's worth of gunships coming in from the north, behind him, stepped into the middle of the road. He assumed a parade rest position, legs apart, hands joined in the small of his back. The combat car's driver, nonplussed by a Marine barring his way, came to a halt.

Brand stared at Decker in puzzlement, then asked, in a querulous tone, "What is the meaning of this impertinence?"

"You'll be doing your parade practice a little later than expected, General. Right now the Commonwealth Armed Services claim precedence."

"What? Are you off your gourd, Marine? What's your name and unit?"

"Major Zachary Thomas Decker, 9th Marine Regiment."

"You're not only far from your garrison, but you also have no business here. Now step aside before I run you over."

"I think not. The Commonwealth Army has priority." He jerked a thumb over his shoulder and was pleased to see Brand's eyes widen. Though Decker had his back turned, his ears told him the gunships were landing in an orderly line on Mannerheim Boulevard to disgorge a highly disciplined battalion of armored and armed soldiers. Troops equipped with ordnance capable of turning the Hamar Brigade's combat cars into scrap metal.

"This is unwarranted offworld interference in the affairs of a sovereign star system." Brand's voice rose to an outraged shout.

A smile spread on Decker's face. Gotcha! "I think we're well beyond protestations of virginity."

Brand's face froze. "What do you mean, Major?" The way she pronounced Zack's rank made it sound like the name of a particularly virulent disease.

"What I mean is we'll let the Scandian parliament hold its vote this morning with no impediments. Whatever orders you received from parties who are not legally entitled to issue them are nullified by my friends blocking your way."

"You wouldn't dare open fire on the National Guard." Her eyes showed the first hints of uncertainty.

"Look at your chest." The red dot of a laser range-finder rested precisely over her heart, courtesy of the H Troop sniper hidden away on a distant rooftop overlooking the barracks gate. "You will stand down and wait for orders from the Scandian Minister of Public Safety, your legal boss."

"Or what?"

"Or I'll resume this conversation with your second in command, and if he isn't inclined to see reason either, whoever is in charge after that."

"You'd murder an officer belonging to a Commonwealth star system defense force?"

"If the officer in question was about to trigger a coup d'état that would precipitate civil unrest causing hundreds, if not thousands of civilian casualties? In a nanosecond. Those Army troops behind me aren't armored and carrying live ammunition for fun, General."

Hera Talyn's voice suddenly filled his right ear.

"You've made the news, Rookie Trooper. There's a camera drone somewhere in your vicinity. Right now, they don't know what's happening but whoever opens fire first will be immortalized. Try to make sure it's not our people." A pause. *"The ground element of the Hakkapeliitta has reached parliament and is deploying. They've exchanged a few harsh words with the police, but are in control."*

"You're insane, Major. And somehow you've infected an honorable unit like the Scandia Regiment with your madness. They won't open fire on us. We're fellow Scandians. Now step aside before I order *you* be shot."

Decker drew his blaster and pointed it at Brand's head. If someone needed to kill her, he might as well do so himself and spare H Troop any public scrutiny.

"The Scandia Regiment's cavalry battalion has deployed around the parliamentary precinct and removed any police presence from the secure zone. Your putsch is over. You will return to barracks, either with, or without your head. I don't care which."

"You won't get away with it, Decker. Scandia will protest this unwarranted interference and demand the Senate take punitive action."

"Be that as it may, but unless you turn around, you won't be alive to witness my punishment."

A deathly silence, underscored by the gentle purr of combat car drives and a soft morning breeze rustling through trees in full bloom, descended on the scene as Decker locked stares with Brand.

"Parliament is about to start voting," Talyn's voice said. *"News commentators are saying the minor parties will side with the government as predicted. It means the new law will pass with two-thirds approval, ensuring*

no single party in power can repeal it unless it holds a two-thirds majority."

"Did you check the news, General? It's too late. The vote is on, and everyone but your Alliance masters will give it a hearty yea. If your Commander-in-Chief, the governor general doesn't ratify the new legislation, Prime Minister Dahlstein will have grounds for asking that Scandia's Supreme Court remove her from office. If you return to barracks, we might get through today without bloodshed. If you don't, the Hamar Brigade will cease to exist."

Brand took another long look at the over eight hundred Scandia Regiment soldiers waiting in silence, backed by their grounded gunships and anti-armor weapons. Then she tilted her head to one side as if listening to her ear bug. She spoke into a throat mike, her words too soft for the Marine's hearing.   Then she gave Decker a most unattractive sneer. "This isn't over, Major."

"For you it is." He slid his blaster back into its holster and assumed the parade rest position again.

At Brand's orders, the rearmost combat cars backed up until the entire column retreated through the barracks' main gate. Decker repressed a long sigh of relief as he felt his shoulder muscles relax. They'd made it through the critical hour without firing a shot.

It was a victory the greatest strategist in human history, Sun Tzu, would approve. But Brand was right. This wasn't over.   Even with its legislation passed, the government couldn't trust the security forces until Dahlstein and his ministers purged the senior ranks, which meant the Scandia Regiment wouldn't return to barracks itself anytime soon.

He switched on his throat mike. "Can someone please organize a meeting with the prime minister? Colonel Salminen, Commander Talyn, and I need to discuss next steps with him. The putsch might be deflected, but we're not done yet."

"I'll take care of it," Talyn replied. *"Stand by."*

"And has anyone heard from Lieutenant Commander Montero, or Ingrid Lagman, or Alisa Berneiser for that matter?"

"Negative."

A sinking feeling tugged at Decker's guts. Montero should have made contact with Ingrid by now. Knowing the *Sécurité Spéciale*, Spaeth wouldn't give up on forcible government change yet, not while things still hung in a delicate balance.

"Did we at least find Ingrid Lagman and Alisa Berneiser's location?"

"No. Berneiser's butler AI keeps insisting she's not at her villa and scans from orbit show no human life signs on the property."

**

"Commander Talyn tells me I should thank you for this, Major Decker." Dahlstein gestured toward a window overlooking Mannerheim Boulevard, where Scandia Regiment armored skimmers stood guard.

"I didn't do it by myself, sir."

"Yes." Dahlstein's gray eyes briefly rested on Talyn and Salminen. "So I gather. And you've created quite a stir. Federal military forces preventing a coup unbidden. The Senate won't be happy at the precedent you've created, for fear it might spread. But please accept my thanks, nonetheless."

"Sir, there's a way to contain the effects of this morning's events. Let me ask you a few questions, and please give me straight answers. Did you expect the Alliance to foment a forcible change in government?"

The Scandian prime minister nodded. "Yes."

"And you took no action to prevent it?"

"How could I? The security services are still stacked with Alliance supporters. Our best hope was for citizens to rise against an arrogant political establishment overturning free and fair elections."

"And watch blood run in the streets."

"Sadly, yes."

"Are you aware offworld interests actively worked with the Alliance to overthrow your administration?"

A spark of surprise flashed in Dahlstein's eyes. "No."

"One of the reasons we — Commander Talyn, Colonel Salminen, and I — undertook to act unilaterally today is because we found incontrovertible evidence of offworld meddling in favor of a renewed People's Alliance dynasty. They've subverted your National Guard, the SSIA, and probably even the Police Authority. We can share this evidence with you and your advisers."

"That sounds rather incredible, Major, but it would explain many things, including several rather strange missives I've received from our senators on Earth in the last few weeks. You mentioned a way to contain the situation..."

"Since Scandia's security agencies seem to be in open revolt against your government, it gives you enough grounds to call for help from the Commonwealth Armed Services under Aid to Civil Power legislation. Backdate your request by a few days and give it to Colonel Salminen, the senior ground forces commander in the Scandia system. That way, what we did this morning will become, for all intents and purposes, completely legal. The Scandia Regiment can continue to protect your administration until you've purged the senior ranks of the Guard, the Police, and the SSIA. And if you want my opinion, you need to do that quickly and with utter ruthlessness before your opposition recovers. I brought a unit of highly trained Special Forces operators with me. They can help with that particular exercise."

A cold smile played on Dahlstein's lips. "You possess the devious mind of a politician, Major."

"As a Marine, I'm not sure that's a compliment, sir."

He chuckled. "No, probably not. Very well. Colonel Salminen, thank you for responding to my request for assistance under Commonwealth Aid to Civil Power legislation. I understand that we still need to place a formal copy on file. My chief of staff will do so at once. Now that the immediate peril has been averted, I would appreciate your working with my Minister for Public Safety to help in restoring order."

"Will do, sir. Might I suggest you issue directives confining National Guard units to barracks until further notice and releasing part-timers from active duty?"

Dahlstein's eyebrows shot up. "The Guard activated its part-time units?"

"Indeed, sir. Yesterday evening. My outlying battalions are keeping them penned in. So far, we've not clashed, but it's only a question of time."

The prime minister reached out and touched a comscreen embedded in his desk. "Harald?"

A few seconds passed. "Sir."

"Did you know General Karlsen activated the part-time Guard units yesterday?"

"No, Prime Minister. The bastard did it without permission."

"Stand them down and tell Karlsen in clear terms that every single Guard unit is confined to barracks until I release them. Those who disobey will be arrested by the

Commonwealth Army and charged with treason. Karlsen needs to choose. If necessary he will make that choice with a gun at his head."

"What choice would that be, sir?"

"Resignation once he's stood his troops down, or prison. I'm suspending the Guard's authority to bear arms except for the minimum necessary to keep order. Our protection will be assured by the Army's Scandia Regiment until we've cleaned house."

"Federal troops, Prime Minister?"

"As you may recall, I asked the Scandia Regiment for assistance two days ago because I feared our own forces would rebel against the government."

A pregnant pause, then, "Of course, Prime Minister. A very prescient call on your part."

"Colonel Salminen, the regiment's commanding officer, will be in touch with you shortly to help restore order in the capital. In the meantime, draw up a list of Guard, police, and SSIA officers whom you know to be unreliable and suspend them from duty.   Find replacements whose first loyalty is to Scandia and not a given political party."

"What about the civil and armed services rules? We can't just suspend or fire people without cause."

"Bugger the rules, Harald. Those pricks tried to overthrow the government. Fire everyone you suspect. We'll deal with the damned rules later. If you need an armed backup to remove them by force, Colonel Salminen will be glad to oblige. He can draw on specialists reputed for their ruthlessness."

"Will do, Prime Minister."

Dahlstein cut the link. "Harald is in his parliamentary office one floor down, Colonel. Now if you'll excuse me, I must face the Scandian people and inform them of what happened this morning. I fear no matter the words I choose, we will see street violence between League supporters and our opponents. We've been a polarized society for years."

"One last question, sir."

"Yes, Major?"

"Do you know where we can find Alisa Berneiser? I'm trying to reach Ingrid Lagman so I can tell her our daughter is safe."

A bark of laughter escaped Dahlstein's throat. "*You're* Saga Lagman's father? Now your presence here makes sense in a strange, surrealistic way. Ingrid and Alisa are in a secure place, Major, and have been since Saga vanished without a trace. Even then we suspected opposition shenanigans."

"You don't know the half of it, sir, but the offworlders behind the attempted coup kidnapped my daughter to blackmail her mother and me. And since their plans failed, I'm afraid they'll try something more direct to squeeze concessions from you. One of my colleagues is looking for them, but he seems to have dropped off the surface of the planet as well, and I fear the worst. Where can we find them?"

Dahlstein studied Decker in silence for a few moments. "Blackmail, eh? I can imagine what they wanted from Ingrid, but what's your angle, Major?"

"They wanted Commander Talyn and me to help precipitate the coup."

"I beg your pardon? In what way?"

"We belong to the Fleet's Joint Special Operations Command and have clashed many times before with the offworld interests that targeted your government. When they discovered I was Saga's father, they hatched a plan to force us into doing their dirty work and thereby compromise the Fleet."

"What sort of dirty work? Or should I not ask?"

"Since their plot failed, it would be best for everyone if you didn't, sir," Talyn said. "We weren't about to carry out what they wanted anyway, in spite of the risk to our and Saga's lives."

Her eyes met the prime minister's, and Dahlstein nodded. "Very well. Alisa and Ingrid are in a safe house north of here." He gave them precise coordinates. "I wish I could tell them you're coming, but with the SSIA compromised, my communications are probably being monitored by the opposition."

Talyn glanced at her partner. "You're taking QD and his troop?"

"Unless Colonel Salminen needs door-knockers to round up putschists."

"We'll be fine," the Scandia Regiment's commanding officer replied. "If we meet a tough nut, we'll wait for you to be done. But I'd appreciate having Commander Talyn with me if that's possible."

"I can manage without Hera, just as long as she stays on call in case I need her NILO magic. But I would appreciate a couple of your gunships as transport."

"Done. They'll be waiting for you across the road from the Guard barracks."

Decker turned to Dahlstein. "With your permission, sir?"

"Of course. Go, Major."

THIRTY-TWO

Still wearing his black dress uniform complete with the holstered Shrehari blaster on his hip, Decker walked up the winding, tree-lined drive leading from Country Road Seventeen to the Villa Three Lilies.

Though he could neither hear nor see them, Decker knew the men and women of H Troop were closing in on the sprawling structure as well, searching for evidence that Spaeth had compromised Berneiser's hideaway.

He finally came around the last bend and into a wide park-like clearing with the single story mansion at its center. Clad in the ubiquitous Scandian gray stone, with a steep, bright red tiled roof, and white, lacy trim, it looked precisely like the one in the simulation. Blank windows stared at him from either side of a double-door that would fit the imperial palace of his fevered dreams.

"I'm here," he sub-vocalized into his nearly invisible throat microphone.

Vinn's reply came through Decker's ear bug almost immediately. "Roger. We see you. Nothing to report. We found and spoofed what we believe are all the security sensors guarding the target."

After a final glance at his surroundings, the Marine walked up a pair of steps and touched the call screen.

"Yes?" A disembodied voice asked.

"My name is Zachary Decker. I've been told Ingrid Lagman, my former spouse and mother of our daughter can be reached at this address."

"Please wait while I confirm." Definitely an AI. It had that telltale neutered tone — again just like the simulation.

A few moments passed, then the door slowly swung aside with nary a sound. "Please enter, Major Decker."

Zack stepped into an eerily familiar broad, high-ceilinged foyer with a marble floor and wainscoted walls. Corridors led off from each side and, as he remembered from the simulator, the doorway facing him opened onto the sitting room. Antique side tables lined the walls, each home to some what Decker's mother used to call dust collectors — statuettes, bric-à-brac, and other assorted ornaments.

"Sera Lagman is in the main room, across the lobby."

Decker thought it strange no human came to meet him, especially since he'd shown up unbidden, though someone probably watched him walk up the drive and confirmed his identity. He stepped through the sitting room door and immediately stopped at the sight that greeted him. The Marine's hand reached for his blaster.

"How nice of you to join us, Major Decker." Spaeth, sitting on a sofa with intricately carved legs, gave him a reptilian smile. "Now everyone's here, perhaps we can put the change of government back on track. I'd also like to hear how you escaped Trulock, the mind bomb, *and* found your daughter, all in the space of a day. We've been unable to locate the lovely Saga since yesterday morning."

Decker ignored the *Sécurité Spéciale* officer in favor of a pale blond woman sitting to one side, watched by a standard issue, dark-suited goon with a large-bore needler in his hand. She stared at him with terrified eyes.

"Hello, Ingrid. Saga is safe from these idiots and under the protection of the Commonwealth Armed Services." He turned to an older woman, also watched by a hired gun, and also scared but not as much as his former spouse. "You must be Sera Berneiser. Prime Minister Dahlstein sends his best. He's fully occupied restoring the rule of law in Hamar after this morning's events, aided by the Commonwealth Armed Services, as per his formal request for federal aid to quell civil unrest."

"We'll see about that." Spaeth's tone held enough venom to kill an entire Shrehari marine division. "One Army regiment and a ragtag bunch of Naval Intelligence agents can only do so much."

"You're pissing in the wind, if you think the situation can be salvaged, Spaeth. It's over. The Guard has retreated back to barracks and will stay there on pain of summary execution for high treason against the Scandian state. Without them, the remaining traitors, such as your SSIA friends, can't do much, not against federal troops empowered to keep civil order by Prime Minister Dahlstein. And once Dahlstein purges the traitors from the top military and civilian echelons, his government will find enough evidence to see the Alliance's senior leadership in prison for the rest of their lives. You lost. The *Sécurité Spéciale* fucked up, and the Coalition can go stick its head into a meat grinder. But you can get out of this. Put down your weapons and walk away. I promise I'll let you and your people leave Scandia unharmed. Resist, and you will die."

"Big words for a man who'll witness two lovely ladies suffer unspeakable agony before they become a slaver's loss-leader." Spaeth glanced at Lagman and Berneiser. "They won't fetch nearly as much as Saga, but perhaps

Dahlstein might agree to compromise with us in exchange for his aunt's life."

"Aunt?"

"You didn't know? Perhaps I shouldn't be surprised. Few people are aware the soon to be ex-prime minister was adopted at birth. Sera Berneiser is his biological mother's sister. And you, Major? I'm sure you'd contemplate a few compromises of your own to spare Saga's mother."

Vinn's voice over the ear bug momentarily stilled Decker's reply. *"We have visuals on four tangos in your location. Confirm."*

"Yes. I'm sure you think so, but perhaps Dahlstein and I might think the lives of five people aren't worth the bloodshed of a civil war."

"Roger. Five tangos understood. One to your right, two by the women, one to your left. No visual on the fifth."

"We'll see how both of you feel after a demonstration."

"I wouldn't do that, Spaeth. You're already in my sights for what you did to Saga. Enjoy that nice sofa because you'll be sitting on something much less comfortable shortly."

"Sofa understood. You'll have to take him yourself."

Decker nodded once.

"Please, Major, do stop this blustering. It didn't do your colleague much good."

"What do you mean?"

"The man — Montero, I believe his name was — you sent here to comfort Sera Lagman. He served as an object lesson in cooperation for our dear hosts."

"What did you do to him?"

"Tested his conditioning. Sadly, it worked. Perhaps I should test yours since it appears Trulock wasn't able to do so. Where is Commander Talyn, by the way? With the prime minister, perchance? Maybe we can set up a link and show her your final moments unless she does as she's already been told."

"Ready when you are."

"I don't think so, asshole." Decker turned a contemptuous grin on his foe. "FIRE."

Four of the sitting room's windows suddenly found themselves the proud owners of precise holes, courtesy of four plasma rounds. So did the four henchmen. They crumpled noiselessly to the ground. Decker drew his blaster and aimed it at Spaeth.

"Game over."

"Come now, Decker. You won't just execute me in cold blood. That's not your style. Let's discuss this like fellow professionals."

"I am not your fellow, and you're not a professional but a criminal. I gave you the chance to walk away. But proposing to sell Commonwealth citizens, especially people near and dear to me into slavery, on top of fomenting the overthrow of a legitimate government and murdering a Navy officer means there's no getting away from the death penalty. Don't worry. I'll let your bosses on Earth know you won't make it back for the annual *Sécurité Spéciale* cockroach ball."

Decker stroked his blaster's trigger. It coughed once. A smoking hole appeared where Spaeth's nose once adorned his face and he keeled over on his side, dead. "We're five for five, Pegasus." He turned to the women. "Sorry you had to witness that."

Berneiser, the more composed of the two nodded.

"You won't find me disagreeing with your actions, Major Decker. Not after what he did to that poor man. It was awful."

Ingrid, still mute, simply stared at him with incomprehension, as if she was still processing the sudden and violent change in circumstances.

"Where did they put Lieutenant Commander Montero's body?"

"You'll find him in the next room." Berneiser pointed at a closed door. "He was a brave man, you know."

Decker nodded. "One of the best. How did Spaeth find this place? Dahlstein told us it was secure."

Berneiser shrugged. "I don't know." But the sudden look of horror in his former spouse's eyes told him everything. The *Sécurité Spéciale* officer had used his hold on Ingrid. He briefly wondered how they communicated, then decided it was a question best left unexplored.

"And Montero?"

"He showed up last night, a few hours after Spaeth. They killed the poor man this morning after trying to interrogate him all night without success."

Vinn's troopers came through the door in matched pairs at that moment, weapons held high. "Is everything clear, Major?" Sergeant Paulus asked the moment she spotted him.

"Five tangos down. There's a dead friendly next door. Lieutenant Commander Garrett Montero."

"Shit. He used to be the 811th Pathfinders' NILO when I served with the squadron years ago. Great guy. Complained more about jumping than Commander Talyn, but as solid as any of us." Paulus pointed at two of her people, then at the door. "Secure the commander's remains." She turned back toward Zack. "QD called for our taxis. He's landing them in the front yard. Commander Talyn says we're to bring Sera Berneiser and Sera Lagman to Hamar. They'll stay with the prime minister for now."

Berneiser nodded and climbed to her feet. "Come, Ingrid. We need to pack our things. I doubt we'll ever come back here. You can chat with Zachary later."

Decker admired the older woman's steely temperament in the face of events that would traumatize most people. That quality likely helped propel the Reform League to power.

**

"Promise you'll come back and visit, Dad. I don't want to wait another twenty years." Saga wrapped her arms around Decker's neck, tears streaming down her face. "And get kidnapped in the bargain."

"I can only promise I'll try, Punkie. The Fleet sends me where I'm needed and not where I want, which is why your mother and I couldn't make a go of it."

"I guess that's all I can ask."

"Promise you'll take care of your mother? She'll need time to forgive herself, even though Spaeth gave her no choice."

"I will. You can be sure of that."

Decker's reunion with Ingrid was as awkward as he'd feared, though they carefully tiptoed around the matter of Spaeth forcing her to betray Berneiser. But after the first few days, during which he oversaw Vinn's Marines helping the Scandia Regiment and loyal elements in the Police Authority arrest traitors, they settled into a reasonably comfortable relationship.

Saga joined her mother at the prime ministerial residence, safe behind a curtain of armored soldiers, two days after the attempted coup, allowing Decker a brief facsimile of family life before orders from Caledonia poured in. To Decker's relief, the Grand Admiral even sent his personal approval of the Scandia Regiment helping Dahlstein's government per the latter's formal request, thereby enshrining fiction as fact.

Talyn, with a few of Vinn's more experienced operators, rolled up the last of Spaeth's operation, though she left the local *Sécurité Spéciale* field office to its own devices. They never found out why the locals were interested in Montero's Mattias Kenly identity, or *Haukka*. But a week after the attempted coup, with the situation on Scandia settling, *Sorcerer* and H Troop were ordered home. Separate orders recalled Talyn and Decker aboard *Phoenix* and instructed both Q-ships to sail in company.

He'd already made his farewells with Salminen, Gulliksen and the Scandia Regiment, promising to visit at the first occasion. When he released Saga, Prime Minister Dahlstein entered the residence's main room.

"I couldn't let you leave without saying goodbye as well, Major. Though you won't get that sort of hug from me." He stretched out his hand. "Thank you for risking your career to keep this planet from erupting in violence, and please thank your superiors for their support, even if it was after the fact. The road ahead will be long and arduous. But things are looking up.

"Viveca Nygaard just announced her resignation as governor general. The Chief Justice of the Supreme Court will fill the position in the interim. I don't doubt the People's Alliance will soon oust Rollo Ilsberg as well. Too many of its members are horrified by his actions. However, I fear cleaning out the security services will take time. Thankfully, we can count on Vaino Salminen to rebuild the National Guard as an apolitical organization. He's just accepted my offer to become chief of staff and replace Karlsen as soon as his retirement from the Army comes into effect."

"General Salminen, eh? I can't think of a better man for the job. The Army's loss is your gain, sir."

"It is indeed. Please pass my government's sympathies to the families of Lance Corporal Dannik and Lieutenant Commander Montero."

Decker, impressed that Dahlstein would remember the names, nodded. "I will." He heard the door open behind him, then Talyn's familiar footsteps. "I believe my commanding officer is about to whisk me away."

"The Fleet waits for no one," Talyn intoned with mock solemnity. "Prime Minister, a pleasure. If offworlders give you grief again, call us. We run a reasonably good extermination service." Then, she turned to Saga. "Honey, I promise I'll try to keep your father safe, but he has a mind of his own. I was glad to meet you, and am a bit jealous Zack has such a lovely daughter. Take care and good luck with your doctoral examinations."

"Thank you, Commander — Hera." Saga planted one last kiss on Decker's cheek, then wiped away the tears. "Fair winds and following seas, Dad."

"Talk to you soon, Punkie."

**

"If I didn't know better, I'd say it was dusty in here," Talyn commented once the Scandia Regiment aircar taking them to *Phoenix* lifted away from the residence. "But then, I've always known there was a tight bundle of emotions beneath that thick shell."

Decker gave her the rigid digit salute. "No editorial comments from the childless gallery."

She winced. "Ouch. Good thing I have no feelings to hurt."

The Marine relented with a sigh. "Those twenty years I lost with Saga bother me more than I thought. But I'll give Ingrid credit. She raised a fine, upstanding human being."

"Who shares your DNA. You're a stand-up guy through and through who was there during her most important early years. I'd say part of the credit is yours as well."

He leered at her. "Flattery will get you everywhere, but let's wait until we've gone FTL."

"How was Ingrid?"

"Afraid I'd bring up the fact she fed the Villa Three Lilies location, among other secrets, to Spaeth and his henchmen. I think Ingrid will live with the guilt forever. But seeing her again like this reminded me our divorce was probably for the better. We can at least be friends now. She wants to step away from politics, for what that's worth, but after meeting the redoubtable Alisa Berneiser, I can only wish her luck."

They watched Hamar fade behind them, then settled back in companionable silence for the rest of the trip north. A few hours later, *Phoenix* joined *Sorcerer* in orbit. By the time Scandia's sun rose over Hamar the next morning both ships were in hyperspace, speeding away from the Rim Sector.

— THIRTY-THREE —

"Commander Talyn, Major Decker, I'm pleased you could make it." Colonel Martinson, the 1st Marine Special Forces Regiment's CO waved them into his office. They, like Martinson, wore full dress uniform, with medals and awards, and carried sheathed swords. "You're here for the funerals, I gather. You heard Garrett Montero is being interred here in Fort Arnhem, right? He had no family and made no specific requests. Since he was a NILO, it seems only right."

"We wouldn't miss it for the world, sir," Decker replied. "As a matter of fact, we have a special request. We'd like to join the escort itself. It's the least we can do for Lance Corporal Dannik and Lieutenant Commander Montero. We owe them more than we could ever repay."

Martinson looked at each of them in turn, then nodded. "Permission granted. Artur Letts, the officer commanding C Squadron, who you might remember, is in charge of the funeral escort. I'm sure he won't object. But I want something from you in return, Major."

"Sir?"

"You know you'll never serve with the 9th Marines again. No one who transfers to special operations ever goes back to his old unit, especially officers who work for Naval Intelligence. I'd say you're truly one of us by now. Don't you think it's time you acknowledged your real home?"

"You want me to re-badge, sir? Put up the winged dagger. Now?"

"That's what I implied. You'll even skip indoctrination week. I'll give you a bye." Martinson smiled at Talyn. "Has he taken a hit on the head recently?"

"Several." She nudged her partner. "The colonel is right, Zack."

Decker drew himself to attention. "It would be an honor to join the 1st Special Forces' regimental family, sir."

Martinson stuck his head through a side door. "RSM, Major Decker has kindly accepted my invitation. If you'd like to help me do the honors."

"Sir!"

When Zack saw his old friend Augustus Vanlith march in, black rosewood cane tucked under his arm, he broke out into a broad grin. "How the hell did you end up as regimental sergeant major without me knowing?"

The two men exchanged a vigorous handclasp in preference to a bear hug, for fear of tangling their impressive medal racks. "They posted me in while you were gallivanting across the Rim Sector. HQ finally stood down the 251st. Kal Ryent's a lieutenant colonel now, over at JSOC, in your neck of the woods."

"Good for you, Gus. It's a deserved honor. And good for Kal, though I'm sorry to see a kick-ass outfit like the 251st struck from the order of battle."

"Our run was longer than most."

Martinson cleared his throat. "You two can catch up later. Right now, we need to outfit Major Decker with the proper insignia so he can escort Reg Dannik and Garret Montero to their final resting place as one of us."

"I have just the thing." Vanlith fished a beret badge, two small collar insignias, and two metallic shoulder titles from his tunic pocket. "If the colonel would take care of the big one, the commander and I can put up the little bits."

Once the swap was concluded, Martinson held out his hand. "Welcome home, Zack. The new regimentals look good on you. I'm sure Reg Dannik would have appreciated you wearing the winged dagger for his last parade."

"Thank you, sir."

"RSM, Commander Talyn and Major Decker will march as part of the escort."

"I figured they might. Major Letts and C Squadron will be glad they're aboard." Vanleith glanced at the time. "We need to head for the chapel. The service starts in ten minutes."

As they were walking out, Decker asked Talyn in a whisper, "Did you know about this regimental transfer?"

"Of course. The commodore suggested it. You won't be an intelligence operative forever, and neither will I. For the good of the Fleet, you're best employed here once the day comes."

"Oh." Decker experienced a brief flashback to his disturbing dreams. "When will that be?"

"Not today, nor even next month. I'm sure we'll be hunting the Coalition as a team for several more years."

******

"Funeral Party, slow MARCH."

Drums began to beat the pace as the long column swung into motion. Two combat cars, each carrying a flag-covered casket on its back deck, rode side-by-side, followed by six pallbearers apiece. Behind them marched two troopers holding black cushions, one with Dannik's jump wings and medals, the other with

Montero's. Two sergeants, each carrying a sky blue beret, Montero's with a winged dagger badge pinned beside the Navy's starburst and anchor insignia, closed the cortege. The escort, three columns of troopers from C Squadron to either side of the combat cars, marched behind Decker and Talyn while Major Letts and a full-sized military band opened the way.

Officers carried their swords reversed, tucked under the arm, right hand holding the hilt high while the left hand grasped the tip in the small of the back. The troopers held their carbines in a similar fashion, tucked under the arm, with the stocks resting in their right hands and muzzles pointing backward.

As the cortege left Fort Arnhem's chapel and wound its way to the cemetery, a single set of bagpipes took up a slow, mournful lament. An anonymous voice in the escort joined the pipes, singing a song of loss and remembrance that was old well before humanity reached for the stars.

When the singer reached the chorus, everyone — the escort and the mourners following behind — took up the refrain, their words echoing over the hills. A shiver ran down Decker's spine at the sheer emotion of the moment.

They finally reached the side-by-side grave sites, where the rest of the regiment and every member of the Pathfinder School waited. Decker was surprised to see the Commandant of the Marine Corps, the Chief of Naval Operations as well as the Chief of Naval Intelligence and Commodore Ulrich among the mourners.

Still marching to the slow beat of the drums and the wail of the pipes, the escort spread out to form a three-sided box around the graves. When the pallbearers lifted the caskets off the combat cars, Letts gave the order to present arms.

The mourners facing them raised their hands in salute until the caskets rested on their lifts over the open graves. As they shouldered arms, another surprise awaited Decker. Instead of the pallbearers removing and folding both flags, the cushion carriers and sergeants carefully placed their charges on the caskets.

"Attention to orders." Colonel Martinson's voice rang out over the quiet, almost bucolic cemetery.

The Commandant of the Marine Corps stepped forward. "In recognition for his selfless act of bravery during a classified mission, an act that without a doubt saved many of his comrades' lives, Lance Corporal Reginald Dannik is hereby awarded the Medal of Honor." He leaned over and placed the medal beside Dannik's other awards on the cushion.

Tears welled up Decker's eyes. The red tape ninjas at HQ finally got something right.

"Attention to orders," Martinson repeated once the Commandant stepped back into the ranks of mourners.

The Chief of Naval Intelligence approached Montero's coffin. "In recognition for a career of selfless service as an intelligence field operative willing to take on the most perilous classified missions, Lieutenant Commander Garrett Montero is hereby awarded the Cross of Valor." Imitating the Commandant, Admiral Kruczek placed the medal on the cushion carrying Montero's awards.

The four bearers retrieved their charges while a lone piper, walking on the ridge overlooking the cemetery, began to play Amazing Grace. The pallbearers then recovered the flags and folded them into precise triangles, with only one of the silver stars showing on the blue background. Since no family members were in attendance, Colonel Martinson accepted Dannik's flag, while Commodore Ulrich took Montero's.

"Firing party, take position."

Ten troopers and one sergeant left the escort's ranks and lined up in two rows of five, one row alongside each grave, with the sergeant taking position between them.

"Firing party, LOAD."

Ten antique chemical propellant-based rifles came up, and ten breech blocks snapped back and forth. The piper segued into Auld Lang Syne.

"Firing party, PRESENT." Five rifles pointed up at an acute angle over each casket.

"Escort, present ARMS." Decker brought his sword up, hilt to the lips, then swung it down in a graceful arc until the tip almost touched the ground.

"FIRE." The thunder of ten blank shots rolled over the escort and mourners.

"RELOAD."

"FIRE."

"RELOAD."

"FIRE."

When the last volley's crash faded away, Decker heard the whine of several gunships approaching the cemetery at low altitude. They popped over the far ridge in two flights of four aircraft from the regiment's aviation squadron.

As they passed directly over the graves, one ship from each flight turned its nose up at the heavens and headed for space, escorting the souls of the dead on the first leg of their final voyage. Decker, tears streaming down his face — and he was far from the only one — watched them go, knowing a pair of frigates waited beyond the atmosphere to fire a final salute once the gunships completed their mission.

Later that night, after an evening spent with QD Vinn and H Troop in the Pegasus Club, drinking and reminiscing, Decker experienced one more dream of the impossible future that had haunted him throughout the mission.

He saw a funeral cortege, not much different from the one in which he'd marched, and instinctively knew he was the one atop a strange looking combat car, with an equally odd flag draped over his casket. Decker didn't know if his dream self died in combat or of old age, but he was being laid to rest in grand style, with countless generals and admirals following the procession.

Even the faceless man he knew as the first emperor of humanity was among the mourners. And so was an elderly woman wearing an admiral's stripes on her sleeves, one who resembled her younger version currently sharing his bed.

A broad smile spread across Decker's sleeping face as the dream faded. Things would turn out okay after all.

Zack Decker and Hera Talyn will return.

About the Author

Eric Thomson is the pen name of a retired Canadian soldier with thirty-one years of service, both in the Regular Army and the Army Reserve. He spent his Regular Army career in the Infantry and his Reserve service in the Armoured Corps.

Eric has been a voracious reader of science fiction, military fiction, and history all his life. Several years ago, he put fingers to keyboard and started writing his own military sci-fi, with a definite space opera slant, using many of his own experiences as a soldier for inspiration.

When he's not writing fiction, Eric indulges in his other passions: photography, hiking, and scuba diving, all of which he shares with his wife.

Join Eric Thomson at http://www.thomsonfiction.ca/

where you'll find news about upcoming books and more information about the universe in which his heroes fight for humanity's survival.

Read his blog at:
https://ericthomsonblog.wordpress.com

If you enjoyed this book, please consider leaving a review on Goodreads or with your favorite online retailer to help others discover it.

Also by Eric Thomson

Siobhan Dunmoore
No Honor in Death (Siobhan Dunmoore Book 1)
The Path of Duty (Siobhan Dunmoore Book 2)
Like Stars in Heaven (Siobhan Dunmoore Book 3)
Victory's Bright Dawn (Siobhan Dunmoore Book 4)
Without Mercy (Siobhan Dunmoore Book 5)

Decker's War
Death Comes but Once (Decker's War Book 1)
Cold Comfort (Decker's War Book 2)
Fatal Blade (Decker's War Book 3)
Howling Stars (Decker's War Book 4)
Black Sword (Decker's War Book 5)
No Remorse (Decker's War Book 6)
Hard Strike (Decker's War Book 7)

Quis Custodiet
The Warrior's Knife (Quis Custodiet No 1)

Ashes of Empire
Imperial Sunset (Ashes of Empire #1)